THE
SHADOW
WRITER

ALSO BY ELIZA MAXWELL

THE
SHADOW
WRITER

ELIZA MAXWELL

LAKE UNION
PUBLISHING

Text copyright © 2019 Amber Carter
All rights reserved.

Published by Lake Union Publishing, Seattle

www.apub.com

Amazon, the Amazon logo, and Lake Union Publishing are trademarks of Amazon.com, Inc., or its affiliates.

ISBN-13: 9781542043496
ISBN-10: 1542043492

Cover design by David Drummond

Printed in the United States of America

This one was for you, Jason,
my all-time favorite human.
Right up until you brought home that
stupid call bell for the kids to play with.
Sadly, it's not for you anymore.
I've written you a haiku instead.

Our love has died, dear.
Death by bell that I dare you
to ring for service.

1

GRAYE

The name inked across the creamy parchment envelope in Sister Margaret's familiar scrawl is an accusation. A skeletal finger reaching out from the past to mark her a fraud.

Graye doesn't go by that name anymore. Sister Margaret knows that, of course. To see it boldly there in black and white can mean only one of two things. Either the nun was so distracted by the contents of the envelope that she slipped and made a mistake, or she did it deliberately.

Neither possibility calms Graye's erratic pulse.

Her morning routine is shattered. As usual, she'd picked up her mail, then stopped for coffee at the café below her tiny apartment before the shop was officially opened to the public.

"Mr. Robbie, you're a saint," she said to the owner, who was also her landlord, when she spied the cup he left especially for her each day.

"Have to take care of my favorite tenant."

Graye smiled. His high opinion has more to do with the fact that she never throws loud parties than it does with affection, but that doesn't bother her.

There aren't many perks of having no friends, but being in the landlord's good graces is one of them.

He never charges for the coffee. Living mostly on financial aid, she can't afford many indulgences, but Graye placed a few dollars in the tip jar anyway, as she does every morning.

The cup now sits forgotten on the outdoor table in front of her, growing cool in the chill of the winter air.

A quiet morning is another indulgence, in spite of the cold. One she normally revels in, but today her solitude is tainted by that name, an uninvited guest pushing its way into her private space.

Graye's hands tremble as she pulls back the flap of the envelope, unaware that she's holding her breath.

She slides out the slim contents. A snippet of newsprint slips from a sheet of folded paper and falls to her lap.

A hoofbeat of high heels clip-clops along the pavement. Graye barely registers the sound. Her eyes are drawn to the headline of the news article. She scans it as the clips and the clops pick up speed, coming faster and closer.

Graye doesn't need to read the words written in the letter to understand why Sister Margaret sent her this.

The headline says it all. Six words. No more, no less. The years she's spent crafting a new life seem suddenly brittle and insignificant, her careful plans for her future no more than a child's fantasy.

She fumbles for the bag at her feet, then stands abruptly, nearly upending the flimsy decorative café chair. The footfalls grow louder, quicker, echoing through the deserted early morning, drumming into her head. Graye stifles the urge to flee.

She isn't Gracie Thacker anymore. That little girl is as dead to her as the family she once had.

Graye slings her bag over her shoulder, the letter gripped in one hand, and grabs blindly for her coffee with the other.

"*Gra-cie . . .*" comes a singsong echo from a dark closet of memories. "*Come out, come out, wherever you are . . .*"

She won't run like prey bounding away from a predator. She is Graye Templeton, and she has a plan.

She turns as the footsteps come to a crescendo, drawing even with her. The crash that follows has an air of inevitability.

In the wake of the collision, two women stand gaping at each other. The differences between them go beyond the coffee that drips down the front of the woman who'd been hurrying past.

"Oh my God, I'm so sorry!" Graye manages to say from behind the hand she holds to her mouth. The cardboard coffee cup and plastic lid have clattered to the pavement at their feet.

The other woman stares at her stained clothing, her mouth hanging wide. Her eyes shine when she raises them to meet Graye's. For a moment, it looks as if she might burst into tears.

Instead, the woman closes her eyes and pulls air into her lungs slowly through her nose. When her eyes open again, Graye braces herself for recriminations.

"I do hope that wasn't decaffeinated," the woman says softly, her voice calm and lilting. "It would be a shame to sacrifice this blouse for anything less than full-caff."

Graye kneels to collect her bag and the woman's phone. She rises, shaking the droplets of coffee from the phone, then wiping it on her own shirt.

"I don't believe in decaf," Graye says. Her gaze darts upward when the woman breaks into a laugh.

"Well, thank goodness for that. A woman after my own heart." With a smile, she takes the phone from Graye's outstretched hand and glances at the screen.

Graye stands mutely, absorbing the unfamiliar sensation of making another person laugh. Especially someone so . . . vibrant. *Yes,* Graye thinks as she turns the word over in her mind. Vibrant *is the right choice.*

Impeccably dressed and immaculately groomed, this woman is the antithesis of Graye, who can practically feel herself fading into the background, blending with the pavement and brick behind her.

The woman's perfectly plucked brows arch, and she shifts her weight from one foot to the other. "I've got to run or I'll never make it home to change then back in time."

She tucks her phone into her purse and exchanges it for a wallet. Slipping out a ten-dollar bill, she offers it to Graye with another smile. "At least let me buy you a replacement before I go. I'd never forgive myself for leaving you under-caffeinated."

"Oh no." Graye shakes her head. "I bumped into you."

"Which wouldn't have happened if I'd been paying attention to where I was going." The woman reaches out and takes Graye's hand. She places the bill in her palm and gently closes Graye's fingers over the money.

"Please," she adds, cupping both her hands around Graye's own and giving her a wink. Her soft smile reveals a hint of a dimple in her left cheek.

This unexpected kindness leaves Graye so befuddled she simply blinks. The woman adjusts the strap of her purse on her shoulder.

"As lovely as this has been, my friend," she says, "I've got to run."

She turns in a cloud of shining blonde hair and has taken several steps back in the direction from which she came before Graye finds her voice.

"Wait," Graye calls.

The woman turns, still taking backward steps as she does.

"I live right here, above the café." Graye gestures to the building where Mr. Robbie is turning the **CLOSED** sign over and unlocking the door, watching the two women curiously.

The backward steps slow.

"I don't have anything as nice as that." Graye nods to the blouse and skirt, now ruined. The outfit probably cost more than Graye spent on clothing in a year. "But I might have something that would work."

The woman stops and tilts her head.

"Really?" There's a hint of hope in her voice. Like she's just been invited to a slumber party.

Graye nods and finds herself smiling back at this gracious woman who sounds so pleased.

"You wouldn't mind?" the woman asks.

"It's the least I can do."

"Oh honey, you're a lifesaver." She hurries back toward Graye. "My name is Laura, by the way."

"I'm Graye. Graye Templeton."

"What a beautiful name."

Graye averts her eyes, but her cheeks warm.

"Gra-cie." A whisper of memory, never far away. *"I'm going to find you, Gracie. You can't hide forever."*

"Thank you," she mumbles. "It's a family name."

She leads Laura toward the stairs that will take them to her apartment. A fading remnant of laughter rings in her head as the lie crosses her lips.

2

LAURA

"What do you think?" Laura spins once to show off the ensemble.

It's more casual than she intended for the day. David won't approve, but her husband's opinion matters less than it once did.

She rather likes it.

"The color looks better on you than me." The earnest young woman who came to her rescue sits cross-legged on the pristinely made single bed placed along one wall of the small apartment.

Laura studies the lavender button-down. It is a pretty color and complements her oversized turquoise necklace. Pleased with the results, she cuffs the borrowed jeans above the ankle before slipping back into her nude heels. The outfit says *confident and approachable*.

"Graye, I can't thank you enough. I hope I haven't made you late for anything."

"No," the younger woman says. "I'm a teaching assistant, but I'm not expected until later."

"Are you a grad student?" Laura asks as she adjusts her earring.

Graye nods.

"A transplant to the East Coast, then?"

Laura is guessing but thinks she catches a bit of the Midwest in the young woman's voice.

Graye tucks a strand of hair behind one ear. She nods again but says no more. Laura doesn't push, but she's intrigued. The apartment gives few clues about its occupant. It's clean, sparse, and neatly organized, but she sees no personal touches.

Laura studies Graye while she gathers her coat and purse. She wonders what hidden depths this nondescript young woman might be concealing. Laura has found that often, the more a person talks, the less they have to say.

Thoughts of David intrude again, but that's unkind. Her husband isn't shallow; he's simply run out of words. Meaningful ones, at least. For a writer, it's a death of sorts, she supposes. A living death. One that David spends a great deal of energy trying to hide from the world.

It must be exhausting.

Laura catches a glimpse of the time displayed in red numbers on the clock that sits perfectly squared on the corner of a desk. She groans.

"As much as I hate to rifle through your closet and run, I need to get going. I'm scheduled to lead a workshop in just over an hour, and I'm completely unprepared."

"Of course." Graye rises immediately from the bed. "I don't want to keep you."

"Keep me?" Laura laughs. "Please. You've done me a favor." She swings her soft brown coat around her, grateful that it, at least, is a good color to hide the splashes of coffee that marred her blouse.

The women exchange phone numbers and promises to meet again soon.

"When we have time to sit and chat longer," Laura says, "I'd love to hear your story, Graye Templeton."

As Laura hurries toward the lecture hall on the Cornell campus, she recalls the smile that bloomed on Graye's lips at those words and thinks of her southern-bred mother.

"Everybody's got a story," Lisette would often say. "Listen with an open heart, and you'll be a better person for it."

Laura had taken that advice and built her life and a successful career around other people's stories.

She'd seen Graye hastily tuck what looked to be a crumpled letter out of sight in the desk drawer when the two women entered her apartment. Laura's curiosity had stirred, raising its head and sniffing the air around them.

She won't pry, of course. Everyone has a right to their secrets. But that doesn't stop her from wondering what the young woman could be so anxious to hide from a complete stranger. Laura has a feeling there's more to Graye Templeton than the still waters on the surface.

3

In another time and place, in a faraway land, there lives a little cinder girl who exists in the shadow of her bright and brilliant older sister. Her sister sparkles where she is dull. She twirls as the cinder girl shuffles, collecting the feathers and glitter that fall from her sister, to hide away in a small wooden box where secrets live.

The cinder girl stows the box of secrets beneath her bed. On quiet days, when Mother and Sister are away, gone in a flurry of color and shine, she reverently unlatches the box. The quiet creak of the hinge is a friend, a co-conspirator whispering in her ear.

The girl touches the treasures, one finger lightly caressing each, and she wonders what it might feel like to live in the light.

How warm it must be, like the square of afternoon sun that moves slowly across the worn quilt of her bed.

She longs to inhabit that space. To live in it until it lives in her, pouring from her eyes, from her smile.

Mother would have to see her then.

◆ ◆ ◆

GRAYE

Graye drops the receiver of the office phone back into its cradle with a clatter. It's the third time she's dialed the number she knows by heart. The third time she's hung up before the first ring has finished.

Her hands shake after the latest aborted attempt.

"Get it together," she whispers. It isn't the right time or place to deal with this.

She's safe. No need to panic.

Graye Templeton is real. A real person with aspirations and goals. Little Gracie is the ghost, not her.

She still has time. She just needs to focus.

"Those marks need to be completely entered in the system by the end of the day, Miss Templeton." The professor barely glances in Graye's direction as he walks by her desk.

"Of course, Dr. West." She finished entering the midterm grades two days prior but doesn't bother reminding him.

He's remembered her name this week, which is a step up.

"You're prepared for the one o'clock lecture?" he asks from his office as he shrugs into his coat.

"Yes, sir." She's been his TA for three weeks. This is the first time he's trusted her with teaching duties. Lectures are one part of the job he doesn't prefer to pass to an underling.

If anything, he seems to enjoy the sound of his own voice.

Dr. West doesn't quite fit the dusty English professor mold. In his midforties, he's too young to be old, slightly too handsome to be bookish, but a touch too short for the classic tall, dark, and handsome. His favored tweed blazer with leather patches at the elbows seems chosen, whether consciously or not, to grant him a patina of intellectualism. An aging surfer transplanted into academia and attempting to dress the part.

Graye tucks her hands beneath her legs to hide the tremor. The lecture is the least of her concerns.

"I'll be back in time for the three-thirty class. You can take the rest of the afternoon off after that if you're caught up." He pats his jacket pockets, then turns back to retrieve his phone.

Graye is always "caught up." She makes a point of it. The professor has yet to notice.

His cell phone rings in his hand.

Please, just go already.

"Can you send my wife in when she arrives? No doubt she'll be running late."

She nods as he answers the call without bothering to shut his office door.

"Isaac," he declares with the polished, robust voice he uses behind the lectern. If a cello could purr, it would sound like Dr. West on a mission to impress. He never uses that tone with her.

Graye watches him out of the corner of her eye as he perches on the edge of his desk.

"Graye?" comes a familiar voice from the doorway of the outer office.

She looks up quickly, hoping her disdain hasn't been showing.

"Laura." Graye sits up straighter behind the desk.

"This must be fate, Graye Templeton. I don't believe in coincidence."

Graye opens her mouth to reply, but she's interrupted by the sound of fingers snapping. Both women turn in Dr. West's direction.

Holding the phone to his ear with one hand palmed over the bottom half, he mouths the words *Two minutes.*

Laura rolls her eyes and dismisses him with a wave. He pulls his office door shut behind him.

"You're working *here*? As David's TA? What a small world." The expression on Laura's face throws Graye off-balance. She appears delighted.

People tend to look through Graye. She's come to terms with that.

There was a time, perhaps, when she hoped things might be different. Before her first lecture she could hardly hold a thought in her head. Seventy-eight pairs of eyes, all focused on her.

With clammy palms and a racing pulse, she'd taken up her position at the front of the lecture hall.

It's not a memory Graye dwells on often. It never fails to bring a flush of embarrassment to her cheeks and a hot lump of something hard to her stomach.

The students who were polite enough to look up stared at her through glazed eyes, chins on their hands, showing no reaction at all. The rest focused on their phones, the furious working of their thumbs across the small screens the only indication of life.

Not being noticed was nothing new for her. But being invisible in front of a room full of people, her carefully chosen words falling on deaf ears, left her feeling foolish for expecting anything else.

Yet Laura's attention doesn't waver.

The tremble in Graye's hands lessens. "I just started a few weeks ago."

"David never tells me anything. What happened to Zoe?"

Zoe Kendrick was Dr. West's teaching assistant before Graye.

"I'm not sure, exactly," Graye says. "Some sort of family emergency."

She'd been too pleased at the job opportunity to worry much about what had taken Zoe Kendrick away from Cornell, but the look of concern that passes over Laura's face makes her wish she had more information to share.

"I hope everything's all right," Laura murmurs. "Zoe's a sweet girl."

The door to Dr. West's office swings open and he joins them. Graye doesn't imagine the slight hesitation or the twitch of his lips before he leans in and kisses his wife on the cheek.

"This is a new look."

The clouds on Laura's face pass and she gives him a sunny smile. "It's a long story. I'll tell you over lunch. I think it's rather chic," Laura says, winking at Graye.

One of his eyebrows rises slowly, but Laura only laughs.

"At least Isaac knows you," Dr. West says. "Anyone else would think I was bringing a student along for a business lunch."

Her laughter dies. "Business?"

He checks the time on his phone before tucking it into his pocket without meeting his wife's eyes.

"David, you didn't tell me we were meeting your editor."

The amusement is gone from Laura's voice, and Graye feels a sudden urge to look busy.

"Didn't I?"

"No. You most definitely didn't."

"Must have slipped my mind." He adjusts his tie and steps toward the open door leading into the hallway. "We should go. I don't want to keep him waiting."

Laura's lips are parted slightly, one hand cocked on her hip as she stares at him.

"Two minutes," she says. She holds up a pair of fingers, then turns her back to him, facing Graye again. Her eyes brighten. "I have the best idea. Why don't you join us for dinner tonight? I'll make pasta and we'll have wine and we can get to know each other a little better."

Graye's expression freezes. Her first instinct would normally be to fumble for an excuse, but Laura's sincerity is a beacon on a foggy shore.

"Are you inviting my TA to dinner?" Dr. West demands from the doorway.

Laura ignores him. "Please say you'll come."

"Do you think that's appropriate?" he asks.

"I don't want to put you on the spot," Laura says, continuing as if he hasn't spoken. "If you have plans already, I understand—"

"Laura—"

"I'd love to," Graye blurts out.

The smile that spreads across Laura's face is equal to the irritation on Dr. West's.

"Seven o'clock," Laura says. "I'll text you the address."

She turns and walks toward her husband, slips an arm into his. It's his turn to stare.

"Come on then," she says. "You don't want to keep Isaac waiting, do you?"

Graye listens to their footsteps recede down the corridor.

Little has changed, yet Graye's edges have smoothed. She's more in control.

If someone like Laura West can see her . . . *truly* see her, then she must be real.

4

GRAYE

Crestview House is always too cold. The residents and nursing staff stay bundled in sweaters regardless of the season.

Maybe the lower temperature keeps the smell of urine and sickness in check, though it can't eliminate it entirely.

Graye suspects nothing can.

She signs the visitors log, and the receptionist passes her a neon-green sticker to affix to her shirt. Proof that Graye isn't some rogue criminal, there to ravish old ladies and steal pieces from the jigsaw puzzles.

The routine never varies, not once in six years. The only things that change are the faces of the residents, replaced as death claims them one at a time, making room for a relatively younger generation.

There's a strange comfort in that. Graye appreciates things that are clear about their purpose. It's all there in the name.

Crestview House. A house for people shuffling toward the crest of their lives, eyes pointed toward the view from the top. A moment's pause, then they'll shuffle forward again, right over the edge.

And someone else will be waiting behind them.

The same end is coming for everyone. Yet some people, younger people, avert their eyes and fill their days with responsibilities and appointments and unexamined expectations that things will be different for them.

In their own way, the elderly of Crestview House are as invisible as Graye. Most of them seem surprised by this. Their bewilderment at finding themselves in such a state, with no memory of how they came to be there, its own form of illness.

Maybe that's what keeps her coming back. Everyone deserves to be acknowledged. The people at Crestview see her, and she sees them.

Ms. Ellis is in the common room playing cards with several other gray-haired denizens.

"Hello, Graye," she's greeted by a few of them. "Nice to see you."

Eileen Ellis glances up from her cards. "We need to finish this hand before you go distracting everyone with that mindless drivel."

She tosses a card into the center of the table, and the players around her follow suit.

"I'll be glad when you finish with this one." Age hasn't quieted Ms. Ellis's complaints. "Why Doris insisted on a bodice ripper is beyond me. You'd think at her age she'd have better things to occupy her mind."

"I heard that," comes a reedy voice from the next table.

"So what if you did?" Ms. Ellis calls over her shoulder.

"It's not so bad, is it?" Graye asks. "Not that different from your mystery novels, really."

"Just with lots of sex thrown in as a bonus," Doris adds.

Ms. Ellis rolls her eyes.

"It certainly draws a crowd." Graye glances around the room. Most of the seats are filled, and more residents, a surprisingly equal mixture of both women and men, are making their way through the door. "Faulkner didn't pull in numbers like this."

"Pooh, Faulkner," Doris says. "With his run-on sentences and stories you have to work to keep up with. Nobody has time for that."

Graye can't help but smile. She once had a particularly fussy American lit professor with a Faulkner obsession. She can picture his face turning an apoplectic shade of purple at the easy dismissal of the literary giant.

Graye takes a seat on the stool in the corner and pulls a battered library copy of *Duchess by Twilight* from her bag. For the next forty-five minutes, Graye, or more accurately, the inwardly tormented and outwardly well-endowed Duke of Cheshire, holds the rapt attention of the audience of septuagenarians.

When Graye comes to the end of a chapter brimming with sexual tension between the troubled duke and his reluctant fiancée's paid companion, she places her bookmark between the pages.

The move elicits groans from the crowd, but Graye resists their pleas to continue.

"Same time on Thursday," she says.

As the audience pulls themselves to their feet and disperses, Graye stuffs the book into her bag and walks back to Ms. Ellis's side.

"A total waste of time," the old woman grumbles as Graye lends her an arm to help her up. "Like we have any to spare. Ridiculous."

Graye raises a brow but doesn't point out that Ms. Ellis gasped along with everyone else when Clarissa, the feisty companion, pushed the entitled duke into the fountain at Vauxhall Gardens.

"Maybe you'll win the drawing to choose the next book," Graye says.

Ms. Ellis snorts. "Ha. Not likely with every Tom, Dick, and Doris throwing their name in the hat."

It's true. The twice-weekly sessions have become a popular attraction at Crestview, much to Ms. Ellis's chagrin. But complaining is part of Eileen Ellis's makeup, a trait that runs straight to her core.

Graye has learned to sift through her grievances and find the ones with meat on their bones.

"Have you had any more trouble with Nurse Jeffries?" Graye asks as she walks Ms. Ellis back to her room.

The other woman's lined face brightens.

"No," she whispers, then leans in closer. "And I think there's something going on there. She didn't show up for her night shifts this week, and the other nurses were clucking about it. Hedda, who's always been nosy, you know, asked if Nurse Jeffries was coming back, but of course, they don't tell us anything."

Ms. Ellis shakes her head. "I hate to get my hopes up, but I'm beginning to think she's quit. Or been fired."

"That would be a relief."

Graye says nothing more. Ms. Ellis is excitable and if Graye stokes that flame of indignation, the frail old thing will get so worked up she won't be able to rest.

"I've been invited to dinner tonight," Graye says, veering the subject to one designed to distract.

"Dinner? As in a date?" Ms. Ellis peers closely at her.

"No, not a date."

"Well, I don't see why not. You'd be an attractive girl if you'd make an effort. I swear, it's like you're trying not to be noticed."

It's a refrain Graye has heard many times. She doesn't bother to explain, again, that spending a large portion of your formative years in the care of nuns doesn't prepare you for the complexities of decorating yourself.

An image of Laura floats up. The classic simplicity of her beauty, so far removed from Graye's experience, may as well be another language. Nothing about Laura sparkled, yet everything shone with a warm and effortless light.

"It amazes me, sometimes, that you and Natalie were such good friends. My great-niece had a shallow streak, you know."

Natalie Ellis was Graye's roommate during her freshman year at Cornell. She vividly recalls the sense of reckless energy that followed Natalie into a room, then lingered even after she'd gone.

They don't speak of her often, the doomed girl whose death brought them together.

Married a jaw-dropping six times, Ms. Ellis reverted to her maiden name after divorcing her first husband. ("Fewer complications when you trade them in, dear.") She never had children of her own, a choice she says she mostly doesn't regret, but she was extremely fond of her great-niece.

Natalie had come to upstate New York at her great-aunt's urging, Eileen willing to pay for her education to have her nearby.

At the funeral, her voice hollowed by loss, Ms. Ellis admitted to Graye that she'd always seen her younger self in Natalie. "Never satisfied, that girl. Always looking for a bigger thrill."

Heroin had proved one thrill too many.

Graye first visited Ms. Ellis at Crestview on a desperate whim a month after Natalie was buried. She couldn't settle into the quiet Natalie's loss left behind.

"I suppose you saw something of your sister in her," Ms. Ellis muses. "Both daredevils, from what you've said."

Graye smiles, touched that Ms. Ellis remembers the stories she's shared over the years. That the details are mostly fiction doesn't matter. To Eileen Ellis, they're real. And to Graye, they're more than real. When she's spinning stories, the boundary between truth and lies fades, and she can paint the past in any colors she chooses. It's the best, the only, form of therapy that helps.

"Alex and Natalie were a lot alike," Graye agrees.

Eileen Ellis is eighty-four years old. At some point, Graye knows, she'll come to sign the visitors log, and one of the nurses will pull her aside to break the bad news with practiced and sympathetic phrases.

One thing Graye has learned, family doesn't always fit neatly into a predetermined shape. Sometimes, family is no more and no less than what you make it.

5

GRAYE

"You're leaving?"

Graye's hand stalls as she lifts the wine glass to her lips.

"Not right away," Laura says. "At least, not David. He'll finish the semester before joining me."

Graye's head is spinning. Whether from the unexpected news or the generous amount of wine the Wests have poured, she isn't sure.

"You're moving to *Texas*?" Graye tries to imagine the couple, so urbane in their red-brick townhouse with jazz playing softly in the background, in Texas.

Laura smiles like she knows what Graye is thinking but finds it all a grand adventure.

"Not necessarily the Texas you might be picturing," she says. "There's a tiny, nearly forgotten island on the Gulf Coast called Port Mary. Not a tumbleweed in sight."

Laura stands and leans over the table to refill Graye's wine glass.

"I spent summers there with my grandmother as a kid. Three magical months every year."

Her voice grows soft, her smile sad and nostalgic. "She passed away last year."

"I'm sorry," Graye says softly.

Laura tilts her head and studies Graye. "Thank you. You sound like you mean that. I loved her very much."

Graye has nothing except broken impressions of her own grandmother. A hoarse voice that frightened her, the overpowering smell of thin, cheap cigarettes. Screaming matches between her and Graye's mother.

Mother. She can go months at a time without thinking about her, then from nowhere, an image will flicker into focus, catching her off guard, always.

In life, Graye's mother was difficult at best. In death, she's a wound that won't heal.

Gracie's, she corrects. Not her mother. Gracie's mother. Gracie's grandmother. They're both gone now. They all are.

"She left us her old carriage house by the beach," Laura goes on. "It's been in the family forever, along with the main house that was converted into a hotel almost seventy years ago."

"She left *you* her house by the beach, you mean," David adds. The slur in his voice has become more pronounced as the evening has progressed.

Laura's gaze flickers briefly toward her husband. Her patience with him is admirable, but Graye can see it's wearing thin.

Dr. West answered the door with a drink in his hand and hasn't slowed down since.

"The hotel is self-sufficient and runs fine without me, but the carriage house has been vacant since my grandmother passed. With David's teaching post coming to an end, there's no better time. I'm going to head down next week to get it set up. Once the semester is through, I'll be ready and David won't have to be bothered with the details."

"What did I ever do to deserve such a *practical* wife?"

Laura turns her head slowly to stare at him as he lounges in his chair, studying the ice in his glass.

"I really don't know," she says.

A dry smirk forms on his lips.

"Enough about us, though." Laura turns her attention back to Graye. "Tell me about yourself. Is your master's nearly complete?"

"Soon."

"Creative writing, you said? Any big plans for after?"

"I . . . I'm not exactly sure yet."

"Miss Templeton is surprisingly circumspect when it comes to her own ambitions," Dr. West states with an emphasis on his consonants. "She went through the entire interview process without once uttering the words *aspiring writer*. It's the reason I chose her."

"Really?" Laura says. "A grad student in creative writing who's not working on the next great American novel? How very . . . extraordinary."

"You and my wife have that in common, Graye . . . if nothing else. She's not a novelist either."

"I wouldn't dare," Laura says in a light but distinctly chilly voice. "One artistic temperament in the house is enough. Two, and there might be no survivors."

"My dearest wife is too humble," Dr. West says to Graye with a wave of his bourbon. "She may never have written a word of prose, but her opinion holds an inordinate amount of sway. She could part seas on a recommendation alone."

Laura's face has grown guarded.

"And thank goodness for that." Her words are no less lethal for the softness of their delivery. "Otherwise, where would we be?"

Dr. West raises his glass in mock salute, then drains it with a grimace.

"Please excuse me, ladies." He struggles to stand without toppling out of the chair. "As stimulating as the company is, duty calls."

He sets the glass on the table with a bang that makes Graye flinch, and gives his wife a long look. Laura's eyes meet his in a silent challenge, a challenge he turns and walks away from without a glance in their guest's direction.

"I apologize, Graye," Laura says once David is gone.

Graye shakes her head and waves off the apology, though the poison-tipped words the couple throw at each other leave her unsettled.

"It's no excuse, but he didn't get the news he was hoping for today. He's been impossible ever since," Laura says. "Is there anything worse than a writer with a bruised ego?"

"You were responsible for his big break, weren't you?"

Laura's eyes swivel to meet Graye's. "You've done your homework."

"I read about him before I applied to be his TA," Graye admits.

It isn't exactly an untruth.

"Well, that's the official story." Laura fans her hands outward in front of her face. "'Book blogger launches career of debut novelist and finds romance made in literary heaven.'"

Laura shakes her head, a rueful smile on her face. "The truth is, David would have made it with or without me. But the association was marketing gold. I got tagged with the label *influential*, and that made me so in the process. David and I both benefitted from that. We still do. Not so romantic when you put it that way, is it?"

"But you got him an agent, then a publishing contract, didn't you?"

"Me?" She shakes her head. "No. All I did was make an introduction. My father's in publishing, that much is true, but David's book sold itself. If it hadn't been so brilliant, I could have made a million introductions and it wouldn't have mattered."

Graye says nothing but senses Laura is downplaying her role in igniting her husband's success. David West isn't the only author she's been the first to champion. Laura's name can be found in the acknowledgments of more than a few award-winning novels. She has an eye for spotting talent.

"And how do you find working for the literary genius moonlighting as a guest professor?" Laura's expression is warm as she watches Graye, like she's equally as interested in the answer as she is in mocking her husband.

"It's fine," Graye mumbles.

Laura's brows shoot up. She leans back in her chair, wine glass dangling from her fingertips.

Graye squirms under the scrutiny. "He mostly ignores me," she admits.

Laura sends her a small, understanding smile in reward for her honesty.

"Don't take it personally," Laura says. "You're not his type. Too astute to fall for his bullshit."

Graye blushes at the compliment. "You did, though," she blurts, then raises a hand to her mouth, eyes widening at her own words.

But Laura laughs. The sound pours down Graye's skin, soothing her nerves better than wine.

"I did, indeed," Laura says. "I'd blame it on youth or naivete, but it's been a while since anyone has accused me of either. Yet here I am."

"His first novel . . . it was stunning."

"It was, wasn't it?" Laura glances in the direction David has disappeared. "Sometimes I wonder where that man has gone."

6

Along the street outside her apartment, Graye walks with her head down. As usual, she's overlooked by most. She's a strikingly unremarkable girl.

But tonight, shadows and plainness can't shield her completely. A pair of eyes follows as she makes her way up the street, moving unobtrusively through the crowd. Graye's shoulders are hunched, her gaze pointing downward, as she steps out of the way of people moving in the opposite direction.

Fascinated, a single set of eyes notices the way she claims no space of her own, only glides like mist around the edges of the space taken up by others.

If these eyes hadn't been seeking her out, waiting for her to appear, she would have slipped past unnoticed by one and all. But for tonight, Graye Templeton claims the full attention of an audience of one.

Once she's gone up the stairs and through her front door, the eyes stay trained on her apartment windows and the play of shadows behind them as Graye moves around the room above.

The sound and laughter of passersby come and go. The watcher remains late into the night. One unseen person who contemplates the house of cards Graye Templeton has built her life on and the aftermath a gust of wind might leave behind.

7

GRAYE

Graye fumbles with her keys as she unlocks the door to her drab little apartment.

She shouldn't have had so much wine, but she relishes the unfamiliar sensations. She spent the bus ride home with her eyes shut tightly, replaying the conversations, the smiles, the barbs.

Dr. West is . . . a disappointment. There have been signs. The pedestal she constructed for him was already shaky. Seeing him in his natural state has kicked it completely away, leaving her preconceived image of him floundering helplessly on the ground.

Graye regrets that before taking the job, she never thought to ask his former TA what David West was like. Unfortunately, there'd been no opportunity. Zoe's departure from the position was sudden, and Graye had been dazzled by the once-in-a-lifetime opportunity to work with the famous author.

She had such hopes.

But Laura . . . Laura is a surprise.

Her phone vibrates in her pocket, bringing those thoughts to a sharp halt.

Graye doesn't need to check the number. She knows who's trying to reach her. She takes her time locking the door behind her before answering the call.

"Sister Margaret." The deference in her tone hasn't changed much over the years. As a child of nine, Graye was in awe of the nun who greeted her on her first day at St. Sebastian's Home for Girls. She still is.

"Graye, my dear." The sister's voice travels many miles and lands in the same vacant spot in Graye's heart it always has.

"I'm sorry I haven't returned your calls, Sister," Graye says. "I received your letter."

As she perches on the edge of the chair at her desk, Graye's posture is unconsciously straight and correct. She runs a hand across the front of the drawer where she shoved the letter and news article out of sight. She can't bring herself to open it.

"I wish you had, Graye. I wanted to tell you by phone, so you'd be better prepared for the news."

She had known, though. Somewhere, in the back of her mind, she'd always known. A perpetual clock had begun a countdown from the moment those bars had slammed closed. Eventually, that clock was bound to stop, and those same bars would swing open again. Graye simply chose not to dwell on it.

Until now.

"But I'm safe here, Sister. Aren't I?"

Graye waits for reassurance from the austere woman she's known for fifteen years.

"Most likely." Sister Margaret sighs. "But you must be aware of these things, Graye. Ignorance serves no one."

Graye rises to pace the small room. She double-checks the lock on the door.

"It was so long ago. I've made a new life. I'm no threat."

Graye moves to the large windows and peeks out through the blinds. She scans the street below. Nothing appears out of the ordinary.

27

"I hope, for your sake, that's true."

Graye lets go of the blinds and they spring back into place with a clatter.

After the evening she's had, the apprehension the nun's letter shook loose in her that morning feels far away. A silly little girl's irrational fears.

She pulls on her bottom lip and debates sharing her news. That she's possibly made a friend.

It's a rare thing.

Graye can count on one hand the number of friends she's had. Natalie, of course. Before that there was Autumn, a girl from the foster home. They'd been so close, in the way only childhood friends can be, yet their lives had taken different paths. They'd drifted apart.

She lives alone now. It's better that way.

In the end, she holds her tongue. Sister Margaret won't understand.

"How are you otherwise, Graye?"

"I'm well, Sister." Graye grasps the opportunity to turn the subject away from the past. "I'm working. My master's is almost finished."

"And you're still writing?"

A small smile flickers across Graye's lips. "Yes."

"Writing has always been your salvation, Graye. But don't forget to pick your head up from time to time. To live."

Graye thinks of Laura, of her warmth and her welcoming smile. Of how easy it would have been to move through one more day without connecting to another person, safely buffered as always by her anonymity and anxiety.

"I'm trying, Sister. I am."

After the nun has said her goodbyes, Graye pulls in a deep breath.

The past is just that. Gone, with nothing but hazy, painted-over memories as reminders.

Most of the time anyway. Except when the memories come alive and crowd in on her. But that hasn't happened in a very long time.

She's safe. She is.

She needs to believe that.

Opening her desk drawer, Graye retrieves the manuscript pages she keeps neatly stacked there.

She sits and removes two felt-tip pens. One black, for words and thoughts to be added.

The other red.

She carefully lifts the cover page and sets it aside as she uncaps the red pen.

Red is to cut.

Graye falls into the words on the page.

These words are her truth. Her life. These words will finally make Graye Templeton a reality, cementing her existence and her worth.

Once these words are published for the world, she'll never again be Gracie Thacker, playing pretend. She'll be real.

Graye can't suppress the hope that her new friend might be able to help her do that.

But first, everything must be perfect. Stunningly, brilliantly perfect.

The red bleeds onto the page. A small cut here. A larger, deeper cut there.

Perfect.

8

MARGARET

Sister Margaret sets the receiver of the phone softly back in place. Quick footsteps patter across the floor above her head.

Janie, out of bed again.

She's spoken with the child time and again about using the facilities before bedtime so she doesn't disturb the other girls in the night, but she can't be cross with her.

Janie hasn't wet her bed in months, and Margaret prefers to celebrate the victories, no matter how small.

Heaven knows the girls have enough battles to fight.

She leans back in the office chair and closes her eyes, replaying the conversation with Graye.

Had there been a hint of secrecy in her words? She sighs. She can't be certain without seeing the girl's face.

But Graye isn't a child anymore. She's a woman now. In truth, even as a child she'd seemed an old soul.

She's never forgotten the look in Graye's eyes when she arrived at St. Sebastian's. A mixture of fragile hope and a foregone resignation that her hope was bound to be crushed beneath inevitable disappointment.

Margaret's heart had cracked down the center as she stood there in the entryway with the sun streaming through the tall double doors. The child was illuminated from behind, as if light were a thing she was headed away from, with only dim and dusty shadows in her future.

But that was an illusion. A darkness lay in Graye's past. A darkness more damning than a little girl standing with her fingers gripped on the handle of a small suitcase could possibly comprehend.

Sister Margaret listens to the sound of Janie making her way back to bed and scrubs her palms across her face. She wonders, as always, if she's done the right thing.

She pulls the newspaper article from her pocket, a copy of the same one she clipped and mailed to Graye, and unfolds it flat upon the desk.

It's dated several weeks prior, and shows wear from traveling in her pocket for so long. She reads the headline again, though she doesn't need to. The words are branded upon her memory.

NOTORIOUS TEEN MURDERER TO BE RELEASED

The grainy photo below the words pulls her gaze, and she stares, hypnotized.

Grace Thacker lost her entire family on that long-ago night.

What followed was a media feeding frenzy. The trial of the decade, they called it. And the lynchpin for the prosecution was the videotaped testimony of nine-year-old Grace, who witnessed it all.

After the trial, the little girl promptly disappeared from the public eye, never to be seen or heard from again. Not that there weren't plenty who tried to find her.

Margaret prays time and miles will be enough to protect Graye now, but the hatred and the emptiness in the eyes peering back at her from the black-and-white photograph mock that hope.

The past is coming for Graye. She can feel it, in spite of her reassurances to the girl on the phone.

It's coming for them all.

9

The cinder girl's sister has found her prince, but Mother isn't pleased.

He hails from a faraway land, filled with dark, dangerous customs, and the road to reach it is long and treacherous.

"He's not the prince for you," Mother declares, and that's where it might have stayed.

But Sister's heart is won, and the prince hoards his prize.

"Let her come with me," he says. "Your daughter will be a conquering queen. It is her desire."

Mother resists.

"If you do not, I will go all the same, and I will take her heart, for it is mine. In its place, I'll leave nothing but a lump of clay, rolled in broken glass. She'll soon wither and die."

Still, Mother refuses. "Leave, then. My daughter doesn't need the heart you've stolen. She can have mine."

The prince shakes his head, confused. "Why do you hold so tightly, Mother? What is one daughter when you have a second?"

The cinder girl stands straighter, her back and shoulders strong. Mother laughs, but there is no joy in the sound.

"How dare you speak of things you don't understand? The one you want has been trained to spin wool into gold. What good to me is the one you'd leave? A pack mule to cart her sister's things."

Mother laughs her mirthless laugh again, but the prince does not return it.

His eyes fall upon the cinder girl, and she sees a sparkle on his cheek.

No, *she thinks,* a trick of the light. Not a tear. No one cries for me.

"You leave me no choice, Mother," the prince declares. *"Your daughter must come. She cannot survive from your heart alone, for you lie. You have none."*

◆ ◆ ◆

LAURA

The slamming door startles Laura from her daydream, and her elbow unbalances a pile of papers and books stacked on the desk. Her hands shoot out to try to stop the avalanche, but it does no good.

She sighs as the detritus of her professional life scatters and slides across the floor, helped along by the breeze from the open windows that carries the scent and murmur of the ocean.

Footsteps approach.

"I thought you were going to get this crap organized." David leans against the doorjamb.

Laura blows back the hair hanging in her face but clamps her jaw on the retort that springs up.

For all his grumbling about moving to a kitschy beach town on the edge of the world, he's shed New York in layers and replaced it with a darkening tan, a continual five o'clock shadow, and a growing collection of linen shorts.

The regular presence of a drink in his hand completes the Hemingway-esque transformation.

Laura has been in Port Mary for six months. The first three, she spent alone, reacquainting herself with the island and the workings of the hotel—she inherited her grandmother's majority shares. But after an initial assessment, she's pleased with the way things are being run. This left her free to spend most of her time unpacking and preparing the carriage house for David's arrival.

His office was beautifully organized before he even set his suitcase down. Laura positioned his antique desk with a view of the beach. She stocked the drawers with the brands of paper and pens he preferred, then added a mini-fridge within arm's reach, filled to his tastes. Not that he noticed her efforts, but there's little else she can do to help David.

The furrow in his brow and distraction in his eyes tells her an organized office hasn't lent him any more creative spark today than it did the day before. Or the day before that.

But asking about his work will only make her a target for his frustration.

When she was younger and cared more, his biting sarcasm could wound, but these days she turns a deaf ear to his tortured-artist moods.

"I think I need to cast a wider net if I'm going to find an assistant," she says, purposely turning the conversation in a direction he'll find tiresome as she leans down to scoop up the mess.

"None of the applicants up to your exacting standards?" He casts a pointed glance around her wreck of a workspace.

She stares at him for a beat, struggling to remind herself of the man she knows he can be—when he isn't being this one.

It's getting more difficult every day to bring that man to mind.

Something of her thoughts must show on her face, and a brief and rare flash of contrition passes over David's own.

"Is there anything I can do to help?" he asks.

An olive branch. And with the precision of a master strategist, he sets her back on her heels.

Laura's stomach tightens as an uneasy guilt fills her. For all his failings, she's far from blameless.

She's betrayed him. In the most elemental of ways, knowingly and deliberately, she's betrayed his trust.

His attitude isn't the only thing chipping away at their marriage.

"David," she says, plunging forward before she can second-guess her timing. "We need to talk."

The concern he's pasted onto his face fades and he stiffens.

She recognizes her mistake immediately.

"If you've found something new to harp on, Laura, I'd just as soon—"

"No," she says. "It's nothing like that."

She's put him on the defensive. She's going about this all wrong.

It's hard to say which of them is more relieved to hear the doorbell chime.

"I'll get it," he says, tossing a darkened look in her direction.

"David," she calls. He doesn't turn back.

She closes her eyes and leans her head back. She knows better than to begin a conversation with him that way. It never ends well.

Voices carry from the front door, and Laura's ears prick. She's familiar with only a few of the neighbors from her childhood summers on Port Mary. Dr. Lawson, an old family friend, is still two houses down. These days, though, many of the homes spread out along the island have been converted to rentals, and the summer season is still in swing.

She stands, curious, and more hopeful than she should be that it's a Girl Scout selling cookies door to door. Nervous anxiety gives her the munchies, and she could murder a box of Thin Mints.

She stifles a sigh when she comes around the corner and realizes the figure in the doorway is certainly not a little girl in uniform. It was a vain hope anyway.

She wanders closer. There's something familiar about the woman's voice, but David is blocking her view.

"I'm hoping you'll be willing to write a letter of recommendation, Dr. West," Laura overhears.

Recognition dawns and she moves to stand beside her husband.

"Graye," Laura says. "This is a surprise."

If she hadn't placed her voice before she saw the young woman, Laura may not have recognized her. Gone is the mousy shrinking violet, replaced with a new, sharper version of Graye. The crisp cream slacks and sleeveless coral blouse, paired with a long silver pendant and leather sandals, certainly hadn't been part of her wardrobe six months prior.

"You could have sent the request via email, Miss Templeton," David says, disregarding Laura's welcome.

Graye blushes and glances at her feet. Laura's heart goes out to her. It's true, but David can be such a jerk.

"I . . . I did, sir," Graye mumbles. "Twice."

Laura glares at her husband, who manages to look mildly embarrassed.

"David—" she begins.

"I had to come to Houston for the interview tomorrow anyway," Graye says quickly. "Once I realized how close Port Mary was . . . I know it's rude to drop by like this, but Cecelia Ainsley was very specific about her expectations. If I mention a position working for David West, she's going to ask to see a recommendation."

Graye pauses to take a breath, then quickly continues, clearly afraid David will slam the door on her at any moment.

"Without one in hand, she'll assume there's a reason you wouldn't give me one, and then I'll have lost the job before I've even opened my mouth."

David's brows have risen at the mention of Cecelia Ainsley, and they remain there until Graye finishes speaking.

"Given Ms. Ainsley's opinion of my work, I doubt a recommendation from me will do you any favors."

Graye opens her mouth, but for a moment no words come out.

"Oh," she says finally. The air seems to leak out of her. Despite the changes to her appearance, Laura sees plainly the awkward girl Graye was when they met months ago on the street.

"Graye, hon, come inside. I'm sure it's not as bad as that," Laura says, though she remembers the scathing review Cecelia Ainsley gave David's last novel and thinks it probably *is* as bad as that.

"You look lovely, by the way." She takes Graye's arm and leads her to the sofa in the living room. "You've done something different with your hair?"

Graye smiles vaguely and reaches to smooth the sleek bob that has taken the place of her unruly frizz.

"Laura, a haircut isn't going to make any difference to that ratty old bi—"

"David," Laura says sharply. "That's not helping."

He shoves his hands into his pockets and leans insolently against the front door he's closed behind them. "I don't know what you expect me to do about it, *dear*."

She glares at her husband. "You could start by going to your office and typing up a recommendation letter."

"It won't do any good. The woman publicly branded me a hack. As if she has any room to talk. She's pumped out the same dystopian garbage masquerading as literature since the early seventies."

"David," Laura forces out through clenched teeth. "Can you set your ego aside for one minute? An endorsement from you may not mean anything to Cecelia Ainsley, but there are plenty of other doors it would open."

The irritation on David's face changes before her eyes.

"I suppose you're right," he says grudgingly. "But you should have called first, Miss Templeton."

He unfolds himself from his indifferent pose and walks toward his office as if he's graciously granting a favor rather than succumbing to flattery.

Graye, who watches the exchange in silence, looks at Laura with large eyes. "He's right, I shouldn't have stopped by unannounced."

"Don't be ridiculous. He wasn't working today anyway. I should be thanking you for keeping him occupied." Laura cocks her head to one side. "Listen, are you hungry?"

"Oh, I don't want to impose—"

Laura nods. "I'll take that as a yes."

"I've been too nervous about the interview to eat much," Graye admits.

"Good, because I'm starving and I have a seat reserved at the best place in town," Laura declares. She's pleased to see the young woman again, and she can't deny the girl has impressive timing.

She saved Laura from a huge misstep. The confrontation with David needs to happen, and soon, but Graye's impromptu visit has bought her enough time to plan a more finessed approach.

It's something to celebrate.

"Let's get out of here," she says with a smile.

10

GRAYE

The best place in town turns out to be a run-down taco stand tucked into the sand like a piece of a shipwreck the ocean has spit out. Graye frowns at one of the corners where it's propped on a cinder block, a stack of gym weights, and what is possibly a boat anchor. She's surprised a stiff breeze hasn't toppled it back into the waves.

A grizzled bear of a man in a stained apron stands as they approach. The whole contraption lists to one side, and Graye reassesses. No breeze is taking the little building anywhere, not with this guy inside it.

"Again, you're back," the bearded man booms, scowling at Laura. His voice has a hint of an accent. French?

The greeting brings Graye up short, but Laura smiles her brightest.

"Antoine, am I starting to grow on you?" she asks with a wink.

"*Oui*, madame. Like a fungus."

"Oh stop. You'll make me blush. We'll take two shrimp tacos each," she says, then glances at Graye. "You're okay with shrimp?"

Graye nods.

"That's good," Antoine says. "The pork—*c'est la merde*."

"I don't know what that means," Graye says softly to Laura.

"He said the pork is shit," Laura translates, not bothering to keep her voice down. "He's right. It's terrible. Stick with the shrimp."

Graye doesn't need to be fluent to get the gist of the angry stream of words that flies from the Frenchman's mouth in Laura's direction. Apparently, it's fine for him to critique his own offerings, but Laura's opinion is another matter.

Unfazed, Laura slaps two bills onto the makeshift counter and turns her back on the big man mid-rant.

She motions to one of the empty weathered picnic tables nearby.

While the taco stand thumps and creaks ominously at their backs, the two women sit facing the Gulf of Mexico.

Even with the grumblings of the surly man peppering her ears, Graye is entranced by the sheer scope of the view.

From where she sits, perhaps she can understand why people once believed the world was flat. An undeniable feeling of insignificance washes over her in the face of such power and beauty. The sand and surf, with their incessant give and take. The sense of being at the edge of . . . well, of everything.

What more could there possibly be?

"It's breathtaking," Graye says in a hushed voice, then glances at Laura, embarrassed.

But the other woman is gazing out at the horizon, where the water blends with the sky. "It never gets old," she says softly. "At night, with the stars overhead and the waves crashing, I can almost picture it the way it must have been hundreds of years ago. Port Mary was a pirate hideaway, once upon a time."

Graye stares at Laura. The wind buffets her hair, and her eyes are far away and shining. She can imagine her there back then, waiting on the shore for her husband to return, or on the deck of a ship of her own.

Laura shakes her head and turns her eyes back to Graye. "I'm sorry," she says. "David would call that sentimental trash, but I've always loved this place. The wonder of it has never faded. Thank goodness."

"If Your Highness so pleases, your order is up," comes the thunderous voice of the Frenchman, breaking the spell. "And don't expect me to walk it out to you."

"God forbid," Laura says with a smile for Graye. She rises and retrieves their food.

When she returns, Laura digs into one of the overstuffed tacos with gusto and Graye follows suit.

"These are good," she says, unable to hide her surprise.

Laura finishes chewing, then swallows. "Of course they're good. Otherwise, why put up with the abuse?"

She polishes off the first taco in two more bites, then wipes her mouth on a paper napkin. "So tell me about this job," she says.

With the taste of salt on her lips, the sun on her shoulders, and the constancy of the ocean in her ears, Graye describes the mundane duties Cecelia Ainsley has outlined for a personal assistant. The juxtaposition is dizzying.

Laura's eyebrows shoot up only once.

"Aren't you a little overqualified to be walking her dogs?" she asks mildly.

"Not really," Graye says. "I've got no experience except as a TA. I was a scholarship kid and couldn't afford to take any of the unpaid internships others could."

"But you must have a solid work ethic if you got through college and grad school on scholarships," Laura says thoughtfully.

"I'm not afraid of work. I know she has a reputation as . . . difficult, but I have to start somewhere." She shrugs and goes back to her food.

"How are your organizational skills?" Laura asks as she breaks off a piece of tortilla and tosses it into the air.

A white gull swoops down and plucks it from the sky with practiced ease. The four gulls that follow in its wake cry their displeasure.

"*Mon Dieu*, no feeding the birds!" comes an explosion of irritation from the taco stand. "Shoo, you filthy animals!"

Antoine lurches out of his cave, waving a broom ineffectually at the sky.

"And multitasking?" Laura asks.

Graye gapes at the chaos the woman has caused and almost misses the question.

"Oh . . . um, yeah. You have to be able to handle all sorts of things as an assistant. Priorities are fluid. It's easier to anticipate problems down the line and plan for them than try and put out fires as they happen."

Antoine almost manages to knock one of the gulls from the sky, but it dodges at the last minute and sends a shrill complaint in his direction before settling farther down the beach.

"No feeding the birds, woman! How many times do I need to say this?" He shakes the broom in their direction as he stomps past them back to his stand, still grumbling under his breath.

Laura never blinks. She's staring at Graye with an intensity that's disconcerting.

"What?" Graye finally asks.

"I have a proposition for you, Graye Templeton."

◆ ◆ ◆

Graye has never lived anyplace luxurious. From a run-down trailer, to a foster home for girls, to cheap student housing, she hasn't even worked her way up to lower middle class yet.

But the motel she's booked in Rockaway is seedy enough to give even Graye pause.

Port Mary, as enchanting as it is, has only the one hotel on the tiny island, and Graye can't afford the rates. She's taken the last ferry back to the mainland.

Not even the bored desk clerk who reeks of marijuana can dampen her mood.

Laura West offered her a job.

"Yeah?" the clerk says when he notices her standing at the counter. His eyes flicker back to the television. Graye studies the nick on his pale neck near his Adam's apple.

When she doesn't answer right away, his gaze swivels back to her face.

"What do you need?" he says with a sigh.

"Am I starting to grow on you?" she asks suddenly. Her voice is overbright, teasing and out of place in the drab space that smells like old mop water.

His eyes widen when Graye sends him a playful wink.

She has no idea where that came from, but the clerk's reaction is worth it, and she stifles a laugh.

"'Scuse me?" he says, leaning forward suspiciously.

"I'd like to pay for another week, if you don't mind. Room 127," Graye says.

"Yeah. Okay," the clerk replies slowly. The name tag pinned to his wrinkled shirt reads *Tripp*.

That's unfortunate.

Graye struggles to hold back a snort of laughter.

"That'll be $255," he says.

Her amusement sours. "But last week it was $215."

Tripp shrugs. "Rates change seasonally."

"The season is the same this week as it was last week," she points out.

Another shrug. "Look, lady, it's $255. Pay it or don't. Whatever."

Graye sighs and counts out the cash from her wallet. The bus ticket from Ithaca to Texas, the rental car, and two weeks' lodging have quickly depleted her savings, but what choice does she have?

She could have told Laura the truth—that she doesn't need an extra week to head back to New York State and collect her things before she can start her new position. But that would only complicate things.

It's better this way.

Graye collects her receipt from Tripp, whose attention is already back on the television screen, and turns to walk toward her room.

One of a group of shaggy men clustered around an old sedan lets out a wolf whistle as she passes, but Graye refuses to let it get to her.

She unlocks her door and drops the keys to the rental car and her plastic keycard onto the small bedside table, then falls back upon the bed and stretches her arms above her head.

Personal assistant to Laura West.

It may not have as much cachet as assistant to Cecelia Ainsley, but Graye doesn't care.

Laura West began her career almost by accident, with nothing but a blog about novels she loved. After she made her future husband famous, she took what was little more than a hobby, combined it with a degree in marketing, and turned herself into a full-fledged institution.

Now she's a sought-after speaker and workshop leader. She founded a book club that includes hundreds of chapters in towns all over the world.

But the crown jewel in her repertoire is an annual themed retreat.

"You handle all of this alone?" Graye had asked.

"And some other things," Laura said. "But I don't want to scare you off, so we'll stick with that for now."

Laura needn't have worried.

A dozen years ago, life had already taught Graye its greatest lesson: everything dies. She'd been a lonely girl enraptured by David West's breakout novel, *Broken Home Harvest*, a gift from Sister Margaret on her birthday. It had swept her away from the cold, dark walls of St. Sebastian's.

David West, for all his faults, has achieved the ultimate impossibility. His published work will carry his voice forward long after he's gone. It is its own organism now, separate from the man himself.

Next week she'll be a cog in the wheel of the machine that created him.

Just maybe, with luck and hard work, that same machine will launch her too.

Things are finally falling into place for Graye Templeton, she thinks with a smile.

Graye drifts off to sleep that night, contentedly unaware that if she'd lifted her head as she walked to her room, she might have noticed a dark car, a rental like hers.

If she'd been paying attention, she might have wondered if she'd seen the same car on the ferry to Port Mary, and again on her return.

But as Sister Margaret knows, there's a strange innocence about Graye. Lost in her thoughts, she doesn't look. She doesn't notice. And if she had, her eyes would have skimmed over the darkened figure without stopping, without any glimmer of recognition.

Over a decade behind bars changes a person.

11

GRAYE

Out of habit, Graye knocks lightly on the side door before she lets herself into the West home.

In the weeks since she's moved into their small detached guesthouse as part of her arrangement with Laura, she's become a fixture in the household.

"The pay isn't great, but the rent is nonexistent," Laura had said.

Graye sets her overnight bag next to the door and wanders down the hallway toward Laura's office.

When she hears her friend's soft, intimate laugh, she stops.

She's been careful not to intrude on the Wests' privacy. She's particularly mindful to give Dr. West no cause for complaint.

He hadn't been pleased when the two women returned late in the afternoon that first day with news there was a change of plans.

His letter of recommendation, typed at his wife's request, wasn't necessary after all.

"No, we didn't waste your time," Graye overheard Laura telling him. "She can add it to her résumé for the future."

"That's not the point, Laura. You could have called to let me know."

"I'm sorry, David. I didn't think about it."

"Clearly. Here. You can give her this, but I'm sure it won't be as impressive as experience working with Laura West, goddess of the *blog*."

Whatever Laura said next was too muffled to hear, but there was no mistaking the flush of anger on her cheeks when she emerged from his office with the letter in hand.

"I don't want to cause any trouble," Graye said quietly.

Laura handed over the sheet of paper.

"Trouble was here before you were. Come on, I'll give you the tour."

Since that day, Graye treads lightly around Dr. West. In turn, he ignores her, much as he did when she was his teaching assistant.

The arrangement suits them both.

"Of course it was perfect." Laura's voice is a low murmur of satisfaction as it drifts from her office. "I know what you like."

Graye takes a careful step backward in the hallway.

She's grown used to the couple's constant sniping, but the rare times they manage to set that aside and share a passing touch or a smile over an inside joke throws Graye off her stride.

Laura laughs again. "Hugo, I don't think your wife would care for that."

Graye stops, the expression on her face almost comical as her eyes widen and her lips fall open.

A thousand competing thoughts careen through her mind. The most pressing one, and the loudest, shouts that she get out of this hallway immediately.

Quickly and quietly, Graye moves back into the living room. She picks up her bag and drops it again with a loud thump.

"Laura," she calls, her voice echoing off the scuffed hardwood floors. "Are you here?"

"Just a sec," comes the reply.

Graye shoves her hands in her pockets and stares out the front window toward the beach while she gathers her runaway thoughts and schools her face into a neutral expression.

So what if she's seeing someone else? Graye tries to tamp down her initial surprise, a childish reaction she scolds herself for.

Why shouldn't she be? David is . . . well, he's David, and he can't be an easy person to love. Not forever.

But what does she know? Romance is a foreign concept to Graye. Relationships never end well, as a rule. She doesn't understand why anyone bothers.

Friendship is hard enough. Throw in sex and love and need, and things just get messy.

A darkened room, fake wood paneling on the walls. Her hands covering her eyes, gaps between her fingers. Just enough to see too much.

Heavy, hurried footsteps pounded, shaking the room, shaking the world. Shaking everything down around them. All coming apart at the seams.

Shouting, shrieking voices, panicked and angry.

"Grace!" A voice close by, hands upon her cheeks.

Everything red.

Red, on the fake wood wall. She stares, watching it drip slowly down.

"Graye?" Laura asks. "Are you all right?"

"Yes, of course," Graye says, turning to smile brightly at her friend. "Why wouldn't I be?"

Laura shakes her head with her phone dangling from her fingertips, forgotten.

"I don't know. You looked . . . strange. Frightened."

"Just thinking about tonight." Graye moves away from the window. "Checking things off the mental to-do list."

Laura pats her arm. "There's nothing to worry about. Janelle's an experienced host, and Mai Linh is funny and smart and charming once she's had a glass of champagne to calm her nerves."

When Laura had floated the idea of attending the Austin chapter meeting of the Wildflower Book Club, all Graye's muscles had constricted at once.

"Oh, I don't know," she'd said, her voice high and reedy. "Book clubs are so intimate and everyone knows each other and . . . and small talk . . . and wouldn't I just be in the way?"

Giving a lecture to a bunch of indifferent students is one thing. She can come into the lecture hall prepared, say what she needs to say, and that's the end of it. There's no need to interact.

"Now you sound just like an author," Laura had said with a laugh.

Graye sat up straighter. "What . . . what do you mean?"

"Well, some of them are extroverts, I suppose. But a lot are just like you—introverted and nervous about social situations. Most hide it better than you're doing now, though."

"Really?" The idea sounded absurd.

"Yes, really. Mai Linh, the guest author joining them? She's nearly mute with nerves until she's had one drink."

"Mai Linh is going to be there?"

"Hmm, yes." Laura was watching her from the corner of her eye. "I thought it would be a good opportunity for you to get your feet wet on the book club side of things, but I understand if you want to skip it."

Laura wasn't stealthy. They both knew she was dangling a carrot and, more so, that she was enjoying watching Graye's whiskers twitch at the temptation.

Graye bit her lip. "Do you think she'd sign my copy of *Songbird*?"

"I'll book the hotel," Laura had said, clapping her hands together.

Now, with a four-hour drive ahead of them, Graye hopes she can maintain a normal facade.

Laura hoists the strap of her bag onto her shoulder and angles her chin toward the door.

"Ready?" she asks, looking for all the world as though she hasn't just been sharing an illicit conversation with a man who isn't her husband.

"Sure." Graye takes a deep breath and determines to set the awkward knowledge aside.

The bright day greets them. Graye is surprised at the touch of sadness that comes with the thought of leaving the island. Silly. They'll be back the following day. But Port Mary, with its postcard views and little pockets of strangers wandering up and down the beach, has quickly begun to feel like home.

She's yet to work up the courage to visit the taco stand alone, though.

The gravel driveway crunches beneath their feet as the two women make their way beneath the carport to Laura's SUV.

"Well, damn," Laura says softly. Her shoulders slump and the strap of her bag slides from its perch there. It falls to the ground with a thunk.

"What's the matter?" Graye asks.

But as she rounds the corner of the car behind Laura, she can see the problem for herself.

"I've never changed a tire," Laura says. "Can you believe that? And David's off fishing somewhere. I doubt I can reach him on his cell."

Graye shrugs and sets her own bag next to Laura's.

"No big deal. I can do it. You have a spare in the back?"

Laura's head slowly turns in Graye's direction. "Well, look at you. A woman with hidden skills. Yeah, I think it's back here."

As Graye shows Laura how to loosen the lug nuts, then raise the car on the jack, she recalls Sister Margaret walking her through the same steps when she was a teenager. Laura's SUV is nicer than the beaten-up van from the girl's home, but the process is the same.

A tug of guilt pulls at her. She should call the nun and let her know she's settled into a new job, but something holds her back. Some sense that she'd jinx her good fortune.

It isn't that the sister isn't supportive. Not exactly. But she has a no-nonsense way about her that prods Graye to examine things from all angles, including potential pitfalls.

Graye is happy here, and that's enough. For now, at least.

As Graye rolls the deflated tire around the front of Laura's car, a figure on the beach catches her eye.

The guesthouse she's living in is tucked beside and a bit behind the Wests' home, leaving little view to speak of, but Graye takes the opportunity to walk along the shore whenever the mood strikes.

Her favorite time is early morning, when it's mostly deserted.

There's something about the man in the red board shorts. Something familiar. She's seen him before, an early riser as well.

He wears a windbreaker in the mornings to ward off the chill, and his hood is usually up when he passes, leaving his face in shadows.

Unlike the other people spread sparsely along the beach, he's turned away from the ocean.

He isn't wearing a windbreaker now, and although it's impossible to be certain because of the distance between them, the man appears to be watching . . . her.

Graye goes cold suddenly, despite the sun warming her shoulders.

"Do you need a hand?" Laura asks, startling Graye and pulling her attention back from the figure on the beach.

"No," Graye murmurs. "I've got it. No need for you to get dirty too."

She glances down at her blackened hands and dirt-smudged clothes. "Do you mind if I wash up and change?"

"Anything for the woman of the hour," Laura says.

Before Graye makes her way toward the guesthouse, she risks a furtive look over her shoulder at the man on the beach, but the spot where he was standing just moments before is empty.

He's gone, like he was never there.

Laura hadn't noticed the long, clean gash in the sidewall of her tire. Graye chooses not to mention it.

"Good Lord, what did you pack in this thing? Bricks?"

Laura lifts Graye's bag from the back of the SUV with an "Oomph."

"Manuscripts," Graye says.

"You brought work? You don't have to impress me, you know. You've already got the job."

"It's my favorite part, though. Leaving them behind felt like abandoning little ducklings."

"Aw," Laura says with a tilt of her head and an indulgent smile. "That's sweet. But here. Your ducklings are heavy."

Graye takes the bag from her and they walk toward the entrance of the hotel.

"Do you miss it?" Graye asks.

"What? Combing through my unsolicited slush pile?"

Laura isn't a literary agent or an editor. Other than a connection to her father, she has no role in publishing at all, but that doesn't stop the stream of unrequested, unpublished work that shows up in her mail and inbox.

"It's my own fault," she'd admitted when she showed Graye the stacks of manuscripts she'd collected but hadn't had time to assess. "I can't stop myself from reading at least the first few pages. And once in a blue moon I've found a rare gem and passed it along to Dad."

One of those "rare gems" had been Hugo Caron's debut, a sweeping historical saga that had gone on to win the National Book Award. The glossy author photo inside the back flap of his book jacket shows a handsome dark-skinned man with a faint smile that hints at mischief.

Is Hugo Caron the Hugo that Laura had been so friendly with on the phone? Graye wonders how many men named Hugo her friend could know.

"I miss it a little, I guess," Laura admits. "But I trust you to pass along anything that catches your eye, and that frees me up to do the things that actually pay the bills."

Laura has no inkling of the fireworks that exploded inside of Graye when she passed the task along to her new assistant.

It's the perfect gift-wrapped, gilt-edged opportunity that Graye had hoped for, and she's determined not to waste it.

Thoughts of the man on the beach intrude, but Graye dismisses them. She imagined his eyes on her, surely. No one knows she's busy working to make her dreams come true on a tiny island off the Texas coast. Not even Sister Margaret.

As for the flattened tire and how it had been damaged, those are thoughts she refuses to even entertain.

What matters, the only thing that matters, is the path ahead.

12

LAURA

Laura sighs as she ends the call with her husband. She leans onto the balcony railing of the hotel room, her mind far from the downtown scene below her. Before she left, David claimed he was going to use the time to rework his newest manuscript, but lingering resentment seeped between his words.

She's grateful he didn't bother to ask for her opinion before he sent the last draft to Isaac. As it was, his editor had been the one forced to tell him it needed work.

She was on the phone checking in with Janelle when he called, so she said goodbye and clicked over to David.

He wanted to know where she'd put the corkscrew. She could hear him fumbling through the kitchen drawers as they spoke.

Laura straightens.

It's time for a serious reassessment of her priorities.

"Mai Linh's flight is late," she says as she closes the sliding glass door behind her, shutting out the blast of heat and the sounds of traffic that push their way into the room.

Laura lifts the hair off her neck and leans over the air-conditioning unit to cool herself.

Graye is hanging her clothes in the small closet, but whirls around with a touch of panic in her eyes.

"It'll be fine," Laura assures her. "The flight wasn't canceled, just delayed. She'll be landing soon."

Graye closes her eyes and takes a deep breath, visibly struggling to relax.

Laura has an overwhelming urge to hug the girl.

"I just spoke with Janelle. She's got everything under control," she says.

An hour later, when the two women step through the doors of the hotel's banquet room where the special book club meeting will be held, Laura can see that, true to form, Janelle Mathis has outdone herself.

A tall, thin woman in her sixties with an elegant braid that falls across one shoulder, Janelle crosses the room to greet them.

"Laura," she says, opening her arms wide and encircling her. "I'm so glad you could make it. Now that you're an official Texan, I'm hoping I'll get to see your gorgeous face more often."

"Janelle, this is Graye Templeton, my new assistant." Laura places a hand lightly on Graye's back with a smile.

"It's a pleasure to meet you, Graye," Janelle says warmly.

"Is there anything I can do to help?" Graye asks, glancing around the room, where hotel staff are busily setting tables with cream and navy linens.

"Well now, since you asked," Janelle begins, taking Graye by the arm and leading her away. She's in good hands, Laura knows. Janelle will keep Graye busy enough that she won't have time to worry about anything else.

That leaves Laura free to wander. She peeks at the gift bags Janelle has placed on the chairs for the guests, smiling at the clean, distinctive dandelion logo she chose when she launched the Wildflower Book Club.

The little bag holds a small leather-bound notebook and pen, along with a blue cardboard jewelry box. Unable to resist, Laura tips up the lid of the box and gasps.

"Do you like them?" Janelle asks as she makes her way back to Laura.

"Janelle, these are beautiful!"

"Thank you. An artist friend of mine made them. I think they turned out well."

Laura holds the delicate silver necklace up for a closer look. It features a filigree version of the same dandelion from the logo.

Laura is surprised to feel tears welling up.

Janelle touches Laura's shoulder. "Good gracious, don't cry. I got one for you too."

Laura snorts and waves a hand in front of her face. "I'm sorry, I'm just so impressed with what you've done here."

Janelle glances around, her eyes bright. "I love an excuse for a party. The regular meetings are wonderful, don't get me wrong, but it's a special occasion when we have a visiting author like Mai Linh. Have you seen the cake?" she asks, linking her arm in Laura's. "The bakery recreated the cover of *Songbird*, and it's perfect, so no blubbering on it or you'll ruin their hard work."

When laughter from the hallway signals the first guests' arrival half an hour later, Graye appears by Laura's side.

"She'll be here," Laura assures her, reading the concern on her face. "Come meet some of the members."

They're making their way toward the entrance of the banquet room when Laura stumbles, her legs wobbling beneath her like a newborn foal. With a sharp intake of breath, she grips Graye's arm to stop herself from tumbling to the ground.

"Are you all right?"

Laura looks down and sees that her favorite pair of shoes has betrayed her.

"My heel," she says, angling her ankle to show the broken piece dangling from the back of her foot. "And this is the only pair I brought."

"I have some that might work. Here, have a seat and I'll run up to the room and get them."

Only a few minutes have passed before Graye returns and places a shoebox in Laura's hands.

"Graye, I honestly don't know how I've survived so long without—" She breaks off as she lifts the lid and catches a glimpse of the shoes in the box.

A gorgeous pair of heels the color of sparkling champagne nestles in the tissue of the box.

"Oh my," Laura breathes out in a low whisper. "These are . . ." She searches for the right word.

"Will they fit?" Graye asks.

Suddenly desperate to find out, Laura slips her feet into them and admires the way they subtly reflect the light.

"Like they were made for me," Laura says with a smile. "Thank you."

She tucks her other shoes into the box and slides it beneath her chair. She glances toward the door and gestures for Graye to follow her gaze.

"I told you she'd make it."

They see a slight woman with chin-length dark hair who looks like she wants to sink into the carpet.

"Let's catch her before she makes a run for it."

Mai Linh's shoulders relax some when she spots Laura heading her way, but only a little.

"I swear to God, Laura, I don't know how you talk me into these things," the newcomer whispers, casting nervous glances at the clusters of women who are beginning to notice her arrival.

"Good to see you too, Linh," Laura says.

"Don't patronize me."

Laura struggles not to laugh. "Linh," she says. "I'd like to introduce you to my assistant, Graye Templeton. Be nice, she's a fan."

Mai Linh rolls her eyes, but her face is kind as she turns to Graye. "I'm always nice."

Laura snorts, and Mai Linh glares in her direction before holding out a hand to Graye.

"I am. I just get twitchy in crowds. Forgive me. You can call me Linh."

It takes Graye a moment to find her voice as she shakes the author's hand. She looks starstruck, but she pulls herself together quickly.

"Can I get you a glass of champagne, Linh?" Graye asks.

Mai Linh graces her with a beatific smile. "I can already see that you and I, my dear, are going to get on like a house on fire."

Janelle, who has joined them just in time to catch the exchange, nods approvingly as Graye turns to fetch the promised drink.

"I don't know where you found her, Laura," Janelle says, "but she's a keeper."

Laura glances down at the heels and wonders if Graye would consider letting her buy them from her. It might break her heart to give them up.

As for Graye, she's quickly becoming indispensable.

"I couldn't agree more."

13

GRAYE

Graye lifts her head and peers across the darkened hotel room at Laura snuggled into the other bed.

She can hear the faint rise and fall of her breathing, which has maintained a steady rhythm for the last hour.

Graye tried to sleep, but the evening kept coming back to her in flashes. The warm, welcoming laughter of the women she met, the applause after Mai Linh spoke. The crisp taste of champagne lingering on her tongue.

Each time she closes her eyes, the sensations fill her head, teasing, leaving her to wonder if she imagined it all.

She eases back the bedcovers and slips from between the sheets.

Laura doesn't stir, and Graye is careful to stay quiet as she slips into her robe and pads to the built-in drawers across the room.

Ambient light filters from the sliding door, just enough for Graye's fingers to locate what she's looking for in the back of the drawer where she tucked her things earlier that day. Turning back to her bed, she sends another glance in Laura's direction before she sheds first her robe, then her pajamas.

She relishes the feel of high-quality material on her bare skin as she steps into the pencil skirt she's taken from the drawer. The zipper gives a faint buzz as she pulls it up. The cream silk of the blouse whispers secretly as she slides her arms into the sleeves, then fastens the buttons.

On quiet feet, she tiptoes to the closet the two women are sharing.

Laura offered to pay Graye for the champagne heels, an offer Graye promptly turned down.

"They're yours if you want them," she'd said. "A gift."

"Oh, I couldn't possibly—"

"Of course you can," Graye insisted. "Please."

So technically, the shoes Graye leans down and grasps with two fingers no longer belong to her, but she doesn't think Laura will mind if she borrows them this one time.

Silently, Graye crosses the room again and picks up the notebook and pen she received in her gift bag from Janelle. Then, with her bottom lip between her teeth, Graye gingerly unlocks and opens the sliding glass door that leads to the private balcony.

It's deep into the night now, so late that things are edging into early, an hour when even downtown is relatively quiet. Graye nevertheless holds her breath as she quickly backs through the doorway with the shoes and notebook in hand.

Laura stirs in the bed across the room as Graye slides the door closed. She watches through the glass as the other woman rolls over, then settles back in. Her eyes never open.

Graye lets out her pent-up breath.

She turns and takes a moment to enjoy the deserted cityscape. The night is warm, but welcoming, unlike the angry heat of the day. A confidante, and an audience, for Graye's sleeplessness.

She smiles faintly as she takes a seat in one of the chairs at the small outdoor table, then arches her feet and slips them into the shoes.

A hair too tight, they bite at her toes. She knew that when she bought them, but they were too perfect to pass up.

Graye scoots the chair closer to the table and straightens her posture.

Slowly, deliberately, she crosses one leg over the other, showcasing the slightly too small high heels.

Graye picks up the pen and flips the small notebook to the first page.

With a blindingly bright smile, she glances upward across the table to the place where another person might stand, if she weren't all alone.

"Whom should I make this out to?" she asks, pen poised and ready in her hand.

"Is that Catherine with a *C* or with a *K*?" she inquires.

With a nod, Graye drops her gaze to the blank page in front of her.

"For Katherine—with a *K*," she says aloud as she writes. "Don't be afraid to follow your dreams. Signed, Graye Templeton."

Graye finishes the signature, bold and loopy, with a flourish, then rips the page from the little book.

"Thank you. I'm so glad you enjoyed the book," she says as she holds the autograph up to no one.

Her fingers part. The night breeze catches the small page and takes it away, eager to claim it, if no one else is planning to.

It flutters and twirls through the dark, finally coming to rest in the street, just feet from the storm drain where it will eventually end up.

In time, rain water will leach the ink from the page, which will slowly disintegrate to nothing but bits and particles.

But Graye isn't concerned. There are more, many more, to come.

Alone in the quiet, amid thousands of sleeping souls, Graye Templeton smiles and signs her borrowed name, wearing borrowed shoes that perfectly complement her borrowed clothes, still stained with coffee, until all the pages in her little notebook are gone.

14

GRAYE

The sun is low on the western horizon when Graye peeks up from the manuscript in her lap. The closer they've come to Port Mary, the quieter Laura has grown, and in the last hour there's been only the swish of turning pages and the buzzing of Laura's phone.

The other woman stopped reading the incoming messages halfway through the drive. Now, as the two of them wait in the parked car for the ferry to dock, Graye notices she still doesn't check. Instead, with each intrusion she's grown more introspective.

"How are your ducklings today, Graye? Any swans hidden among them?" Laura asks, breaking the silence that's settled over them.

The casual question causes Graye's pulse to quicken, but she forces herself not to visibly react. It's the opening she's been waiting for. She chooses her next words with care.

"There is one," Graye says. "I'm not done reading yet, but it has promise."

"Really?" Laura glances over, interested.

That simply, the hook is set. Graye nods and looks back at the pages, not trusting herself to make any sudden movements.

"Let me know how you feel about it when you're finished. If you're impressed, I'd love to see it." Laura's phone buzzes again.

Graye's heart does somersaults while the other woman sighs and finally checks her messages. Two spots of color rise on Laura's cheeks and her mouth tightens.

"That man," she mutters under her breath. "I swear, sometimes . . ."

Laura doesn't finish the thought, at least not aloud. Graye's heart is thumping too hard in her chest to make intelligent conversation anyway.

Laura pulls the car forward onto the ferry and kills the engine while Graye marvels at her luck.

Somewhere in the back of her mind, she realizes she could have sent the manuscript out on submission the traditional way, querying literary agents or publishers. But she knows enough to know that way is paved with rejection slips and heartache.

She can't take that chance, can't bear the polite form responses. *Thank you for your submission, but . . .* Or worse, the yawning cavern of no reply at all.

Her words mean too much to her to consign them to an overworked, underpaid aide in the basement of an agency, to be lost among the piles of slush.

They are her proof of life.

Once her words are published, Gracie Thacker will fade into nothing, where she's always belonged. But Graye Templeton will matter, and no one will be able to take that from her.

The sting on her cheek burns.

"What do you think you're doing? Get out of that dress before you ruin it," the voice hisses.

She covers her face. "I'm sorry, Mother." The words are muffled by snot and tears.

"Sorry? You're always sorry. What good does that do? You think money grows on trees, little girl?"

"No, Mother."

There is someone else in the room, but their judgment is silent.

"Your sister's going to be a star, Grace. Everyone knows it." Rough hands on her shoulders, turning her toward the dark. A shove at her back. "But you don't have it and you never will, so stop pretending. You're making a fool of yourself."

The ferry shifts on the water, and Graye puts out her hand to brace herself on the interior door of the car.

"I know we have some video work on the schedule for tomorrow, Graye, but I think it can wait until later in the week."

Laura has closed her eyes and leaned her head back against the headrest.

The car sways beneath them.

"All right," Graye says, taking note of how exhausted Laura looks. "I can work on getting the latest batch of reviews up."

"Why don't you take a day off? I'd feel guilty about you working while I spend a lazy day catching up on my to-read list."

"But that's still working for you," Graye points out.

Laura opens one eye and peeks over. "Don't tell anyone, but it's really not. I love reading days. I live for them."

The ferry gently bumps into the dock, and Laura shifts the car into drive.

Once she's pulled onto the main road that encircles the island, the Mary Read Hotel passes on their right. Laura slows as a couple crosses the street in front of them, heading in that direction. The woman's skin is a delicate shade of pink, but her smile is bright as she waves to them and hurries past.

The hotel, named for a famed lady pirate, is the epicenter of the tiny island community. There are worn paths between the houses lining the interior of the island that converge around it.

Even Graye, an avowed introvert, can see the appeal of the converted hotel's casual back patio strung with café lights. The sound of waves accompanies the band that often plays on the small wooden stage into the wee hours.

More importantly, the bartenders are friendly and don't mind mixing yet another margarita. Or if they do, they hide it well, at least while the tips flow freely.

The patio lights twinkle and sway in the breeze.

Just past the hotel, the West home is visible. The windows glow through the darkening twilight. It should be a welcoming sight, but Laura's grip on the wheel tightens and her eyes narrow.

"What's wrong?" Graye asks as the car slows and Laura prepares to make the turn into the driveway.

Laura shakes her head. She's staring at the lights blazing, and Graye is staring at her face, trying to decipher her reaction.

"The door . . . ," Laura says quietly.

Graye's eyes swivel to the carriage house.

It stands just as they'd left it, an elegant, if aging, structure, like a woman who's achieved a certain maturity yet embraced the time that's passed rather than fought against it. Her pale-blue paint is faded nearly to white and peeling in places. But she has good bones, and age only adds to her charm.

Still, too many lights are burning for one person home alone, and the front door, which faces the street, is open wide.

Distracted by the wrongness of the scene, neither woman sees the figure that stumbles in front of the car until it's too late.

Laura slams her brakes with a gasp and Graye lets out a startled scream. The papers she was holding neatly in her lap slip from her fingers and plunge forward, loose and messy on the floorboard as the car grinds to a halt.

For a split second the women stare at each other, each hoping she imagined the sight of something—or someone—that had materialized out of nowhere.

Then Laura flies, all her limbs seeming to move at once. She jams the gearshift into park and grapples with the door handle, then lunges out of the car and slingshots her body around the front of the vehicle.

Graye isn't far behind.

She stands, gaping as Laura falls to her knees next to a crumpled body in the street.

"David!" Laura shouts. "Oh my God, David, are you okay?"

Her hands flutter, touching, then hovering over him as she searches his body, assessing it for damage.

"David!" she shouts again.

There's no response.

"Graye, call an ambulance," Laura says, shifting suddenly to an unnerving calm and clarity.

Graye stands, mute and immobile, entranced by the heap that is Laura's husband, an acrid smell burning her nose.

"Graye!" Laura shouts.

The voice shocks her out of her head, and Graye runs back toward the cab of the SUV, where both doors are still hanging open. The cross-breeze, uncaring of their all-too-human emergency, has taken hold of the manuscript pages and begun to scatter them across the road.

Her pages. Her words. Fluttering in the wind.

She fumbles through the car, searching futilely for the phone that went flying when Laura slammed on the brakes. She finally finds it beneath the mountain of papers and runs back to Laura's side.

Her fingers are trembling as she tries to unlock the phone to dial 911.

David groans.

"David, can you hear me?" Laura asks, leaning in close.

Slowly, he sits up, pushing his wife's hands away as he does.

"Ge' off me," he mumbles. "Fell, that's all. Didn't see you coming."

With a sudden burst of clarity, Graye realizes the crunch beneath her feet isn't just the road. She spies the broken glass from the liquor bottles David was carrying scattered about, explaining the overpowering smell that surrounds them.

He sits up fully, then manages to rise mostly to his feet, though he stops midway to lean his hands against his knees and catch his balance.

David West, esteemed and award-winning novelist, wasn't hit by the car at all. Instead, he's shit-faced drunk.

Graye sees Laura's face change the moment she realizes the same.

She stands, her body stiff and her face a frozen mask. Another car slows as it passes.

"Everything okay?" an older woman asks, leaning her head out the driver's side of the car. "Laura, do you need help?"

Laura glances toward the car and a flush colors her cheeks.

"Dr. Lawson," she says in embarrassed recognition. She shoots a glare in David's direction, then forces a weak smile for the woman in the car. "No, I think we're okay. My husband's just had too much to drink. I'd introduce you, but . . ." She trails off, finding no dignified way to salvage the situation.

The woman in the car waves off Laura's attempt at niceties. "I can see this isn't the best time. Come by sometime, though, and we'll have coffee," she says. "If you need anything before then"—her gaze rakes up and down David's swaying form—"anything at all, I'm only a phone call away."

"You got a cure for an angry wife in there, Doc?" David asks loudly.

The woman doesn't smile. "I'm afraid not. Best thing you can do is sleep it off."

Clearly mortified, Laura sends the neighbor another tense smile. "Thank you, Dr. Lawson. I'll come visit soon."

"I look forward to it," she replies with one last glance in David's direction. Slowly, she pulls the car down the street.

"Thanks for nothing, Doc!" David shouts, his hand raised in mock salute. The sudden movement upsets his balance, and Laura, stone-faced, reaches out and steadies him.

David lays his arm across her cold shoulders and leans into her steady weight, oblivious.

"Wha' are you looking at?" he tosses in Graye's direction.

"N . . . Nothing. Nothing at all," Graye mumbles, casting her eyes back to Laura.

"Watch the tone, David, or I'll leave you in the street," Laura grinds out between clenched teeth. "Do you have any idea who that was? That woman was my grandmother's oldest friend. She's the nearest thing to family I have on this island, and *you* are the world's biggest ass."

She turns, still bearing his weight, and the two of them move toward the open front door.

"Graye, can you—" Laura begins, strain in every syllable of her words.

"I'll get the car," Graye says, grasping the chance to be useful.

"Thank you."

While Laura wrangles her husband and his embarrassing proclivities into the privacy of their home, Graye runs back to the car and shuts the passenger door before jogging around to the driver's side.

She catches a glimpse of white blowing down the street. Sending a quick glance toward the house, Graye dashes into the road and grabs an errant page, then another. She collects all the pages she can see before striding back to the car, resentment at Dr. West simmering all the while.

Graye pulls the vehicle under the carport, which is open on all sides. From the driver's seat, she spots a few stray pages that have somehow made their way between the houses and are now fluttering down the beach.

Graye sighs. The wind has taken them. There's no way she's getting those back.

She restores the scattered manuscript pages she managed to salvage into a loose stack before collecting the rest of her things from the vehicle.

Deliberately taking her time in order to give the couple some privacy, Graye walks slowly to the detached guesthouse that sits nestled between the hotel and the carriage house and drops off her things.

But she can't just abandon Laura. What if she needs her?

Graye sighs again and walks back to the SUV. She gathers Laura's overnight bag, her purse, and the keys from the ignition.

She can hear the couple arguing before she raps lightly on the kitchen door.

"You don't understand what it's like."

"Oh stop already. It's an excuse, David, and a tired one at that."

Graye cracks open the door. The pair is nowhere in sight, but the insults they hurl at each other ricochet around the old house.

"Creativity is a mystery, my dear. It needs to be nurtured, not scheduled. It can't be forced!"

"Is that what you've been doing for two years? Nurturing your creativity? Because from here it looks like you're trying to drown it."

Graye steps into the kitchen on quiet feet and carefully sets Laura's bag on the floor.

"You're the one who signed up to marry a writer, honey. For better or worse. It's not all award banquets and book signings. You're my wife, Laura! You're supposed to be here to support me."

Graye's stomach churns at the self-pity in his voice. There was a time she respected this man.

"Support you? By paying your liquor bill? I've been here the whole time, David. Waiting on you to get your head out of your ass."

"Afraid of losing your investment?" David asks bitterly.

Graye freezes as something crashes in the living room. She doesn't know if an object was hurled across the room or if David simply fell over again.

Laura's keys are cutting into Graye's palm as she grips them tightly.

"I'm not doing this," comes Laura's tired voice. "Get over yourself, David. There are more important things than the next book."

David laughs. It's a harsh, ugly sound.

"That's fine, then. Off you go," he says.

With rising panic, Graye realizes his voice is closer than she thought. Seconds later he stumbles into the kitchen.

"More important things," he mutters, oblivious or uncaring of her presence. "More important things, she says. Not to me."

She shouldn't be here, but her limbs refuse to move.

David throws open a cabinet door and rummages inside, then pulls a bottle out. He holds it up, trying to focus, then unscrews the cap and tips it over a glass sitting along the edge of the counter.

A trickle of clear liquid dribbles out.

"Not to me," he says again, louder this time as he tosses the empty bottle onto the counter next to the glass. It spins, and Graye watches, entranced, as it drifts closer and closer to the edge. It comes to a halt at last, precariously close to crashing to the floor, its neck pointing directly at Graye.

"What about you, little sparrow?" David says softly before he lifts his glass and tips the meager drops into his mouth. "With your freshly framed diploma on the wall? What do you long for, if not immortality?"

Graye jerks her gaze to his face. "I . . . I should go."

David laughs again, a bitter sound of failure and decay.

"You know what your problem is, Miss Templeton?" His words are slurred and disjointed, but she can understand them just fine. "You lack conviction."

He waves the glass around, a king making a great proclamation. "You with your meekness and all your disgusting hesitation. *'I, I, I should go,'* she says like a peasant. No one with an MFA *aspires* to be a personal fucking assistant."

A knife twists inside of Graye, but David has a grip firmly on the hilt, and finds pleasure in turning it.

"That's right. Don't think I don't hear you clack-clacking away at night on your vintage typewriter you probably bought at a pawn shop because you're a romantic who thinks it grants you some sort of magical gravitas that a ballpoint and a spiral notebook can't. You don't fool me."

He peers at her, his eyes squinting, trying to pin her down through the haze of alcohol, as if she were flitting about the room rather than stock-still in front of him.

"A scared, insecure closet writer, just like everyone else, with big dreams and no follow-through. But you think to yourself, if you work hard and clack away, someday, maybe, luck will smile down and your big, big dream will fall from the sky and land smack in your lap. That's what you're hoping for, isn't it? What you all hope for? To take a giant bite out of that apple. But the trick," he says, dropping his voice to a whisper, "the part no one tells you, is not to take *too* big a bite, my eager little birdie, or you might just choke on it."

He tosses the empty glass into the sink, and Graye flinches as it shatters.

"I'm sorry," he says, though he sounds anything but. "Did I scare you? Are you scared now?" He sends her a satisfied smile and a glance beneath hooded eyes.

"Fly away then, little gray bird, back to your nest," he says with a flutter of his hand. "Fearful wings will take you there safe and sound."

Graye's spine stiffens. "I'm not afraid of you."

"No?" He tilts his head and grabs at the kitchen island that separates them to catch his balance. "Resting on the crocodile's back is a nice place for a little bird to be, is it? Fun for everyone?"

David lurches toward her, faster than she would have expected him capable of. She takes two quick steps away from him, but her back hits the wall. It still isn't far enough to stop him falling against her. The keys in her hand drop to the floor with a clatter. He smells of salt and booze, sweat and inadequacy.

She stares at the red veins that radiate through the whites of his eyes.

"And what happens when the crocodile gets hungry, little bird?"

Graye, immobilized by his weight pinning her, paralyzed by this man who's fallen so fast and hard from his self-satisfied pedestal, feels a hot hiss of breath as his wet lips part.

Teeth close upon the lobe of her ear.

Her stomach rebels and a thick ball of bile and revulsion pushes its way up her chest, then explodes outward. She shoves, heaving the carcass of this useless man out of her space.

He stumbles, a ridiculous mask of boyish surprise mingling with the drunken slackness as he tumbles over a chair pushed out from the breakfast table and lands clumsily on his back.

Graye stands over him, her hands clenched into fists.

"Are you done?" she asks, fighting for calm.

The shock in David's face slowly banks. His eyes shutter and his lip curls, exposing a glint of teeth.

The loathing on his face might be directed at Graye. It might be directed at himself. She doesn't care which.

Holding her muscles taut and exerting all the control she can summon, Graye crouches next to where he sprawls across the floor.

He tries to open his eyes, but his head falls back with a thud and his lids flutter closed, a puerile refusal to face her.

Perhaps he's just too drunk to try.

With a soft hand, Graye reaches out and caresses the cheek of the man whose words once gave her wings to ride away from her cold, dreary life.

Her thumb moves gently back and forth, feeling the stubble and aged roughness that time and poor choices have etched there.

His eyes don't open, but the weight of his head shifts toward her palm, a cat leaning into a scratch behind the ears. A child looking to his mother for comfort.

Her fingers stiffen in support. She tilts her head and watches his face as she moves her thumb upward to stroke the pink eyelid that's closed against a world in which a big man has become small.

Graye raises her other hand and places it opposite the first. A sigh escapes him as, without thought to why, he takes the touch she gives.

Slowly, purposefully, and with marked restraint, Graye increases the pressure of her thumbs against his closed eyes.

David twitches. She feels the moment exactly when his stolen comfort becomes confusion. When his confusion becomes fear.

It runs up her arms and feeds the anger that awoke when he put his mouth on her.

She smiles slowly and increases the pressure.

Balancing the weight of his head in her hands, she leans her face closer to his. Her lips part inches from his ear.

"Touch me again," she begins, her words slow and concise, "and this little bird will peck your eyes from your head and have them on toast."

The smallest gasp escapes him, enough for Graye to know she's pierced his drunken fog.

His hands come up, presumably to pry hers away. Instinctive, but futile in his state.

One last squeeze, then she opens her fingers wide. His skull falls back against the floor.

If he opens his eyes to stare at her, she wouldn't know. She's moving to pick up Laura's keys.

She tosses them on the counter, then Graye walks out of the house without looking back.

15

At the prince's insult, Mother smiles. She braces her feet with might and rage and pulls a deep breath in, collecting all the winds and the clouds inside of her, until she's as full as she can be.

She purses her lips and cocks her hips and she blows. Such a mighty gale neither the cinder girl nor her golden sister has ever seen. It lifts the prince, a rag doll on the wind, and away he flies, growing smaller and smaller still until he tumbles over the hills and treetops on the horizon, gone from their sight.

Gone from their lives.

Mother rights her dress and tucks a stray strand of hair into place. "That's quite enough of that."

Away she strolls, leaving the sisters to stare at the empty skies.

The cinder girl, expecting tears of grief, lays a skinny arm across her sister's shoulders.

"Don't be sad," the cinder girl whispers. "Someone loved you. It's more than I've ever had."

But the cinder girl sees, to her great surprise, there are no tears on her sister's cool cheeks.

"I'm not sad, you little fool," Sister says. "What good is a love so easily blown away?"

She stands and her face is as hard as Mother's, two women now without a heart between them.

"I need no prince," she says as she turns her back and walks away.

GRAYE

For most, a day off work is a reason to relax, even celebrate, but Graye finds herself at loose ends.

She's gotten a late start after another long night, "clacking away," as Dr. West so patronizingly put it.

There are about a dozen pages missing from her manuscript, long gone, probably floating in the Gulf by now. She could have replaced them from older drafts, but in the end, she retyped the book entirely, finally falling into bed for a few hours' rest as the sun began to lighten the sky.

The pristine new draft is just where she left it when she wakes to the cry of the gulls and the distant laughter of beachcombers.

Graye rubs her dry red eyes, hair still tousled from a troubled sleep. She lays her fingers lightly upon the cover page.

The Orphan's Ashes, a novel by Fiona Boyd.

There's a tug on her conscience at the fictitious name.

But Graye is risking everything, every single thing that matters, on Laura's opinion of this work. She can't afford to let their connection cloud her unfiltered response.

If Laura likes it—more so, if Graye allows herself the fantasy that Laura might love it—then it will be a pleasant surprise to discover the true author. A funny story to share in interviews or at book signings.

If, God forbid, she hates it . . . then Graye will have to adjust her plans. At least she'll have saved them both from the embarrassment of a polite yet heartbreakingly awkward conversation.

David's voice echoes uninvited through her mind.

"You know what your problem is? You lack conviction."

She tries to shake the words off before they can find a weak spot to latch onto and burrow in, but they're persistent.

Graye takes a deep breath and walks toward the bathroom, then twists the faucet on the shower.

Cecelia Ainsley is right. David West is a hack. A man who struck gold once, then proceeded to piss it all away.

She doesn't need Dr. West's approval, and she certainly doesn't need his permission. She is Graye Templeton. That's going to mean something soon.

Graye steps into the steaming shower. When she steps out again, she leaves her doubts behind. But not her conviction. She dresses in running clothes and ties her hair back, then heads out the door and takes the short walk to the Wests' kitchen door.

Laura sees her coming through the glass and waves her in. She's standing at the counter in a T-shirt and worn gray sweatpants that have been cut off at the knee. She's bobbing a tea bag in a cup.

"Good morning," Laura says, her forced cheerfulness almost believable. "Do you want a cup of tea?"

Graye shakes her head. "No, thanks. I'm heading out for a run, but I thought I'd drop off that manuscript we talked about yesterday. I finished it last night." She holds up the ream of papers, secured with rubber bands.

Any sign of David's few days of debauchery has been cleared away, the chairs righted, empty bottles stowed in the garbage, the broken glass gone from the sink.

But the feel of his teeth, sharp on Graye's skin, remains.

"The swan among the ducklings," Laura says with a distracted smile. "Listen, Graye. About yesterday—"

Graye shakes her head and looks away from Laura's earnest expression. She fiddles with the rubber band on the manuscript and gives it a snap. "You don't need to—"

"But I do," Laura interrupts. "You've been so kind. A rock. I owe you an apology."

"No need, really. You've been nothing but generous, and—"

Graye breaks off as David, bleary eyed and unkempt, stumbles into the room. Her spine stiffens, but she refuses to look away as his gaze travels around the kitchen.

"Thank you, Laura," Graye says, her words stiff and too formal, even to her own ears. "But *you've* got nothing to apologize for."

She doesn't miss the way Dr. West's eyes widen just a fraction, or the way his body goes suddenly still. She hopes he's reliving the memory of pressure against his closed eyes. That her words are replaying on a loop in his head.

She thinks perhaps they are, and that's enough to improve her mood.

"Coffee," he says with a croak. "Just want a cup of coffee."

Both women stare at him. Neither moves.

He clears his throat. "I . . . I'll come back later," he says and steps backward out of the room without meeting Graye's hard eyes.

Once he's gone, Graye busies herself by pulling her hair down from its ponytail and retying it, something to do with her hands while she schools her face into a more casual expression.

She doesn't see the way Laura's gaze flickers back and forth between Graye and the doorway her husband has retreated through, or the frown of concern she can't hide at the exchange.

"I've got to run," Graye says. "But you should read this when you get a chance. I'm curious to hear your thoughts."

Conviction, Graye thinks, even as her hands tremble at the idea of taking such a big step. She fights an overwhelming urge to snatch the pages back, to run and hide them in a dark closet forever. To burn them, to toss them one by one into the waves.

Who is she kidding?

Conviction. She forces her hands to stay casually by her sides.

"Of course," Laura is saying, unaware of the battle raging inside Graye. "I'll add it to the stack."

"Great." Graye turns to make a hasty exit before the tremor in her voice gives her away. She's reaching for the door, but Laura isn't done.

"Hey, so I know today is supposed to be a day off, but I got a call from the manager at the Mary Read. She has some questions about the setup for the retreat."

Graye's hand stalls and she turns back.

"I was going to head over later and talk it over in person if you'd like to come along."

"Absolutely," Graye says with no hesitation at all. "Days off are overrated."

Laura shakes her head. "I swear, we were separated at birth. We're only three weeks out from the event and everything's looking good so far, but days off might be hard to pin down between now and then, so if you want to make the most of this one, I completely understand."

Graye rolls her eyes. "What time?" she asks.

Laura brightens, clearly pleased. "Lunchtime? We'll call it a working lunch. My treat."

"It's a date. See you there."

As Graye heads down to the beach, a faint smile lingers.

Conviction. It's going to be a good day. She can feel it.

16

LAURA

Even with the constant ocean breeze, the sun is intense, and Laura appreciates the extra blast of air from the wide bamboo fans that whirl from the beams of the pergola over the Mary Read's outdoor bar.

She spots Graye seated at one of the high-top tables, sipping from a frosty pink drink that Laura's mouth waters at the sight of.

For once, the other woman is looking up rather than down at a book in her hands, though her face seems drawn as she stares toward the beach.

"Can I get an ice water with lemon, please, Mike?" Laura asks the waiter who converges on the table at the same time she does.

"Coming up," Mike says obligingly.

"Thanks for meeting me." Laura slides into the empty seat across the table from Graye.

"Wouldn't miss it," Graye says. "And it *is* my job," she adds with a smile.

"Fair enough."

They order lunch, and Laura fills Graye in on some of the details for the upcoming event. This year she's planned a mystery theme, complete with an Agatha Christie–inspired murder mystery dinner on Saturday evening to round off the weekend.

"It's the highlight of the year for me, without a doubt, but it never fails that something goes wrong. My job, and yours too this year, will be to adapt to whatever emergencies crop up."

Graye nods. "And the meeting with the hotel manager?"

"She wants to go over the placement of the tables for the Friday Noir Poker Night and the Saturday events, so this is a good opportunity for you to get the lay of the land as well."

Graye nods again, but Laura can see a cloud has settled over her.

"Having second thoughts about taking the job?" Laura asks. The question may sound like a joke, but in truth, Laura has come to depend on Graye. The young woman has a way of stepping up to a challenge that Laura appreciates.

Graye's eyes lift. "Are you kidding? Not a chance. It's the opportunity of a lifetime."

Laura lets out a breath she didn't realize she'd been holding. "But something's on your mind."

Graye pushes her salad away. She doesn't disagree as she wipes at the condensation gathered on her glass.

"It's nothing," Graye says. "It's not my place to pry."

It was inevitable, really. They can only tap-dance around the elephant in the room for so long.

"Graye, can I ask you something? As a friend?" Laura says, tackling it head-on.

"Of course."

"When you dropped off my bag and keys yesterday . . . did David say something to upset you?"

Graye takes a deep breath and meets Laura's eyes, but she doesn't speak.

"Did he . . . did he make a pass at you?"

Graye's lips turn down in a frown, and that's all the answer Laura needs.

"Not exactly," Graye says. "I mean, sort of, I guess. Maybe. But not really. He was drunk and . . . well, it doesn't matter. I dealt with it."

The food she just ate sits like lead in Laura's stomach. Damn him.

"Graye, I'm so, so sorry. I understand if you're not comfortable continuing on—"

"Oh God, no," Graye interrupts. "It's fine. I took care of it. I don't think it will happen again." Graye's face is flushed and her eyes have gone wide. "This is where I want to be. Please don't let me go over this."

Laura is surprised by and a little ashamed of the rush of relief she feels. It's selfish, but she likes Graye.

"I'm not firing you, if that's what you're thinking," she says. "If you're sure you want to stay."

Graye nods emphatically. "I want to stay."

"I'm really glad to hear that." Laura reaches across the table and squeezes the younger woman's hand. "But I will talk to him."

"No, please don't. That'll just make things awkward. Can we just forget it happened?"

Laura won't forget. She can't, but if it will set Graye's mind at ease for her to agree, it's the least she can do.

"If that's what you want."

She'll deal with David all the same, without dragging Graye into their mess. She's been avoiding it for too long.

"Thank you," Graye says, but judging by her face, there's more on her mind. Laura waits.

"Can I ask *you* something? As a friend?" Graye finally says.

Laura sighs. Inevitable. "Why I stay with him?"

Graye nods.

Laura twists the wedding ring on her finger and looks away from Graye's searching gaze. How can she explain to this young woman with her whole life ahead of her the fire David used to ignite in her? The thrill she'd get from the brush of his hand across hers, or the way their eyes would meet across a room, communicating their thoughts in just a glance.

She can't describe the scent of a thousand flowers. But she can remember.

She can remember the glow in David's face when she came home to the first apartment they shared and found it filled with endless bouquets of daisies, peonies, roses, chrysanthemums, and so many more. Flowers she didn't even know the names of.

"What in the world?" she whispered, dropping her bag at her feet. "David?"

He grabbed her, swinging her legs around in a circle, laughing with the purest joy she'd ever witnessed.

"We did it," he said, kissing her fiercely. "We did it, Laura. We sold the book. And I have you to thank."

"By buying every flower in the state?" she cried, laughing along with him.

"Yes," he said. He held her gently and put both his hands on her cheeks. "I was searching for just one that could compare to my incredible wife, but none of them came close, so I had to buy them all."

Things are different now, and have been for a while, but Laura doesn't know exactly when or where that crumbling shift began.

Was it after David's second novel was released, to much fanfare, followed by a universal sigh of disappointment?

Was it after she broke their agreement? No kids, they'd both said. We don't need kids to be fulfilled, they'd said, young and arrogantly unaware that things wouldn't, couldn't, continue down the same charmed path forever.

Or was it before that? Was it the decaying scent of a thousand cut flowers inevitably dying in their vases, no matter how hard she tried to extend their life?

David dealt with success far better than failure. He allowed failure to change him.

And the thing is, she'd have loved him to his dying day as a washed-up novelist. What she can't find it in her heart to forgive is the way he's giving everything he is, everything they are together, over to bitterness.

It makes her feel cheap. It makes her love cheap, so easily traded—not for something new and better, but something poisonous and hurtful.

How can she ask Graye to understand, when she herself doesn't?

Laura and David are flying toward the finish line in a race she's set in motion without David's knowledge, and she's holding on only to give him one final chance. A chance to choose her, and a future, and step away from the mire their life together has become.

To start over. To be a family.

She feels she owes him the chance to make a better man of himself.

Not that she expects him to take it. She doesn't even know if he can, but when he makes his choice, she will know at least that she's seen it through. And maybe, in the end, she can forgive herself for changing the rules on him.

But she can't say any of this to Graye.

"It's complicated right now," she says instead, an inane phrase that sounds exactly like what it is. A big fat excuse. Yet it's true.

Life with David has never been anything *but* complicated. Yet she can't leave Graye with that. She deserves more.

"There are changes coming," Laura says. "I'm not sure exactly when, or what form they'll take, but they're coming all the same."

Again, too vague, but Laura's stomach flutters in recognition of the unbending honesty of those words.

She should say more, knows she should, but Graye's face has softened, and Laura doesn't dare continue for fear she'll sound like a bigger idiot than she already does. She keeps her mouth shut and watches the other woman take it all in.

"Okay," Graye says softly, accepting the inadequate explanation without further questions.

"In the meantime," Laura says, glancing at the clock on her phone while she composes herself, "you and I have some murder to plan."

17

GRAYE

The hotel manager is a small woman, and younger than Graye expected, but she's enthusiastic and eager to bring the event off without a hitch.

"We're fully booked for the weekend, Mrs. West, and your party makes up the bulk of the reservations. The staff and I are, as always, at your disposal."

"Thank you, Yolanda."

"We've never hosted a murder mystery dinner, and I'm intrigued," the hotel manager says.

"You guys just do what you do best. Graye and I will take care of steering the guests when it comes to Saturday night."

"I've set aside a room on the first floor for the staging area as you requested."

"That's wonderful," Laura says.

Graye must admit, the small historic beachfront hotel is the perfect backdrop for what Laura's cooked up.

Yolanda and Laura move to the far side of the ballroom. The hotel manager's hands wave as she speaks, directing Laura's attention. Graye stands back, building the evening in her imagination, searching for potential problems they haven't considered.

She glances around, filling in the practical details.

"Where are the restrooms from here?" she calls to Yolanda.

"Just out those doors and to your left," the manager calls back.

Graye glances over her shoulder and cranes her neck to peer out the doors. A figure, standing too still in the hallway by the elevators, turns his back to her suddenly.

But Graye has seen his face. Her world begins to spin. She'll never forget that face. It's been in her nightmares for years.

She stares at his back, willing herself to be wrong.

The red board shorts. The man she passes in the mornings on the beach, never looking too closely, never making eye contact, because that's what she does. She always keeps her head down, not drawing notice to herself.

He's been watching her. The day Laura's tire was slashed, that morning from the beach. It was him.

No, her mind screams. Not this. Not now, just when things are finally coming together.

The elevator dings and the door slides open. The man steps casually inside.

Nothing to hide. Nothing to see here.

And Graye wants to believe it. Wants to be wrong.

But she isn't wrong.

When the man turns to press the elevator button, his face is angled away from her, but she sees the quick flutter of his eyes, sideways, seeking her out. Just a millisecond slip, to check if he's been found out, gives him away.

When he catches her watching him, his eyes narrow and he stands straighter, facing her head-on.

There's no mistake.

A dizzying sense of vertigo takes hold of her as she stands with her future on one side, and her past staring her down on the other.

Without thought for the consequences, Graye bolts toward the elevator.

The doors begin to slide closed between them, but Graye reaches them just in time to thrust her hand out. They open again, whether she truly wants them to or not.

Heart pounding, she steps inside without a word, facing the man she hasn't been this close to in more than fifteen years.

He doesn't speak, doesn't smile. Not that she expects him to. His eyes are shrouded in mystery, but Graye refuses to give in to terror.

She's no longer the little girl she once was.

The elevator doors slide closed, oblivious to her pounding pulse or the way her skin prickles at being closeted in such a small space with nothing between her and him.

"Hello, Grace," he says quietly.

The softness of the words doesn't fool her.

His voice is deeper than she remembers, his skin lined, his hair shorter, but otherwise, he's the same.

"What are you doing here, Nick?" She forces the words from her lips, hating how they sound. Weak. Shaky.

Will he lie? Pretend his presence on this little island is some sort of cosmic joke they can laugh about together like old friends?

If he does, Graye doesn't think she can stop the scream that's building in her throat.

"I've been watching you," he says instead.

A chill courses through her at the words. The scream lingers too near the surface.

"What do you want?" she demands.

He tilts his head, studies her like a bug beneath a magnifying glass.

"You've grown up, Grace," he says, sidestepping her question.

She chokes back her response as the elevator pitches to a stop and the doors slide open. A young couple, laughing and happy, steps into the elevator with them. Graye moves to stand at the back, making room, and stares down at her feet.

She can feel his eyes on her, even while the elevator continues along its way. She bites at the inside of her cheek, tastes blood, while they ride inside the mechanized box that's begun to feel like a cell.

The door dings again, and the couple steps off. Graye glances up and meets his eyes, but he makes no move toward her, though she doesn't feel any safer for it.

"Don't run from me, Grace. There's nothing to be afraid of," he says.

Her mind conjures an image of a sharp, glinting blade slicing into a sidewall of rubber.

Nick, silent on the beach, observing the aftermath.

He's lying.

She reaches over and again thrusts her hand between the elevator doors, stopping them before they can close her in once more.

"Stay away from me," she hisses. "There's nothing here for you."

She steps out, free from the confines of his presence, and forces her feet to keep a calm pace as she walks away.

"You can't hide forever, Grace," she hears him call.

She quickens her pace, but that's the thing about ghosts. They're impossible to outrun. They travel in the heart of the people they've hurt the most.

She should know. She's been running from ghosts her whole life.

Now she's been found, and she's nine years old again. Little Gracie, who is always afraid.

Little Gracie, who put a murderer behind bars.

But there are no bars to protect her now.

18

MARGARET

Sister Ursula does a poor job masking her curiosity when she hurries to find Sister Margaret in the garden.

"You have a phone call, Sister," the small, round woman says, out of breath from her rush to share the news. "A young woman. She sounds quite upset."

Margaret frowns, ignoring Ursula's overly bright, probing gaze.

Life is quiet at St. Sebastian's. One could even be forgiven for calling it dull.

This suits some of the girls, and frankly, some of the nuns, better than others.

"Carrie, have the girls take the vegetables you've gathered into the storeroom when you're done. And two baskets to the kitchens, if you don't mind," Sister Margaret says.

"Yes, Sister." Carrie is one of their older girls, and a responsible sort.

Margaret brushes the soil from her hands and walks toward the home office, where their only phone is located.

Ursula hurries along beside her.

"I believe it may be Graye Templeton," she chatters. "I do hope the child hasn't found herself in a pickle."

Margaret sighs. Ursula has a penchant for colorful phrases better suited to children's television programming than real life. *In a pickle* is a favorite.

"What do you suppose the trouble might be?" the other woman continues.

"I don't have the faintest idea, Sister, as I've yet to speak to her."

"Yes, of course. That makes sense. Mustn't get the chickens before the horse."

"The cart," Margaret corrects.

"What's that?"

"Mustn't get the cart before the horse, dear. Not the chickens."

"Oh. Yes, yes, of course. Although I'd think getting the chickens before the horse wouldn't be a good thing either. Chickens underfoot like that." Ursula shakes her head, clucking. "Someone could get hurt."

Margaret stops in the large entryway and turns to face the other woman, who stumbles to a halt. "Sister Anna mentioned she could use some help in the kitchens."

Sister Ursula's shoulders droop.

Margaret keeps her features polite until Ursula finally turns to shuffle slowly off in the other direction. She stays put until Ursula has disappeared, then walks briskly to the office, where the receiver of the phone lies waiting on the desk.

"Graye?" Margaret says into the phone. Ragged, heavy breaths come from the other end of the line. "What's wrong?"

There's a choking hitch that might have been a sob before the young woman speaks.

"How could you, Sister?" the voice asks, low and pleading.

"How could I what, Graye?"

"Nick," she cries. "Nick is here. Did you tell him where to find me? You must have."

The unease that's been lying heavy on the nun's mind since she heard Graye's voice cracks open, becoming full-fledged panic.

She struggles to hold it in check. Histrionics won't help.

"Graye, take a breath and slow down."

Margaret's heart pounds. Graye has tried so hard to put the past behind her, but the nun's greatest worry for the girl has always been that she'll never be able to run far or fast enough.

It would appear she was right.

"If Nick is in New York, he certainly didn't find you through me."

"He's not in Ithaca, Sister. I'm in Texas. If he can find me even here, I'll never . . . I'll never . . ." Graye's voice breaks.

"Texas?" Margaret says, confused. "What are you doing in Texas?"

"You didn't know. No, of course you didn't."

"You haven't returned my calls or answered my letters in months, child."

"But . . . but how did he find me then?" Graye asks.

"I don't know, but if you're sure it's him, you should go to the police. Tell them everything, then pack your things and get out of there as soon as you can."

"No!"

The vehemence in the girl's response leaves Margaret shocked.

"What choice do you have, Grace? You can come here. We can protect you, just like we did before. We'll get you a new name, a new identity, if we need to. You can start over—"

"No, Sister!" Graye shouts. "No. Not now, I can't leave now."

"Grace, be reasonable—"

"Stop calling me that!"

The slip was accidental, but Margaret is struggling to stay composed.

"I'm sorry, Graye," she says slowly, in a soothing tone. "Take a breath and explain to me exactly what's going on. Why can't you leave?"

"I've got a job. A real job with a future."

It's the first Margaret has heard of this, but it isn't unusual for Graye to go long periods without contacting her. She's no longer a child, and the nun has no claim on the girl's time, as much as she might worry.

"What job could be worth putting yourself at risk this way?" she asks.

"You don't understand."

Margaret takes a deep breath. "Then explain it to me."

"I'm an assistant for an important woman in the book community. She's reading my novel. I can't just pack up and leave now. This could be my shot, Sister."

Margaret opens her mouth to disagree, then stops. Her words, she knows, will make no difference.

Writing has always been more to Graye than simply a dream. It's the thing, possibly the only thing, that pulled the child from the depths.

When Grace arrived at St. Sebastian's, the care workers told them she was capable of speech. She *could* talk. She just chose not to.

For months, Margaret despaired of ever getting through to the little girl who'd witnessed such a horrific crime. She explained that for Grace's own protection and privacy, she had arranged to have her name legally changed. She expected the child to have some sort of opinion about that, but she got no response. Margaret chose the name Graye herself, as similar as she could devise to Grace's birth name, hoping it would make the transition easier.

Yet still, the child didn't speak.

Then one day, on a wing and a desperate prayer, Margaret retrieved a notebook and a pencil from the office. She sat next to Graye on the bed in the room she shared with several other girls, a few of whom had tried to befriend the newest resident.

She'd spoken to none of them.

"Graye, I know you've been through a terrible ordeal," Margaret said gently. "And I want you to know that it's just fine if you don't wish to speak. I won't ask you to. One day, I hope you'll be ready, and when you are, I, and the others, will be waiting."

The child didn't answer, but her wide eyes were sharp and Margaret believed she understood.

"Until then, I thought you could use this." She placed the notebook on the bed between them and laid the freshly sharpened pencil on top.

Graye looked at her but didn't reach for the offering.

"Sometimes it can be hard to know what to say to other people, but here, on these pages, this is just for you. No one else will read it if you keep it well hidden.

"Here you can pour out everything that's scary or sad or ugly. Every bit of it. And maybe, when you're done, you'll feel just a little bit better."

The nun tilted her head and studied the girl. Would this work? Possibly not, but she couldn't stand by and do nothing. Margaret had poured her own hurt out when she'd given her life to the church, becoming an empty vessel for Christ to fill with his light.

But she'd been older then, old enough to recognize the sense of coming home that a life dedicated to the service of God offered. Graye was only a child. A little girl searching for her way.

"That's how we do things here, as you'll soon come to know. We work hard every day in the hope that, the next day, things will be just a little bit better. And then we do it again. Because with enough time and effort, every little bit adds up to a great deal."

She placed her hand on the girl's cheek, then tucked a strand of limp brown hair behind one ear. Graye didn't pull away, which was something.

"A little bit each day can add up to everything."

Graye accepted the notebook that day hesitantly.

The weeks passed, and Graye seemed to calm and settle into a routine at St. Sebastian's, even if it was a silent routine.

Then one day, after evening prayers, Sister Margaret was shepherding the girls up to their rooms. Graye dawdled at the back of the group.

"Come along," the nun said, holding out her arm.

The child walked up to her and stopped.

Margaret squelched the urge to kneel and pull the girl into a hug.

For one thing, it wouldn't do to show favoritism among the girls, but more importantly Margaret had learned that many of the children who came to them needed to find their footing and understand they were safe before they could accept affection.

So she waited.

Graye looked up at her with large, imploring eyes.

"Please, Sister," she began in a low whisper. "Can I have another notebook, please?"

Margaret bit her lip and cleared her throat before she trusted herself to speak.

"May I," she said finally. "It's *may* I have another notebook, dear."

Graye nodded, so serious for such a young face.

"May I have another notebook, Sister? Mine is full up."

Matching the child's serious expression, Margaret nodded as well.

"I see," she said. She considered her words before she spoke again. "In that case, I must tell you, everyone at St. Sebastian's is expected to lend a hand in one way or another. If you feel you're ready, then we can meet tomorrow and discuss where you believe you might be most helpful."

"And the notebook?" the little girl asked.

A soft smile formed on Margaret's face.

"Of course, Graye. We'll find you as many notebooks as you need."

It had been a big promise, but Margaret was true to her word. For the following few years, those notebooks were everything to the little girl. Her entire world.

Autumn came to St. Sebastian's when Graye was eleven. By that time, the nun had given up trying to get the child to engage with the other girls, so it warmed her heart and eased her worries to see the two become fast friends. Even then, though, a notebook was never far away. It stayed close at hand as the girls made up stories together, acted them out, and Graye recorded their secret worlds in looping pencil script.

The hurt and abandonment in Graye's face when Margaret had given her the news that Autumn was leaving still brought on a heavy, hollow sadness. A distant family member of Autumn's had been found and, after a little over a year at St. Sebastian's, the girl would be going to California to live with them.

Graye never again connected with another of the girls. If anything, she retreated even deeper into her notebooks.

When Graye left St. Sebastian's many years later to attend university, she did so alone, save for her boxes of notebooks, each filled with a girl's words, which had become a woman's dreams.

"Graye, I'm pleased for you," Sister Margaret says carefully now into the phone. And it's true, but the single-mindedness of Graye's preoccupation with being published is concerning. "But there are many roads to becoming an author. There's no need to put yourself at risk for—"

"You're not listening, Sister. Laura West is the key to my future. I can't explain it, but I know it's true. She's influential and she knows people. She put her own husband on the map. David West was an unknown, unpublished nobody before Laura, and then he wasn't."

Margaret's breath seizes in her chest. What is Graye playing at? Her words, almost religious in their fervor, cause a new level of concern to blossom.

"If she likes my book, she can do that for me," Graye continues. "And I won't let Nick or anyone else get in the way of that. Not now. Not ever."

19

LAURA

Laura studies her reflection in the vanity mirror.

Her hair is up in rollers, her skin pale. And not in the perfect-complexion-for-a-1940s-film-star sort of way that would complement her outfit for the evening's event.

Instead, the shade is sickly. Pasty. The kind of face you'd expect to see on a woman who's come to the end of her endurance. A woman forced to take stock of the life she's leading and add up the mistakes that brought her to this point, counting them out and lining them up in a row, one by one.

She sighs.

That's why God created makeup. To cover fine lines, dark circles, and regrettable choices.

Laura begins with concealer, though it can't hide the disillusionment in her eyes when David walks into the room holding a suit on a hanger.

"You expect me to wear this?" he says, one eyebrow lifted in disparagement.

Laura twists the cap back onto the tube and tosses it onto the vanity with a clatter. She says nothing.

"All that's missing is a fedora and a dog collar for you to clip your leash to."

Uncharacteristic heat flares in her. "Trust me, that's not all that's missing."

"I suppose Hugo Caron will be dressed to impress. Did you choose a matching suit for him too?"

Laura stares at him through the mirror. "You're drunk. Again. And I will not do this with you right now."

"Oh, I'm not drunk. Not yet. But the night's still young."

She swivels in her chair to face him. "You don't have to come, David. And if this is the attitude you're going to have, frankly, I'd prefer you stayed home."

He tosses the suit across the bed and begins unbuttoning his shirt.

"And miss the opportunity to watch you flirt with Caron? Not a chance, sweetheart."

They've barely spoken all week. David had plenty of opportunities to pick a fight during that time, so she has to wonder if he's deliberately chosen this moment for another confrontation. She wouldn't be surprised.

Six days have passed since he stumbled into her office and tossed a handwritten note across the keyboard of her laptop.

"Must have been a damn good time if he's sending you a thank-you card," he said.

The note, which read, *Thanks, love, for a weekend I won't soon forget. —Hugo*, had been tucked into a beautiful leather-bound copy of *Jane Eyre*. It was among the many stacks of books that wobbled precariously around her office.

"Where did you get this?" Laura asked.

Jane Eyre wasn't David's taste. Had he been rummaging through her things?

"Not the most pertinent question, *love*."

She stared at him openmouthed, holding the card in one hand. He was sloppy, his words blending together, and he was having trouble remaining upright.

"This isn't what . . ."

No. She stopped. She wouldn't go on the defensive to justify herself to a man who'd put her through the hell of an affair himself. Even if it had been years ago, that kind of hurt takes a long time to fade, if it ever does.

If the shoe was on the other foot, then so be it. Let him see how it felt.

They had bigger issues.

"David, it's time to do something about the drinking. There's an AA chapter that meets on the mainland—"

His arm shot out and swept the stacks of papers and books to the floor, pulling a sharp intake of breath from her.

"Don't change the subject, Laura!"

A fierce drunken anger had overtaken his features. There was no semblance left of the man she loved.

From someplace unexpected, her own fury rose to meet his. She stood suddenly and took a step toward him.

"I will not have this conversation with a drunk."

She moved to walk past him, but he reached out and grabbed her arm in a viselike grip.

She stared, even as pain radiated up her forearm, shocking her to her core. David had plenty of faults, but he'd never laid a hand on her in anger.

"Drunk or not, I am still your husband," he hissed. A fleck of spittle landed on her cheek.

Laura narrowed her eyes and leaned in close to him. "A situation that can be remedied."

She pulled her arm from his grasp, aware she'd have finger-shaped bruises to mark her there in the coming days.

She walked away from him, seething at the new depths to which he'd sunk. At the door, she turned back, an ugly resentment fueling her parting words.

"What bothers you more, David?" she asked. "The idea of me sleeping with another man . . . or that it's a man whose reviews are better than yours?"

It's no wonder he's barely spoken to her since.

Things can't continue this way.

With a deep breath, Laura crosses the room to where he's fumbling with the buttons on his shirt.

"Let's just get through this weekend, please," she says. Her voice is soft, pleading. "After it's over, we'll take some time together. Maybe go away somewhere for a few days."

He glances up at her in surprise, then narrows his eyes at her tone.

He's right to be suspicious. She simply doesn't have the energy to host this event and fight with him at the same time.

Selfish of her.

"We'll talk," she says, sliding her arms around his middle and laying her head against his chest. "We'll make things better, if we can."

God, she hates herself for the flicker of hope she still has for them. It lingers in the memory of the man who used to bring her coffee in bed, before he began most mornings hungover, waking on his office couch after drinking himself into a stupor the previous night. His smile was easy and warm then. Before a desperate frustration stole it from him.

But wishing for what they once had won't make it materialize in the present. Some things, once they're gone, will never come again.

Realistically, she knows he won't forgive her. Not once she tells him the whole truth.

Gently, hesitantly, David raises his arms and places them around her.

And that small hope clings to life, refusing to die.

She breathes in the smell of him. For better or worse was their promise. But then, they'd promised a lot of things.

"Let's just get through the weekend first."

"Okay," he says, surprising her with his quiet agreement. She leans her head back to search his face.

"You mean that?" she says.

He nods, but his jaw is tight and he doesn't meet her eyes. A delicate truce, like a bomb they're tossing back and forth. One slip could destroy them both.

Still, it will have to be enough. For now.

20

GRAYE

The ballroom of the Mary Read glitters beneath strategically darkened lighting, a small version of a casino floor. Graye believes even the pirates who once roamed the island would approve.

Caterers are armed with plenty of food and drink, the blackjack and poker tables are ready, and the walls are lined with slot machines, each vying for attention in louder and flashier ways than the next.

Every detail, down to the vintage movie posters that hang on the wall, is sheer perfection.

If only Graye could set aside her anxiety over Nick, check it off like another item on the to-do list, maybe she could relax and enjoy the evening.

He disappeared after their tense exchange in the elevator. She checked at the front desk, hoping to discover what room he was staying in on the pretext of returning a lost wallet. But he was gone.

Gone from the hotel, gone from the island, but still front and center in Graye's thoughts. There's no logic to the idea that he would somehow track her down, travel all this way, then simply vanish because she'd told him to.

He must have an agenda. Everyone does. Nick has had fifteen years with nothing but time to reflect and home in on exactly what it is he wants from Graye.

She's a tightrope walker, balancing knives while traversing a wire suspended over a pit of hot coals. And Nick's unexplained disappearance has killed the lights, leaving her in pitch darkness.

"This looks fantastic," Laura says, clapping her hands together at her side.

Graye hadn't heard her approach, but as distracted as she's been these past few weeks, that's no surprise.

Her eyes widen at the sight of Laura. Dressed in a vintage-style red dress with a straight skirt and peplum flare at the waist, she's arranged her hair in a deep side part. Glossy waves curl in around her face. Her lipstick is a fiery shade that matches the dress.

"Wow," Graye says. "So do you. All you need is a black-and-white film crew and a foggy train station."

"And Bogart waiting at the end of the line?" Laura jokes. Graye looks closer. No amount of makeup can mask the circles beneath those eyes.

"Did you get any sleep at all?"

Laura shakes her head. "Not a lot."

"Listen, everything's under control here," Graye says. "Most of the guests have checked in already and picked up their name tags and welcome bags. Everyone's excited about tonight."

Laura nods distractedly and drops into a seat behind the check-in table by the entry of the ballroom. Graye takes the one next to her.

"So what's bothering you?" Graye asks.

Laura meets her probing glance in surprise, but her eyes slide away. "Is it that obvious?"

"Only to me," Graye says.

"Nothing," Laura replies. "And everything. David and I . . ." She shakes her head and looks across the room.

"Have you told him yet?" Graye asks gently. "That you're pregnant?"

The expression on Laura's face freezes, then her eyes grow wide. She slowly turns her head to stare openmouthed at Graye.

"How . . . how did you—?"

Graye gestures to the other woman's hand, which has crept up to protectively guard her midsection.

"You do that more often than you realize," she says. "How far along are you?"

Laura blinks and shakes her head. She looks like someone has sucker punched her.

"Nine weeks," she whispers. "Graye, I—"

A pair of women materializes in front of the table.

"Laura, I still don't understand how I let you talk me into these things."

Laura looks up quickly and to her credit, Graye thinks, hides her distress well.

"Linh! And here I was convinced you were going to back out at the last minute."

"I considered it, believe me," the author admits as Laura stands and steps around the table to hug the tiny woman. "But I heard a rumor you're planning to bump off Cecelia Ainsley. I couldn't miss that."

Laura laughs. "You know I can't give you any details. That would ruin the fun. You'll just have to keep your bloodlust in check until tomorrow night."

"Spoilsport. I'll bet Graye will tell me." She raises an eyebrow in Graye's direction.

Graye is inordinately pleased Mai Linh has remembered her name, but she smiles and shakes her head. Ms. Ainsley isn't on the guest list, but she doesn't want to disappoint Linh. "Sorry, my lips are sealed."

The women chat for a time and pick up their welcome packets before they excuse themselves to go get ready for the kickoff event.

Laura waves, then sits again.

When the two of them are alone once more, Laura fiddles with her necklace.

"David doesn't know," she says quietly, in answer to Graye's question.

Graye nods. She assumed as much.

"I'm going to tell him soon, but David . . . he's never wanted kids."

Graye studies the woman beside her that she feels she's come to know so well. "And you?"

Laura sighs. "I agreed with him. At first. And then I didn't. I knew from the beginning what I was getting, so to try and play the part of the wronged spouse is hypocritical of me."

"So what changed?" Graye asks.

Laura gives a dry chuckle. "Him. Me. Our expectations. Our marriage. What didn't change is a better question." Laura sighs again. "I guess I got tired of being alone."

Graye reaches over and squeezes Laura's hand. Loneliness is as familiar to her as her own reflection.

Laura looks up with misty eyes. "I'd like to think he'll rise to the occasion, but deep down I know that's wishful thinking."

Laura sits up straighter and takes a deep breath. She dabs at her eyes and gives Graye a lopsided smile.

"Let's talk about something else," she says with a wry twist of her lips. "Anything else."

"All right."

Laura's face brightens slightly. "The upside to feeling so crappy lately is I've had lots of time to lounge in bed reading. I've been meaning to tell you, I started that manuscript you recommended."

Every cell in Graye's body reacts at once, electrified, as if she's risen from a hundred-year sleep.

Another guest arrives at that precise moment to sign in, which is both a blessing and a curse. Graye has time to compose herself, but she also has to endure the small talk and introductions with a smile.

Once the guest is finally done and on her way, Graye forces herself to pause for what she can only hope is a reasonable amount of time before she brings the subject up again.

"So . . . you were saying?" she prompts. Casual. Calm. Collected. Those words play in her head and she struggles to listen.

"What?"

Graye bites back a scream of frustration.

"The manuscript? *The Orphan's Ashes?*"

"Oh yes!" Laura says. "I'm only about halfway done, but I have to say, I'm really impressed with your taste."

Graye is barely breathing.

"You . . ." Deep breath. "You like it then?"

Can Laura hear the thread of desperation that runs so wide through the question?

Calm. Casual. Collected.

Hold it together.

"Like it?" Laura says. "Are you kidding?"

Graye's befuddled brain doesn't know if she's supposed to answer or not.

"I absolutely love it," Laura continues.

Oh God. Oh God. She loves it. Graye is suddenly dizzy, disoriented.

"It's got such a compelling voice," Laura goes on, oblivious to Graye's spinning thoughts. "A little rough around the edges maybe, but the sense of menace, it's so subtle and powerful. And the unreliable narrator—while a bit overdone in the last few years, it feels like a fresh take."

It's so much to absorb. Too much. Laura's words march around in Graye's mind like soldiers in an army band, clanging about as they each play a different tune.

Compelling—Rough—Menace—Powerful—Fresh.

It's everything Graye could have hoped for. Everything, and so much more.

"The fairy tale sections especially. The story within the story? So intriguing. I don't know where she's going with the rest of it," Laura went on, "but honestly, I think Fiona Boyd has the potential to be a big new voice in fiction."

A shadow looms over them.

Graye's emotions are shredded. For once, she's grateful for an interruption, but when she looks up and sees Hugo Caron standing there, tall, distinguished, and even more handsome in person than in his photo, she's overwhelmed with a sensation she has trouble naming.

"Hugo," Laura says with a gasp. "You made it!"

"Laura." He gives her a slow smile. "You're looking smashing, as usual."

And then Graye knows. Impending doom. As if someone or something is positioning them as players in a game where the rules are a mystery and the stakes are growing higher and higher.

Laura's face lights up as she greets her friend. Her lover.

"Graye," Laura says, "would you excuse me?"

It's all too good to be true, and dangerously precarious. First Nick, showing up in her life after all this time, and now this? Will Hugo Caron be the thing that tips the delicate balance?

Laura has risen from her seat and joined Hugo. She slips her arm into his and speaks quietly, words Graye doesn't catch, and the two of them walk together out of the ballroom to a secluded corner of the hotel lobby.

Graye stands and moves as casually as she can manage to the entryway of the ballroom and watches them discreetly over the top of a checklist she picked up from the welcome table. They pay her no mind.

Graye tries to focus. She's just received the greatest of gifts, confirmation her story resonates with the person whose opinion matters the most.

She should be over the moon, and she is, but the higher she soars, the more acutely aware she becomes of the distance to the hard, rocky ground beneath and the looming presence of Nick below, waiting. Watching.

If she falls now, it could break her.

Graye studies the pair, but a tall potted plant partially blocks her view. They're deep in conversation, and from the look of concern on Hugo's face, the discussion is intense.

Graye busies herself pretending to study the clipboard in her hand and tries not to stare at the two of them. The evening will begin soon, regardless of Laura's personal life, and Graye can do nothing except help ensure the event runs smoothly and seamlessly.

She wonders for a moment how Laura, a woman who can juggle such minute details with ease, has landed herself in such a mess.

Graye tucks a strand of hair behind her ear and keeps her eyes downcast as Laura walks with Hugo to the elevator. The two of them share a hug, and Graye watches beneath hooded eyes.

Laura is swiping at her eyes when she joins Graye again.

"An old friend," she says by way of explanation. "I'm sorry, I should have introduced you."

Laura's pallor has worsened, if that's possible, and her features are taut. Graye waves away the apology.

"Are you okay?" she asks.

Laura nods with a stiff smile. "I'll be fine. Just not feeling myself."

"Is there anything I can do?" Graye asks.

Laura lets out a sigh of relief. "There is, actually, since you offered. I wrote some notes for a welcome speech on a few cards, then ran off and left them on my desk. I could wing it, but—"

"I'll take care of it," Graye says. The other woman doesn't look capable of making it through the party on her own two feet, much less winging anything.

"Thank you. And while you're there, would you mind grabbing some ibuprofen from the medicine cabinet? This headache is going to be the death of me."

"Absolutely."

Graye isn't about to let anything be the death of her friend. Not now. She has too much to lose.

21

GRAYE

It's a short walk from the hotel next door to the West home.

The floral-printed shirtwaist dress she ordered online just for tonight flows around her knees in the breeze. It isn't as fancy as Laura's, but Graye rather likes it. Especially with her pillbox hat.

Unfortunately, pillbox hats aren't designed to stand up to island winds, and Graye reaches up with a gasp as the pins she used to secure it give way. It tumbles, rolling happily between the houses, then onward toward the beach.

She races after it as it rolls across the sand, but someone else gets there first.

The smile of gratitude dies on her lips when she recognizes the man clutching the little blue hat.

"I told you to leave me alone," Graye hisses. Her pleasure at the near-perfect day and excitement about the coming weekend drain away in an instant. Dread seeps in like grains of sand pouring into her shoes.

"What do you want from me, Nick?" she demands.

He holds the hat out to her, but stays rooted in place, a wolf waiting for the chance to pounce on his Red Riding Hood. She forces herself to close the distance between them despite the warning bells clanging in her head.

She snatches the hat from his outstretched hand.

"Why are you back?"

"I've tried to forget you, Grace," he says. Another person might call his tone gentle, but Graye knows what this man is capable of. She isn't fooled. "But that's been more difficult than I expected."

"You're nothing to me," she says. "Grace is nothing. The past is gone. I have a new life now, a future."

He shakes his head as if he pities her. "It's not that simple, Grace. I know what your family did to you."

"I don't have a family anymore!" Her voice is rising, but he's unmoved.

"It's a dangerous game, to play with people's lives. Not everyone has the stomach for it."

He slides his hands into his pockets and stares at her long and hard. Her cheeks warm. She feels exposed beneath his gaze.

"What do you want?"

He considers his reply before he speaks again. "I want you to be honest with me."

He's lying. He's always been a liar. She hasn't forgotten.

"And you think I owe you that? You think I owe you anything after what you did?"

His face changes, his mask of politeness slipping just a notch.

"You should be careful, Grace," he says quietly. "Every act has consequences, even if they take a lifetime to catch up with you."

Graye's heart is thumping, but she can't back down now. She's done nothing wrong. Not when she was a girl, and not now. Whatever he believes he's owed, he's mistaken.

"Are you threatening me? All I need to do is walk into a police station and file a complaint, Nick. You shouldn't be anywhere near me, and you know it."

An empty threat he sees through right away. "And you're going to do that? Expose yourself to the world? Give up this life as Graye Templeton?"

The press, who'd searched for little Gracie Thacker relentlessly, would find her, and they wouldn't hesitate to pounce. Her life, her future, would be ruined more quickly than if she'd doused it in gasoline and flicked a match.

"You've settled in. You're making something. Something good, you hope. You don't want to jeopardize that, do you?" he says, his voice like velvet, concealing the razor-sharp edges of his words.

"Your boss seems like a nice woman. Laura, right? Beautiful name. A tire can be repaired, Gracie. A life? Not so much."

The threat lands heavily between them, all pretense swept away.

"You stay away from her!" Graye screams. "Stay away from us both!"

Graye backs away in horror, desperate to put as much distance between her and this man as possible. It can never be enough. There's nowhere left to hide.

"Stay away!" she cries. Out of options, Graye turns and runs. She doesn't look back to see if he's following her. She doesn't need to. He's always been there.

No matter how fast she runs, he always will be.

◆ ◆ ◆

Dr. West may not be the absolute last person Graye wants to face at this moment, but he's close.

Her shoulder jostles his as she passes him on her way into Laura's office. She doesn't bother to apologize.

"Did the lady of the manor forget something?" David asks. "She sent her maidservant to retrieve it?"

He's dressed haphazardly, his shirt untucked and his tie hanging loose.

Graye ignores him and heads to the desk where Laura said she left her notes.

She doesn't have time for this.

Her damn hands are shaking again as she swipes the notecards from the surface of the desk. Several flutter to the floor. She kneels to collect them as David darkens the doorway at her back.

"She could have called me," he says, indignant at the perceived slight. "I would have brought them to her."

Graye rises to her feet and stares at his mulish face.

"Am I supposed to respond to that?" she asks. Her patience is at a breaking point.

"I'm sorry," David says, raising his palms as if to ward her off, though she hasn't moved. "Is that too much to ask? Or do you just repeat what you've been told? Independent thought above your pay grade?"

Graye crosses her arms. "Does that make you feel good?" she asks. "Do you feel like a big man now that you've put the underling assistant in her place?"

David's eyes widen slightly, and she sees his throat work as he tries to swallow. There might even be remorse there, if she cares to examine it.

Instead, she walks toward him, closing the distance until she faces him eye to eye.

"Does that make up for the pathetic waste of your life?" she asks, wielding her words with precision. She cocks her head to one side and studies him. "Your marriage and your career are circling the drain. The only question is which will go first. I suppose it's understandable to lash out, and I'm an easy whipping boy."

Graye turns sideways and squeezes past him with his shocked expression and his clenched jaw. God forbid he step out of her way.

Graye moves down the hallway to the bathroom.

"It's easier that way, isn't it?" she calls over her shoulder.

Graye should stop, but her frustration at yet another man in her path—unmoving, unbending, unrepentant in his ignorance, unrelenting in his confidence that he's earned the right by virtue of his existence—it's enough for one day. Enough already.

"Excuse me?" David whispers. He's followed her to yet another open doorway and stands there gaping like a fool. Worse, a fool who believes he's a king. A fool who mistakes the bells that jangle from his jester's cap for applause each time he opens his mouth.

She turns away and begins rummaging through the medicine cabinet.

"I said, it's easier that way, isn't it? Easier to take it out on me? Who am I, after all? Because to put all that contempt where it belongs—squarely on your own shoulders—you'd have to be a better man than you are."

Graye finds the ibuprofen, but her hands still aren't steady and several other bottles fall to the sink and floor below with a clatter.

Gripping the bottle of pills in one hand and Laura's notecards in the other, Graye walks up to David again.

His nostrils flare, and he has a wild, wounded look in his eyes.

"Did I hurt your feelings?" she asks calmly.

David's breath is ragged, and she can smell the booze he had for lunch. His hands clench into fists at his sides. She wonders dispassionately if he's going to hit her.

"Get out of my way," she says slowly.

Surprisingly, he does, stepping back suddenly as if he's only just realized how close he's been standing to a contagious disease. She brushes past him, unable to hide a curl of her lip and unwilling to try.

Graye hurries back toward the hotel, head down, her mouth a grim slash across her face. Her thoughts are consumed by worries over Nick and his threats, leaving her jumpy and wired.

If she had the mental real estate to spare on thoughts of Dr. West, she would assume he began pouring his rage down his throat using the closest alcohol at hand after she slammed the door behind her.

She'd have been right.

What she wouldn't have imagined was the way he took his drink of choice into the bathroom she'd just left. The way he gripped the bottle by the neck like a lifeline as he slowly slid his back down the wall.

His legs splayed out as he took a swig, then set the bottle on the tile floor with a comical amount of care.

Graye couldn't know the despair that smoldered beneath the veneer of a lost man who's turned to alcohol out of nothing but cowardice and knows it.

David picked up one of the pill bottles that had fallen onto the floor and felt the weight of it in his hand. So light, yet so heavy.

Graye couldn't know because even David couldn't have said whom he loathed more in that moment—his wife, his wife's bitch of an assistant, or himself.

22

LAURA

Laura rinses her mouth with water from the sink in the hotel restroom.

The doctor she visited on the mainland had warned her that so-called "morning sickness" was a misnomer. That each pregnancy was different and nausea could hit at any time during the day. For the particularly unlucky, it could be an all-day affair, though it didn't often last past the first trimester.

Laura sighs and forces herself not to dwell on the negative aspects of a situation she's consciously chosen.

She had other choices. Choices she walked right to the edge of.

For the first ten years of their marriage, Laura hadn't questioned David's assertion that he didn't want kids. She hadn't wanted kids either. They were young. They were busy building careers, basking in each other's early successes. They were drunk on each other.

Naively, she'd believed them so in sync that the vague possibility she might *one day* want children didn't bother her. She assumed David would be in step if that day ever came. It was a foolish assumption to make.

Her twenties were gone in a blink, and she found herself reconsidering once her thirties had taken hold. Laura once broached the subject after meeting a friend's new baby, wondering aloud over dinner what a child of her and David's might look like.

His fork stilled halfway to his mouth, his eyes suddenly dark and wary. He placed the fork carefully on his plate with a clink.

"Like a mistake," he said softly. "A big one."

He stood and walked away without another word, leaving her speechless and alone. She'd been too shocked by the coldness of his reaction to broach the subject again.

On the surface, things went back to normal, but Laura suspects that was when the first crack appeared beneath their feet. The birth control pills she swallowed each night took on new gravity, and other people's children an unattainable lure.

Which is why Laura doesn't know with any certainty how *accidental* it truly was when she became pregnant ten months later. What she knows, with great certainty, is the fierceness of David's anger when he found out.

Within forty-eight tumultuous hours, David drove Laura to a clinic to "take care" of the situation. He remained in the waiting room while she endured the procedure alone, silent tears running from the corners of her eyes.

He'd been kind on the drive home. Solicitous. A far cry from the volatility she'd seen in him over the previous days.

"My father was forty-eight when he died," David said as Laura stared out the window, her eyes unfocused on the passing scenery. "A heart attack. He left behind six kids who hardly knew him. At his wake, friends and coworkers spoke about a man who was a stranger to me. He accepted every hour of overtime offered, left before we woke up, and came home too exhausted to be part of the family he was working so hard to support. But what choice did he have?"

Laura glanced across the car, searching her husband's features for something, anything, that could help her forgive him. That could help her forgive herself.

"What choice did my mother have when she remarried within the year? She couldn't support six kids on her own, and the months of trying had stolen her savings, her smile, her beauty. Her hope. She needed a husband. But the only thing she had left to attract one was a house full of unsuspecting victims."

Laura's breath caught in her throat.

"What kind of man do you suppose she found?" he asked without looking at her.

She was grateful he didn't expect an answer. There was nothing she could have said to erase the past. Not the distant past, and not the recent one either.

They never spoke of children again. As long as they didn't, Laura could ignore the expanding web of cracks in the foundation of their lives.

Until now.

When Laura watched the stick turn blue for the second time in her life, she was a different person. Gone was the younger woman willing to sacrifice the possibility of a child for the sake of her marriage. Gone was the seemingly perfect marriage that made that choice seem reasonable.

Her first thought, as uncharitable as it was, had been irritation. If children were such a deal breaker for David, why had he never bothered to get a vasectomy? But she knew the answer to her unvoiced question.

Because it was Laura's responsibility to ensure David lived the life he felt he deserved. It always had been. And it was a role she was tired of playing.

Distracted by her annoyance, she hadn't noticed the tendrils of something else creeping around her heart. Something that felt like joy. Something that felt like hope.

Laura doesn't expect a child to fix her marriage. If anything, it will probably end it. The difference now is that the woman staring back at her from the mirror is a woman willing to take that chance.

She can hear laughter drifting from the ballroom as she repairs her makeup and fishes a breath mint from her purse.

The door opens a crack and Graye pokes her head inside.

"Are you all right?" she asks, letting the door swing closed behind her. The young woman swallows hard before she asks, "Do you need me to give the speech?"

Graye looks petrified at the prospect, but she offered. *Bless her heart,* Laura's grandmother would have said.

Laura pulls in a deep breath and takes stock. "I feel a little better now, actually. I probably have a good twenty minutes before I turn green again."

Graye holds up Laura's notecards, though the furrow in her brow gives away her doubts. "I guess you'd better hurry then."

The crowd is rowdy as they make their way back through the mock casino, just the way Laura likes it. She thrives on the smiles and the noise.

She flips a switch on the microphone Yolanda set up for her earlier in the day, and it lets out a shrill whine that draws the attention of the room.

"Good evening, everyone, and welcome to Port Mary," Laura says.

A cheer goes up, the crowd having warmed already thanks to a busy waitstaff and their trays of drinks.

"I won't keep you long since I can tell by the way Olivia is jiggling her foot that she has a good hand." She shakes her head. "Don't bother trying to bluff her, boys. She'll take you to the cleaners and leave you with the bill."

One of the players, a portly white-haired man whose name is no stranger to bestseller lists, tosses his cards onto the green felt table.

"I fold," he declares loudly, holding up his hands in surrender and eliciting a good-natured laugh from the crowd.

"I just want to thank you all for being here," Laura goes on. "It's my absolute pleasure to have the honor of working around books, and by extension their authors. It turns out you're as lovely as the words you write and the stories you create."

She wags her finger at a tall man near the back of the room. "Except for you, Walt. But there's always one, I suppose."

She winks and Walt dips into a showy bow, pulling more amusement from the group.

"I'd also like to give the warmest of welcomes to the book bloggers, the booksellers, and the super-readers among us. The tireless champions who are the nerve center of what we do."

Glasses raise around the room, and Laura joins the group in a hearty round of applause.

"As my father likes to say, a person writes a book out of ego, reads a book out of hope, and recommends a book to another out of love."

When the applause dies down, Laura continues.

"For the truly brave among you, I look forward to seeing you at the Bestseller Breakfast Charades in the morning, where we'll judge what you're *really* made of."

Laura prefers to keep things short and sweet, but she has one last thought to leave them with.

"A moment more, and I'll let you get back to it," she says. "You all received a character card in advance for the Christie Murder Mystery dinner tomorrow night."

Nods and whispers.

"Each included a backstory, complete with a few instructions and a clue. Our mystery will kick off tomorrow afternoon, when we'll gather for cocktails before dinner.

"Just a piece of advice. Question everything. Mingle. Compare notes. Band together, if you like. But remember—things aren't always what they seem. Trust *no one*."

There are slow smiles across the room as the guests turn to consider one another with exaggerated suspicion.

"Anyone could be the next victim. And anyone a killer."

As she replaces the microphone, Laura breathes a sigh of relief. She made it through the speech without running to the bathroom to puke.

She catches Graye's eye. Ironically, Laura is feeling better. Graye, on the other hand, who seems more nervous than she is, has gone a sickly shade of pale.

Bless her heart.

23

GRAYE

Despite the lateness of the hour, as the two women make their way back to the West home, Graye can't help but notice that Laura seems energized. Her pallor is gone, replaced with a moonlit brightness in her eyes fueled by the success of the evening and anticipation of the next day.

Graye, though, is a bundle of exposed nerves. The need to keep up the illusion of a calm facade is beginning to take a toll. Inside, Graye is battling her growing apprehension about Nick and his intentions. If there weren't so very much at stake, she'd run as far and fast as she could manage. But she can't do that.

Not yet.

Side by side, the women have chosen to walk along the beach rather than the road. Shoes dangle from their fingertips. Occasionally a crab scuttles past. The moon throws jeweled reflections off the sea.

At night, the shore is a world of its own, a unique and private landscape inhabited by creatures that shun the glaring sun of the day. The faraway bell of an unseen buoy rings in the darkness, answered by the low foghorn of a distant ship, and the constant gentle rush of surf. The flicker of a campfire farther down the beach is the only sign they aren't the last two people left in the world.

It should be a pleasure. But Graye jumps at shadows, real or imagined, moving among the row of houses standing tall and silent along the seaside.

Neither woman mentions David's conspicuous absence that evening, which is fine with her. Graye has enough on her mind with thoughts of Nick. She's been unable to shake the foreboding that's settled around her.

"There's no way I can sleep. I'm too amped up," Laura says as they draw close to home. "And a glass of wine isn't an option. I think I'll read for a little while, distract my brain. That manuscript has been whispering my name since I set it down yesterday."

Graye's pulse jumps. There will be no sleep for her now either, knowing Laura will be just yards away, traveling the path that Graye's words have paved.

They veer up the beach to the faded blue house.

"See you bright and early for the big day. I have a surprise or two up my sleeve for tomorrow," Laura says as she lets herself in her kitchen door, leaving Graye to continue the few steps farther to the guesthouse.

A surprise? Graye tries not to let her disquiet show at the idea.

"And Graye?" Laura says at her retreating back.

She stops and turns.

"I don't know if I've said it, but thank you for your help today. For everything, really."

"That's my job," Graye says.

"It's not part of the job to be a friend. I couldn't have made it through tonight without you, you know."

She's grateful for the darkness that hides the blush rising on her cheeks.

"Good night, then," Graye says.

"Good night."

And Laura is gone.

But it isn't a good night. Not for Graye. She sits alone in the dark, with only her racing thoughts for company, alternately imagining Laura enthralled by her book and Nick waiting to ruin it all. Sleep is impossible, until eventually even the dark gives up and fades into day.

◆ ◆ ◆

Sleeplessness adds a surreal layer to the following day that's impossible to escape. Like a child's kaleidoscope, the view shifts suddenly, sending light and color careening at Graye while her fuzzy head struggles to keep up.

The collective mood of the group is too cheerful, conversations too loud.

Staff of the Mary Read set up tables and chairs beachside, extending the party of the night before with brunch and a mimosa bar staged on the outdoor patio. Laura's guests have officially renounced their responsibilities at home, giving themselves over to the relaxed frivolity Laura offers with an abandon that leaves Graye both befuddled and a bit envious.

The laughter that rings out while a group of adults indulge themselves in a decidedly un-adultlike game of charades on the beach is a vague irritant, a grain of sand in her dry, tired eyes. Graye tries to concentrate, creating lists in her head of what needs to be done for the day, but thoughts of Laura's opinion of *The Orphan's Ashes* creep in.

Has she finished it? There hasn't been an opportunity to ask, and the question sticks in Graye's gut like a rusty fish hook she's swallowed by accident.

Thoughts of Nick are never far away, and she surreptitiously studies the crowd, searching out the specter at the feast.

It's going to be a very long day.

Graye stares at a patch of sky far in the distance and the barely discernable shadow that mars the otherwise wide, clear horizon.

She's read the weather report. Her head knows it will bring nothing more than a few thunderstorms. They'll be gone as quickly as they arrive. Nothing to worry about. But her heart is uneasy.

"Earth to Graye," Laura says at her side. The group of guests has begun to disperse, finished with the parlor game at last.

"I'm sorry." Graye straightens immediately, pulling her thoughts back from the edge. "Hey, did you have a chance to finish that manuscript last night?" Graye asks, reaching for a casual tone she doesn't feel.

Real subtle, she thinks. *Way to go.*

"I did," Laura says, brightening. "It was—"

"Laura," a voice calls out. Laura breaks off and turns her head. A warm smile fills her face.

"Hugo," she says. "This is my assistant, Graye."

Graye dredges up a smile and shakes the man's hand even though she's dying inside, a little at a time.

"I was hoping to catch you in between events. Could you spare a few minutes?" he asks Laura.

"Of course," she replies. "Just give me a second, okay?"

Laura turns to Graye. "All the guests are doing their own thing for the afternoon, but they know to be back for the big dinner by six. That means you're off the hook, barring any emergencies. Meet you back here by five thirty and we'll go over any last-minute issues?"

Graye nods, though she wants to howl in frustration. Instead, all she can do is watch the couple walk off together toward the hotel, their heads bent toward each other.

It mystifies Graye, the peculiar way people complicate their lives.

She's been on dates. A few anyway. There was a guy she went out with several times during freshman year. Her roommate, Natalie, had set them up.

He was nice enough. Attractive even, she supposed.

When he kissed her after their third date, she didn't stop him, thinking maybe it was time to find out what all the fuss was about.

Books are riddled with characters who defy logic and reason to chase that elusive thing called love.

Or, at the very least, sex.

But after fumbling through the clumsy machinations, gamely attempting to do her part, Graye realized there was a lot books never mention.

Like the feel of someone else's sweaty back beneath your hand. Or the need in their eyes as they watch your reaction to their efforts, hoping for confirmation they're not as bad at this as they fear.

Nor do books talk about the moment when biology takes over and they no longer care, so focused on their own grunting, panting release.

The books skip right past the uncomfortable moments after, when you know that even if he bothers to call again, you won't answer the phone.

Graye tried it. She's yet to cross paths with another person, man or woman, who's tempted her to try it again.

No, thanks. Hard pass.

It was a stance Natalie found incomprehensible and more than a little funny. But Natalie's quest for collecting all the pleasure the world had to offer slowly took over her life. Her plans to leave college and go to Los Angeles with her latest boyfriend, cooked up after a late-night drug-infused bout of mania, ended not in stardom, but her death when she overdosed on drugs provided by the same guy who'd promised to make her famous.

As different as the two girls were, Natalie and Graye were friends.

Such a needless waste of a life. And it never would have happened if Natalie hadn't been so ready and willing to complicate her world. Men, sex, drugs. All so pointless.

It isn't that Graye doesn't understand what people are searching for. Belonging, acceptance, validation, a cure for loneliness, to scratch an itch.

She longs for the same, but more than that, she longs to be *heard*. To have a voice. The rest will flow from there.

Far in the distance, a silent flash of lightning arcs through the air, warning of what's headed their way.

Graye clenches her jaw, determined to weather whatever the storm might bring.

24

LAURA

"Laura—"

"Hugo—"

They speak at the same time, the words bumping against one another in the awkward space between them.

Hugo smiles gently and places his hands into the pockets of his shorts.

"Ladies first," he says.

"No, you go."

He leans his back against the wall and crosses one foot over the other. Laura's eyes slide past him, landing anywhere but his too-perceptive gaze.

"Have you told him?" Hugo asks.

Laura shakes her head, then tucks a strand of hair behind her ear. "I'm working up to it."

"Laura," he says, the word drawn out. There's so much disappointment in those two syllables. A world of disappointment.

"I am," she says.

"You can't go on like this."

"Don't you think I know that?" she replies, more sharply than she intended.

He's silent, a silence that does nothing but allow her time to regret the way she's spoken to him.

"Who are you angry at?" he finally asks quietly.

"Myself, mostly," she says with a sigh.

"And there's your mistake. He doesn't deserve you. He never did."

Maybe, she thinks. *Maybe not.*

She walks toward the elevator and pushes a button on the panel to open the doors. She steps into the empty waiting space and looks again to where Hugo is standing, hands still deep in his pockets, concern etched on his face.

"You coming?" she asks.

He sighs. "Where else would I go?"

When the doors slide closed, she presses the button for the second floor, where his room is located. In the moment of privacy, he pulls her into a hug.

Laura lays her head against his chest, an echo of the way she laid her head against David's chest just the day before. The difference is, instead of seeking some sort of truce, with Hugo, she can take comfort for herself from this man who knows her so well. He gives willingly, without hesitation.

"He doesn't deserve to be lied to either," she says, glancing up at Hugo, meeting his eyes at last. "No one does."

25

GRAYE

With the afternoon free from responsibilities, Graye considers returning home for a quick nap. She dismisses the thought almost as soon as it comes to her.

It's not that Laura would mind. She'd probably encourage her if she had any idea how long it's been since Graye has slept.

But she doesn't want to risk getting tangled up in dreams of Nick and Alex and the family she used to have.

Those memories stayed firmly locked away for years, but with Nick's sudden return they've joined forces, breaking down her defenses. Now, she's powerless against them.

She hates the familiarity of that sensation.

And even if her personal ghosts, both living and dead, left her in peace for once, Graye wouldn't risk oversleeping and letting Laura down.

She settles for stretching out on one of the hotel's beach chairs beneath an umbrella for a few moments instead.

The little bruised patch of sky has grown slightly larger, darker, but perspective on the coastal horizon is tricky, making the storm look closer than it is. Supposedly, they have hours yet before it will reach them.

Graye closes her eyes and focuses on the wind caressing her cheeks and pulling at her hair. If third-date guy had felt half as good, there might have been a fourth.

She wishes the wind could carry her worries away.

Nick and what he wants with her is a problem she can't escape.

Does he mean her physical harm? Or worse?

If she's exposed as Grace Thacker now, when she's so close to her dreams she can feel the shape of them brushing her hand, it will ruin any chance to earn respect as a writer. If the truth comes out before she's published, no one will ever take her seriously. She'll forever wear the stain of tabloid trash. Worse, trash with delusions of grandeur.

They'll laugh. They'll all laugh at her, getting ideas above herself, grasping for a brass ring she has no chance of reaching. Her opportunities will wither on the vine, leaving nothing within her reach except potentially a stint on a B-list celebrity dance show.

And Graye is a terrible dancer.

After she's published, things will be different. After, she'll have a career established as a successful novelist to wave as a white flag. Once that happens, her past is nothing but a tragic backstory.

This is the mountain she's been climbing her entire life. She's so close to the peak now, she can feel the air growing thin.

Only Nick stands between Graye and the future she's meant to have.

But she has faith in Laura. Nothing Nick could say will change anything if Laura has already seen she has talent. But first, Laura has to fall in love with the book.

By tomorrow, the guests will be packing up and checking out of the hotel with enough time to catch the afternoon ferry and return to their homes. There will be nothing left to get in the way of a long discussion with Laura about the merits of "Fiona Boyd's" work.

Graye imagines the pleasure that will fill Laura's face when she reveals her secret. She'll be thrilled for her assistant. Her friend. She'll forgive the small untruths, and understand why Graye had no choice.

Of course she will.

Truth, lies, it won't matter what Nick says after that.

Her work will speak for itself.

"You're a fool," a familiar mocking voice whispers in her head. *"You've always been a fool."*

Graye's brow furrows as she squeezes her eyes shut tighter.

"Haven't you learned anything? People only love you for what you can give them, Gracie. You have nothing to offer."

She gives a small shake of her head, denying the voice, denying the words.

Lost in a maze of insecurities, Graye gives a shriek when a voice, a real voice, speaks at her side.

"Tell me something, Miss Templeton," David West says. He seats himself on the lounge chair next to Graye, sitting upright and studying her profile. "What is it you hope to gain out of your association with my wife?"

He holds two glasses in his hands, both cheery and garish with bright paper umbrellas perched at the rim. They're a stark contrast to his colorless features.

David thrusts one of the drinks at her, but she shifts away from his outstretched hand and eyes him warily.

"A little early for me, thanks," she says.

"It's a smoothie. Nonalcoholic."

Slowly, she takes it from him and watches as he takes a long sip from a fat straw.

"Supposed to be good for you," he says with a shrug. "It would be better with a few shots of rum."

"What do you want?" Graye asks. David West and all he represents has fallen far and fast down her list of concerns.

He raises an eyebrow and takes another sip. "I asked you first."

"Nothing," she says, inwardly cringing at the defensiveness in the word. "To do my job, that's all."

He doesn't reply, but the doubt is clear on his face.

There's too much perception in those eyes, the only part of him that looks alive. The rest a wax imitation of a man who's been left in the sun too long and has woken to find himself in an unwanted state of sobriety.

Graye likes him better drunk.

His hands shake as he raises the straw to his mouth again and pulls in the blended fruit concoction like it might cure his tremors.

It doesn't.

Graye takes a drink of her own smoothie and watches from the corner of her eye as he swings his legs around to stretch out on the lounger. He lays his head back, closing his eyes against whatever tug-of-war rages inside of him.

He doesn't seem to notice or care that he's intruded on the only moment of solitude she's likely to find today.

Grudgingly, she accepts his presence and his peace offering, though she much prefers the frozen drink to his company.

With her eyes closed and his silence, she can almost forget he's there. At least until he speaks again.

"Laura has a soft heart," he says without opening his eyes.

Whatever Graye might have expected him to say, that isn't it.

"It makes her easy to take advantage of. I should know, I've been doing it for years."

Graye gapes at him.

He tilts his head toward her and opens his eyes for just a moment.

"Why so shocked? You think I don't know what I've done?"

He shakes his head and closes his eyes again.

"I didn't set out to use her, but she made it easy."

Somehow, he manages to make it sound like it's Laura's fault he's an asshole.

"Laura and I have our problems, none of which I feel the need to justify to you, but her happiness is entangled with mine. We've decided, together, to put new effort into making our marriage work."

"Why are you telling me this?"

"Because frankly, you're in the way. You've overstayed your welcome and it's time to move along."

Graye's jaw falls, the sweetness of the drink curdling on her tongue. The breathtaking gall of the man.

"You'll have my recommendation and hers as well, I'm sure. I don't expect you to go away empty-handed, but I do expect you to go away."

"You're serious," Graye says.

He meets her shocked expression directly.

"Do yourself a favor and accept this gracefully. Laura's loyalty was spoken for long before you came along. If you attempt to put that to the test, you'll only humiliate yourself."

He moves back into a sitting position and finishes off his drink with the same finality he finishes the conversation.

"No hard feelings, Graye. I'm doing you a favor, really."

He stands. There are things she could say, things she should say, but her words are lodged behind a seething ball of revulsion that fills her throat.

He pats her on the shoulder, once, then twice. Fatherly, almost, if one's father happens to be an arrogant prick. Then he walks away.

Stone-faced, Graye stares at the waves that crash just yards away. Moments ago, she'd taken solace in them, but not anymore. Now they're as unstoppable, as unforgiving, as her rage.

David West would dismiss her with a wave of his hand, just as she's been dismissed by everyone she's ever known.

Not this time. Not when she's so close.

Nick DiMarco and David West can both go to hell.

Graye stands suddenly, so suddenly she has to steady herself with a hand around the pole of the large beach umbrella. The combination of exhaustion and determination is wreaking havoc on her equilibrium.

She marches up the sand, away from the beach and surf.

She won't give in.

Graye stares at her feet, forcing them forward, and nearly collides with a figure crossing her path. The blonde waitress who carries a tray of drinks sidesteps her and manages not to spill her tray, but a wave of dizziness sweeps over Graye at the sight of the woman.

The past and present overlap, confusing her in her sleep-deprived state.

It happened a lot when she was younger, after Alex was gone. She'd see a stranger with the vaguest resemblance and think of her sister. It hasn't happened in years. Not while she's awake, at least.

She has been dreaming of her sister lately, though. It's one reason she fights so hard against closing her eyes. Once sleep has claimed her, she has no control over where her mind and her memories go.

She shakes her head, grasping for the real, for the now. Her eyes seek out the waitress, now handing the drinks to a pair of guests in beach chairs, but she looks nothing like Alex. They never do. Not really.

Get it together, she thinks, rubbing her fingertips along her temple.

There's too much on the line to begin losing track of what's real and what isn't.

Not now.

Not again.

26

Night has drawn its dark curtain over the cinder girl's bright and beautiful sister.

Where once there was sparkle to rim her eyes and jewels for her golden hair, a darkness has descended, unrepentant, as Sister gives herself to the lure of twilight and shadows.

Mother rails against this new cloak of melancholy, but try as she might, her eldest daughter either cannot or will not spin gold from despair.

Mother's honeyed words do nothing. Threats and punishments yield the same. Further and further her golden sister retreats into the dark, unmoved by Mother's machinations.

"Refuse me if you dare," Mother hisses, her voice as cold and deadly as a viper when she turns the lock on Sister's chamber door. "But here you will stay until you come to see things my way."

There comes not a sound, not a whimper of protest from the chamber. With the thin key on a red ribbon around her neck, Mother stalks away.

That night, the cinder girl creeps up the tower stairs to her sister's locked chamber. She passes a tray of bread and gruel, her own supper, through a slit in the door.

"Sister," she whispers urgently, for she's frightened and cold, alone in the dark. "Do as she asks and she'll let you be free."

There is no reply.

The cinder girl might have thought her sister asleep—or dead—had it not been for the sound of a soft, low whisper repeating a chant or a prayer.

"Sister?"

The shadows move on the stone walls, alive even without light. They encircle the cinder girl, reaching out their spindly dark arms to ensnare her.

The chant grows louder, coming from everywhere and nowhere. From the shadows, from the stones, from the very air.

Two words she hears in her sister's hard new voice.

"Come closer," the words demand.

She can't do as her sister asks. Her legs are frozen in fear.

"Come closer!" echoes inside her head.

Afraid her heart will burst, or she'll go mad, the cinder girl turns and runs.

GRAYE

Graye is seeing ghosts—a situation made more awkward by the fact that her ghosts aren't the silent kind.

Confusing a random waitress for Alex is bad enough, but when one of the retreat guests asks her in passing if the hotel has a gym, Graye sees only her mother's face, judgmental and sneering.

"Why would anyone care what you have to say?" are the words the innocuous question becomes in her mind.

"Stop," Graye whispers in response.

"Excuse me?" This from the woman, coupled with a look of confusion, translates into *"If you don't learn to keep your mouth shut, I'll just have to teach you,"* followed by a familiar soul-crushing laugh.

Graye puts her hands to her ears and squeezes her eyes shut, just as she did as a child.

"Are you all right?" the woman asks, her face a picture of growing concern.

"You've got a mighty high opinion of yourself, don't you, Grace," comes the snide version, delivered from the mouth of a dead woman.

"Leave me alone," Graye mumbles, backing away from the outstretched hand of a stranger who only wants to help. "Just leave me alone."

Graye retreats quickly, practically running from the woman, who looks more confused than ever.

Something is wrong. Something is very wrong.

An occasional voice from the past is nothing she hasn't experienced before, but faces to go along with those voices are a new and disturbing twist.

Graye stumbles down the hotel hallway, no specific destination in mind. She only knows she needs air, and there's a door leading to sunlight at the end of the hall.

But when she bursts through into the light, Graye finds herself surrounded by noise and more laughter. The hotel pool is filled with a small crowd of people. Their voices become the voices of the girls at St. Sebastian's.

"What's the matter? Cat got your tongue, little gray mouse?"

"Come here, little mousey. We're not going to hurt you," the voices taunt. A memory of the stinging yank on a ponytail that doesn't feel like a memory at all.

Graye reaches up and rubs her scalp, gripping her hair between her fingers as she does.

Breathe. Just breathe in and out. This isn't happening. You're delirious from worry and lack of sleep. That's all.

"Creepy little mouse, creeping to the church house." The whispery singsong voice that drips with ugly derision makes the hairs stand up on the back of Graye's neck.

"No," Graye moans. "Not this. Not now."

She misses the curious stares of a few of the guests who can't help noticing her odd behavior. She's lost inside her maze of memories, desperately searching for a way out.

One thing Graye knows for sure, she has to get out of here. Laura can't see her this way.

She's worked so hard to craft this persona, built her from the ground up, layer upon layer. Confident, chic, efficient, indispensable. Each a brick carefully created and settled into place, just so. If she loses that now, there will be nothing left but dust.

Home, then. Home. She'll lie down, combat the dizziness, the confusion. She'll pull herself together.

She will.

Through the gates that lead away from the pool and the audience of prying eyes, Graye moves toward safety. A little peace and quiet, some privacy—that's all she needs.

A laughing man on the path turns and smiles.

"I can't stop thinking about you, Grace." Nick's face, his lips forming the words.

She shakes her head. No. Not Nick.

"This isn't real," Graye whispers again and again as she forces herself not to run down the street that leads to home. Once she makes it there, once she's alone, she can find her center, stop this spiral before it spins further out of her control.

A woman steps from a car parked in the hotel lot, a woman with Sister Margaret's face.

Graye veers away, ducking her head as she avoids looking at anyone else.

She's so close.

She's Graye. Not Grace. She's real. She *is*, and she can prove it.

Her book. The manuscript is her talisman.

She's written everything down, shaped and molded it, given it a new ending. She's turned the tables on the truth. With the wave of a magic wand, Gracie's reality has become Graye's fiction.

Her manuscript is all she needs. To hold its weight in her hands, see the words on the page, listen to the sentences sing in her head.

Graye walks past her own door without pause, past the guesthouse that holds nothing more than an impersonal bed and a desk. She goes straight to the Wests' kitchen door. It's unlocked and she doesn't think twice about letting herself in.

Laura is busy with Hugo for the time being, leaving Graye free to steal through her home like a thief.

She isn't a thief, though. She has no intention of taking anything. By rights, the manuscript is hers. She's only placed it in Laura's care for a time.

Besides, Laura would understand.

And if Dr. West comes home, she can deal with him. Think up some excuse, some forgotten thing she's been sent to fetch, if necessary.

Luck is on her side. She sees no sign of him. Not in the kitchen or the living room, not down the hallway that leads to the open doors of Laura's office, the bathroom across from it, and Graye's destination beckoning at the end.

Laura's bedroom. Laura and David's, really, though Graye knows Dr. West spends most nights in his office at the other end of the house, as far from his wife as it's possible to get and still be under the same roof.

He may even be there now, home from the beach and attempting to write. Struggling to recapture something that's long since abandoned him.

Graye realizes she doesn't care.

She needs her manuscript, and nothing is going to stand in her way.

"Graye." Sister Margaret's voice holds a note of disapproval.

Graye leans her shoulder against the wall outside of the bedroom doorway.

"Don't, Sister," she begs. "Please don't. You don't understand."

"You're not thinking clearly, child," Sister Margaret chides.

And a child is exactly what she feels like. A child who is losing control, running away.

The nun had calmed her when she was young. Cared for her. The first and only person who believed Graye was special. Until Laura.

"You're not here," Graye says. "And I'm not a child."

Graye straightens from her slump and walks through the door into another woman's bedroom.

The space is light, airy, with a lingering scent. Clean sheets and Laura's perfume. Graye closes her eyes and breathes deeply. It's a hug when she desperately needs one.

There, on the bedside table, the stack of pages Graye has come for sits waiting.

She walks slowly to them and carefully removes a pair of reading glasses from where they've been placed on top. She lifts the manuscript, hugs it to her.

Her center. Her new truth.

This is what she's come for.

Now she can go.

But her legs have lost their strength. Instead, Graye slowly sinks onto Laura's side of the bed.

Holding the pages tightly in her left hand, she flips through them with her right, words flying past. Years of work and tears and dreams, woven carefully together, recreating Graye as the master of her past, no longer its victim.

The weight of the pages, solid in her lap, anchors her, and the voices in her head grow quiet at last. The soothing balm of relief washes over her.

Anxiety over Nick, over Dr. West and his ridiculous demands, over everything, drains from her limbs, leaving little behind.

She's never been so tired.

Without thought, Graye holds the manuscript close and lifts her feet from the floor to tuck them under her. She lays her head on the pillow that belongs to her friend.

It smells of Laura. It smells of kindness and new beginnings and hope for the future.

Graye closes her eyes, just for a moment. She won't stay, of course. She'll get up and leave Laura's private space, place the manuscript back where she found it.

No one will know.

But first, she'll rest. Just for a moment.

Laura won't mind.

27

GRAYE

The peace that Graye falls asleep with doesn't last.

Plagued by strange dreams full of the same cast of characters who fill her waking thoughts, though in bizarre new combinations, she wakes with a gasp.

Glancing sharply around, Graye struggles to regain her bearings. The bedcovers are twisted tightly in her hands.

Her grip has loosened in sleep and the papers she'd been clutching have fallen. Scattered along the edge of the bed and across the floor, they're undeniable evidence that Graye has intruded someplace she has no business being.

How long has she slept? She can't say. Light still fills the room, but it doesn't have the brightness of afternoon sun, she realizes with rising panic.

At least she hasn't been discovered. Yet.

In a burst of movement, Graye pulls loose pages to her, gathering them as quickly and quietly as she can manage. She drops to her knees and continues to do the same on the floor.

Her hands stall when she hears sounds traveling down the hallway from the front of the house. If Graye was alone before, she isn't any longer.

She makes out a voice, muffled and indistinct, but undeniably male.

It's Dr. West, and he's upset about something, that much is clear. It sounds as if his stint at sobriety was brief as well.

With her heart pounding in her throat, Graye straightens and stacks the pages together, no time and no thought given to their order or neatness.

She has to get out of this room.

As carefully as she can manage, Graye puts the manuscript back on the nightstand, replacing Laura's glasses on top of the messy, disorganized heap.

That will have to do.

Graye holds her breath as she creeps out of the room with quick, light steps.

The house is old. Creaky. But Dr. West's voice is raised, and he doesn't hear the floorboards announcing Graye's passage.

Closer now, she can make out his words a little better. He's making no effort to keep his voice down.

"You don't even know me," he yells. "What makes you think you can come here and ruin my life?"

She's never heard him so angry. Drunk and pathetic, yes. Sarcastic. Biting. But this is new and unnerving.

There's a muffled response that Graye can't make heads or tails of, but David's reply is loud and clear.

"Pregnant? That's ridiculous," he says with a hoarse laugh. "You need to leave."

Graye's breath catches in her throat. Laura's closely guarded news isn't a secret any longer. She peeks around the corner of the hallway, trying to catch a glimpse of the person who has betrayed Laura's trust, but David is standing in the front doorway, blocking her view.

He steps forward, pushing whoever is at the door farther out and away from his home.

". . . need to talk . . . can't ignore this."

A female voice, muffled and impossible to identify.

"I don't think you understand what I'm saying," David says, violence in his voice. "I *can't* be the father. That's impossible."

Graye sucks in a breath, then ducks down and hurries through the living room while David's back is turned, catching little more than an impression of a figure out front.

Slipping into the kitchen, Graye heads immediately for the door that leads outside. She doesn't let out her breath until she's quietly closed it behind her and made her way quickly across the carport and through the door of the guesthouse.

But her relief is short-lived.

Laura.

She needs to find Laura, to warn her. David's anger was palpable, and if he decides to turn that on his wife, Graye can't begin to predict the outcome.

Checking the clock on her desk, she sees she didn't sleep as long as she feared. There's still time, but she has to hurry.

◆　◆　◆

The wind has picked up and the day has taken on the strange, illuminating glow often called the "golden hour," with the added dimension of the still-looming storm.

Graye hurries back to the hotel, casting a wary eye at the distant skyline. The darkened clouds have paused, stopping to observe those below, curiously perhaps, before crashing the party.

And a curious sight they must be.

While the breeze dances with the strings of patio lights at the hotel bar, the group casts a glow of its own as the partygoers spill out onto the sand. The women are glittering caricatures of a bygone era, the men austere and sharp in black and white tuxedos.

Graye scans the crowd, searching for her friend. Her eyes pass over the waitresses, also dressed in black with ruffled white aprons and caps, paid extra to work the event in costume.

She spots a woman in a nun's habit, but despite the madness that overtook her earlier, doesn't confuse this woman for Sister Margaret. She's a guest dressed as the character she's been assigned, and the habit is different than the ones worn by the sisters at St. Sebastian's anyway.

There's Hugo, whose magnetism is only enhanced by the formal clothing and the highball glass in his hand. His teeth sparkle like the string of pearls looped around the neck of the woman next to him.

A woman who isn't Laura.

Graye pushes her way into the group, her eyes open and searching. Where is she?

Conversations buzz around her, most concerning the narrative that will dominate the evening.

"Rumor has it she's going to name a successor. That she plans to walk away from the business entirely and travel the world."

"No husband or children, right?"

"Not officially, but—"

An urge comes to turn to the gossipy women and ruin the mystery, just to see the disappointment on their faces. Only the care Laura has put into building the suspense for her guests stops her.

"Everyone will have a little piece of the story," she'd explained to Graye. "Only by mingling and asking questions can they gather enough information to find the truth."

At the time, Graye shared Laura's excitement. She'd been anticipating how the story, which centers around the indomitable Baroness Lyttleton, a prominent businesswoman at the helm of a textile empire, would play out as much as anyone. Perhaps more. But now, with real concern churning, the incessant chatter about a fictional character grates on her.

Graye spots Mai Linh, a glass of champagne in hand, deep in conversation with two other women.

Graye shoulders through the crowd, making her way to the author's side.

"Hi, Graye," Linh says when she sees her. "Have you met—"

"Have you seen Laura?"

Surprise crosses Linh's face, but she quickly recovers.

"No, not recently. Is something wrong?"

"I just need to . . ." She trails off as her eyes search the crowd again. A light-blue sparkle catches her eye.

"Excuse me," Graye mumbles, then pushes her way through the crowd again, this time toward the hotel. She doesn't spare the trio of women a second glance, missing the raised brows and exchanged glances she leaves behind.

Once through the wide double doors, Graye turns her head quickly from side to side.

More guests. More staff.

She jogs forward, checking the lobby, the ballroom, the corridors. Laura is nowhere.

The mechanical rumbling of the elevator catches her attention. A couple dressed in period clothing steps off. Not Laura, but the ding of the elevator door reminds her of the text alert on her phone.

The phone lies heavy in her pocket, waiting for Graye to remember it exists. When she palms it, the screen lights up. It's a quarter past six and there's a message waiting from Laura.

Just checking in. Let me know when you get back to the hotel. ☺

It was sent thirty minutes ago.

Graye's fingers fly as she types out a reply. If David is headed this way, he won't be far behind her. His anger was a hot blast of heat radiating from him. She can't let Laura walk into that blind.

Where are you?

Graye hits "Send" and listens to the digital whoosh that says the message is heading to its target. Thankfully, after only a few seconds, she sees the dialogue bubble that shows Laura is typing a reply.

On the roof.

Graye shakes her head and reads the message a second time, but it doesn't change.

The roof?? Need to talk. Important!

"Send."

Her eyes stay trained on the small screen in her hand as the dialogue bubble appears again.

And then it's gone.

Graye is already typing when the bubble reappears, followed by Laura's message.

OK. In the middle of something though. Call you when I'm done.

Graye lets out a growl of frustration that elicits a side-eye glance from a passerby.

I can come to you.

"Send." Her toe taps impatiently. She's not even sure how to get to the roof.

No need. Be down in a few. Gotta go.

Like a dam approaching its critical tipping point, Graye's frustration pushes against the walls of her control. With no care for the scene she's creating, she runs back outside and elbows through the crowd again, bumping into bodies and jostling drinks along the way.

Once she's far enough out, Graye turns and scans the roofline of the hotel. The clouds begin to rumble at her back, but faintly, far in the distance. Time still, before the rain arrives.

There. Along the side of the building and around a corner from where the crowd stands unaware, Graye sees a shadow of movement. A hint of sparkle from a light-blue sequined dress.

Then, a scream.

A body falling.

The deafening silence that remains when the scream cuts short.

A darkness crashes around Graye.

And the dam bursts.

28

GRAYE

For the barest moment, silence reigns. There's no sound at all other than a sharp collective intake of breath that sucks the oxygen from around them. The crowd is a living snapshot, a sea of frozen faces.

It doesn't last.

The moment passes and time speeds up, the seconds ticking past at double the pace, covering for the missed step, hoping no one notices.

No one does.

All around Graye, people react. Shock. Fear. Panicked voices saying, "Oh my God." Bodies begin to rush toward the hotel, a wave of humanity that will crash against it.

Graye can't move her legs.

Her mind tries to stretch itself around the terrible impossibility of what she's just witnessed and fails.

She stands rooted in place, jostled as people flow around her.

"Laura." Two syllables of breathless sound, a voice she doesn't recognize.

"Laura!" she says again, louder, stronger this time, full of a contagious urgency that finally, finally spurs her limbs forward.

Once moving, she can't stop.

Coming against a wall of people, each craning to see, Graye doesn't slow but pushes her way between them.

After the mad dash, why are they all just standing there?

"Get out of my way," she says, shoving a tuxedo-clad man aside.

Graye absorbs the sight in front of her, but understanding is slower to come.

A body sprawls upon the ground at their feet. The body of a woman.

This is wrong. All wrong. Graye shakes her head, not trusting her eyes, not after the day she's had.

Nothing makes sense.

She feels it. The very moment the energy of the crowd changes. The whispers begin and, like smoke, drift outward, flowing from lips to ears, then back again.

"It's her," the whispers say.

Who? Graye wants to scream.

A man walks forward and leans over the prone form, blocking the woman's face from view.

"Is she . . . is she *dead?*" asks a woman nearby.

The moment stretches as he glances over his shoulder, confusion evident on his face.

"I don't understand," he says, shaking his head.

"Oh for goodness' sake."

The words elicit a gasp from the gathered onlookers. They come from the mouth of the woman stretched out on the ground. The woman who's apparently just fallen from the roof.

A woman who definitely isn't Laura. And doesn't appear to be the least bit harmed.

"Of course I'm dead," she says. "Now help me up, you idiot."

"Is that . . . ?" the whispers ask, this time with more excitement than fear. The woman rises with help from the man at her side. She brushes a hand down her elegant red pantsuit, then pushes a mane of silver hair back from her face imperiously. *"Yes, I think it is,"* they answer.

"Oh, oh," says a voice from the back of the crowd. "This is my line."

Heads turn as a small woman Graye recognizes as the proprietress of an independent bookstore bursts through the line at the front of the group.

"It's the baroness!" the bookstore owner says, her voice breathless with excitement and theatricality. "Someone's pushed her from the roof! She's been murdered!"

A chain reaction begins. Frothy delight bubbles up, which quickly morphs into laughter. Guests turn to one another in embarrassed relief, eyes rolling toward the sky, sheepishly admitting they've been had. They bring their hands together, applauding their own deception.

The woman in red bows low, then stands with her shoulders back, her chin high, until the applause lessens.

"Now if you'll excuse me," she says, nodding in acknowledgment, "I'll be at the bar, where, before you ask, I will *not* be answering any questions, because I am, obviously and unfortunately, deceased."

The man next to her holds out his arm, upon which she places a bejeweled hand. The crowd parts for them to pass as she makes an exit grand enough for any Gilded Age screen goddess.

Graye watches them, though her mouth can't form a smile. She's not as enchanted as the others by the turn of events. There's no room for her to be. Terror—honest, real terror—isn't easy to let go of, and she's still clamped in its fist. Visions of Nick pushing an unsuspecting Laura from the roof are too fresh.

"I had no idea she was going to be here," a woman's voice says. "Did you?"

Graye overhears Mai Linh's amused answer.

"Not for sure," she says. "But I did suggest to Laura this weekend wouldn't be complete without the murder of Cecelia Ainsley. And she actually pulled it off."

29

LAURA

Laura doesn't immediately register that she's been slapped across the cheek.

The signs are there. Graye's quick, darting hand, out and then back again, like the tongue of a frog licking a fly from the sky. The sting that's left behind. Her assistant's wide, frightened eyes as it dawns on her what she's done.

They're standing just outside the ballroom. More than a few of the guests who are headed through the doors see the exchange. They give the two women a wide, cautious berth.

It doesn't occur to Laura to be angry. She's never been slapped before, so surprise has its foot firmly in the door before anger can gain any traction.

"Graye?" She raises a hand to her face. She's about to ask why, when it bursts upon her like fireworks. Again, the signs are there, if she'd only look.

"Oh God," Laura whispers. "I'm so sorry."

Tears pool in the bottom of Graye's eyes. "This was your big secret? I thought . . ."

"Graye, I'm so, so sorry. I didn't think."

"You didn't tell me . . ."

Laura reaches for the other woman's shoulders, pulls her into a one-sided hug, even as Graye keeps her own arms firmly wrapped around her middle.

"I wanted it to be a surprise, that's all," Laura says. "It never occurred to me you'd think it was me."

"You told me you were on the roof! What was I supposed to think?"

"I was on the roof to help throw the dummy over." Laura backs up, her hands still on Graye's forearms as she tries to get the girl to meet her eyes. To see the humor in the situation. Graye's not ready for that yet. "Someone from the hotel staff was at the bottom with Cecelia. They tossed the dummy behind the bushes before the crowd arrived."

"You should have told me," Graye whispers. She shakes her head back and forth, her hand pressing against her lips as she takes several steps backward.

Laura steps forward.

"Graye, I'm sorry," she says again. It's the only thing she can think to say, and it's clearly not enough.

"I thought . . . Oh God. I think I'm going to be sick."

Graye turns away. Laura takes a step forward to follow, but a voice at her side stops her.

"In my experience, once they're angry, you may as well let them go. If they come back, they come back. No need to waste your breath."

If Cecelia Ainsley understands that comments like that one have sustained her reputation, she doesn't appear bothered. And while it's hardly Laura's style, there is an inescapable truth to her words.

Graye just needs some space. She can give her that, at least. The guilt sticks around, but Laura tries to set it aside for now.

"Ms. Ainsley." Laura turns to the woman at her side. "You were magnificent."

The award-winning author dips her head in recognition of the truth of those words.

"I usually am, dear," she says. "I admit, I wasn't sure your little farce was going to be particularly dignified, but I'm quite enjoying myself."

"I really can't thank you enough," Laura says as the two women turn and walk into the crowded room. Long lines of tables set for dinner sparkle in candlelight. "It's an honor to have you here. Beyond what I could have hoped. Especially considering everything."

Cecelia raises her brow. "Whom you choose to be married to is your business, Laura. I decided a long time ago that love must be an evolutionary adaptation."

Laura hadn't been referring to David, though clearly Ms. Ainsley's opinion of her husband hasn't changed since she wrote the scathing piece about his last novel.

"It's nature's way of allowing even mediocre men to find a mate," Cecelia continues.

Laura isn't sure if the woman is serious or simply playing up the persona she's created.

"Doesn't that contradict Darwin's theory?" she can't help asking. "Survival of the fittest shouldn't leave much room for mediocrity."

Cecelia's eyes are dancing, and Laura has a rush of satisfaction that her renowned guest is enjoying herself so thoroughly.

"Oh child. How naive you are." Cecelia grins with a touch of malice. "If procreation were reserved only for extraordinary men, the species would have died a slow, sputtering death centuries ago."

Laughter bubbles up. "I can't argue with that," Laura admits. "But no, I meant the situation with my assistant, Graye. She was going to interview for you, and it was unprofessional of me to steal her away."

Cecelia glances at Laura with a truly withering stare. Perhaps her reputation isn't only for show after all.

"I assume you're speaking of the assistant who just slapped you? Whatever makes you believe I'd hire someone like that?"

"That's not a regular . . . I mean, she wouldn't normally—" Laura breaks off, realizing how ridiculous she sounds.

"I should hope not. Husbands are bad enough. It's quite another to put up with nonsense in an employee."

"She's actually quite good at her job," Laura hears herself say, though she's not certain if she's defending Graye or her own judgment in hiring her.

"I'm sure I don't care in the least," Cecelia says, holding up a hand to stop her. They've arrived at the table of honor where Laura has seated Ms. Ainsley. "If I have a motto, it's this: 'Not my monkeys, not my zoo.'"

If Laura expects something more profound from the author, she's destined for disappointment. Cecelia Ainsley pulls out her chair and takes a seat. Several of the other guests notice and stop at the table to praise her performance.

Laura recognizes when she's been dismissed.

She turns and studies the crowd. Everything is going well. Everything except the alienation of her assistant, of course. She considers texting Graye but decides to give her more time.

Mai Linh steps into her line of sight and hands her a glass of white wine.

"Congratulations," she says, her voice a low whisper. "That was quite impressive."

Laura smiles. "I thought you'd enjoy that." She glances over her shoulder, noting how close they are to Cecelia's chair. But the older woman is holding court and couldn't care less what gossip is being passed behind her.

Laura gestures with her chin anyway, and they step away from the table.

"How in the world did you get her to agree—"

A disturbance near the back of the room pulls their attention in that direction. A woman named Veronica, a blogger with thousands of social media followers, is sobbing into her hands while several people attempt to comfort her.

It doesn't appear to be working. Her sobs only grow louder.

"What the . . . ?" Linh mutters, squinting to see better.

Laura puts one hand on Linh's arm and holds the other up, palm facing outward, the universal signal to *just wait a minute.*

Linh gives Laura a quizzical glance, but her mouth soon turns into a silent *O* of understanding, and she turns back to the scene with anticipatory glee.

"She can't be dead!" says the distraught woman who's caught the attention of the crowd. "I've come all this way to meet her."

"And who are you, deary?" asks someone from the crowd.

"I'm her daughter, given up for adoption nearly twenty-five years ago!" Veronica declares. She holds the back of her palm to her forehead with an impressively campy amount of showmanship.

There are a few gasps and a round of surprised laughter. Linh glances at Laura, who holds up a finger. *There's more,* that finger says.

"You can't be the baroness's daughter," rings out a voice from across the room, and heads swivel in that direction.

Veronica stands up straighter, recovering quickly from her exaggerated swoon.

"Well, I'd like to know why not?" she demands, hands on her hips.

"Because *I'm* her daughter, that's why! And I can prove it." Daughter number two, a romance author named Rose, holds a folded sheet of paper high in the air as she steps forward through the crowd to confront the woman. "I've got a letter from the baroness, begging for my forgiveness and inviting me here to claim my birthright."

"That's impossible," Veronica scoffs as she opens her bag and pulls out a sheet of paper of her own. "I'm the one with the letter, you golddigging imposter!"

The two women face each other down as the crowd looks on, absorbing the scripted drama playing out in front of them.

Several of the people around Cecelia Ainsley's table turn to her, as if looking for an explanation.

"Well, don't expect me to sort it out for you," she says loudly as she leans back in her chair and folds her arms across her chest. "I'm dead, remember?"

"Are you calling me a liar?" Rose asks, full of mock offense.

"I most certainly am! And you're not going to get away with it."

Taking two steps toward her nemesis, Veronica is still waving her letter in one hand, effectively distracting onlookers from the small black pistol she holds in the other.

It's not a real gun, of course. It's a cap gun that Laura sent herself with the character packet she'd mailed months ago. But when the little toy lets out a distinctive *pop, pop* and Rose jerks backward, once, twice, someone in the stunned crowd lets out a little scream of fright.

Playing her moment for all it's worth, Rose clutches her chest and crumples gently.

The toy gun clatters from Veronica's hand to the floor. "Are you okay?" she asks in a loud whisper.

Rose opens her eyes and says, "Shh! You're spoiling my death scene," then gives her a wink and squeezes her eyes shut once again.

Laughter erupts from the group, and Rose's head lolls on the floor for just a moment before she leaps from the ground and takes a deep bow.

"Bravo, my dear!" Cecelia says, clapping loudly. "Now come join me for dinner at the table of the deceased."

The mood in the room is festive as Veronica is led out by the arm, loudly proclaiming, "Get your hands off me! Do you know who I am? I'm the true daughter of Baroness Lyttleton!"

"You really do have a flair for the melodramatic," Linh says at Laura's side. "Are you going to tell me who had the honor of pushing the old bat from the roof?"

"Not a chance." Laura laughs.

"Come on, just a hint."

"No, but I'll walk you to your seat. Dinner will start soon and you don't want to miss it. Grilled salmon with a side of poison for a chosen few."

"Sounds delicious," Linh says, grinning and rubbing her hands together.

"Be nice, or I'll have you eating at the death table with Cecelia," Laura warns.

Graye still weighs on Laura's mind, and after she leaves Linh at the seat with her place card, she scans the room, hoping to spot the girl. She's nowhere in sight.

Laura checks her watch. She has a few minutes to spare before the next round of dinner theatrics is slated to begin. She wonders where Graye would have gone to compose herself.

Waitstaff begin bringing out the first course, and the group buzzes with gossip and anticipation. Silverware clinks and glasses are raised as Laura makes her way toward the door, planning to step out and track down Graye. She stops here and there to smile and check in with her guests along the way.

She's made it halfway across the room when she spots Graye along the far wall.

Her assistant looks up and meets Laura's eyes. She gives a tremulous smile, raising Laura's hopes that she's been forgiven for her thoughtlessness. Laura sends the girl a small wave.

"Would you excuse me?" she says to the two men beside her as she heads in Graye's direction.

With her focus on her assistant, Laura doesn't immediately realize there's a problem. Her back is turned to the big double doors, so she doesn't witness her husband stumble into the room. David's entrance doesn't go entirely unnoticed, though. She glances around to see what's causing the stir and stops midstride.

He's left the jacket of his tuxedo behind. The black bow tie hangs loose from the collar of his stark white, halfway untucked dress shirt.

With the neck of a bottle gripped in his hand and an unsteady gait, he looks like he's come from an after-prom party for the middle-aged and washed up.

Laura's breath catches in her throat before it all leaves her at once.

With an unwanted burst of clarity, she's nearly blinded with a new perspective. Like the shift when an optical illusion changes before your eyes, becoming a zebra instead of the butterfly you thought it was, the two images flicker back and forth in her mind for a moment, superimposed upon each other, before the old image fades, replaced with a zebra she can't unsee.

David's state isn't shocking—it's hardly the first time she's seen him like this. But he's always been careful with his public image. It's one thing to destroy your liver in the privacy of your home. Another entirely to put your vices on such blatant display in a gathering of your peers.

He stops to speak to an author he recognizes, leaning too close as he grips the back of her chair and talks loudly into her horrified face.

"Olivia, my dear! I hope my wife . . . is treating you with all the deference your *impressive* reputation deserves."

His words are slurred, and the woman pulls back as he waves the bottle high in the air.

"Share a drink with me, Olivia," he says, leaning over to pour some of his liquor into her glass of wine, splashing it across the tablecloth as he does. "A toast to my wife. My incomparable, always *welcoming* wife."

Olivia, to her credit, recovers quickly. "Why don't you sit down, David," she coaxes in a calm voice.

Conversations gradually hush as David gains the undivided attention of the room. It's clear to most that this isn't part of the planned entertainment. Olivia remains gracious and attempts to salvage the man's tattered dignity. It's more than he deserves.

Paralyzed by an overwhelming surge of embarrassment for him, Laura can only watch as things go from awkward to worse.

"Everybody!" David says, swinging his bottle around and addressing the room. "Raise a glass to my wife! And if you're one of the lucky ones . . . I'm talking to you, there, Hugo, buddy . . . to whom she's . . . *extra* welcoming, well then, why don't you raise two."

Hugo Caron's face is a chiseled stone as he watches David West light a match to his marriage and possibly his waning career. Hugo rises, but the woman at his side places a hand on his arm, shaking her head.

Laura's feet come unstuck from their place on the floor, and she rushes toward her husband.

"David, that's enough." Her voice is a plea he won't heed.

"Enough?" he asks, swinging wildly around and attempting to focus on her face. "That's enough, my lovely wife tells me," he declares, laughing as if everyone is in on the joke with him.

"Do you know the definition of *enough, dear*?" he asks. "Do any of you? Come on, a room full of writers, surely you do. I'll tell you, Laura."

He turns back to her and slings an arm along with too much of his weight across her shoulders.

"'To the required degree or extent,'" he says carefully. "'Adequately.' Do you feel I've *adequately* addressed the situation?"

"I'll take you home, David."

"You didn't answer the question. Do. You. Feel?" The index finger of the hand holding the liquor bottle comes up and touches her nose, punctuating each of the last three words. Drops of alcohol spill across her cheek. "That I've adequately *addressed* . . . the fact that my *wife* . . . has been *fucking* . . . another *man* . . . ?"

Gasps and whispers of outrage begin circulating around the room, and Laura's cheeks burn. Not for herself, but for the asinine display David has placed them in the center of.

Alcoholism is a disease. Laura knows this. She's not looking at the man she married. Not all of him, at least. But the ugliness that hides beneath the surface, the rocky, jagged edges of him that drinking exposes, have become impossible to navigate.

From the corner of her eye, Laura sees Hugo jump again from his seat, unwilling to be dissuaded this time. The woman next to him doesn't even try.

"Oh, and look," David says, turning to watch the man come to her side. "There he is, your knight in shining armor, stepping up to defend your honor."

David smiles to the stunned crowd. He's lost the goodwill of his audience, if he ever had it, but he doesn't care.

"Isn't that impressive, folks. Just look at him. Give him a hand, everybody." David brings his hands together in a slow clap, not an easy thing while holding a bottle of vodka. Somehow, he manages.

"David, you need to leave," Hugo says. "Now."

Hugo is calm, but there's anger banked just behind his eyes, fueled by righteous indignation on Laura's behalf.

"Wait, did I hear you correctly?" David drops his arm from around Laura's shoulders and lurches toward Hugo, who sidesteps him easily. "I need to leave? *I* need to leave?"

Laura can't forgive this. She'll never forgive this.

"David—"

He doesn't hear her, doesn't register she's spoken. She steps in front of him, placing both hands on his chest, attempting to turn his attention back onto her, away from Hugo. This can't end well.

"David, stop. Please."

Graye, her face filled with concern, has materialized at their side. David pushes Laura out of his way. In typical Graye fashion, she's in just the right place to catch Laura before she stumbles into one of the tables. The two women hold on to each other for support as they watch David tumble farther and farther from grace.

"Tell me something, Caron. Were you sleeping with her before or after she launched your career? Was it a thank-you fuck or a bribe?"

"It's time to go, West," Hugo says. He takes David by the arm that holds the bottle and pulls him toward the door.

Laura quickly moves to follow.

"Get your goddamn hands off me!" David attempts to pull out of his grasp, but Hugo holds tight.

They're moving together toward the exit, whether David wants to or not, when he resorts to jerking his arm upward, letting loose the bottle he has, up until now, held tightly in his grip.

The heavy glass container rises in the air. It has little momentum, but it's uncapped and doesn't need much to splash an acrid spray of liquor into Hugo's face before it crashes to the floor, breaking into shards of wet glass. Hugo loosens his hold on David and runs a sleeve across his eyes to wipe the stinging liquid away.

David stumbles, but even in his wasted state recognizes the only opportunity he's likely to get. In a move that looks as if it were choreographed for a surreal Laurel and Hardy sketch, David pulls back an arm, his hand balled into a tight fist. He nearly falls over backward, but rights himself and manages to shift all his weight forward, putting everything he has into landing the sucker punch.

As he does, Hugo bends at the waist, hands still wiping at his eyes. He can't see David lunging toward him, but the crowd around them does. Shouts of warning and the scrape of chairs fill the room even before David's body connects with the other man.

His fist swings comically wild as he tumbles over Hugo's back.

It might have been a fitting end for David's shameful behavior, to end up sprawled across the floor at the feet of people who once respected him. Few would have pitied him, not after the performance he'd subjected them to.

Showing his ass, Laura's mother would have called it.

But the little sympathy he could have gained by a dose of divine justice goes up in a puff as he flips over Hugo's back and slams directly into Laura, knocking them both to the ground in a tangle of arms and legs.

Laura absorbs the force of her husband's body. She dimly registers the screams of outrage enveloping her, Graye's the loudest of all, in the moment before her head hits the hardwood floor with a crack.

Then her world goes dark.

30

GRAYE

Graye makes her way to the front of the ballroom, past the guests milling about. The first course sits cold and forgotten on the tables.

Snippets of conversation pepper her ears.

". . . absolutely excruciating."

". . . feel so sorry for her."

". . . had no idea he was this far gone."

At the head table, the one designated for guests who've met their demise, Graye stops and picks up a wine glass. She clinks it with a fork to get the attention of the group. Dutifully, they quiet down, and all eyes turn to her.

"If I could have your attention, everyone, I'd like to make a quick announcement. First, and most importantly, Laura is doing fine. She has a bit of a bump on her head, but the doctor is checking on her now, and she's well enough to insist she doesn't need a doctor, so that's good news."

Relief passes across their faces.

"She's regaining her bearings here at the hotel while Dr. West has been escorted out of the building."

There are nods of approval along with a few shaking heads.

"Most of you know Laura personally, so it shouldn't come as a surprise that her first concern is ensuring this unfortunate incident doesn't ruin your evening. She's asked that everyone please enjoy their dinner and the rest of the mystery theater. She plans to rejoin you shortly and sends her heartfelt apologies for the disruption."

Graye motions the waitstaff to begin clearing the first course and serving the second while the guests slowly make their way back to their seats.

Mai Linh flags Graye down as she's heading back out of the room.

"She's really okay?" Linh probes.

"She is," Graye says. *For now,* she refrains from adding aloud. Between the combined threat of Nick and Laura's own husband, Graye wonders if she's going to have to guard Laura in her sleep to keep her safe.

"That bastard," Mai Linh says, her arms crossed protectively around her middle. "She's too good for him."

Graye agrees, but doesn't want to gossip about her friend. "She just needs to catch her breath."

"Send her my love, and let her know if she needs anything at all . . . an aspirin, a shoulder to cry on . . . the name of a killer divorce lawyer, I've got her back."

Graye nods. There are others who stop her to send similar sentiments, and Graye collects their good wishes to pass along, but she's itching to get back and check on Laura.

The room that's been set aside to use as a staging area is on the first floor, and that's where Graye heads.

She arrives just as Dr. Lawson is leaving. They've interrupted her evening, evident by the robe she's thrown on over a pair of pajamas, but her eyes are clear and bright.

"She'll be fine," the doctor assures Graye. "As stubborn as ever. I don't believe she has a concussion, but keep an eye on her. Any signs of nausea or mental fuzziness and I'd like you to call me right away."

"Thank you, Dr. Lawson."

The woman nods and tightens the belt on her robe. They're standing in the hallway. Hugo is inside with Laura, and the door is cracked open.

"Call me Bridget," Dr. Lawson says. "I'm glad she has you, Miss Templeton. There are times in our lives when we need friends around us."

The doctor pats Graye on the arm and turns to walk down the hallway. Touched, Graye watches her go.

Words filter through the crack in the open door. Hugo's voice, low and insistent.

"This can't continue, you know."

"Of course I know. I just . . ." Graye can feel Laura's hesitation, her worry. "I thought I had more time."

"Time for what?" Hugo presses. "What more can you possibly need from that man?"

Graye doesn't want to interrupt, but she doesn't intend to stray far from Laura's side. Not again.

She knew David was stewing in his anger, that he'd aim it in Laura's direction. She knew, but she'd let her emotions run away with her. She'd had the chance to warn Laura about Nick and David both, but she'd let the chance slip away, lost in her own wounded feelings.

Graye won't allow that to happen again.

Laura needs her.

Now more than ever.

She waits outside the door.

"You don't understand," Laura says.

"Explain it to me then." His voice is hard now, insistent. "And don't give me any more excuses. No more of that 'It's complicated' bullshit."

"It *is* complicated. And I don't owe you any explanations."

"Owe me? Is that what you think? I'm not here because I expect anything from you, Laura. I'm here because I care about you."

It's not a comfortable feeling, eavesdropping on the two of them. She paces outside the door. Graye won't hesitate to interrupt if she hears any indication that Laura is ready for the conversation to end.

A woman rounds the corner of the hallway, glances around, and bears down in her direction.

Graye recognizes her, though she doesn't recall having been introduced and can't put a name to the face. It's the woman who was standing next to Hugo during cocktails. The same woman who was seated next to him at dinner, who placed a hand on his arm when he first rose to intervene.

She's not happy.

Graye meets her halfway, just feet away from the room.

"Can I help you with anything?" Graye asks.

"Are they in there?" The woman gestures to the door Graye has stepped away from to protect Laura and Hugo's privacy.

"They'll be out shortly," Graye says. "Would you like me to pass along a message?"

"No," she replies slowly. "I don't want you to pass along a message. I want to know if they're in there."

"Well, yes, but—"

The woman moves to step past her, but Graye takes a step as well, blocking her path.

The woman looks at Graye as if she's no more than a bug beneath her shoe. "I'd appreciate it if you'd get out of my way," she says.

"I'm sorry. I can't allow you to disturb them right now."

The woman's brows shoot up, nearly grazing the ceiling. "You can't *allow* me? I wasn't asking your permission. Now get out of my way."

She shoulders her way around Graye, who reaches out to grip the woman's arm. Laura's reputation has suffered enough. She can't allow random strangers to walk in and interrupt her with the man she's been cheating on her husband with. There's no telling what kind of gossip that would kick off.

The woman stops in her tracks and turns back to Graye, her eyes wide and fiery. "I don't know who you think you are, but I can promise you this, if you don't get your hands off me, you will regret it."

"I'm Laura's assistant and it's my job to make sure—"

The two women, still locked together by the arm, turn their heads in unison when Hugo's dumbfounded voice escapes from the room. "Pregnant? Are you serious?"

Graye pulls in a breath. The woman faces her again, her gaze sharp enough to draw blood.

"You may be Laura's assistant," she says, her voice rising as she pries Graye's fingers off her arm. "But I am Hugo's *wife*, and there is absolutely no way you're going to stop me from going in that room."

Suddenly the door in question swings wide and Hugo stands there, his face stricken. Clearly, he heard and recognized his wife's voice.

"Rachel." He hardly spares a glance for Graye.

The woman pushes past him into the room. The door swings wide and Graye can see Laura sitting on the bed, her shoulders slumped, face hidden in her hands. Graye moves to follow.

"Not you," Rachel says, turning and pointing at the door.

"Excuse me?"

"You heard me. Get out."

"I don't take orders from—"

"It's fine, Graye," Laura says, dropping her hands from her face. She stands, and unease courses through Graye at the state of her. Her eyes are puffy and strained, her cheeks streaked. Most of her makeup is gone, leaving nothing to mask her pallor.

"Would you mind checking in on the guests? I'd like to salvage as much of the evening as . . ." She trails off.

Graye scans the three people in the room, each standing stiffly, none willing to meet her eyes.

"I don't want to leave you like this."

"It's fine," Laura says in a curt tone that makes Graye flinch. "I'm sorry," she goes on, more gently.

"No, it's okay." Graye takes a hesitant step backward. "I'll go. If that's what you want."

"Thank you," Laura says, giving her a tired smile that goes some of the way toward soothing the hurt.

As she closes the door behind her, Graye can't stop a final glare in Rachel Caron's direction. The woman stands unflinching, her hands upon her hips as she watches Graye go, chin held high.

There's something about her demeanor that rubs Graye the wrong way. She came down that hallway ready for a confrontation, Graye is sure of it. It was clear in the way she walked, the way she held herself.

She knew she'd find Laura and her husband closeted together.

More than that, Graye recalls the expression on her face when she heard the news that Laura West, her husband's lover, was pregnant.

She wasn't surprised. Not the least bit.

Graye would stake her life on the fact that Rachel Caron already knew.

She reaches the end of the hallway and throws a concerned look over her shoulder, but the door remains closed to her. Whatever's being said between the three of them, Graye's been shut out.

She won't lie and pretend it doesn't sting, but that doesn't mean she can't see the glaring question hanging in front of her face.

Earlier this evening, someone went out of their way to visit David, to purposely spill Laura's secrets. Someone who *knew* she was pregnant.

It doesn't seem possible. The woman couldn't have known already. Could she?

But someone had. Someone with a grudge and a tall, handsome incentive to cause problems. And yet another threat that Graye hadn't considered.

31

Prison isn't like the movies. You're not going to find Morgan Freeman and Tim Robbins bonding over a harmonica, debating the value of hope and secretly tunneling through the wall.

Prison is a scouring.

If it can be taken away, it is.

Your desires? Kiss those goodbye. Dignity? First thing to go. Comfort? Forget about it. Prison is cold, except when it's hot enough to bake in.

Your future? What future?

All of it. Gone.

Layers are stripped away until there's nothing left but what you carry with you, and all the time in the world to marinate in it.

The lucky ones have something to hate. Something other than themselves. The system, their abusive stepfather, the guard who gets off on pain.

Or the girl who put you in the hellhole in the first place, walking free. Pretending to be someone she's not.

One day, if you're lucky, prison will spit you out like an old piece of gum that's lost its flavor, chewed up and ill equipped for a world that's forgotten about you.

Hate, though. It's the strongest part of you now, and it feels good, so good. It feels alive, an impeccably maintained piece of machinery waiting patiently for you to take it for a spin.

And that is how you end up on an island where a snotty little nobody is nursing delusions that she's escaped a debt.

But some debts can't be outrun.

So you watch.

You're patient. No need to rush. Anticipation is a drug, and you can wait until the time is right. You know why cats play with mice before they devour them. Because it's fun.

You watch little Gracie skitter this way and that, licking the boots of the blonde woman who has no idea who Gracie really is, where she comes from. How easily she'll betray, given the chance.

Grace was always weak. Names can be changed, but not a person's nature. Grace needs someone to tell her what to do, tell her who to be. She's looking to Blondie to fill that role. That much is clear.

But she isn't built to live a happy life. You're surprised she hasn't figured that out yet. Some families are born in clean, pretty places. They live their whole sweet-smelling lives never looking down, in case they lose their balance and fall into the shit that runs through the gutters.

But Gracie was born down there, and there isn't enough perfume in the world to mask that stink forever. Every once in a while, people sitting next to her will catch a whiff. Their noses will wrinkle and they'll wonder who forgot to take the trash out.

You know this, but Gracie, poor naive Gracie, she's hopeless.

Watching Grace scamper, with no clue her sins have caught up with her, is the most fun you've had in years. The most fun you've had since that long-ago night that seems like a dream from someone else's life.

You're in no hurry. You've got time. You give her the lead and let her run. You can yank her back whenever it pleases you.

She doesn't know this, but you do.

And it's intoxicating.

32

LAURA

Hugo is gone. Off somewhere with his wife. Laura shut down the tense conversation in the hotel room by rising and walking to the door.

Holding it open for the pair, she motioned them out. "I have an event to host."

"You can't intend to—"

"It would probably be best if you call it a night," she told Hugo firmly, cutting him off. "There will be enough gossip as it is."

She didn't miss the look of agreement that passed across his wife's face.

Laura doesn't need anyone to hold her hand, nor does she have any right to ask even if she did.

Laura may not be a novelist, may not have magic at her fingertips, but she's a master showman.

It doesn't matter that the heated words in the hotel room leave her bruised, or that even if she can smooth things over with her guests, she still has David to contend with when she gets home.

Her mother taught her well. Her heart is battered and bloody, so she crams it into a heart-shaped box. She fixes her face and pummels her features into a relaxed guise.

Because that is what Laura does.

There's a hush when she returns to the party. To be expected, really. But Laura digs deep for a smile and a little wave designed to let them off the hook. *Everything is fine here, nothing to see,* her smile says. That easily, they're free to enjoy their evening without the guilt of believing their hostess is busy having a breakdown.

Even if she is.

Graye has kept all Laura's balls in the air, and she gives a silent prayer of thanks for talented, effective women. With Graye's help, she can at least attempt to hide how quickly things are falling apart.

The body count has risen while Laura's been distracted with her personal life. By the time dessert is served, the table of death has become an exclusive club, rowdy with men and women whose responsibilities have been satisfied.

Cecelia, comfortably regal in her role as queen of the dead, waves away a woman found strangled earlier, her feet extending from the bottom of a ladies' bathroom stall. When the other woman rises, Cecelia motions for Laura to join her in the newly vacated seat by her side.

Not Laura's first choice for companionship, but Cecelia Ainsley is the unspoken guest of honor and it would be beyond rude to ignore her.

"How's your head?" the older woman asks, getting straight to the point.

"I'll survive," Laura says.

Cecelia is watching the crowd, a benign expression on her face that masks whatever opinions she might have about Laura's domestic problems.

"That you will," she agrees. The hush is gone, the noise level risen again, perhaps even beyond where it was before.

"They're relieved the danger has passed and giddy that it brushed so nearby," Cecelia observes.

"That's not a very kind thing to say."

"Is it not?" She looks at Laura, pity in her eyes. "People put so much stock in kindness. Truth is infinitely more interesting."

Laura sighs. The woman can be downright unpleasant.

"You believe I'm harsh." It's a statement, not a question. Certainly not an apology. "I was married once too, you know," she goes on.

Laura didn't know, but says nothing. Her head is pounding and the woman is a magnet that continually flips, pulling in, then suddenly pushing back with no notice at all.

"I won't bore you with details, but I will say this, because you're too polite to get up and walk away. A bad marriage is a forge. Once you're in it, your only choice is to push forward and find your way out of the flames, scars and all, hopefully stronger for it." She shrugs. "The alternative is to sit there and be burned to nothing."

A chill passes over Laura. Her chest tightens, and she stares at a spot along the far wall. Anywhere other than the woman's eyes.

"I should see to the other guests," Laura hears herself say. She can't rise from the chair quickly enough.

"You do that," Cecelia says.

Her eyes are on Laura's back as she walks away. Runs away, both from the author's presence and her pointed words, aimed with precision. Words that ring with a detached, uncaring truth and no hint of kindness.

And now Graye is coming at her with worried, overly sympathetic eyes. Laura forces professionalism into her voice, speaking first to head off the personal questions she'll have to deal with soon enough.

Not yet. Not with an audience watching my every move and pretending they aren't.

"How are things coming along, Graye?" she asks cheerily. "Everything ready for the grand finale?"

Her assistant stops, visibly swallowing back what she'd planned to say. Some question about Laura's well-being, no doubt.

"Ah. Um, so far, so good," Graye says.

Good girl.

"One of the poisoning victims stole the spotlight. She had a fit of giggles and nearly choked, but she's fine now." Laura nods as Graye glances at her watch. "We're gearing up for the final act any moment."

"Wonderful," Laura says, rubbing her hands together and resolutely muting all thoughts that don't have to do with finishing this evening off with a bang.

"Laura, are you—?"

"Not now, Graye. Please." She's making a herculean effort to hide the strain. Graye is perceptive. She sees what Laura's trying to hide but concedes and drops the question.

Laura can't decide if she should hug her or give her a raise. Maybe both.

At that moment, the lights flicker once—quickly, almost imperceptibly.

She glances at Graye, who suddenly stands straighter. The childlike anticipation that fills Laura is mirrored on her assistant's face.

She sends Graye a wink.

Showtime, Laura mouths as several things happen in quick succession.

The lights cut out completely, enveloping the room and its occupants in nothing but shadows, tossed crazily about by the candles burning low on the table.

Murmurs of unease and more than a few gasps of surprise flutter about in the darkened space.

The gasps morph into full-blown shrieks as, seconds later, a boom of thunder makes its presence known by shaking the walls around them.

Neighbors instinctively grasp the person sitting next to them, and the collective pulse rate of the room jumps tenfold. A rush of sound overtakes them—a susurrus, for those in a literary frame of mind.

Pure chance. With impeccable timing, the rain has arrived. More thunder heralds its presence.

A slow, satisfied smile, hidden in the dark, snakes across Laura's face. A showman to her bones.

Nervous voices begin to twitter, coupled with great heaving sighs of relief.

". . . power's gone out."

". . . nothing to be—"

Their reassuring whispers to one another are cut short by a muffled shout and the unmistakable sound of flesh connecting with flesh.

Chairs scrape as people peer around, half rising and craning their necks as they attempt to see what the latest fuss is about.

And the lights come up.

It was only dark for a short time, but people blink and peer at one another, nocturnal creatures suddenly blinded by the light of day.

Then someone lets out a high-pitched, warbling scream.

A woman seated at the table next to Walt backs away quickly. His prone form is sprawled on the ground next to his overturned chair.

He groans and red liquid bubbles from his mouth, as red as the stain spreading across his tuxedo shirt, where a knife protrudes from his chest.

Laura shakes her head and places a hand upon her hip.

She thought she'd dissuaded him from the fake blood.

"I don't think that's necessary," she'd said on the phone just last week. "This is dinner theater, not Broadway, Walt."

Apparently, she hadn't been as successful as she thought.

Guests rush to his side. Mr. Peterson, for his sins, simply raises an eyebrow and leans back in his chair, enjoying the spectacle.

"Only a flesh wound. No need to be dramatic."

But Walt has waited all evening for his moment to shine. He seizes the spotlight. Grasping the plastic theater prop stuck to his shirt, he leans onto his side and coughs a spray of red onto the floor. Droplets land on the ankle of the woman nearest him, and she pulls back with a grimace.

Now someone's going to have to clean that up, Laura thinks.

Walt's head falls back to the floor and his arm drops, a marionette whose strings have been cut.

And Walt has finally earned his round of applause.

Mr. Peterson speaks over the noise.

"What's that on the ground next to him?" he asks loudly. He glances over at Laura, a question in his eyes.

She nods, recognizing his contribution to their little tableau with thanks.

"No, there," he says, pointing again, when nothing is found. "Move over, Walt, you great fool," he scolds. "You're lying on top of it."

Opening one eye, Walt scoots a bit to the right, then lets his head fall to the floor again.

"There," Mr. Peterson says.

All eyes turn to the folded paper that's been revealed, stained with red, but no one moves toward it.

"It's not a snake, people," Mr. Peterson says. "Someone pick it up. It's past my bedtime."

The woman with blood on her ankle reaches down and grasps the paper, holding it away from her body with two fingers. In Walt's enthusiasm for all things bloody, it's dripping with red.

"Pass it over, then," Mr. Peterson says with a sigh. The woman leans past Walt's sprawled legs and hands it off as asked.

He unfolds the sheet of paper and squints at it, pulling it closer to his face. With a sigh, he pats his pockets, and eventually pulls out a pair of reading glasses.

"What's it say already?" Cecelia calls out.

"Patience, my dear," Mr. Peterson says with a glare over the top of his glasses.

Laura tries to hold back a smile.

"Let's see here," he mumbles. "It appears to be the last will and testament of Baroness Abigail Lyttleton."

"So who gets the dough?" someone yells.

Mr. Peterson holds up the crumpled, stained paper again. "It's got a minor bequest to the Humane Society, and after that it says . . . *I, Baroness Abigail Lyttleton, do hereby bequeath the remainder of my worldly possessions to . . .*"

He pauses, turning the will over to check the back.

"Oh, come on!"

Mr. Peterson drops the hand holding the will and glares. "A little respect for one's elders wouldn't go amiss."

"Elder, my foot. I'm as old as you are, you cranky old ass."

Mr. Peterson grins. "Yet you don't look a day over ninety, Olivia, my dear."

She tosses a balled-up napkin at him and the crowd groans.

"Get on with it!"

"Well, I'd be happy to," he says as he folds up the paper and removes his glasses. "But that part has been ripped away. See for yourself, you savages."

He holds the will up with one hand while he replaces his glasses in his pocket with the other.

Seeing her cue, Laura steps forward and claps her hands together.

"And that, my friends, brings this evening to a close."

"But what about the murders? Aren't you going to tell us who did it?"

"Ah," she says, holding up a hand. "It's up to you now to figure that out. What fun is it if I tell you the answers? Suffice it to say, the clues are all there. The question is, how many of you have been paying attention?"

She smiles and shakes her head as they pepper her with questions.

"You won't get another word out of me. My lips are sealed. The outdoor bar is closed, given the weather, but drinks will be served in the breakfast room for those of you not quite ready to call it a night."

Laura takes a breath and feels the need to continue.

"I'd like to thank you," she says, her voice no longer playful, "each and every one of you, for being here. I'm grateful to know you all. My life is richer for having you in it."

She clears her throat.

"And with that, I wish you good night. Join us in the morning for the Book Hangover Brunch, where we'll get down to the bottom of things once and for all. I look forward to seeing everyone there."

She pauses and drops her voice to a low and foreboding tone. "Those of you who make it through the night, that is. Sleep well," she adds with a smile.

She continues to smile through the laughter and the applause. Past the well-wishers and their whispered, unveiled concern, she attempts to make her way out of the room.

"Will you be okay?" they ask quietly.

"Of course," she replies reassuringly.

"If you need anything at all . . . ," they say.

"Thank you, I'll be fine," she replies reassuringly.

"I'm just a phone call away . . ."

"I'm touched, but that won't be necessary," she replies reassuringly. And on it goes.

By the time she breaks free of the crowd, exiting the room of people she herself brought together, the weight of their worry for her and what she may be going home to is suffocating.

She makes a beeline for the front door of the hotel. It's clear through the glass that rain is still lashing at the building, the wind kicking around the fronds of the palms and any detritus not nailed down.

It looks like heaven calling to her. A sanctuary.

Laura steps out into the cool, cleansing wind and fills her lungs fully for the first time in hours.

It's shocking, how close she is to tears. How shaky her foundation has become.

She steps away from the door, finding her way to the wall of the building, barely covered by the roof over the entry. She can't go farther. Not yet.

In her sequined party dress, with a mostly successful evening at an end despite David's best efforts, she slides her back down the wall and curls her arms around herself.

Spray from the wind and rain finds her, but she doesn't care. Her limbs have lost the ability to carry her. Her mind, the ability to shield her.

Nerve endings stripped bare, Laura is coming apart.

How did she get here?

She doesn't hear the footsteps approach but senses Graye's quiet presence at her side.

The girl doesn't speak.

She simply sits beside her, quiet and calm.

Laura bites back a scream. *Go away. I don't deserve your kindness.*

But oh, does she need it.

She leans her head against Graye's shoulder, and her silent tears mix with the spray of rain, indistinguishable from one another.

33

GRAYE

The storm passes, as storms tend to do. The rain and the tears come, then go, leaving nothing but questions in their wake.

Graye's heart hurts for Laura, but the other woman is too strong, too capable, to stay so low for long. Once she's through the other side, she takes a deep breath, then lifts her head and swipes at her face.

"I'm sorry, Graye." Her voice is hoarse and she gives a lopsided ghost of a smile. "Your job description doesn't include mopping up your boss's tears."

"Please don't do that," Graye says quietly.

Laura glances at her. "Do what? Apologize?" Laura forces a laugh, and Graye can see her mask falling back into place, bit by bit. "You're not being paid enough to deal with emotional meltdowns."

"That," Graye says. "Don't do that."

Laura's face clouds. Does she not realize?

"Don't put up walls between us and hang a sign with a job description on it. I'm not sitting here because you're paying me to."

Laura looks slightly abashed, and Graye regrets that her words put the expression there.

"Okay," Laura murmurs.

"You can stay with me tonight, if you want," Graye says. "Or here at the hotel if you're more comfortable with that. You don't have to go back."

Laura sighs. "I wish it was that easy."

"It is."

Sadness is etched in the tiny lines around Laura's eyes.

"No, it's not. If I sleep now I avoid it all. When I wake up, the edges will be dull, the cuts already beginning to heal. I'll find some excuse, some reason to put it off one more day. Then another."

Graye opens her mouth to speak, but Laura shakes her head.

"No. I know myself. I *like* the path of least resistance. That's what got me here." She stares out into the darkness, where drips fall from the palm fronds and rainwater has pooled. Graye studies her profile. There's still sadness there, but a new determination as well.

"I have to face this now, head-on, before I lose my nerve."

She sends Graye a small smile.

"Don't worry. David's probably passed out anyway. I'm going to go home and pack his suitcases while he sleeps it off. No muss, no fuss. And tomorrow . . . well, tomorrow I'll have the last day of the retreat to distract me."

Now is the chance Graye has been waiting for. She should warn Laura that David isn't the only threat. She should tell her about Rachel Caron's visit to her home earlier this evening. She should spill everything about Nick and her past and the fact that he could be stalking them right now, skulking in the shadows waiting for a chance to . . . do what? She still doesn't understand exactly what it is Nick hopes to achieve.

It's a vital question and, without the answer, is Graye willing to risk jeopardizing everything she's building here? Laura hasn't even told her what she thinks of the book yet. She *needs* Laura to be on board.

And what would Nick have to gain by harming Laura anyway? Graye rationalizes. Wouldn't it make more sense for him to target her? Laura's not in any real danger.

Is she?

Graye just needs a little more time. Complicating things now with talk of wronged spouses and convicted killers while Laura is already trying to deal with ending her marriage will only muddy the waters.

There will be time for that later.

"What can I do to help?" Graye asks, shoving her internal debate aside.

Laura gives her a stronger smile, with shades of the woman Graye is used to shining through. She leans over and nudges her gently with her shoulder.

"Nothing you haven't already done."

"Are you sure?"

Laura places her palms on the concrete walkway.

"You can help me up off the ground," she says. "My butt has gone numb."

Graye rises and grasps her by the hand to help her up. Laura straightens her dress and slips out of her heels to wiggle her toes.

"You can walk me home," she says. "You can talk to me about anything other than men."

"That's not hard," Graye says. "I don't *know* anything about men."

Laura laughs. "Me either. Every time I think I have them figured out, they prove me wrong."

And Hugo? Graye wonders. *Has he proven you wrong too?* She hasn't seen him or his wife since Laura emerged from their private tête-à-tête.

But that's a line Graye's not willing to cross.

With bare feet, they cross to the back of the hotel and walk along the beach, neither in a hurry to arrive at their destination.

"Do you regret coming here, Graye?"

The air tastes fresh again, and Graye won't taint it with a lie.

"Not most days. You?"

Laura looks out into the distance. The moon is small tonight. A sliver of hope hanging in the darkness.

"I have plenty of regrets, but that's not one of them. If I have a true love, it's this little island."

Despite the terrible day, despite what tonight and the next day will bring, Laura looks content. At peace.

"And books, of course." She smiles. "Always books. It's just disappointing when you learn the worth of a person can't necessarily be judged by the depth of their talent."

The sadness is encroaching again, and Graye would give anything to push it back.

"With books, though, there's always another one waiting," Graye points out.

"With men as well?" Laura asks, but she's smiling again.

"You're asking the wrong girl."

"And I said I didn't want to talk about men anyway." Laura rolls her eyes at herself. "So let's talk about books. I finished the one you recommended last night."

Graye should be used to the sensation of her stomach clenching and her nerve endings beginning to crackle. Yet she's not.

Laura has finished her book.

She's not looking at Graye, but instead at the light shining in the distance from the windows of her home. That's good, because Graye is sure the expression on her face would give away her panic.

"Oh yeah?"

Does she sound as casual as she intends, or is there a hint her entire world is hanging on Laura's next words?

"It was . . ."

One of Laura's shoes slips from her hand and she stops to pick it up from the sand.

Graye's breath leaves her in a silent rush and she can't get any of it back. The air won't come.

Laura straightens, pushing her hair back from her face. Her home draws her gaze back toward it, eyes hazy and too far away from the conversation Graye has waited so long and so patiently for.

"Did you like it?" she hears herself ask in a voice laced with desperation.

"Um . . ." Laura tilts her head, considering her words. "I'm not sure, actually."

Not sure? How can you be not sure?

Graye forces a small laugh. It's brittle, and fragile, and alone in the night.

"What . . . what does that mean?"

"Ms. Boyd has potential, but there was just something about it." Laura stops again, shaking her head. Graye's going to be sick. "It's compelling, and the unreliable narrator works, but . . . I don't know. The payoff wasn't there. It left me feeling like something was off, you know?"

Laura's eyes finally land on Graye, who feels as if she's watching herself from a distance. She's nodding along, accepting this knife in her heart that beats wildly while it struggles not to bleed out on the sand.

"Even the supposed truth comes across like more lies." Laura shrugs and Graye is dying. "I just didn't trust her, I guess. The narrator."

"Oh," Graye says. It's a small word, an inadequate throwaway word. It's all she has left.

Sounds are emerging from Laura's mouth. They must be words, but the syllables are jumbled and they blend together. Meaningless, meaningless noise.

She's hugging her now, pulling Graye close. Her touch is a branding iron, leaving burns that will fester in her wake. She's walking, her arm looped through Graye's. Toward her home. Toward her life.

A life that isn't Graye's. That never will be. She's been fooling herself, playing a game she couldn't afford the ante for.

"I'll see you in the morning, okay?" Laura is saying. "And don't worry about me. I'll be fine."

Worry? About her? Why would she do that? Graye nods, an instinctive response, but doesn't speak. Can't speak. She's been silenced, her words illusions swept away in the wind, leaving her to wonder if they were ever there in the first place.

Graye stares at Laura's back as she climbs the wooden steps from the beach to her house. Her posture is straight, shoulders squared. A warrior into battle, and Graye is nothing. A page boy left holding her horse.

Her skin is tight, her tongue caught between her teeth, fitting into a groove left by a long-ago scar. She tastes the dark copper-penny tang of blood.

The sound of Laura closing the door behind her registers, and Graye is left mute in the dark. Alone, so she believes. Again.

She twists, turning away. Laura West is an iceberg that has slowly, silently, ripped a gash along Graye's side, then left her here to sink into the frigid waves with no one to mourn her passing.

All this time, Graye believed Nick was the biggest threat, but with Laura's words thoughts of Nick fade to useless murmurs in the distance.

Graye stumbles. Not toward the guesthouse, but away, back to the beach. Away from the broken promise of Laura and away from her own ridiculous dreams.

One foot moves in front of the other until she's at the edge of the earth. Salt water licks at her ankles. Waves rush in her ears.

She stares, eyes wide, at the stars winking, light traveling from years in the past only to mock her on arrival.

34

In sleep the cinder girl dreams, but dreams can't shield her from the whispers.

"Wake up, little sister," they say with a tickle in her ear that becomes a tap, then turns to a scratch. "Wake up now."

The cinder girl bolts upright in her bed, her hand batting at her ear and her heart beating fast.

A spider, soft and black with eight long, prickly legs and as many eyes, scuttles down her body. But the spider's not afraid, for it stops and turns to stare in her direction. Waiting.

The cinder girl's breath is short and fast, and she scrambles backward, moving faster than the spider bothered to go.

No one speaks, but the spider's pincers widen slowly, then snap back together fast.

Though she's never seen this creature, as big as the palm of her hand, the cinder girl somehow knows without question—her sister has called.

Nearly two full cycles of the moon have passed since her golden sister became a golden prisoner, locked away in the tower keep. Mother delivers her meals and guards the key.

The cinder girl does not wish to go, as memories of the shadows swirling around her are fresh and terrible, but she can't help a leap of wonder that she's been sought out.

Why would her sister want her?

The spider moves languidly to the icy stone floor, and the cinder girl tosses the bedcovers back. The spider waits, and she doesn't hesitate. She's used to the cold.

Out the door and down the hall, past the great room and Mother's chambers, the spider scuttles and the cinder girl follows behind.

Into the tower and up the long and winding stairs they climb, her foggy breath rising into the night the only sign of their passing.

Up and up they climb.

Near the top of the stairs, the cinder girl stops. Chanting pours from her sister's prison cell, low and insistent like it was before.

The spider continues farther than the cinder girl can go, disappearing beneath a small crack below the door.

The cinder girl is alone.

Except for her sister.

"It is time for you to do something for me, cinder sister," the voice says from behind the barred door.

Sister does not sound weakened from weeks under lock and key. Her voice is rich and persuasive, as it always was. Perhaps more.

"Anything, Sister."

"There are things I need. You will get them for me."

The shadows swirl again, but this time the cinder girl is not afraid. Her golden sister's voice whispers in her ear once more, telling her exactly what she requires.

GRAYE

The party is an unexpected complication. Normally, Graye would have heard them laughing, or seen them building their campfire on the wet sand long before anyone got close enough to interact. But she's lost in her head, suffocating beneath her wasted hopes, and they're upon her before she can think to retreat.

"Is there someone over there, sitting by the water?" she hears a woman's voice ask.

"Don't know, maybe."

It's a couple, broken off from the group for a stroll down the deserted beach. Deserted, save for Graye.

"Hello?"

She doesn't answer. She barely registers the darkened figures moving toward her. Only when they're close enough to touch does she slowly turn her head and stare up at them.

Graye has no idea how she looks, but she knows how she feels, and that must show in her face because it triggers a response.

"Hey." The woman kneels at Graye's side. Her voice is kind. Soothing. She's speaking as a mother might to a lost child found wandering alone.

"Are you okay?" she asks. Her concern is real. Graye struggles to find a way out of her own head to give an answer.

No, she thinks.

"Yeah," she whispers.

"Are you by yourself?" the man asks. He's standing by their side, looking around to see if anyone else is with her.

"Yes," Graye says. "But I live just over there." She gestures with her hand somewhere in the direction of her guesthouse but doesn't turn around.

"I know you," he says, snapping his fingers and pointing at her. He's too happy, too laid-back, and Graye recognizes the sweet, skunky smell wafting off him.

"You're with that book lady," he says. "The one with the asshole husband. I waited tables at that fancy dinner tonight. Man, that was wild." He's smiling and nodding before it occurs to him to ask, "Is she okay?"

Graye nods slowly. "She's fine."

Better than me.

"We're just hanging out," the girl says. "Our friend Tom's got a guitar and we've got drinks. Why don't you join us?"

Graye shakes her head. "No, I don't want to intrude."

"No way, the more the better," the man says, happy again now that he's forgotten about the book lady's asshole husband.

Near the campfire in the distance, the group is growing larger and Graye can hear laughter and a strum of strings. She glances out at the waves and mulls the idea of not being alone, just for a little while.

Just this once.

"Okay," she concedes. "If you're sure."

"Come on then." The woman stands and holds her hand out for Graye to grab hold of, just as Graye did not so long ago for Laura. Graye hesitates only a moment before reaching out to grasp the girl's warm, welcoming palm.

Just for a little while.

Jesse and Karina, the couple are called. They're engaged but haven't set a date. He's an architecture student. She's pre-med. They're staying with friends for the summer, picking up odd jobs for spending money and squeezing the last drops out of their final days on the island before real life intrudes.

What will it hurt to pass an hour, that maybe stretches into two, with people she's never met? There's nothing to stop her. Nothing to stop her accepting when she's offered a bottle of beer. No one to contradict her for weaving a backstory for herself, fabricated from the sea air, when they ask.

The lies trip off her tongue. No one claims they don't trust her. They don't stare, squinty-eyed, like she's not being straight with them.

So she smiles and listens to Tom, who plays guitar better than he sings.

When the "cigarette" is passed around the first time, she declines and passes it along, and no one cares.

And this little island of light on an island of darkness becomes an oasis. Graye is someone new in the warm glow of the embers, with the laughter of strangers caressing her. Not Gracie Thacker. Not even Graye Templeton, heavy with disappointment, but someone wholly fresh, her possibilities endless and intriguing.

She smiles and accepts the offer when it comes her way again, though the smoke squeezes her lungs, and she coughs once, then again.

The night grows fuzzy and soft, and Laura's earlier words lose their edge, no longer razors cutting her from the inside.

She makes new friends.

Time abandons her and Graye is content just to be, here on this bit of sand with the fire burning low and the waves muffling the world.

Faces lose their distinction and Graye's thoughts drift, but she knows she'll never forget this night. Karina and her kindness. Jesse's gentle presence at his fiancée's side, like a happy Labrador.

The faces in the dark, at the far side of the circle, aren't staring, examining every move she makes and every lie she tells, no matter what her imagination is whispering to her. She's a stranger here, to herself and to everyone else.

The moon has moved lower in the sky by the time worry starts to creep in. Her words won't come. Not the ones she wants. Sentences fall from her mouth in jumbled nonsense, nothing like what she wants to say.

The others are laughing and she tries to laugh as well, but her attempt is weak. Her smile falters.

No matter who she is, no matter who she's ever been, words are the thing she can count on.

She takes a deep breath and pictures them in her head. Slowly, she arranges them in the order they should be and carefully speaks them aloud. The effort it takes is unsettling and her high begins to fade.

Graye stands, then sways on her feet.

"I should go home," she says, then pulls in a deep breath of relief and smiles wide. There. Her words are still there. She just needs to sleep. Sleep and everything will be fine.

"Oh, don't go," Karina says and reaches up to squeeze her hand.

She kneels to hug the woman who gave her this gift when she needed it most.

"Thank you," Graye whispers in her ear.

"Anytime," Karina says. "Do you want Jesse to walk you home?"

"No."

Jesse is happily stretched out on the sand debating with Tom whether Bob Dylan should have been given a Nobel Prize. "Man, nobody can say he's not a poet."

She shakes her head. "I'm just up the beach. I'll be fine."

She's lost her fear of who might wait on her, unseen in the night.

"Okay, then. It was nice to meet you, Graye."

And perhaps her path back home is a winding one, but Graye is too numb to be unhappy.

The steps from the beach to the West home are harder to navigate than she remembers, and she concentrates on her footing, each step taking her away from the sounds of the sea and closer to her bed.

Light still burns from the windows, but Graye can't bring herself to get worked up over how Laura is faring as she packs up one half of her life, to be cut out and left for dead the next day.

Laura and her problems loom less large in her mind now.

Graye veers left, heading for the guesthouse. Maybe it's time to exorcise herself from Laura's life as well. Things haven't gone as planned here. She needs to consider whether anything can be salvaged, or if it's time to move on.

But not tonight. She's done thinking tonight.

From several yards, her door swims into focus. Almost there. Only a few more steps.

Muffled, as if from a great distance, the sound of shouting reaches her ears, causing a hitch in her step.

Graye stops and tilts her head.

A crash follows.

Laura and David, at it again. Apparently, Laura's assumption that her husband would be passed out was wishful thinking.

She stands beneath the carport, her gaze torn between the Wests' kitchen door and her guesthouse. Her bed is calling to her.

She's in no condition to help anyone. And Laura's made it clear she can take care of herself.

The sound Laura's skull made when it connected with the hardwood floor of the ballroom reverberates in her mind, and Graye realizes she's taken two steps toward their door.

She's reaching out a hand when another memory intrudes.

"I just didn't trust her, I guess. The narrator . . . Something was off, you know?"

Her hand falters.

Whatever is going on inside the West home, it isn't her problem. It isn't her fault either, and she can do nothing to fix it.

Besides, Laura knows where to find her if she needs her. With determined steps, Graye turns back to her own door.

She won't give in to guilt. A friend, a good friend, wouldn't turn their back, but her friendship with Laura has soured. How much more can she afford to invest in such a one-sided relationship? She'd give anything to make it not so, but she can't do that. It wasn't her choice.

Graye opens her door. She gives one last look at the West home, where the shouting continues.

Slowly, Graye closes the door, shutting out the sounds.

35

GRAYE

"If I've told you once, I've told you a hundred times. If I want to hear your voice, I'll tell you what to say!"

The ripping sound of silver-edged tape being pulled from the roll fills her head, and she scrambles backward on her heels and bottom.

"No, Mother. I'll be quiet, I will."

The hard grip of fingers that clamp in her hair, forcing her head to turn, isn't as bad as the tight, sticky seal the duct tape makes when it's slapped over her mouth.

Graye wakes with her lips clamped over her teeth, a stifled scream caught behind them.

Her eyes wide but bleary, she shakes her head, trying to break free from the grip of memory.

"It was so long ago. So long ago," she tells herself. "I'm not that little girl."

She has to say it a few more times before her breathing begins to slow. Once it does, there will be no more sleep for her, regardless of the early hour.

Dawn isn't quite ready to break over the horizon when Graye peeks out of the blinds, but the darkness is fading a little at a time.

She reaches for her phone, but it isn't on the table where she normally places it.

Graye's head is already pounding, but when she bends at the waist to check if her phone has fallen beneath the bed, blood rushes to her brain and she squeezes her eyes against the onslaught.

Groaning, she takes a seat on the floor and drops her aching head into her hands.

What was she thinking, getting wasted on the beach with a group of strangers?

Whatever had been going through her head, she's paying the price for it today.

Slowly, Graye drags herself from the floor and heads toward the small bathroom. Dizzy, and possibly still a little drunk, she searches blindly for a bottle of ibuprofen and pulls some water from the tap into the palm of her hand to swallow two of them down.

She splashes cold water on her face and avoids examining her reflection in the mirror.

Today is going to be one of the hardest days of her life.

Somewhere between Laura's hurtful words the night before and falling into her bed after a night of indulgence, Graye has come to a decision.

Things can't go on like this.

Laura won't be the one who helps her voice be heard.

If Graye has any doubts, she needs only to recall Laura's easy dismissal of her work. The hours since haven't lessened the blow. If anything, her sense of abandonment and betrayal has deepened into a chasm that can't be bridged.

Graye will tell Laura the truth and deal with the consequences.

After that, it will be time to move on.

It will mean a change of plans, but Graye will just have to adapt. She's no stranger to disappointment. With enough time and distance, she'll figure it out. She'll make new plans.

It's all she knows.

With the decision fresh in her mind, Graye takes Laura's own words to heart.

I have to face this now, head-on, before I lose my nerve.

She brushes the grit from her teeth and pulls her hair into a messy ponytail.

Laura first. Everything else will fall into place after.

Graye still can't find her phone, so there's no clock to chide her for the ungodly hour. She pulls on a fresh pair of jeans and a T-shirt, then collects what she'll need before walking out into the gray breaking dawn.

From the outside, the carriage house is quiet. No shouting spills into the dawn, as it did the previous night. The entire island is quiet, in fact, save for a few gulls near the beach.

Laura is probably sleeping at this hour, but Graye doesn't let that stop her. She knows where her bedroom is.

Considering the state of things between the couple, David is no doubt passed out on the couch in his office again.

No second thoughts trouble her as she opens the unlocked door to the West kitchen and lets herself in. Graye carries a sadness inside of her, but it's a resigned sadness.

Laura isn't the first friend who's let her down.

A clock ticking somewhere in the depths of the house is the only sound that reaches her.

How vulnerable we are in sleep.

Anyone could walk in off the street.

This island, it casts a spell. It's an existence that hinges on the good-will of the elements. Time may pass. Years turn into decades, and the deadliest storms veer right or left, allowing the decades to stack upon one another. But eventually, as though it were all castles built of sand, another storm will come and wipe everything away. It's only a matter of time.

And still, people build their castles taller, more ornate, thumbing their noses at Mother Nature. They'll lose in the end, but the defiance makes them careless. Distracted.

Not all storms come from the sky. Even at the edge of the world, the heart has an infinite capacity for darkness.

Laura should really lock her doors.

Graye releases the handle carefully behind her. She doesn't want to startle anyone.

On soft feet she moves through the kitchen. The light is slowly gaining a foothold outside the windows, and the dim glow that filters through reveals nothing out of place. A dishtowel is folded along the edge of the sink. A drip builds at the faucet, growing fat before dropping into the basin.

At the entry to the living room, Graye pauses, one hand on the doorjamb. Unconsciously, her fingers tighten, gripping the wall for support. Only her eyes move as she scans the room in front of her, struggling to make sense of what she's seeing.

Something is wrong. Something is very wrong.

Furniture is overturned. Throw pillows and lamps are tossed across the floor, books and papers scattered. There's not a space to be seen that hasn't been defaced by some sign of violence.

An echo of screams dances through Graye's memory, raising the hair on her arms.

Did she sleep through this destruction, just yards away, safe in her bed? It doesn't seem possible, regardless of how tired she was.

This must have happened as she was drowning her sorrows on the beach with a group of strangers.

"Help me," a woman cries in her head. *"Oh Jesus. Help me."*

Laura?

Graye shakes the plea from her mind. She's imagining things. She would have woken if Laura had come to her for help. She's sure she would have.

A short hallway to the left leads to David's office. Graye has never been inside and has no desire to now.

She needs to find Laura.

Gingerly, she steps into the room, pushing a broken picture frame away with her foot. Glass crunches beneath her shoe.

The silence that was a comfort just moments before is heavy with unanswered questions. The anger that must have raged, fueling this disaster, still hangs in the air, and Graye can't shake the sense she's being watched.

As quietly as she can manage, she heads toward the hallway that leads to Laura's office, then to her bedroom at the end.

Nothing stirs.

Nothing and no one.

Graye's heart is beating heavily in her chest, worry growing by the second, when her foot slides out from underneath her.

Her hands whirl, grasping for something, anything, to catch herself, but it's too late. She's falling.

With a sharp intake of breath, Graye lands on her butt. Her jaw clamps down over her tongue and the sudden shock of pain brings tears to her eyes.

Graye squeezes her eyes shut and shakes her head, fighting a wave of nausea, then wipes a hand across her lips.

One glance at herself, though, and the throbbing pain in Graye's mouth fades into the background.

Blood.

It's on her hands, on her clothes. It's smeared across her pant leg.

An image of Walt comes to her, with a fake plastic knife protruding from his belly, colored corn syrup spraying from his mouth.

But this isn't corn syrup, dyed to a bright, candy-apple red.

There's no mistaking the dark, brownish scarlet that marks Graye's skin and clothes.

If she had any doubts, the sickeningly familiar smell fills her nostrils. Graye's stomach and throat constrict at once, a gag reflex she has no control over.

Nothing smells the same as blood.

It's a scent she'll never forget.

Screams again fill her head, and Graye fights back the panic threatening to engulf her. She can't distinguish where the memory is coming from. In the grip of terror, one scream sounds much like another.

Through the growing cloud of anxiety, a single thought cuts past the fog.

Laura.

Graye is panting in fear as she pulls herself from the ground. She almost loses her footing again in her haste, but manages to stay upright as she runs down the hallway, uncaring now about the sounds of her footsteps echoing through the century-old home.

Laura's bedroom door is hanging ajar, and Graye skids to a halt just inside.

Upheaval is evident everywhere. The bedcovers are thrown from the bed and drawers are pulled out, their contents emptied across the floor.

A suitcase lies open where it's fallen, a man's shirt balled up in one corner.

Graye swings her gaze around to look back down the hallway, but stops short.

Just inches above where her hand is gripping the open bedroom door, there are three dark brownish-red streaks.

Slowly, she raises her hand, still marred with blood from her fall, and lines up her shaking fingertips with the spot where the streaks begin. They fit perfectly.

The sound of short, sharp gasps reaches Graye's ears and it takes a moment to realize the sound is emanating from her.

Someone, someone with a small, feminine hand, has left a bloody handprint smeared across the door of Laura's bedroom.

Her empty bedroom.

Laura is gone.

Her gasps turn to whimpers, trapped behind lips incapable of opening.

The taste of blood is still fresh in her mouth when Graye turns and runs.

36

GRAYE

The voices are back. People long gone fill Graye's head as she struggles to navigate the minefield she's stumbled into.

Alex is laughing. Her mother is screaming. And the blood, so much blood.

Graye slams open the door of the guesthouse. It bounces off the wall and swings wide behind her as she runs straight for the shower, cranking the water as hot as it will go. She doesn't wait for it to warm but steps in even as she strips the stained clothing from her body. Her T-shirt and jeans end up in a sodden heap on the floor of the tub as the water goes from cold to hot, scalding her skin. Red swirls circle and reach for the drain.

She's crying, silently, behind a jaw so tightly locked it may never open again. Her body struggles to pull enough air into her lungs through her nose, but in the grip of panic, she begins to grow dizzy.

"I said you'd never amount to anything. What have you done, Gracie?"

"Nothing!" she cries, her jaw finally loosening. Oxygen rushes to her brain. There's no one to hear her. She's alone in the room with only a reflection disappearing in the mirror as steam pours from the blindingly hot shower.

Her hands shake as she tries to hold on to the bar of soap. It slides from her grip, like everything else does.

Graye wraps her arms around her middle and bends at the waist.

The smell of blood won't leave her, and she has no idea how much is real and how much is a memory that's come to life like a child's monster in the closet, ready to eat her alive.

"No, no, no," she whimpers. "This wasn't the plan. It wasn't supposed to be this way!"

"She's the monster, Grace," a voice whispers in her ear. *"She deserves it."*

"No!" Graye's hands flail outward in front of her face, warding off the invisible, untouchable forces that batter her defenses.

"They're going to find you, Gracie. It's all going to come out. The truth about who you are, and all your lies. You can't hide this time."

Graye's eyes fly open.

The full implication of those words rains down upon her.

The past she's tried to hide like a weighted-down corpse is rising to the surface. The fiction of Graye Templeton will be exposed to the world.

She'll be forced back into the skin of Gracie Thacker from the wrong side of the tracks, who watched her mother get murdered and lived to tell the tale. That can't happen. Not yet.

Graye stumbles out of the shower, not bothering with a towel.

I have to get out of here.

Now.

On wet feet, she skids across the floor in her rush to get out of the bathroom.

There's no time. No time to think, no time to prepare. Everything is spinning out of her control.

Throwing open a drawer, Graye pulls out the first piece of clothing she puts her hands on and slides it on over her wet, dripping skin.

It's Laura's silk blouse, the coffee stain still evident on the front.

The irony brings a choked sob to her throat, but she'll mourn Laura later. Later, when she's safe and gone from this place that builds up dreams only to push them from a cliff.

With the buttons of the blouse only partially fastened, she pulls on a pair of jeans and glances quickly around, wet stringy hair slapping her cheeks as she does. Her eyes land on her bag.

The only way off this island is by ferry. She could ride to the mainland as a passenger, but that won't get her far enough, fast enough.

There's no way around it. She'll have to take Laura's car. God knows, Laura doesn't need it anymore, and Graye knows where she hangs the keys. There's enough cash in her own wallet to pay the fare. Nothing else matters. Everything in the guesthouse is baggage, easily replaced.

Each one of Graye's senses balks at the idea of walking back into the bloodstained carriage house, but she can't see any other way.

Graye grabs her bag and slings the strap across her shoulder, then runs back out the door, quickly, before her fear has time to catch up with her.

In her haste, she's forgotten shoes. The gravel of the driveway digs into the soles of her feet, but she won't turn back.

She must keep moving forward. Anything else would be a terrible mistake, and Graye can't afford mistakes. Her existence depends on it.

The kitchen door to the West home is hanging open, as she must have left it when she ran out. Graye doesn't pause.

Through the tidy kitchen, the sun now streaming through the windows, Graye moves toward the living room. She keeps her eyes focused upward, avoiding the blood, avoiding the destruction. Her only goal is the little wooden plaque with four hooks hanging by the front door where the Wests keep the keys to their vehicles.

It swims into focus and Graye moves toward it as a drowning man to a life raft.

She cries out as a piece of broken glass slices the bottom of her bare foot.

"Don't be such a crybaby!"

Graye doesn't slow down until she grasps the keys of Laura's car and pulls them from the hook.

Finally, finally, she can breathe.

Back toward the kitchen she heads, limping on her bleeding foot. The keys are gripped so tightly in her palm that her knuckles turn white. On the other side of the kitchen door, she'll step into Laura's car and drive away from this place forever.

It's unfortunate, but things in Port Mary haven't worked out as she'd hoped.

She's halfway across the kitchen when Graye freezes.

There's one more thing. One thing she can't leave behind.

It's the only thing that matters anymore. The only thing that ever mattered, and she can't walk out that door and leave it for whoever is left to clean up the mess the Wests have made of their lives.

Her manuscript.

It was still in Laura's possession. Graye doesn't write on a computer, doesn't have a file saved on a cloud somewhere. It's an old-fashioned affectation she now regrets.

The open doorway and the car waiting for her just feet away call out, begging her to go. Go now, while she still has time, but Graye can't walk away.

That manuscript is everything. Without it, Graye Templeton is nothing at all.

Laura may not have been willing to champion it, but that's a hurdle she can overcome. Graye will find someone else, someone with a sharper eye, who can see the potential in her story. She will.

But not if she leaves it behind. Left behind, it's nothing but trash to be thrown out. Just like little Gracie was.

Her heart races as she turns and runs back into the living room, crossing it without thought to the broken things she's walking over.

She steps around the pool of blood, prepared for it this time. All her senses are focused in the direction of Laura's office. She's already seen the bedroom. If there had been typed pages scattered across the floor, she would have noticed.

Laura must have put it back in her office.

At least, she hopes so. If not, Graye doesn't know if she can face the seemingly insurmountable task of an anxious search through the house while the clock ticks away, marking the miles she should be putting between herself and this hated island. Miles between herself and the wounds the Wests have inflicted, both on her and on each other.

Her eyes skim past the streaks of blood on the bedroom door. She can't help Laura now.

The door to the office is closed and Graye grasps the knob and twists, breathing a sigh of relief when she sees that this room, at least, is untouched by whatever took place between the couple the night before.

Her eyes fall on it straightaway, tied with an oversized rubber band that holds it together.

The Orphan's Ashes, a novel by Fiona Boyd.

Graye rushes across the room to pick it up and hug it against her chest. The weight of it in her arms grounds her, and strangely, her panic recedes.

This is all she needs.

With a satisfied smile she'd be surprised to realize is on her face, Graye hurries back down the hallway.

Halfway across the destroyed living room, joy begins to sing again in her heart. Faintly, it's true, but it's there.

Everything is going to be all right. Maybe not for Laura, but she can't do anything about that. For Graye, at least, things are going to be fine.

There's no warning before the police burst through the door, guns drawn.

"Get down!" they shout into Graye's stunned face.

She doesn't move.

"Put your hands in the air and get down on the ground!"

Slowly, Graye raises her hands, the manuscript still gripped in one.

Pages slip from between the rubber band and begin to fall fast and thick on the ground at Graye's feet.

More shouting from the men in black uniforms, but their voices become static in her ears, like a radio station between signals.

Her gaze settles on a single white sheet of paper, filled painstakingly with her words, as the breeze from the open door catches it and it whirls lazily through the air before sliding to the floor with the others.

Her eyes are still on it when a black boot steps on the page as the boot's owner rushes in her direction.

Graye's eyes fill with tears as the men converge on her. One of them pulls her hands behind her back to slip handcuffs around her wrists. It hurts, but she doesn't cry from the pain of being confined.

Black marks in the shape of a foot mar her words. The utter disregard for everything she is, everything she's worked so hard to be, is everything she always knew it would be.

Tears cloud her eyes, but they remain locked on that boot print until she's pulled away toward a future meant for a little girl with a different name. A future she never wanted and can't escape. She stares at that boot print until she can't look any longer.

37

GRAYE

She's been sitting in this room alone for what feels like days, though it can't have been more than a few hours. There's a clock on the wall behind her. She can hear it ticking but doesn't turn to see. Time makes no difference now anyway.

Graye lays her forehead on the cool, scuffed surface of the table, then turns her cheek against it and stares at the wall. She picks at a jagged scratch in the surface with her fingernail.

Her hair has dried into stringy clumps.

The officers didn't allow her to go back to the guesthouse for shoes, but they did loan her a pair of oversized men's rubber boots.

She slipped them off an hour ago when the cut on the bottom of her foot had begun to throb. She should ask for some antiseptic and a bandage when they come back.

If they come back.

There's a window that looks out on the rest of the police station, but she lost interest in the activities taking place on the other side a while ago. If her head is turned, she won't have to see the way people cut their eyes to peer in as they walk past.

Two plainclothes officers escorted her into the room when she first arrived at the station. Port Mary has no official police force of its own, she's learned, only a rotation of patrols from Rockaway.

To her surprise, they brought her across the bay in a police boat rather than a car that would need to use the ferry to get back to the mainland.

The boat ride might have been interesting, under different circumstances, but Graye couldn't find any joy in the experience.

A stone-faced uniformed officer had unfastened her handcuffs before helping her into the craft, which was a small comfort. But with one officer positioned on either side of her, she was squeezed between them. Graye wasn't going anywhere, not even over the side of the boat into the bay, had she been so inclined.

Not that she hadn't considered it.

How long would it be before they discovered who she really was? Is that what they were doing now, as she waited in this cold, institutional room?

Reporters had lost the trail of Grace Thacker many years ago, but the deceit surely couldn't be maintained when it was hammered from the opposite direction. Not by police who had more effective resources at their disposal than journalists.

The two who brought her in here—a woman who looked only a bit older than her, and a balding middle-aged man—had been politely professional. She couldn't remember their names, but the man offered her something to drink while she waited.

She declined, but her parched throat was beginning to regret the easy dismissal of an unwarranted kindness.

"Am I under arrest?" she asked.

"Should you be?" the older man replied, sounding almost as if he were teasing a niece or nephew.

Graye wasn't used to teasing, in any form. She had no idea if that meant they knew she'd done nothing wrong, or if it was simply a calculated tactic to lull her into letting her guard down.

Graye had only shaken her head. The less she said, the better off she'd be, a lesson she'd been taught early and often.

And so she waits, alone, in silence, once again tucked away from those with more power who will decide her fate.

The door opens and Graye straightens in her chair.

"Miss Templeton, I'm sorry about the wait."

The same officers who escorted her into the room are back at last, but they're too relaxed. Too casual, given the circumstances.

The older man places a bottle of water and something wrapped in foil onto the table and slides it over to Graye. It gives off a scent of bacon and she struggles not to gag.

The woman takes a seat and places a notepad and pen in front of her. They both take their time settling into the chairs positioned across the table from her. The female officer meets her eyes and gives her a small smile.

"Have you found Laura?" Graye asks.

She recalls the slippery sensation of blood between her fingers and shudders.

They don't seem to have heard her or, more likely, simply don't bother to answer.

"Let's get a few formalities out of the way. First, I want you to know we're recording this conversation." The officer points to the corner of the room where a shiny black orb is mounted.

Graye doesn't care about that.

"Fine," she says with a wave of her hand.

"For the recording, it's nine twenty-three a.m. the morning of Sunday, August twenty-sixth, two thousand eighteen. This interview is in reference to an initial investigation concerning a suspicious death at four fifteen Oceanside Parkway, Port Mary, Texas. Now, can you tell us your name for the record?" the woman asks.

Grace Ann Thacker. Daughter of Crystal, sister of Alexis.

"Graye Templeton," she answers without hesitation. *Daughter of no one.*

"Miss Templeton, I'm Detective Foster and this is Detective Branson," he says, gesturing to his partner. "We're with the Rockaway Police Department. At this point in time, you are not under arrest, simply a person of interest in this investigation. However, we want to do this right. Cross all the i's and dot all the t's, if you know what I mean, so I'm going to go ahead and read you your rights."

He proceeds to do just that, never losing his gentle, casual tone.

Graye shakes her head, uninterested in either an attorney or the detective's easy banter, designed to tempt her into believing he's her friend.

"Do you know why you're here?"

Graye nods. "Because of the blood," she says in a quiet voice, nearly a whisper.

Detective Foster's features remain relaxed, but his eyes take note of every twitch of her facial muscles.

"That's right," he says. The kindly uncle tone of his voice never wavers. "Can you tell us about that? Can you tell us about the blood?"

His partner looks up, her pen poised to jot down whatever Graye might say next.

Her foot throbs. She focuses on the pain so she doesn't have to think too deeply about the words they want to hear.

"There was so much of it. I slipped and fell. Can you tell me if you've found her?"

"You're speaking of Laura West?" Detective Branson asks with a tilt of her head.

"Yes. There was blood, so much of it. David must have killed her. Have you found David?" She doesn't mention the troubling possibility plaguing her that it could have been Nick. That admission would just complicate things. There would be so many questions.

"Dr. David West, Laura West's husband?" the female detective asks.

Were they seriously playing games with her right now? Did they not realize the severity of the situation?

"Yes! You need to be out looking for him! He killed her, I know he did."

"You believe Dr. David West killed his wife?"

Graye stares at her in disbelief.

"That's what I've been saying! It was David, it had to be." Or Nick. Or Rachel Caron. But that's their job, not hers. Why aren't they doing their jobs?

Graye is horrified by the growing tightness in her throat. She's going to cry. She promised herself she'd never cry in front of anyone with authority over her again, but the tears are there and she can't stop them.

Once they start, there's no holding them back.

Eventually they pass, leaving her broken and humiliated. Drained of her final drops of self-respect.

"I'm sorry," she says. For what, she can't say, but apologizing is a difficult habit to break.

"Would you like to take a moment?" Detective Branson asks.

Graye shakes her head. She's stronger than this. She is.

"No. I just want this done."

Detective Foster leans forward and places his elbows on the table. "Why don't we start from the beginning?"

Graye knows this man is her enemy. In her heart, she knows. But that voice. It's so very kind. Kindness is Graye's weakness. She's known so little of it in her life.

"It's all my fault," she says. "I knew David was dangerous, and I left her alone with him. It's my fault."

Tears threaten again at the thought of what Laura must have suffered. Detective Branson speaks, and Graye focuses on her words, refusing to allow herself to break again.

"How is it your fault?"

Graye shakes her head. Why don't they understand?

"Don't you see? I knew he could be violent. I'd seen it. I was her friend, and I let her down."

How she wishes she had the power to turn back the clock, to warn Laura, but she never imagined . . .

Detective Branson briefly meets her partner's eyes. Graye can't read what's exchanged between the two of them but senses it's not good.

"Miss Templeton," Detective Foster says gently. "I can assure you, David West didn't kill his wife."

Graye's stomach drops. Nick. They're going to find out about Nick.

"That . . . that can't be right," she says, stunned. "He was so horrible at the party. Laura was humiliated and angry. She *told* me she was packing his bags. He'd knocked her to the ground in front of sixty witnesses, for God's sake."

The two officers watch her closely.

There's something going on here. Some piece of the puzzle that Graye can't quite see.

She's reeling, shuffling through the possibilities. Had Nick done this just to hurt her? She can't face the implications of that. "It couldn't be Hugo. He loves her. Anyone can see that."

Detective Branson flips through her notebook without meeting Graye's eyes.

"Would you be referring to Hugo Caron?"

"But he would never hurt her."

"What makes you believe Mr. Caron could be involved?" Detective Branson prods.

"Nothing!" she says. "I just told you, he couldn't be. He loves her, and she loves him."

"Laura?" Detective Foster asks. "Laura West, in love with Hugo Caron?"

The man's slow, smooth delivery that had lulled her just moments before is beginning to grate.

They're detectives. Why are they having so much trouble keeping up?

"Why don't we slow down and back up just a bit," Detective Foster says, leaning back in his chair and running his hand across his nearly bald head.

But Graye doesn't want to slow down. She can't.

The female detective speaks, her voice all corners and edges.

"Mr. Caron may or may not have been having an affair with Mrs. West, but Hugo Caron didn't kill anyone. He has an alibi for the time in question."

Graye was almost relieved they sounded so certain. For Laura to face such violence at the hands of someone she cared so deeply about would be the worst sort of betrayal. She must have been so afraid.

"She was pregnant, though," Graye says, leaning forward and placing her hands on the table. They're not taking her seriously and she feels like she's nine years old again, about to be dismissed with a pat on the head.

"That has to be the key. Laura was pregnant and Hugo's wife knew about it, I'm sure of it. I was there. I overheard her telling David."

Agitation has overtaken Graye's nerve endings, and her skin warms, as if a stove burner has been switched on inside of her.

"It must have been Rachel. Rachel Caron. If she's his alibi, he could be protecting her. Talk to Rachel."

"Miss Templeton, I think maybe we're getting a bit off track. Perhaps we should start with how you came to be acquainted . . ."

He continued to speak, but Graye lost track of his words. Her eyes were drawn behind him, to the window that opened onto the rest of the police station.

211

A man was walking past, headed from another room Graye couldn't see. He stopped and spoke to the receptionist behind the desk.

His back was turned to her, but she knew that man.

Graye rose from her chair slowly.

The detectives met each other's eyes, but neither made any move to stop her as she stepped carefully from behind the table.

At a torturous pace, Graye walked to the glass and placed her hand upon the cool pane.

The man turned, glanced in her direction.

It was Hugo.

"You're just going to let him walk out of here?" Graye asked. "He must know something!"

"Miss Templeton, perhaps you should sit back down."

But she's not listening.

The double glass doors at the entrance to the station that hold back the scorching August heat are opening.

A woman enters. Rachel Caron.

Hugo turns and greets his wife, holding an arm wide for her to slip next to his side. She, in turn, wraps an arm around his waist.

"That's her! She did this, I'm telling you!" Graye says, tapping on the glass with her index finger and whipping her head back around to face the detectives. "He's protecting her, the bastard!"

They're staring at her with a mixture of confusion and empathy.

"Miss Templeton," Detective Foster says gently. She wishes he'd stop using that solicitous tone. It's lost its appeal.

"Miss Templeton, Rachel Caron didn't kill Laura West."

She gapes at him.

"You can't know that," she says, shaking her head at their incompetence. "You've had me here for what? Two hours? That's not enough time to make those kinds of decisions. How could you possibly know that?"

A flurry of movement pulls her gaze back to the lobby of the police station.

Someone else is crossing the lobby, heading in Hugo and Rachel's direction, practically running.

Graye stares as the three people embrace. They speak to one another for a moment, words Graye can't possibly make out due to the distance and the glass between her and them.

Then the newcomer turns and meets her eyes.

"Miss Templeton, Hugo Caron didn't kill Laura West, and neither did his wife," the voice of Detective Branson says at her back.

It can't be. It doesn't make any sense.

But there's no mistaking that face, the shining blonde hair, the blue eyes set against pale skin.

"We know this because Laura West isn't dead."

Graye turns back to stare at the woman in the lobby and her shock turns to something else entirely.

Graye stands straighter as a massive weight dissipates from her chest. The anxiety that's dogged her since she first saw the blood drains away. She's as light as air.

"Now, Miss Templeton. Why don't you have a seat and we'll start again."

"Of course," she says, her entire demeanor shifting in an instant.

A dazed smile she can't contain blooms. She bites her lip, but that doesn't hide her joy, her relief, so she drops her gaze to the floor and walks on lightened feet to take her seat.

"Miss Templeton, we've brought you here as a person of interest in the investigation of the death of David West, Laura's husband."

A girlish giggle escapes her lips and floats into the room, as out of place as a jazz band at a funeral.

She can't help it. She's been haunted by visions of Laura being murdered in a savage, bloody rage. Haunted by the fear and despair she must have felt, realizing this person she trusted completely could subject her to such horrors. Haunted by the thought that, in her final moments, Laura saw nothing but the eyes of an animal who'd never cared for her at all.

The sight of Laura has swept that all away.

She's alive. Laura is alive and David is dead.

That was certainly never part of Graye's plan, but she can't deny there's an alluring beauty to it. The stricken expressions on the detectives' faces tell her she should stop, and she raises a hand to her mouth, trying to shut the laughter in, but it's insistent.

"Laura's alive," she says, exuberance in every syllable of the words. She reaches a hand out across the table, but neither officer is inclined to take it as they stare back at her, shocked by her outburst.

She pulls her hand back and cups her palms around each other, pulling them and her joy close beneath her chin.

"Miss Templeton?" Detective Branson says slowly. "A man is dead."

"Yes," she says, struggling ineffectively to tamp down the happiness. "Yes, of course."

"What can you tell us about what happened to David West?" Detective Foster asks. His tone of voice, while still low and soothing, is more reserved this time, guarded. It's clear he's been thrown by her reaction.

"Oh, I don't know anything about that," she says with a wave of her hand. She sighs happily and leans back in her chair, dropping her hands into her lap.

This may not be exactly the case. Graye sometimes struggles to tell the difference between what's real and what's imagined, even to herself. That's especially true in times of stress.

But there's no need to share her personal idiosyncrasies.

Police officers deal in facts, and there's only one fact Graye can share that matters.

"Whatever did happen, I can tell you this. David West deserved it."

38

LAURA

"Laura, you shouldn't be here," Rachel says, placing a gentle hand upon her upper arm and peering closely at her face. "Have you told them what you went through last night?"

Laura shakes her head, too close to tears at Rachel's concern to say more.

"They need to know," Hugo insists.

"I'm fine," Laura says. She's not fine. Not by a long shot, but the words come automatically.

Rachel crosses her arms and gives her a disgusted look. "You are the absolute worst judge of whether or not you're fine."

Rachel has known Laura since their days in college, and she's not wrong. But it makes no difference.

"I have to stay. They're not going to let me go anywhere until I've been interviewed by the detectives."

"They will if I call my attorney," Rachel insists. "And they will if you *tell them what happened.*"

"I'll tell them. I promise," she says. "But please don't call a lawyer. Not yet."

"Legal representation does not make you guilty. It makes you smart."

Rachel is an attorney. She specializes in tax law, thankfully. Laura has no doubt that if she were a criminal attorney she'd have already made a scene.

The last thing Laura wants is a scene.

David is dead.

Murdered.

She has trouble wrapping her mind around it. It sits like a stone in the middle of every thought as she tries to skirt around it, avoiding looking directly at it.

"I'm fine," she says again. "How did everything go?" she asks Hugo, deflecting Rachel's ire.

It works.

"I still don't understand why they questioned you first," Rachel exclaims to her husband.

He leans over and squeezes his wife's shoulders. "Because I got into a public brawl with the man less than twenty-four hours ago," he says quietly.

"Were they treating you like a suspect?" Rachel prods. "Because if I get a single whiff that they're trying to pin this on you, I swear to God—"

"Rachel," Hugo says. His voice is smooth and steady, a counterpoint to his wife's fiery one. "They're just gathering facts. You need to let them do their jobs."

"From what I heard, the facts are pretty damn clear," Rachel points out. "She was picked up standing in the room with David's dead body on the floor beside her."

The words steal the breath from Laura's lungs, and the blood drains from her face.

"Oh God, I'm sorry," Rachel says, holding her for support. "You need to sit down."

They move to a bank of uncomfortable plastic chairs lining the wall of the station lobby, and Laura drops into one, then lets her head fall into her hands.

The visual hits her like a battering ram. Her friend rubs a hand up and down Laura's back as she tries to catch her breath.

They sit in silence until she does.

"What kind of questions did they ask?" Laura says quietly.

Hugo's focus is on Laura's well-being rather than the police interview, but she needs to know. She needs to know if she's placed her friends in danger by dragging them into this mess. Her mess. If she's placed *herself* in danger.

He takes one look at her determined face and sighs.

"They asked about the fight," he admits. "About what caused it."

"What did you say?" Rachel asks.

"I told them the truth, didn't I. That David was an insecure drunk who'd somehow gotten it into his head I was sleeping with his wife."

"Hugo," Rachel chides.

"What, Rachel? It's not like it's a secret. There are a thousand and one witnesses that heard him accuse me. It would have been a waste of time to play dumb. Jesus, Laura, I *knew* we shouldn't have left you alone last night, no matter what you said."

"You told them the real story, I hope," Rachel says.

"Of course I did. But don't be surprised if they want to confirm everything I said with you."

"Oh, I'll be happy to tell them what's up."

Laura lets out a choked laugh.

"I've no doubt you will," Hugo says and leans across Laura's back to give his wife a kiss.

Introducing them had been a whim Laura considered one of her greatest accomplishments. Hugo and Rachel were two of her favorite people, and somehow she'd known they'd fit perfectly together.

She'd sat back and watched their love grow into something real, something tangible, that went deeper than surface attraction.

If only she'd been so perceptive when it came to her own life.

But could she honestly take the blame for what David had become? Should she have somehow known what kind of man he would turn into? Worse, was she somehow, at least partially, responsible?

She remembered the handwritten note from Hugo that David had tossed accusingly at her. It had said something like, *Thanks for a weekend I won't soon forget.*

Hugo had sent it to her along with a collector's edition of *Jane Eyre*, her favorite novel, after Laura had helped arrange a surprise getaway weekend for the couple in Saint-Tropez.

She could have told David so. She should have, but it was so . . . demeaning, to be forced to explain herself that way. She could have shown him the emails between her and Hugo discussing the arrangements. But by God, she'd *never* cheated, which was more than she could say for him. She'd be damned if she was willing to validate his insecurities by playing that game.

Rachel told her she should tell him, but Laura had refused to listen, instead standing high on her useless principals.

When David caused a scene at the dinner, Rachel didn't hesitate to tell her oldest friend, "I told you so, didn't I?"

And yet, everything in Laura rebelled at the idea that she might have had a hand in enabling David's downward spiral.

But was that fair, or was she simply unwilling to shoulder her share of the responsibility?

And what kind of person, what kind of wife, was she, that her husband was lying dead on a medical examiner's table somewhere and she was desperately trying to absolve herself, even in her own mind?

39

MARGARET

Margaret hasn't stopped shaking since she heard the news.

David West is dead.

It's only by chance that she catches the tail end of the breaking report. The crowd in the breakfast room of the hotel where she's staying turns up the television playing low in the background after someone notices a picture of David flash across the screen.

The room, boisterous prior to that, grows quiet to a person, riveted by the drama unfolding before their eyes.

The reverence with which their gazes turn upward, coupled with the number who hold a hand to their mouth, eyes wide with shock, reminds her of the day the *Challenger* exploded.

It's a surreal moment to share with a room full of strangers, especially for a woman who's spent the last two and a half decades surrounded by a bevy of orphan girls and a handful of fellow nuns.

She planned to leave the island this morning. It was a mistake to come here, to meddle in things best left in the past. She should have learned her lesson by now.

Margaret has a rare talent for making decisions that only ever worsen an already bad situation.

And now this.

Graye must be terrified.

The reporter, standing outside a short white-brick building with a few scattered palm trees in front of it, claims the police are speaking to several persons of interest.

Margaret can't reach Graye on her cell phone, though she tries the number half a dozen times.

Fear unlike any she's ever experienced courses through her.

The group in the breakfast room begins to whisper among themselves.

"Shh," she says loudly, hushing them without a second thought, as she would the girls before prayer.

"I'm Sally Monahan, reporting live from Rockaway, Texas. And now back to you, Blake."

The scene cuts to a handsome man with a weak jaw and perfect haircut who's pasted an expression of grave concern on his face.

"Thank you, Sally. Sad news for the literary world today."

Margaret shocks herself by wondering how many times the news anchor had to practice that somber look in the mirror before he was satisfied.

Apparently, leaving her nun's habit behind has shaken her mind loose from the strict regimen of charitable thoughts the Church expects.

And now she's coming unmoored, in more ways than one.

"Where did they say the police station was located?" Margaret asks a group of women sitting at the nearest table, interrupting their conversation. "Is it here on the island?"

Something of her desperation must have shown on her face, because none of the three women seem bothered by her rudeness.

"No, it was on the mainland, wasn't it?" one of them asks another.

"I'll google it," another woman says, picking up her phone and typing something into it.

Margaret is grateful. She'd made a trip to the local cellular store before leaving home and purchased her first ever mobile phone, but other than entering Graye's phone number, she hasn't taken the time to learn how to use it.

"Rockaway," the woman says. "That's on the mainland. I can give you directions, if you like."

"Yes, please," Margaret says. "Thank you. I'll call a taxi."

"I have a better idea," another of the women says, an older woman with an elegant chignon of white hair. "We're planning to catch the next ferry. Our morning plans haven't exactly gone as expected, to say the least. We could take you."

Humbled by the offer, Margaret asks, "Are you certain? I don't want to be a bother."

"No bother at all, dear. Were you a guest for Laura's retreat? I don't recall seeing you at any of the events."

"No," Margaret says. "No, I'm . . ." She doesn't know what to say. Doesn't plan the words that fall from her mouth. "I'm a nun who's run away from home."

The trio of women blink in unison.

It takes a moment for any of them to speak.

"Okay, now you have no choice," says the youngest of the three, a brunette with large-framed glasses. "You have to let us give you a ride so you can tell us the rest of that story."

Margaret shakes her head, regretting her thoughtless words. She doesn't have time to socialize with strangers. She has one goal, and only one. She must find Graye.

"I'll tell you everything if we can leave right away," she says.

All three of them stand quickly, gathering the bags at their feet.

"You may not realize what you've done," the older woman says. "We're all writers, so you've essentially held up a feather on a string to three cats."

Writers. Of course they're writers. Margaret hadn't realized when she'd decided to make the trip, but she'd quickly discovered that the woman Graye was an assistant to was hosting a book event on the tiny island. She'd been able to secure a reservation at Port Mary's one hotel only due to a last-minute cancellation.

Margaret can't explain her sudden need to see Graye in person. They don't have the kind of relationship that would lend itself to impromptu visits.

But her worry has only grown over the months. Graye stopped returning her calls. With the knowledge that Nick tracked the girl down weighing heavily on her mind, Margaret stopped sleeping nights.

She hasn't suffered such severe insomnia since before she took her vows.

She was sitting in chapel last week and realized she hadn't offered up a single word of prayer. Her thoughts were blanketed with images of Graye. The girl she was, the woman she's become. The danger she faces.

For days, she tried to hide her distraction and focus on the tasks in front of her, but her hands went through the motions by rote, having performed the same ones for decades.

Nothing freed her from the endless whirl of worry.

Finally, she gave up as she stared at the ceiling in the sparse, utilitarian room that had granted her comfort and peace once upon a time.

She could lie to herself. But she was forced to accept that God knew what was in her heart better than she did.

She called a taxi service to pick her up and take her to the nearest bus station early the next morning.

Telling no one her plans, she slipped away unseen, dressed in secular clothing pulled from the donation box. The garments felt too light. Insubstantial, compared to what she was used to. But her habit is miles away now, left neatly folded on her bed, with a note sitting on top. A note which won't even come close to a proper explanation of her reasons.

Because she can't put those reasons into words herself.

She only knows that Graye needs her and, for once in the girl's life, Margaret needs Graye to know that someone is in her corner.

Is she willing to share this with three strangers in exchange for the quickest route to Graye?

Yes. Yes, she is.

"My name is Rose, by the way," the brunette says. "And this is Penny Southerland and Olivia Hart."

The other two women nod.

"Olivia is our resident murderer," Rose says with a smile. Everyone goes still.

"Oh." She raises a hand to her mouth. "That wasn't . . . I didn't mean—"

"What Rose meant is that I played the role of the villain in our little murder mystery this weekend," Olivia clarifies. "We revealed the clues and unmasked the killer, Poirot-style, at brunch this morning. But with the very real death of David West, the exercise lost its appeal. And now we know why Laura West didn't show up."

"It's a shame, really, we couldn't give it more attention. The story was quite convoluted. Olivia was the long-supposed dead sister of Baroness Lyttleton, and she'd come back to expose her sister's lifetime of treachery and lies. It was . . ." Rose trails off and the light drains from her face. "I suppose it doesn't really matter now. Considering."

"No, Rose. I suppose it doesn't."

Margaret can't help but wonder what she's agreed to by allying with this trio.

But they are moving quickly, and soon the three, which have become a reluctant four, are leaving the hotel and closing the distance between Margaret and Graye.

It's a strange sensation for Margaret, to talk about herself. The Church encourages the sisters to accept God's will, his hand as a guiding force. Even the concept of self is eventually lost, and the sisters, if they're lucky, will grow to see themselves as vessels for God's love.

Margaret, however, made a bargain, and she keeps her word. The women prove to be exceptional listeners as she shares her story. Providing more detail than she'd ever intended, she begins to see them as confessors.

By the time Rose pulls her rental car into the parking lot of the Rockaway Police Station, navigating around the news crews stationed outside, Margaret is shaking with nerves again, but she's also lighter somehow. Less burdened.

"Good luck to you, Margaret. And to Graye," Penny says, the quietest of the group. "I hope the two of you find strength in one another, and that your path forward becomes clear."

It's so like a prayer, such a gentle gesture of care, that Margaret feels tears gather in her eyes.

"Thank you," she whispers.

"Now go," Olivia says. "That girl needs you now."

She nods and waves after she steps out of the car. The women wave in return and drive away, three angels sent to help her along her way when she most needed guidance.

The Lord does, indeed, work in mysterious ways.

Margaret turns and faces the station. She pulls in a deep, strengthening breath. She grasps the handle of her battered suitcase, the same with which she'd entered the convent as a young girl, so many years ago.

When she pushes open the double glass doors, a blast of cool air hits her, invigorating her senses and her purpose here.

There are several people seated in the line of red plastic chairs in the lobby, talking quietly among themselves.

She meets the eyes of the blonde woman who sits in the middle. She's never met the woman, but there's grief and more than a touch of fear in her eyes. Margaret realizes with a shock that she must be Laura West, David's wife.

David's widow, now.

Margaret's gaze skitters away and she turns to walk toward the officer stationed at the front desk.

"Excuse me," she says quietly.

The woman behind the desk is wearing a crisp uniform and a badge. She's typing something into a computer screen in front of her and looks like she's had better days.

She glances quickly in Margaret's direction, but the telephone rings, pulling her attention back to the desk.

"One moment," she says.

Margaret waits while the officer takes the call.

"No, there's no official statement at this time. A press conference has been scheduled for three o'clock this afternoon, and members of the press are encouraged to attend."

A pause, and two faint lines appear between the officer's brows.

"We have no further information to release. No, I'm afraid not. You're welcome to attend the press conference, and I wish you a good day."

With that, the officer replaces the receiver and pushes a wisp of hair away from her face, the only sign of her frustration.

"Can I help you?" she asks in a harried tone.

"Is Graye Templeton here?" Margaret asks.

The woman cuts her eyes to a large window toward the back of the station almost imperceptibly.

"I'm afraid I can't release that information," the officer says, and it's Margaret's turn to sigh.

She has already spotted Graye in the room behind the window speaking with two other people as clear as day. What's to be accomplished by obfuscation?

"Are those the detectives in charge of David West's murder?" she asks, lowering her voice. She doesn't wish to garner the attention of the other people in the room, particularly Laura West.

"What is this regarding, ma'am?" the officer asks.

"I need to speak to them."

"In regard to the death of Mr. West?"

It was Dr. West, not mister, but she doesn't correct the officer.

"Yes," she whispers, glancing over her shoulder. The trio is still talking, but the eyes of David's wife are on her, as Margaret had sensed they would be.

Quickly, she turns back to face the desk.

"I have some information that could be important."

"Could be?" The officer raises an eyebrow.

"Yes. It's about Graye . . . and it's something I don't think she's going to share willingly. But . . . but it's important."

Margaret has debated this course of action for weeks. Ever since Graye told her Nick had found her. The girl's vehement refusal to put her past up for public display Margaret can understand. They'd worked so hard to shield the child from the aftereffects.

But if she's in danger from that very same past—and given their current predicament, it certainly seems that's true—then it's time for Graye to come clean.

Perhaps that's what she's doing right now, sitting in that closed-off room with people who could protect her, if they knew the truth. Perhaps.

But Margaret knows Graye. She's single-minded in her determination, and Graye is determined to shed the skin of Grace Thacker permanently.

Even if that means withholding pertinent information from the detectives in charge of a murder investigation.

The female officer is studying her closely, probably debating whether she's a crank.

"Ma'am, why don't you have a seat. I'll let the detectives know you're here."

"Thank you," Margaret says, breathing a sigh of relief that causes her shoulders to sag.

She picks up her suitcase and finds her way to a seat as far removed from the other three people as she can manage without making eye contact.

And she waits.

She clasps her hands together in her lap and wishes she'd chosen a chair positioned where she could see Graye in the interview room. But to do so she would have had to sit next to the trio who are also waiting.

Occasionally people enter, but the desk officer swiftly instructs all media to remain outside the station. The town is small, the police force as well. She sees only two other uniformed officers moving about. The lobby remains relatively quiet considering there's been a murder in their jurisdiction just this morning.

Margaret does her best not to call attention to herself, though it's difficult in the small room with so few occupants.

At last the door to the interview room opens and two plainclothes detectives walk out, speaking quietly to each other after the door shuts behind them.

Margaret straightens in her seat. From the corner of her eye, she sees Mrs. West do the same.

The pair notice as well and say a few more words to each other before they turn and head in the direction of the lobby. The female detective stops to speak to the officer behind the desk, and the man walks past Margaret without a glance.

He stops in front of David's wife, who stands to greet him.

"Mrs. West, I'm sorry to have kept you waiting for so long. I know this is a difficult time," he begins in a voice that could soothe an angry bear. "It will just be a few more moments and—"

"Did she do it?" Laura West interrupts. "Did she confess?" The question is asked without malice, but rather a desperate need for understanding.

"The investigation is ongoing. We'd like to interview you next, if—"

Margaret has stood without realizing it. She finds herself walking toward the small group on unsteady feet.

"Graye didn't do this," she says.

All heads turn to Margaret. Even the officer behind the desk stops midsentence and gapes at her.

Perhaps she's spoken more loudly than strictly necessary.

"And you are?" the male detective asks.

"I raised that girl. I know her. She didn't do this," she says, more quietly this time, utilizing all her effort to control her voice.

The man's expression changes, morphs into what Margaret can only describe as sympathy.

"Ma'am, if you'd like to have a seat, my partner and I will be happy to speak with you soon. For the moment, I'm afraid we have more pressing matters to see to."

If he'd spoken in a less gentle tone, Margaret might not have been so inclined to automatically acquiesce, but his voice has a touch of magic. The pied piper of the Rockaway police, and she finds herself backing up and taking a seat again, just as he requested.

Margaret stares down at the hands gripped in her lap as the others turn away, back to the business at hand. She doesn't hear what they're saying, as a cacophony of revolt is taking place in her mind.

They *will* listen to her.

Margaret stands again suddenly, and the female detective at the desk raises a hand to her waist, where her weapon is holstered.

"I know who killed David West," Margaret announces loudly, interrupting the conversations yet again. "And it wasn't the girl in that room."

This time they all gape at her.

At last, she has their full attention.

40

MARGARET

Detective Foster leans back in his chair and runs a hand through the few strands of hair left on his head.

"That's quite a story, Sister," his partner says.

"I'm not lying, Detective."

The man and the woman glance at each other, some silent communication she's not privy to.

"Of course, we'll have to verify this."

"Verify all you want," she says. "But I'm telling you, Graye Templeton isn't real. I should know. I helped create her. Graye Templeton is Grace Thacker. She has her own reasons for being on this island and involved with the Wests' lives, but those reasons, as misguided as they may be, have absolutely nothing to do with any wish to harm them. The very idea that Graye had anything to do with this is, frankly, absurd."

Margaret ignores the doubtful voice that whispers in the back of her mind.

Are you sure about that?

But she is sure. Of course she's sure.

"Nick DiMarco was on that island. He approached Graye. She was frightened of him, and with good reason."

Detective Branson leans forward and places her elbows on the table between them.

"The part I'm having trouble with is why Graye didn't volunteer this information to us herself."

Margaret sighs. "Graye is . . . she's *different*. Special. You have to understand the situation she came to us from. Her picture had been plastered across the news outlets, and she was never going to live down the infamy of what happened to her family.

"Graye was created purely from a need to escape that. Her name was legally changed, and we petitioned the courts to seal all records pertaining to her new name and whereabouts. Graye spent the rest of her childhood closeted away from her past, and I, along with the other sisters, encouraged her to branch out, become someone new."

"That's all well and good, Sister Margaret, but she's being held in a cell on suspicion of murder. Now would seem to be an occasion to tell us the truth."

"You have her in a cell!" Margaret can't hide the shock in her voice or the way her heart sinks into her belly. She didn't see them remove Graye from the interview room, as they asked Margaret to wait in one of the detectives' offices before they began her interview.

She didn't believe Graye even knew she was here, but she had held on to a slim hope that the police had set her free already.

Instead, she's been locked away like a common criminal.

"Yes, Sister," Detective Branson says. "We do."

"But Graye didn't do this! She couldn't have!"

But are you absolutely, completely sure of that?

"Sister Margaret, we will certainly look into the things you've shared here today and take them into consideration, but this investigation is ongoing and our job is not to sort out a fifteen-year-old grudge. Our job is to determine how and why David West was killed."

"But Nick is a murderer! He's a convicted murderer and he was there, on Port Mary, and now someone else is dead!"

"According to the woman suspected of committing the crime," Detective Branson says.

"She didn't kill anyone!" Margaret says, banging the flat of her hand onto the table and causing the female detective to flinch.

"Sister Margaret," Detective Foster says in that smooth tone Margaret's come to loathe. "We have approximately"—he glances at his watch—"forty-six hours left to determine whether we're going to charge Graye Templeton with this crime. If you believe so strongly in her innocence, I suggest you allow us to do our jobs unimpeded. If she is innocent, then the evidence will surely bear that out."

Margaret feels the first stirrings of real panic. She'd thought if she could just explain, then they'd see who was responsible and let Graye go. The answers are staring them in the face, but they've said nothing about releasing Graye. Nothing at all.

"You'll verify what I've told you? You'll find Nick DiMarco?"

"I can assure you we will."

Margaret sits back in her chair, defeat deadening her limbs.

"I'm not a liar," she says in a low voice.

"I have no doubt of that, Sister. But unfortunately, what we believe to be true doesn't always line up with the facts at hand."

The two detectives rise.

"But thank you for coming in."

41

BRANSON

Branson leans back against the wall in the hallway as Foster walks the nun out of the station.

She pushes her hands deep into her pockets as a frown creases her face.

What the hell has landed in our laps?

"Whew," Foster says quietly when he returns.

Mrs. West is still waiting in the lobby. Branson can see her around the edge of Foster's hulking form. The woman looks worse with every passing hour.

"We need to get the wife in, then send her home. She looks like she's about to fall out of that chair. And I give it about twenty more minutes before Caron's wife loses her shit and calls in a fleet of attorneys."

Foster glances back over his shoulder. "Yeah. I just need a second to absorb that last one. Jesus, the Thacker case. I guess that was before your time."

"I think I was in junior high, but I vaguely remember something about it. Made a big splash nationally."

"The little girl, mostly," Foster says. "She looked so lost and sad. Tugged on every last one of America's heartstrings. Not surprised she had to go into hiding to get out from underneath that kind of notoriety."

Branson glances down the hallway toward the cells. There are three, and Graye Templeton's is the only one occupied after they let old Billy Cobb go home this morning once he'd sobered up.

Nobody had time to mess around with him today.

"Why don't you call and check in with the crime lab," she says. "I'll have Graham start digging up everything he can find on the Thacker case, then we've got to get Laura West in to interview."

"While he's at it, have Graham track down Nick DiMarco."

Branson lifts a brow. "You know that's probably wishful thinking on the nun's part, right?"

"I know." He shakes his head. "But we've got to check. If DiMarco was on Port Mary, that throws a great big kink into what was looking like a pretty solid case."

"A solid case against Grace Thacker, America's sad little sweetheart?"

Foster takes a deep breath and blows it out in a low whistle. "Geez, Branson. I should have gone fishing today."

"You and me both."

"Bad enough, a dead author on our hands, but this ices the damn cake. I don't want to be surprised again. We need everything there is to know about this woman. Every rock kicked over, no matter what name she's been using. Tell Graham his overtime and vacation depend on it."

"The press are gonna go wild over this, you know."

"Branson, right now, the press is the least of my concerns. Get Graham busy kicking rocks, and I'll meet you in the interview room with Mrs. West in ten."

42

LAURA

Laura fights back the dizziness that threatens to overwhelm her and focuses on the two detectives across the table.

She's seated in the same chair Graye was.

Do the detectives see her as a suspect as well? It's a question that won't leave her in peace.

"Mrs. West, can you take us through the events of last night please."

She nods. Detective Foster doesn't sound like any policeman she's ever seen portrayed in movies or television. Even books tend toward brash, confrontational murder cops. This man reminds her of her father's best friend, Sal, who'd kept butterscotch in his pockets for her each time he visited.

"Well, there was the mystery dinner, of course. Where David made a scene."

The two detectives nod, but say nothing.

"I suppose Hugo's told you all about that," she says, ruffled under their scrutiny.

"Can you tell us what happened after?" Detective Branson asks.

"Graye walked me home. I'd decided enough was enough. I mean, there's only so much a woman can be expected to put up with, and

David had crossed that line so many times. The fight with Hugo, in front of all those people. It was the last straw."

"What time was this?"

"It was late. The dinner ended around ten, I guess. We probably got home about ten thirty or ten forty-five. I'm sorry, I didn't look at my watch."

"Did Miss Templeton enter your home with you?"

"No, I left her outside the door. I assume she went to the guesthouse."

"And what happened then?"

She sighs. This was all so personal.

"David was passed out. At least, I thought he was. I expected him to be. I was planning to pack his bags and have them ready for him when he woke up the next day."

"And did you? Pack his bags?"

"I started to. But . . ."

Laura bites her lip, needing to feel the pain to keep her focused on their questions.

"But he woke up. Or maybe he was never asleep, I don't know. He would closet himself in his office a lot, then come out drunker than he'd gone in. I'd been home for a while by that time. An hour, maybe two? I just assumed he'd be out for the night, considering the state he'd been in at the dinner."

She shakes her head, remembering the rage on David's face when he'd seen what she was doing.

She'd never seen him so angry.

"He . . . he wasn't happy," she finishes weakly.

Unconsciously, she crosses her arms around herself, rubbing the bruises where David had grabbed her.

She wouldn't repeat the vile things he'd said to her. She'd never repeat those words to anyone.

"There was a confrontation?"

She looks away, down at the table, where she picks at one of her nails.

"He was angry, and he went a little crazy, throwing things. Breaking them. We were screaming at each other."

"Did things get physical at any point between you?"

But she won't share that humiliation either. Laura has always sympathized with women who've suffered physical abuse at the hands of their partner, but from a semidetached, safe distance. She's never imagined the sheer terror of looking into the eyes of a person you loved, a person who'd professed to love you back, and wondering at the core of your soul if you were going to survive the night.

She'd had no idea. But she does now.

"No, not exactly," she lies and takes a deep breath. "I'd sworn to myself I wouldn't be the one who left. It's my home, and it was my grandmother's home before that. David could go. I was staying. But that all changed, when—"

The lump that forms in her throat makes it impossible to push words past.

She fights another wave of dizziness, along with a pain in her heart.

The detectives wait while she gathers herself.

"That all changed when I began to bleed."

Detective Foster goes still, and his partner sits up straighter in her chair, peering at her.

"You were bleeding?"

"Yes," she whispers. "I'm . . . at least, I *was*, pregnant. For a little while."

Their surprise is evident, and Laura wonders if this nightmare will ever end.

"I'm not anymore."

"Mrs. West," Detective Branson says, "I'm sorry. Are you telling me that you miscarried last night? Less than twenty-four hours ago?"

"Yes, Detective. That's exactly what I'm telling you."

There's a moment of silence for that to soak in before Detective Foster speaks again.

"Mrs. West, I'm no expert, but shouldn't you be under the care of a doctor?"

"I am," she says. "I saw a doctor last night, and that's where I'm headed back to when I leave here. Dr. Lawson is an old friend of my family and she lives on Port Mary as well. Just two doors away. I went to her last night when I realized what was happening. That's where I spent the remainder of the night. But David was alive when I left him, I swear to you."

Branson doesn't bother to hide her confusion as she shakes her head.

"I'm sorry, can we back up just a little? You said you were arguing with your husband, then began to miscarry. Out of the blue?"

If being knocked down with a suitcase and kicked repeatedly in the stomach could be considered out of the blue, Laura thinks, numb now to the horror of the night before.

She stares at the woman, but the officer is young and Laura can guess she's never been forced into such a vulnerable state. She herself wouldn't have understood yesterday.

She hopes this woman never learns firsthand that terror.

"That's correct."

"Mrs. West," Detective Foster says. "You frankly don't look well. Would you like to postpone this interview and seek medical attention?"

Bless him. She wonders if he keeps butterscotch in his pockets too.

"No," she says. "I'd like to get this over with, if that's okay."

"If that's what you'd prefer," he says slowly, but his tone of voice implies he's not happy with her.

Well, he can stand in line.

"So once you realized you were bleeding, what did you do then?" Detective Branson asks.

"I left, like I said."

It was true. She had. She simply skips over the part where she's begging David to stop, screaming that he's killing their child. The part where she flees her home, running from the horror story their marriage has become.

Something had changed in David. She'd been aware of his gradual descent, aided and abetted by the alcohol he'd come to depend on. She'd known he'd eventually hit rock bottom, but never expected to find a monster waiting there.

"And you went to your neighbor's house." The detective consults her notes. "Dr. Lawson?"

"That's correct."

"And what time was this?"

"I'm sorry, it didn't occur to me to check the time," she says, unable to keep the strain out of her voice. "Dr. Lawson may know."

"How did you get there?" Detective Branson asks.

"I walked."

"I'm sorry, you walked?" The woman is struggling with Laura's story, and strangely she's stumbling over the parts that are completely true. She had walked.

"Yes."

"You're bleeding from a miscarriage, and you walked two doors away to your neighbor's house?"

"That's what I said."

"Why didn't you call 911?" the detective asks, incredulous.

Laura sighs. "Because Port Mary is an island. An ambulance requires the ferry, which doesn't run in the middle of the night, or a helicopter."

"Are you telling me you didn't dial 911 because you didn't want to inconvenience emergency services?"

"Look, Detective," Laura says. "You may find this difficult to believe, but unless you've ever been in that situation, I'd appreciate it if you'd refrain from judgment."

The woman has the grace to look slightly chastised, but still not satisfied with Laura's answers.

"I was bleeding. Not a little blood, but a lot of blood. I knew what that meant. It was too early in the pregnancy to lose that kind of blood and still be . . . viable." Laura nearly chokes on the last word. Such a clinical, cold-blooded word for the end of a life before it even had a chance to begin.

"Even if I'd called 911 and they'd sent a chopper out immediately, there was no chance I was still pregnant. I knew it in my heart. In my bones.

"So, yes, I walked to my friend's house. I walked to the house of a doctor and a woman who's known me since childhood. A woman who's bandaged my knees and nursed me when I was sick and comforted me when I was in pain. A woman whose very presence reminds me of my grandmother, whom I would give everything I have just for the chance to hug one more time."

Tears are forming and Laura doesn't bother to try and stop them. She's earned every one of those damn tears. Let them fall.

"I walked to Dr. Lawson's house, and I did it slowly, crying every step of the way. A funeral procession of one for a baby I was never going to hold, or kiss, or watch grow into a unique little person. But that doesn't mean I didn't love her, and it doesn't mean I didn't mourn her."

Laura doesn't know when her lost child became a *her*, but it feels right. It feels true.

The detectives leave a moment of silence after she finishes speaking—out of respect, Laura supposes. But they are still detectives.

"Why didn't you knock on your assistant's door?" Detective Branson asks finally. "She was closer, wasn't she?"

Laura sighs.

"I did, actually. She didn't answer."

"Did you see or notice anyone else along the walk? Can anyone confirm that?"

"I have no idea," Laura says, out of patience. "I was too upset to notice. Look, I've answered your questions to the best of my ability. Why exactly are you making me feel like a suspect? I've lost my child. I've lost my husband. When I left my home, David was drunk, he was angry, but he was alive.

"Speak to Dr. Lawson, if you don't believe me. Speak to Rachel Caron. They'll both confirm what I'm saying."

Detective Foster tilts his head. "Where does Mrs. Caron come into this?" he asks.

"I called her. She and Hugo were staying at the hotel for the retreat, and she came to be with me."

Detective Branson's pen stalls over her notepad, where she's been jotting down every personal detail Laura's been forced to reveal.

"You called a woman whose husband you were purported to be having an affair with?" she asks.

"I wasn't having an affair! Hugo is a friend, nothing more. Rachel knew that. She was my friend first. For God's sake, I was the one who introduced them."

Branson raises her eyebrows but points her gaze back in the direction of her notepad as she continues to take notes.

"So you called Mrs. Caron in the middle of the night?" Detective Foster gently prods, ignoring his partner's clearly dubious opinion of Laura's answers.

"She came right away. She stayed with me. I have several witnesses who can verify where I was at the time David was killed."

"And how would you know what time Mr. West was killed?" Branson asks.

Laura's nerves are at a breaking point.

"Well, obviously, I don't know the exact time, but if he was alive when I left him and dead by the time police swarmed my house the next morning, then it's not much of a leap to say I have an alibi for the hours in between."

The young detective simply stares at her.

"You were at Dr. Lawson's home until late this morning?" Detective Foster asks.

Laura nods. "We heard the commotion," she says, in a calmer tone of voice. It doesn't take a genius to realize the two detectives are playing off each other. The age-old good cop/bad cop routine, but Laura can see why. It's surprisingly effective, even when you can see the manipulation for what it is.

"Dr. Lawson walked outside to see what the fuss was about. When she told me, I rushed over to the house, but there were people in white coverall suits going in and out of my home."

"Crime scene technicians?" he asks.

"I suppose. I'm afraid I became a little hysterical. That's when I realized David had been . . . that David was . . . dead."

"And you never left Dr. Lawson's house, from the time you arrived until that moment?" Detective Branson asks.

"That's what I've said."

Branson sets down her pen and leans back in her chair. "Then can you explain to me, Mrs. West, why a blonde woman matching your description was seen walking on the beach between Dr. Lawson's house and your own near dawn this morning?"

Laura's breath stops, but only for a moment. A miniscule moment that the detective couldn't possibly notice.

"It wasn't me."

The moment of silence stretches long and tight between them.

"You're sure of that?"

"Port Mary may be a small place, Detective, but somehow I doubt I'm the only blonde on the island."

Detective Foster gives her a warm smile. For the life of her, Laura has no idea if it's sincere or if he's simply embodying his good cop role.

"I think that's all for now, Mrs. West," he says and she finds she doesn't care which it is. "You're free to go, but we have to ask you not to leave the area."

Laura nods, her relief immense.

She stands, too quickly, and the dizziness that's remained waiting on the sidelines seizes the opportunity and overtakes her.

Laura falls to the ground.

"Goddammit," she hears Foster say. "Branson, get an ambulance," he shouts, before everything goes blessedly dark.

43

BRANSON

"It's leaked, boss," Graham says, and Branson marvels at his ability to state the obvious. "They've figured out who the girl is."

The phone is ringing practically nonstop, and the crowd of reporters they've banished to the parking lot is growing by the minute.

Apparently, a dead author coupled with the resurrection of "America's sad little sweetheart," as Branson has come to think of their guest, is an entirely new level of newsworthy.

The ambulance has come and gone, whisking Laura West away to Cresswell Memorial Hospital, once it navigated the news crews parked outside.

Branson prays they haven't left themselves open for a lawsuit. Even with Mrs. West on record denying she needed to stop the interview, it had been plain to see that the woman wasn't well.

But that didn't mean she was telling the truth.

"What did you think of her story?" Branson asks her partner.

Foster balances on the edge of his desk. His eyelids are droopy, and anyone else might think he were about to nod off.

"Something's off there," he says slowly.

Branson can't hold back the tiny rush of satisfaction at those words. She'd been afraid she was the only one to see it.

"She's lying about something," Branson says.

"The question is what. And does it make her a killer?"

"So what do we do now?"

Foster picks up a pencil and taps it on the desk. She's worked with him long enough to patiently wait him out.

"The crime lab in Cresswell says they need more time. Graham, stay on them. Make sure this is their number-one priority. And call Dr. Lawson. Confirm Laura West's story. And while you're at it, get me a list of attendees present at this mystery retreat too. They're probably scattered all over the country by now."

He glances over and meets his partner's eyes, then sets the pencil down and stands up from the desk. "You and I need to find Nick DiMarco."

"I can maybe help with that," Graham says.

"Yeah? You find an address for him yet?"

"Not exactly. He's waiting in the lobby."

Branson rolls her eyes. "Think you could have mentioned that a little sooner, Graham?"

He shrugs.

"Looks like it's our lucky day, Branson," Foster says. "Let's go have a chat with a murderer."

◆ ◆ ◆

Branson peers at the man sitting calmly in the seat across from them.

Of all the interviews they've done today, Nick DiMarco, a convicted killer, is the subject most at ease. At least, that's the impression he gives off.

In his early thirties, he's casually dressed in linen pants and a light-blue button-down shirt, but his shoes are expensive, and no doubt his haircut as well.

244

Not handsome, exactly. Not in any way that would stand out in a crowd, but not unattractive either.

Nick DiMarco blends in. A man you'd expect to see working in the tech industry, or maybe an engineering field.

Not a man you'd expect to see behind bars.

"I appreciate you coming to us, Mr. DiMarco," Foster says. "Saves us the trouble of tracking you down."

"When I saw the news this morning, I had a feeling you'd want to speak to me. I've learned it's easier to face these complications head-on."

"Complications?" Branson's brows lift. "Mr. DiMarco, a man is dead. I'd call that more than a complication."

He shrugs. Branson decides she doesn't like him.

"You must have been nearby if you were able to travel here in a matter of hours."

"I was in Houston," he says. "A work conference."

"And what work would that be?"

"I'm a web-based graphic designer."

She'd called that one.

"Fancy," she says, unable to keep the snideness out of her voice. He probably made three times her salary. Or more, judging from those shoes.

"I was always interested in computers and art, and I was lucky enough to be housed in a facility that had training programs. I've worked very hard since my release to become a contributing member of society. No easy feat for a felon."

"My heart bleeds for you," Branson sneers.

Foster doesn't blink at her confrontational tone. They play their roles well, and he either doesn't realize her distaste is real or, more likely, doesn't care.

DiMarco doesn't blink either. "I was a young man who committed a terrible crime. I've paid the debt society demanded in return for that."

"Nice words. Do you suppose they're much comfort to Grace Thacker?"

"I don't suppose so, no. Perhaps you could tell me what exactly I can do to make that up to her?"

Branson definitely doesn't like him.

"Is that what you were attempting to do by tracking her down on Port Mary? Make things up to her?" Foster asks mildly.

DiMarco tilts his head and studies Foster, and Branson has the impression she's been dismissed.

"In a way," he says.

"So you admit you were present on the island?" she pushes.

"Yes. Why else would I be here?"

"And did you speak to her directly?"

"I did. She was frightened to see me. Which is to be expected, I suppose."

"Did you interact with David West as well?" Foster asks.

DiMarco shakes his head. "Never met the man."

"It's a small island. You never passed him on the beach or ran into him at the hotel bar?"

"Not that I'm aware of."

"Mr. DiMarco," Branson says, "I can't help feeling you're yanking our chain. I'm going to need you to explain *exactly* what you were doing on that island, and how you discovered Miss Templeton was residing there. Unless you're going to try and sell me on the highly unlikely probability that it was a coincidence—and I should warn you, that's one line I'm not going to swallow."

DiMarco frowns and sits back in his chair. "I wouldn't dare insult your intelligence, Detective."

And that is just about enough.

"*Why* did you follow Graye Templeton to Port Mary, Mr. DiMarco?"

"I wanted to check on her," he says. "Make amends, if I could."

"You wanted to mend fences? After what you did?" Does he seriously expect them to buy this steaming pile he's shoveling?

"I'm trying to rebuild my life. *Am* rebuilding my life. I'm a different person now."

"Why did you think she'd have any interest in seeing you again?" Foster asks.

"I knew she wouldn't. Of course she wouldn't."

"Then why come?"

DiMarco sighs and pulls his chair closer to the table, leaning his elbows on it.

"I was worried about her," he says, glancing up and meeting their eyes in turn. He really is trying to convince them.

"Worried?" Branson says. "She was responsible for putting you in jail. She took your freedom from you, and you were worried about her?"

DiMarco leans back again and sighs. They're beginning to rattle him.

"Grace was a child," he says. "A child who didn't have an easy life."

"You're trying to tell me that, given your conviction, given the years you spent locked up, given the part Graye played in that, you tracked her down, traveled all the way to Port Mary, and sought her out because you were *concerned* about her?"

He glares at her. "Look, I've served my time. I don't have to explain myself to you."

Branson leans in and waits for him to meet her eyes. "Maybe you don't understand the gravity of the situation, Mr. DiMarco. We've got a dead man. We've got a convicted killer. It doesn't take much to draw a big black line from one of those to the other."

Nick DiMarco runs his hand through his expensive haircut and appears to be struggling to decide what to say.

"Look, I came to you. I came to you because there are things you need to know."

"Oh yeah? Like what?"

"I'm not the one with reason to hate Grace."

Branson knows what time it is. They all do it, everyone suspected of a crime. A time comes when they each, to a man, try to deflect suspicion onto someone else.

"And is this the part where you tell us who really did it?" Branson asks.

Disgust passes briefly over DiMarco's face, and she's almost amused that the man guilty of murder has a problem with her manners.

"Look," he says, after he's schooled his features back into an expression of apathy. "If you've decided to arrest me, go ahead. I'm not concerned. I told you already, I've never met David West. There will be no evidence that even remotely ties me to his death, because I've never set foot in his home.

"I was in Houston last night, trying to decide if I should fly home and wash my hands of this mess or come back and try one more time.

"There are witnesses that saw me there. Hotel employees, a woman I talked with for an hour or two at the bar. I had a pizza delivered. I assure you, I wasn't on that island last night.

"If you're planning to try and take the easy way and put me in the frame for David West's murder, you should know, science is not going to back you up."

There's a moment of silence as his words settle.

"Okay, then, Mr. DiMarco," Foster says. "I'll play along. Who do you believe has more reason to hate Grace than you?"

DiMarco looks at Foster like the answer should be obvious.

"The person who told me where to find her, Detective. That's who you need to talk to."

"And that would be?" Branson asks.

"Alexis Thacker, of course. Her sister."

44

LAURA

Laura bites her lip and watches Dr. Sukawala absorb her strange request.

"Mrs. West, I'm not sure I understand what you're asking. You want me to release to the Rockaway Police—"

"*If* they call and ask you," Laura interjects. "Although I'm guessing they will."

"Okay." Dr. Sukawala's eyes cut over the top of her glasses and meet Laura's own. "*If* the police call and ask, you want to give your permission to release a partial account of your medical records? Is that correct?"

"Yes," Laura says, keeping her voice low. Rachel has gone to the hospital cafeteria for coffee, but she'll be returning at any moment. Laura doesn't wish to deal with her friend's reaction any more than she wants to deal with the reaction of the police.

Rachel knows only that Laura lost her baby. She doesn't know the role David played in that loss any more than the police do.

"They'll want to confirm that I was pregnant and that I suffered a miscarriage last night. My husband, he . . . he died last night, and there's an investigation, and . . . it's all very complicated, but my blood is going to be found in our house, which is now a crime scene, and I need them to know I'm not lying."

The doctor's eyes narrow.

"I had nothing to do with my husband's death, Doctor, but the thing is . . . if they discover the miscarriage was brought on by trauma to my midsection—"

"Rather severe trauma, I must say," Dr. Sukawala says softly.

A woman has no secrets from her obstetrician.

"They'll have questions. Personal questions I'm not comfortable answering unless I have to. Questions that have nothing to do with their investigation, though that won't stop them from prying."

Dr. Sukawala removes her glasses slowly and folds them before placing them in her pocket.

"Mrs. West, you do understand the police could get a warrant for your full medical records, in which case, I'd be compelled to release them?"

"Yes, I do, but there's no reason for them to do that."

The purse of the doctor's lips and the creases in her forehead give away her opinion of the situation.

"I am bound by the laws regarding medical confidentiality," she says. "If the police come to me with a warrant, I will do nothing to circumvent those laws."

"Of course, Doctor. I would never ask you to do that."

There's a pause, and Laura waits uncomfortably for whatever the doctor might say next.

"But if I receive a call from the police in search of confirmation that you've suffered a miscarriage, *and* I have your signed, written permission to confirm that information, I will do so."

Laura draws in a huge breath of relief and closes her eyes, letting her head fall back into the pillow propped behind her.

"I know nothing about the death of husbands, Mrs. West. What I know is women's bodies. Until I'm told otherwise by a court of law, your body is your business."

Laura gives her a small, grateful smile as tears warm the corners of her eyes.

"Thank you, Doctor," she says.

The door to her hospital room opens and Rachel is back with coffee. Her attention is trained on the phone in her hand.

"Laura, you're not going to believe this," she says, glancing up, her eyes wide.

Laura's heart drops. She can't take anything else. Please, nothing else.

But Rachel doesn't see the anxiety that settles on her, or the fear that freezes her limbs.

"Graye Templeton isn't really Graye Templeton," Rachel says.

Laura shakes her head, unable to unravel that cryptic statement.

"What does that mean?" she asks.

"That's what it says." Rachel holds up her phone, although she's too far away for Laura to make out what she's reading.

"You're not making any sense. Let me see that."

Rachel closes the distance between them and hands over her phone before she drops down into the chair by Laura's hospital bed with an inappropriately satisfied smirk on her face.

"I told you there was something strange about that girl, didn't I?"

45

BRANSON

Branson grimaces as the cold, stale coffee hits her tongue.

She places the cup in the microwave. Bad coffee she can live with, but bad, cold coffee is one insult too many.

Foster's on the phone with the crime lab again, trying to cajole them into sending a preliminary report. He has better luck at those sorts of things than she does.

Branson doesn't ask as nicely.

"Graham, did you call and check on Laura West?" she asks the sergeant.

"Yeah. They say she's stable but referred us to her doctor for any more questions."

"You have the doc's number?"

"Right here," he says, pulling a scrap of paper from beneath a growing pile. Graham's desk drives her crazy. How he can work in the middle of such a disorganized heap is beyond her comprehension.

She moves to her own desk, more welcoming with its clear surface and black-and-white desk calendar. She picks up the receiver of the phone and begins to dial the number Graham has jotted down for Dr. Tara Sukawala.

Mrs. West's story doesn't add up.

"Psst," Foster says, catching her attention. He covers the receiver of his phone with one hand and tells her in a low voice, "You've got to hear this."

Branson sets down the receiver in her hand. Mrs. West will have to wait.

"Yeah, okay. Thanks, Sam," Foster says into the phone. "I owe you one. Just fax that over if you don't mind. I'll be waiting on it."

Foster hangs up and hauls his bulk out of his chair. He rises to stand next to the fax machine, then turns to face Branson, a spark shining in his eyes.

"They have something?" she asks. She knows they do, though, by the way her partner is leaning backward against the counter, one foot crossed over another with his hands shoved into his pockets.

She wouldn't be surprised if he suddenly started whistling.

"You could say that," he says with a slow nod.

She stares, but he apparently doesn't intend to say anything more.

"Spit it out then," Branson says. She's hungry. She's irritated, and she's tired of this case already.

The fax machine starts to make that god-awful noise she hates. Luckily, she doesn't have to hear it often. Nearly everyone communicates via email these days.

Sheets of paper begin to slowly roll out, and Foster picks them up, scanning them one by one without speaking. She glances at Graham so they can roll their eyes at Foster together, but he's on another phone call.

Branson's little brother, Randy, is thirteen. He thinks he wants to be a cop when he grows up, just like her. She doesn't have the heart to tell him how much of the job is paperwork and telephone calls.

She takes appreciation where she can get it, though, even if it's from a preteen with questionable hygiene.

"Well?" she says, her patience at a breaking point.

"This is just preliminary," Foster says.

"Yeah, yeah." Branson twirls her hand in the air. "Get on with it."

"First of all, they've identified certain areas of blood at the scene that testing indicates is most likely to be from the loss of a pregnancy." He glances up and meets her eyes. "That backs up Laura West's story," he says, almost apologetically.

"Doesn't mean she's not lying about something else." She's not ready to let Mrs. West off the hook just yet.

"There's more. They've lifted prints from the scene. They're still working on it, but they've run them through the system."

"They had a hit," Branson says, her face lighting up. She'd love to put this case to rest and go back to DUIs and petty vandalisms.

Foster nods. "But this is where it gets weird. They matched on a partial lifted from an unsolved in Ithaca, New York."

Branson stands up, frowning.

"Let me see that." She takes the report from his hand and scans the information.

"Wait a second," Graham says. "I've got a call here. Ithaca." He turns back to his desk and starts rifling through the mess, eventually coming up with another scrap of paper and holding it up in the air.

"Yeah, Ithaca," he says. "A woman named Eileen Ellis. Says she knows Templeton."

Branson waits, but Graham doesn't say any more.

"Is that it?" she asks. "She say anything else?"

Graham shrugs. "Just that we must have made a mistake. Says the girl she knows wouldn't do anything like this. Apparently, she reads to the elderly twice a week at the old folks' home." Graham glances at the scrap of paper he'd jotted notes on. "Crestview House."

Branson's eyes shoot up. "You said Crestview House?"

"Yeah."

She holds the report up to Foster and taps an index finger on the middle of the page. "We've got her."

Foster nods slowly. His excitement has faded as her own has grown.

"America's sweetheart," he says with a shake of his head.

"Oh, and I tracked down Alexis Thacker like you asked," Graham says. "She's in Missouri, according to her parole officer. Hasn't missed a check-in since her release."

Foster stares down at the report in his hand, as if he's willing it to say something different.

"Doesn't look like the sister had anything to do with this, boss," the sergeant adds.

Foster shakes his head again. "No, Graham. I don't think she did. According to this, I'd say there's no question who killed David West. Between the science and the 911 recording, this case is a slam dunk."

"Thank God," Branson says.

"Yeah," Foster agrees.

He sets the report on the corner of Branson's desk and sighs.

She doesn't miss the way his shoulders sag as he shuffles out of the room.

46

MARGARET

Margaret studies Graye, searching for a sign, the barest hint, that the girl understands the precariousness of her situation.

But Graye looks . . . serene.

It boggles her mind. In spite of the orange jumpsuit provided by the State of Texas, which washes out her already colorless features, in spite of her unkempt hair and ragged nails, Graye appears calm. At peace.

It brings to mind the bearing of the young girls who choose the path of the church. There are fewer these days than there used to be, but to a person, there is a contentment immediately following their vows. Whatever internal strife and indecision might have plagued them up to that moment is released. They live, for a time at least, secure in the knowledge that there is a power greater than themselves they've embraced, and who has embraced them in return.

It doesn't last. The deprivations of monastic life are difficult to adjust to, and in most cases, there will be a time, usually within the first few months, when the permanence of their choices will bring about a quiet storm of regret.

Some weather the storm. Some do not.

But Graye isn't there yet, and Margaret can't quiet the fear that awakens inside of her at the girl's placid, accepting features.

"Graye," she says slowly. "I've spoken with an attorney who's willing to take on your case pro bono."

The girl tilts her head and pulls her gaze back to Margaret from where it had been wandering around the room.

"That's good, then," she says.

"She's going to come by to meet you tomorrow, and together you can decide how best to move forward."

"Okay."

Margaret frowns.

"Graye, do you understand what's happening?"

"Yes, Sister," Graye says. "Of course." She bestows a small smile on Margaret.

"You've been charged with the murder of David West, Graye. The New York district attorney is also going to charge you with the murder of Inez Jeffries."

Graye nods. "Okay."

Margaret shakes her head and grips the edge of the table. If she could, she'd grab the girl by the shoulders, shake her.

"Graye, who is Inez Jeffries?"

At last, this solicits a reaction. Graye's face darkens slightly.

"Nursing isn't for everyone, Sister Margaret," Graye says. "Some people just don't have the temperament for it."

Silently, Margaret sucks in a breath, and the fear roars in her ears.

"Graye," Margaret says quietly, fighting to keep her voice calm. She shouldn't ask the question. She knows she shouldn't. The answers have the potential to destroy her.

"Graye, did you kill David West?"

Again, the child tilts her head and considers the answer. Again, Margaret's breath stalls, and the only thing that moves is her heart, pumping blood fiercely through her veins.

"Maybe," Graye says. "I'm not really sure."

Margaret swallows back the dry, hot lump in her throat, and seizes on that seed of doubt. If there's any chance, any chance at all, that this isn't true, Margaret is duty bound, both to Graye and to God, to forge ahead.

"There was a phone call. The morning of the . . . the murder." She still had difficulty wrapping her tongue around that word. "It came from your phone, Graye."

Graye considers this.

"I don't know, Sister. I don't think so," she says with a shake of her head.

"Graye, you confessed to killing him."

"Did I? I don't remember that. I couldn't find my phone. I looked for it, though. I did."

Tears are just below the surface, but Margaret has no time to spare for them and ruthlessly pushes them back.

"It was found at the West home. Graye, it had your fingerprints on it."

Graye mulls this over, then maddeningly, she shrugs.

"Maybe. If that's what they say."

"No, Graye!" Margaret says, shocking herself and Graye with the volume of her words. The girl flinches and focuses her gaze on Margaret's face.

For the first time, she appears just the slightest bit frightened.

"The knife," Margaret says, forcing her volume lower. "They're saying the knife came from the guesthouse. That it also had your fingerprints on it."

Graye stares into her eyes.

"Yes," she says quietly. "Yes, the knife. But . . . I didn't . . ." She trails off and stares upward at a spot behind Margaret's head again. "At least, I don't think I . . ."

"You need to tell me what happened, Graye. If you don't tell me the truth, I can't help you."

At last, the girl's gaze comes back to Margaret.

"It wasn't part of the plan, Sister. I swear."

Margaret had believed her heart couldn't possibly fear more, but those words open a chasm at her feet.

"What plan, Graye?" she whispers.

Graye shakes her head. "It wasn't supposed to be this way."

"Graye, you need to tell me. Tell me what you've done."

Later, when Margaret leaves the building, a lifetime will have passed. She's white-faced as she stumbles to the driver's side of the car she's rented. She lays her head against the steering wheel and gives in to the devastation.

Before she left, Graye made a request.

"I have some money in my bank account, Sister," she'd said, her eyes brightening. "Could you arrange for it to be put into a commissary account for me?"

"Okay," Margaret replied, her voice deadened with grief.

"Thank you." Graye smiled, unaware of Margaret's pain. "There are notebooks and pencils here we can buy."

Margaret has spent fifteen years trying to protect Grace. Trying, and failing.

No one can protect Grace from herself.

47

LAURA

Laura's nerves sing in chorus with the doorbell.

She's not sure she's made the right decision and was up late into the night debating all the ways she could call this off. But it's too late to back out now.

On soft feet, she pads to the door and opens it slowly to find a woman she's never spoken to directly waiting for her.

"Sister Margaret," she says.

The woman is thin and appears to have aged in the last year, since that day she and Laura sat in a police station lobby and waited, united by nothing except uncertainty.

"Thank you for agreeing to speak with me, Mrs. West," her visitor says quietly. "I'd have understood if you'd refused."

"It's just Laura," she says as she steps back and opens the door wide for her guest to enter.

"And please, call me Margaret," the woman says. "I'm no longer a member of the order."

Laura's brows rise. "That's quite a big decision."

Margaret nods. "Yes. The last year has brought many challenges, both inside myself and out. Redefining my relationship with the Lord has been a part of it."

Laura's not sure what to say to that. "Can I get you something to drink?"

Margaret stands awkwardly in the center of Laura's living room, redecorated in the last year, to a style more reminiscent of the original design.

"Coffee, tea?"

"Water is fine, if it's not an imposition."

"Of course. Why don't you have a seat?"

Laura steps into the kitchen and takes the opportunity to pull in a deep, shaky breath. Her hands tremble only slightly as she places ice in two glasses and pours water over the top.

By the time she rejoins Margaret, sitting upright along the edge of the sofa, Laura has schooled her features into a mask of false serenity.

As for Margaret, she's obviously ill at ease. Laura wonders if she's aware that this is the room David died in. Most likely, she is.

It was difficult for Laura as well, at first.

She didn't even want to enter the house after it happened, preferring to stay in Dr. Lawson's spare room. The Carons had graciously offered to let her stay with them as long as she liked, but Dr. Lawson was practically family.

Her parents had come to Port Mary as well. Her mother, in fact, had overseen the renovation of the carriage house. After they received the go-ahead from the police, of course.

"Mama, I don't know if I can go back," she said, hoping she'd understand.

"In that case, it will still need to be done for when you decide to put it on the market."

The fact that her mother hadn't balked at the potential sale of her family home had gone a long way to assuaging Laura's concerns.

When she'd hesitantly walked through the door the first time, months after David's death, she expected chills. She expected fear. But her mother had a warm and welcoming touch. The room was the way Laura remembered it from the time her grandmother was alive.

There was even a quilt thrown over the back of the sofa that Laura recognized from her parents' home in New York. It had been a gift from her grandmother to her mother, hand stitched with care, given at a time when Lisette was beginning a new chapter in her life, far from home.

"No matter where you go, child," she could remember her grandmother's voice saying, "you carry home with you."

Instead of fear, she'd felt her grandmother's arms surround her. She'd felt love.

She'd never again discussed selling the house.

Her family was there to support her, no matter what, and she couldn't be more grateful for that.

But this woman isn't Laura's family. She's Graye's.

"I admit, I was surprised to get your message," she says. "I'm not exactly sure what I can do to help you, Margaret."

The ex-nun takes a long sip from her glass and positions a coaster perfectly squared with the corner of the coffee table before setting her glass down.

She clears her throat and Laura waits.

"Have you ever carried the weight of something so big it affected everything that came after?" Margaret stares intently at Laura, gauging her reaction. "Like a car with one low tire, you drift. Without even realizing it. And if you're not careful, you're heading straight for the side of a cliff, so you jerk the wheel, overcompensating. And sometimes you get lucky and manage to get the wheels back between the lines. Keep moving forward."

Margaret glances down at the hands clasped in her lap, then up toward the windows with a view of the beach. Everywhere but Laura's eyes.

"But it can't last," she continues softly. "One too many overcorrections and you flip the car, tumbling end over end."

She trails off and stares at some place in the distance, some place Laura can't see. Nor does she want to.

"Sister Margaret, I'm sorry. I don't understand."

Margaret sighs and turns her gaze back to Laura, her eyes clearing to a sharp focus.

"I know, and I'm the one who should be apologizing. I've intruded upon you and now I'm talking in riddles. There are things you have a right to know, Mrs. West. Some of them will come out at the trial, and there's nothing I can do about that, but I can at least give you the time and space to absorb them privately."

Laura sits up straighter. "What are you talking about?"

"I need to tell you a story. A story about a girl."

Without warning, Laura hears an echo of her mother's voice in her mind. *"Everybody's got a story, Laura. Listen with an open heart, and you'll be a better person for it."*

Unconsciously, she picks up her glass of water and scoots farther back into the sofa. She tucks her legs beneath her, entranced by the simple words.

"The girl was a sad girl, and lonely. She was the youngest of two sisters and lived in a home that held little love or kindness.

"One day, when the girl was still young, but not so young as she had been, she fell in love with a boy. A boy with dreams too big for the small town they'd grown up in."

Margaret locks eyes with her and Laura can't look away.

"When the summer was through, he left to go back to college, and the girl was heartbroken. She never told him she was pregnant."

Laura's heart breaks a little. It's an age-old tale, told by many and in many ways, but the unfairness of it never lessens.

"Graye had a child?" she asks quietly.

Margaret never looks away. "No, dear. The girl was me."

Laura's mouth falls open, but Margaret's not through.

"The baby was given to my older sister to raise. She already had a child of her own. I didn't want to do it, but I had little choice. The only thing my daughter had of me was the name I'd given her before my mother took her from my arms. Grace."

Laura shakes her head. The dots are beginning to connect, but there are so many questions left unanswered.

"As soon as the opportunity arose, I left, determined to put my faith in a gentler place. I joined a convent, gave my life to Christ, and for a time, I found peace."

An old pain flared in Margaret's eyes. "In some form of divine irony, I was placed at St. Sebastian's Home for Girls, where I spent my days caring for other people's daughters."

"That must have been . . . difficult," Laura says, though she knows the word can't possibly describe how it must have felt.

"I chose to see it as God's will. His granting me a chance for redemption. Thinking of it any other way would have driven me mad."

She sighs. "But then my sister was murdered. My mother was already gone by that time. My own daughter had no one left."

Margaret leans forward and takes another long drink from her water.

"I called in favors and pulled strings and petitioned the courts and the foster system to have her sent to St. Sebastian's. For her own safety, and a chance at a seminormal life, Grace became Graye, and I became her guardian in the only way I could."

"You never told her?" Laura asks, though she suspects she knows the answer to that.

A darkness settles over Margaret. "I prayed time and again for guidance. I begged God to show me the way forward. But, in this instance, he was stubbornly silent. Perhaps he was waiting for me to make the right decision on my own. But I failed his test."

Margaret rises and hugs her arms around her middle. She walks to the window to get a closer look at the view, perhaps pulling some of the ocean's calming presence into her heart.

"When Graye was twelve, I gave her what I hoped was a gift. She was enamored of words. She read voraciously, and when she wasn't reading she was filling page after page with her own writing. It was a novel, newly released to great acclaim, written by an author named David West."

Margaret turns, and Laura stares into the face of a woman aged by her own choices and the repercussions of those.

"She fell in love with his prose, with the beauty of his words. I never told her he was also her father."

The glass in Laura's hand falls to the ground, shattering between them.

48

LAURA

Laura jumps from the couch and grabs the broom from the kitchen, stopping for a moment to lean against the pantry door and catch her breath.

The broken glass gives her the opportunity to step away for a moment from the extraordinary story Margaret has just placed in her hands.

Thoughts are whirling unchecked. It's almost too much to believe. An underage girl forced to give her child away, a child who later becomes unknowingly obsessed with her own father's words? A child who will eventually grow into the woman who is now facing trial for the murder of that same man?

Briefly, Laura wonders if Margaret might be deranged. What does she really know about her anyway? And she just opened the door to her, invited her in.

But that line of thinking quickly loses steam. The woman in her living room has been buffeted by life, battered by abhorrent circumstances, most of which were out of her control. But no matter how implausible the things she's saying, Margaret seems perfectly, unfortunately, sane.

Laura avoids Margaret's eyes as she returns to the living room with the dustpan. She sweeps up the wet glass, the actions achingly reminding her of David's final few years. The wife of an alcoholic becomes proficient at such things.

She stands and finds Margaret studying her.

"Are you okay?" the woman asks.

Laura thinks about it for a moment. "It's a lot to take in."

Margaret nods and takes the dustpan with the broken glass from her hands.

"And an unfair way to tell someone, really. For myself, it's been a lifetime of poor decisions, separated by years to accept the consequences of each. To see them together, lined up in a row like dominoes falling into one another, must be overwhelming."

Margaret takes the dustpan toward the kitchen, giving Laura a few more moments alone to digest everything.

When she returns, she sits once more on the edge of the sofa, her posture straight, and she takes a deep breath.

Laura realizes Margaret's not done. Incredibly, there's more to come.

"I've made mistakes. So many, many mistakes in trying to protect Grace from the truth. She's lived a life full of loss. She lost her real mother before she was a full day old, and my leaving allowed my mother and sister to forget I existed. I doubt I was missed, even for a moment. As far as I'm aware, my name was never mentioned in my family again, and certainly not to Grace, even in the role of an aunt who'd run away from home."

Laura shakes her head. "That's crazy. What kind of people would do that?" she asks. She's not so naive that she doesn't realize there are dysfunctional families in the world, but her own experiences are so far removed that it's like examining an alien life-form.

"I was a late baby," Margaret says. "One my mother didn't want. Nor apparently my father, as he abandoned my mother before I was born. I'd always known my mother despised me, but it wasn't until

I was five that my sister explained why. I was the result of an affair Mother had had, an affair that ended up costing her the security of a husband, who was a successful bank manager, and her upper-middle-class lifestyle.

"We lived in a small town. Mother was ostracized, thrown into poverty, shunned."

"But that wasn't your fault!" Laura says.

"No, but I was a living reminder of all she'd lost. They blamed me, both my mother and my sister. Her husband moved on, marrying someone else and starting a new family. He hardly had time for my sister. As for me, he never acknowledged my existence."

Laura can't imagine the isolation, the loneliness, of a child forced to bear the brunt of an adult's mistakes. And yet, they do. All the time.

"When I left, I have no doubt my family was relieved to see the back of me. And I'll admit, the feeling was mutual. But my deepest regret, in a life filled with regrets, is leaving Grace behind to become their surrogate whipping boy."

Laura knows the basics of what happened after that. She's read the reports that threw the national press into a feeding frenzy of sensationalism. Once the news broke that Graye Templeton, the young woman accused of murdering renowned novelist David West, was actually the long-lost darling of the Thacker case that held the nation in thrall fifteen years before, Laura hadn't been able to go anywhere without seeing Graye's face splashed across a front page.

It was often placed side by side with a photograph of Grace at nine, an iconic shot of the little girl looking back over her shoulder on the steps of a Missouri courthouse. There's fear in her face, and sadness in her eyes.

There was even a documentary, though Laura couldn't watch more than twenty minutes before she shut off the television and went for a run along the beach. She ran miles farther than usual that day, past the point of her endurance. She circled the entire island, then managed to drag herself, exhausted, into her bed.

"Grace had so much loss in her life," Margaret continues. "Witnessing Crystal's murder, the only mother she'd ever known. Alexis and her boyfriend Nick jailed for the crime.

"I couldn't give her David. Not in any real way. He didn't know she existed, and I couldn't risk telling her in case she tried to contact him. We'd tried so hard to hide Grace from the press, to give her some chance at a normal life, and I couldn't put that at risk. I thought I could be enough."

Margaret's shoulders drop.

"I was wrong."

She glances around the room, her eyes sliding over things, searching for someplace to land, and Laura's stomach begins to knot. She can sense there's more to come, and she braces herself for it.

"Grace was an exceptional student. Scholarships would have allowed her to go to a number of different universities. She chose Cornell because it was David's alma mater. She had dreams, such big dreams, of following in her literary hero's footsteps."

Margaret's face tightens.

"I told myself it was harmless. There was no cause for concern. Young girls often fixate on idols. But then David took a job as a guest professor and Graye was over the moon. Then this, here, working for you, living in your guesthouse. It was a snowball barreling down a hill, and I couldn't stand by and watch it happen."

The tension inside of Laura is at a breaking point, and she fights an urge to shout at Margaret to stop, to put her hands over her ears and throw the woman out in the street. She's tried so hard to heal. Her body, her heart, her mind were all left in tatters after the events of last summer.

Yet here she is again, following the white rabbit with a pocket watch, wherever it leads. She's falling, and she knows it's too late to stop.

"I traveled here, to Port Mary, to tell David the truth," Margaret says. Her hands are picking at a corner of her secondhand sweater.

"I came to this house and rang the doorbell the day before . . . the day before he died. He didn't recognize me. Refused to allow me inside to explain. He tried to shut the door in my face, and I was forced to tell him there on the doorstep, through a crack in the door with my foot wedged inside to keep him from shutting it. I told him he had a daughter."

Laura's heart drops. "David knew?" she whispered.

Margaret nods, and swallows visibly. "I could see the moment he recognized me."

Laura raises a hand to her mouth, biting her lip. Margaret meets her eyes.

"I've never seen rage like that in a human being. It had been a very long time since I'd seen David, but still, it shocked me.

"I saw a flicker of fear in his eyes, just for the briefest moment, a spark that lit the fire of his anger. He was shouting, accusing me of lying, of attempting to blackmail him, of trying to ruin his life."

Chills run down Laura's arms, and she pulls up her legs and wraps her arms around them. She remembers too clearly the incredible violence that had awoken from some sleeping place inside of David that day. She'd never known what triggered it. Blamed herself for not seeing his potential for hate, for hurt, prior to that night. There'd been hints, but never anything to the degree she witnessed.

"He never even asked about her," Margaret says, disbelief heavy in her words. "Not a single question about the daughter he never knew he had. The daughter living right under his nose. His only concern was the loss of his reputation if it became known that he'd impregnated an underage girl."

Margaret sighs and shakes herself from the place her mind has gone. "I knew then it would be an even bigger mistake to tell David who Graye was. And I'd already committed a grave error by telling him as much as I had, so I left. I went back to the hotel without ever telling Graye I was here. I planned to go back home the next day, but then . . ."

"Then David was killed," Laura says softly, completing her thought.

"Yes. And Graye was discovered standing next to the body of the man she never knew was her father."

She sighs and the silence stretches between them. Laura's mind is readjusting the perspective she's always had of that night, but it's a difficult shift to make.

A horrifying thought occurs to her.

"Have you told her yet?" she asks in a low voice.

A look of pain crosses Margaret's face, so great that the cracks in Laura's heart open even wider.

"Not yet," she admits, shaking her head. "When I leave here, I'm traveling to Houston to be there for the trial. I've put it off for so long, but I have to try to speak with her before the trial begins. I don't want her to find out that way."

Laura's face goes white. The trial is scheduled to begin the day after tomorrow. Her parents and the Carons are flying in to be there with her. But Laura is dreading it.

"But why would . . . ?" She trails off.

"Graye cut her foot on a piece of glass," Margaret says. "Her blood was at the scene along with David's. The connection was inevitable. The prosecution is aware of the situation. Graye's lawyer too, though we've had many discussions about whether Graye knew the truth. The attorney feels we should withhold the information from Graye for now, and wait and see if the prosecution chooses to use it as motive. It's a risky move, but there's a chance they feel it will weaken and complicate their case, and will leave it out. If not, Graye's lawyer claims her sincere initial reaction to the news could work in her favor. I think she's wrong."

The attorney's cold-blooded reasoning behind denying Graye the truth of her parentage isn't lost on Laura. Nor the high-stakes games lawyers are willing to play with people's lives and emotions.

"That's . . . that's disgusting," Laura says, unable to hold back her unvarnished opinion.

Margaret closes her eyes slowly and squeezes them shut for a moment.

"It is quite vile, isn't it? The defense attorney took Graye's case free of charge, which is no small matter, but I've come to realize she did it with her own agenda."

"Is that why Graye is pleading not guilty?" Laura asks. She's wondered time and again, given the supposed strength of the case against her, if the press can be believed, why Graye has chosen this path.

"To some degree," Margaret admits. "The attorney denies it, but I saw the glint in her eye when she heard Graye claim she wasn't guilty. This trial is going to be a circus, and Graye's attorney is going to be the one with the flashy coattails, holding the bullhorn and the whip. Even if Graye loses, the lawyer wins."

The horror of the situation isn't lost on Laura. No wonder Margaret looks as if she hasn't been sleeping.

"Can I ask you a question, Margaret?"

She meets Laura's eyes and slowly nods. Laura has a feeling Margaret knows what she's going to ask.

"Do you believe she's guilty?"

Margaret bites her lip and takes a few moments to consider her words before she speaks.

"I believe that, in Graye's mind, there is a difference between innocent and not guilty. And her attorney has encouraged that distinction for the sake of her own celebrity. But if you're asking if I believe Graye killed David . . . then yes, I do."

Laura's at a loss for words, her mouth falling open just a bit. Yes, the case appears to be strong, though they won't know the full extent of it until the prosecution has a chance to lay out the evidence at the trial. But this woman is Graye's *mother*. The woman who raised her for half her life.

"Do you believe she killed the nurse as well?"

Margaret takes a deep breath before she speaks again.

"I think she must have. Graye became friends with an elderly woman named Eileen Ellis after the death of her roommate, the woman's niece, her freshman year. They were very close, and Inez Jeffries, by all accounts, was rather a poor excuse for a caregiver. She was reportedly abusive, both emotionally and perhaps physically, to the residents under her care."

"My God, that's terrible," Laura exclaims.

"Yes."

Something nags at her. Something Margaret said.

"How did her roommate die?" she asks slowly.

If possible, Margaret's face grows even more drawn.

"An overdose," she says. "So they say. But . . ."

She stops and takes a deep breath, perhaps searching for the strength to continue.

"You don't believe that?" Laura asks softly.

"There was a little girl. A little girl at St. Sebastian's who came to us after Graye had been there a few years. Autumn. Surprisingly, the two became friends. Graye hadn't really connected with any of the girls before that. The two were inseparable, as close as sisters. They even called themselves sisters. They played games and made up stories in their own pretend world for hours on end."

Without realizing it, Laura is holding her breath.

"But then a distant relative was discovered, and Autumn was leaving to go live with them in California."

Margaret's face clouds, and she runs a hand across her forehead.

"The night before they were set to arrive, there was an accident. Autumn was found at the bottom of a nearby ravine. Her neck was broken in the fall."

Laura stands suddenly and rushes out of the room. She manages to make it to the bathroom before she's sick in the sink.

49

LAURA

Once her stomach is empty, Laura washes out the sink, then splashes cold water on her face. She sees herself in the mirror's reflection, her skin a sickly shade of white, beads of water clinging to her cheeks.

She backs up against the bathroom wall and slides down until she's sitting on the floor.

She can't go back out there. Not yet.

Perhaps not ever.

Maybe if she hides in here long enough, Margaret will leave and Laura can open a bottle of wine and lose herself in it, drowning out the horrors the woman has brought into her home and into her mind.

There is a very real possibility that Graye Templeton is a serial killer. David's daughter. A woman she befriended, worked side by side with for months, depended on, and brought into her home.

She sits, alone, and struggles to find a way to come to terms with that.

Margaret came here for a reason. If it was to share insight into Graye's past and her own, Laura can't say she's happy to know the things she does now, but it *is* true that she's thankful for the privacy to process the revelations.

She can't fathom learning some of these things in court, with the cameras of the press pointed at her face.

Once Laura manages to pull herself up from the bathroom floor, she washes and dries her face one more time, then tucks strands of wet hair behind her ears.

Slowly, she walks back to the living room.

She's surprised, and honestly, a bit relieved to see that Margaret is nowhere in sight.

Her gaze lands on a white sheet of paper lying on the coffee table she recognizes from the notepad that hangs on her refrigerator door.

Slowly, Laura walks toward it and picks it up, then drops down into the place where Margaret had sat on the sofa not so long ago. Beneath the note, there's a white envelope, fat with pages folded inside.

> *Laura,*
>
> *I know you probably want me gone. I would, if I were you. But as much as it pains me to say so, there's more you need to know.*
>
> *This letter is from Graye. She asked me to give it to you, and after much hesitation, I told her I would, but only if she allowed me to read it first.*
>
> *She agreed.*
>
> *The contents are not easy to stomach, and for that I offer my sincerest apologies. I considered burning the pages, or throwing them from the highest peak of a mountain, but in the end, I've had to accept the truth for what it is. I've spent a lifetime trying to hide from it, but no more.*
>
> *It can be bent, shaped, and molded, but only in our own minds.*
>
> *Sometimes we're forced to step back and see the whole for what it is. Only then can we come to accept it.*

I've gone for a long walk along your beach. I will be back, only because I feel you may have questions. I owe you answers to whatever those might be.

After that, I'll leave you to live your life, and God willing, find peace.

Margaret

Laura stares at the envelope sitting in front of her like it's a snake that might strike at any moment.

In a way, she supposes it is.

She hasn't seen or spoken with Graye since David died. She can't imagine what the girl might want to say to her now. Apologies? Excuses?

Does it even matter?

Laura considers if she has it in her to pick up the envelope and burn it herself, unopened.

But she knows she doesn't.

Graye is behind bars, at least for now. The chances that she'll be released are slim to none, considering the evidence against her.

Graye can't hurt her.

At least, not physically.

Everyone has a story. Listen with an open heart.

"Oh Mama," she says aloud. "I don't think this is what you meant."

But perhaps she did.

Hesitantly, Laura reaches out and picks up the envelope. She slides the sheets of notebook paper from it and carefully unfolds them in her lap.

Then, she begins to read.

Dear Laura,

I hope this letter finds you well.

I know it's been some time since we've spoken, but I have nothing but time on my hands now, and I wanted to take the opportunity to reach out to you and perhaps explain, if I can.

I've always expressed myself better through pen and paper, but now I find my hands are shaking. Perhaps because I know you don't have to listen. But I hope you do.

People say "Start from the beginning," but that phrase has always struck me as silly. There are many beginnings. An infinite number. The trick is knowing which one best serves the story.

Dr. West understood that. Or he did once. It was part of what made him one of the greats. For a time.

Cracking open the spine of his novel Broken Home Harvest *was a watershed moment for me. By the time I finished, his voice had claimed ownership of my heart. He was a wizard. A word voodooist, fearless in his power and sorcery.*

Learning to be as great a writer as David West became my singular goal, and I set about making it happen. Even if I fell short of the bar he'd set, there was no worthier metric. It sustained me for many, many years.

If I'd only known the man behind the golden words would prove to be such a disappointment, I never would have suggested extending Dr. West an invitation to become a guest professor.

Of course, I can't be held wholly responsible for that. The head of the English Department made the ultimate decision, but when he asked the graduate students for suggestions, I couldn't not speak up. After all, who else could compare?

I was quite devastated, as you can imagine, when the position as Dr. West's teaching assistant was initially filled by Zoe Kendrick. She was singularly unsuited for the honor. Instead of supporting Dr. West's nomination, she bemoaned the fact that Kurt Vonnegut was dead, and hence couldn't be approached for the position.

Luck was not on my side, in that instance. But I'm a great believer in making one's own luck. As a successful businesswoman yourself, I'm sure you appreciate the value in that sentiment.

The accident that ended Miss Kendrick's time at Cornell was regrettable, but necessary. Unfortunately, being hired as her replacement was directly responsible for the painful death of my fascination with David West.

The man, as I'm sure I don't need to tell you, of all people, did not live up to the legend.

On a positive note, you'll be happy to know Zoe Kendrick's physical therapy is reportedly going well. There is even a chance, albeit a small one, that she may one day walk again.

Laura drops the page in her hand and fights another wave of nausea. She remembers Zoe, David's teaching assistant prior to Graye. She was a bubbly girl, always ready with a wave if Laura stopped by to drop off lunch for David.

Tears form and Laura chokes back a sob.

There are at least four more pages of Graye's letter.

If she doesn't read it, she'll always wonder. Yet the price of those answers is allowing Graye's voice back into her head. She's not sure it's a price she can afford to pay.

She halfway rises from the sofa, then drops back down. There's no other way. She needs to know what other damage Graye's obsession has caused.

She owes it to David. She owes it to Zoe Kendrick.

Laura closes her eyes tightly and pulls in a deep breath before she picks up the next page.

They do say that when one door closes, another opens. It may be a cliché, but in this instance, it proved to be an accurate one.

You see, Laura, in my exhaustive research of Dr. West, I'd always been intrigued by the story of the woman behind the myth. And from the moment I heard you speak at the first workshop you presented on campus, I knew.

My plans hadn't been in vain. I'd been wrong, but not by so very much. It wasn't David I was destined to connect with, but you.

Familiarizing myself with your habits unfortunately involved a bit of stealth, and for that I sincerely apologize. Stalking is a word with such negative connotations. It implies some intended malice, and I want you to know I never wished anything but good for you.

I hope you believe that.

The morning we "officially" met, I must admit I was surprised by your gracious nature. I was wary, considering my recent experience with learning there is sometimes a vast difference between a person's public persona and their true self.

Yet you were even more charming than I'd imagined.

I do owe you a long-overdue apology, however. If I'd realized the blouse you chose that morning was silk, I'd have arranged our meeting for another day. It's a shame it was ruined.

But you, Laura! Oh, how you reinvigorated my hopes and dreams.

And then, you left.

I was hurt, of course. At first. But it didn't take long for me to come to understand that you were giving me the time I needed to prepare myself.

I'd spent many, many years honing my writing skills. I owe Dr. West a debt of gratitude for that. I couldn't have done it without the inspiration he provided.

But through you, I learned there is so much more that goes into the business of being a published author. Image matters as much as content. Isn't that what you always say?

So I set out to put your advice to use. I hope you don't mind that you were my inspiration while I crafted a new image for myself. If you'll forgive the use of another cliché, they also say imitation is the sincerest form of flattery.

I'm afraid I had to tell a few white lies to ensure our paths intersected again. When I discovered Cecelia Ainsley was interviewing for a personal assistant, it was an opportunity too perfect to pass up.

I must sheepishly admit I never forwarded my résumé to Ms. Ainsley. It's not that I wished to mislead you. Rather, I took it as a sign. Sister Margaret is a believer in signs from the Almighty, but I've always preferred a solid plan of action.

In this case, there was no denying the timing and location were right.

My apologies for droning on. I doubt you're interested in the specifics of how I set about making myself indispensable to you.

A punctured tire, the weakened heel of a shoe, a rather lovely replacement pair in just the right size. None of that seems terribly important now.

I would like to say, though, for the record, I had no idea that leaving Hugo's sweet note for David to find would lead to such an extreme response. Perhaps I should have anticipated it, but I'm afraid I underestimated Dr. West's capacity for violence.

For that, I take full responsibility and beg your forgiveness.

I didn't wish you harm, but sought only to give you an excuse to end your marriage free from guilt.

He was not good for you, Laura.

I suppose, in the end, it worked out. Now, you doubtless have more time and energy to devote to the cultivation of unrecognized talent.

But no life is without regret, including mine.

I regret that the manuscript I gave to you wasn't ready. I've come to realize that criticism, when coming from a place of love, is not meant to wound, but to strengthen.

It took some time to understand that, but it was an important lesson. One of many ways you've enriched my writing process.

I'll never forget your words to me. "Compelling," you called it, but "even the supposed truth comes across like more lies."

I've taken your advice to heart and put my time in this place to use. The original manuscript has been lost, unfortunately. I assume it's moldering in some police storage locker somewhere, filed away as evidence. I've come to see that as an opportunity, rather than a tragedy. The Orphan's Ashes *has been entirely rewritten, with an eye toward revision. I've aimed my pen for a more honest narrative and feel it's a much stronger work now.*

For that, I owe you a debt I can never repay.

I'm aware the chances are slim, but if there ever comes a time you could see your way to reading the new manuscript,

I would be most grateful. Though, of course, I'd expect and understand if you were to say no to such a request.

They tell me I killed David.

At first, I admit, I couldn't see how they could be right. Killing Dr. West was never part of the plan.

But as time passes, I'm beginning to believe it may be true, though my memories of that morning are still somewhat hazy.

Perhaps one day, they'll come into focus. Until that time, I'm afraid we may never know.

I know, Laura, how much store you put by honesty, so I've gone to great lengths to include nothing here but that. The truth, as I know it to be.

You've been the dearest of friends to me. More like a sister, really.

It is my fondest hope that one day we can rebuild the trust we once had.

Warmest wishes,

Graye

Laura looks up from the letter and angrily swipes the tears of horror from her eyes.

Her breath is coming quick and shallow, and she can't get enough air into her lungs. She begins to panic, or perhaps she already was and she's only now realizing it.

"Cup your hands around your mouth," Margaret says, and Laura shrieks in surprise. She didn't hear the woman return, lost as she was in Graye's eloquent insanity.

Margaret sits next to Laura and places a hand on her back.

"You're having a panic attack," she says calmly. "Bend at the waist and cup your hands over your mouth. I'm going to count backward from ten. I want you to hold your breath until I'm done."

Wide-eyed and dizzy, Laura obeys.

Within a few minutes her pulse begins to calm. Her initial anger fades, and in its place a sadness unlike any she's ever known rushes in to fill the void.

Margaret holds her silently as she cries.

She cries tears for Graye, for Margaret. For herself and David, and the marriage they should have had. Tears for Zoe Kendrick. Tears for the baby that almost was.

She cries until she has no tears left.

Margaret hands her a fresh glass of water and she takes it gratefully.

"She was haunting us," Laura says hoarsely, looking up at Margaret with puffy, red-rimmed eyes. "Like a ghost in the shadows, she was haunting our lives, and I never saw it. I never imagined—"

She breaks off and sits up straighter.

"She's still lying," she says, incredulous.

Margaret frowns slightly and takes a seat in the chair perpendicular to the sofa, understanding intuitively that since her tears have passed, Laura will want to reestablish the boundaries of her personal space.

"I'm not saying you're wrong, but can I ask what makes you say that?"

Laura frowns and shakes her head. "She said she never intended to kill him, but that can't be true."

Margaret tilts her head, her own frown deepening.

"The knife. I had to identify the knife for the police, to confirm it came from the set in the guesthouse. If she didn't plan to kill David, then why did she bring the knife?"

Margaret closes her eyes slowly, then opens her mouth, but whatever she intends to say stalls on her tongue. She remains silent for a beat. "Ah," she says finally. "I see what you mean."

But there's something in her tone, something in the way she no longer meets Laura's gaze that causes Laura to squint at the former nun.

Margaret bites her lip, and her eyes skirt around the room. Her mouth twitches once again, as if she's decided to say more after all. Yet she stops herself a second time.

Instead, she stands, patting her pockets and glancing around as if checking to make sure she's not forgetting anything, even though she brought nothing with her except the letter from Graye.

"What is it you're not saying?" Laura asks slowly.

And still, Margaret won't meet her eyes, confirming Laura's suspicion.

"Margaret," she says. "Look at me."

The older woman sighs, then slowly turns to look at Laura.

"After this, after all this," Laura says, sweeping her hand at the six-page letter scattered across the coffee table, "what more could you possibly have to hide?"

"I . . . ," Margaret begins, then stops.

But Laura's had enough. "Say it!" she shouts, and Margaret flinches. "Jesus, just say it already!"

"She's not lying!" Margaret shouts back, surprising herself.

They're both panting, staring at each other with wild, hurt-filled eyes.

"She's not lying," Margaret says, quieter now, visibly trying to gain control of her emotions. "She never intended to kill David."

"Then why bring the knife from the guesthouse?" Laura demands, refusing to let her off the hook.

A strange combination of emotions flickers across Margaret's face. Exasperation, sympathy, pain. Guilt mingled with grief. All of them, together, meld into a look Laura will remember for the rest of her days, along with the words that follow it.

"The knife was never meant for David, Laura. It was for *you*."

50

MARGARET

"Me?" Laura says, her voice barely above a whisper. "Graye meant to kill *me?*"

The fight visibly drains from her, and she melts backward into the cushions of the sofa. Her face has gone slack and uncomprehending.

"I don't . . ." Laura shakes her head, her eyes closing in confusion. "I don't understand."

Margaret hadn't intended to share this particular insight. It isn't something likely to come out at the trial, and she saw no reason to add to the woman's pain.

She searches for words to cushion the revelation, but there are none.

"She admitted as much to me," Margaret says, rubbing her hands up and down her arms. She's shaking again.

Taking in the wide eyes of the woman staring back at her, Margaret sighs and plunges on. Better to get this over with.

"Graye has . . . *difficulties* with friendships. Especially female friendships. She doesn't connect well to most people, but when she does, she becomes attached to the point of obsession."

Thoughts of Autumn and the sound of the girls' combined laughter flit across her mind.

Margaret is to blame for this. For allowing Graye to be taken and put into the care of her sister in the first place, a hard woman without a conscience. And for everything that's followed. Margaret knows full well what sort of life she left her infant daughter to. She'd lived that life.

Grace's childhood in Crystal's home mirrored Margaret's own so closely that there's no escape for her from the knowledge that Grace stepped into Margaret's place, enduring torments that were meant to be hers. Patterns of abuse that continued upon an innocent and unknowing child.

While Margaret eagerly grasped religion as her salvation, Grace never had that option.

The truth, as unchristian as it may sound, is that when Margaret received news that Crystal was dead, she was glad. Overjoyed, in fact, that her child was finally released from her sister's grasp, free now to live a life Margaret never had a chance to know.

She ignored the signs that, for Graye, it was too little, too late. Irreparable damage had already been done.

One day, Margaret knows in her heart, she'll have to stand before her God and answer for her failings.

"It's easier to see in hindsight, as I suppose most things are. But I can't pretend there weren't clues. Graye's jealousy if her friend Autumn played with, or even spoke to, any of the other girls was extreme. She insisted the two of them spend every waking moment together, inseparable. She became agitated if they were separated. Once, while Autumn was visiting the dentist, Graye had a tantrum in the kitchen, breaking dishes and ruining the evening meal, because she wasn't allowed to go with her friend. When Autumn died so suddenly, just hours before she was meant to leave us, to leave Graye, I should have questioned her more closely. The girls were alone, in a place they were expressly forbidden to be.

"But I buried those suspicions deep. They were ridiculous. Of course Graye wouldn't harm Autumn, her dearest friend and confidante. She was devastated by the girl's death."

Margaret trails off, lost in her memories.

"And the roommate?"

She'd almost forgotten Laura was there.

"I don't know for certain," Margaret admits. "I haven't managed to bring myself to ask her. But I believe the girl's overdose may not have been accidental. Graye told me she was making plans to leave. To run off with her boyfriend, leave school. Leave Graye."

Laura sits up straighter and leans forward, the tightness returning to her features.

"But I wasn't going anywhere, Margaret," Laura says. "Why would Graye want to hurt me?"

Margaret meets her gaze. "She told me . . . She said she had a plan. You were going to help launch her career as a novelist. But when that didn't appear to be working out—"

"The book," Laura says on an exhale of pent-up breath. "She was waiting for me to read the book. But once I had . . ."

Margaret nods. "She felt you'd let her down. Both her aspirations for the future and the friendship she'd invested in you. In Graye's mind, those things are twisted together into one. By dismissing her writing, you abandoned her too. In your own way."

Margaret says this with a hint of apology, but it does little to lessen the impact her words have on Laura.

"I don't know how she thought she'd get away with it. I don't even know if she'd thought that far ahead. She's done so for so long, it was hardly a consideration from what I can tell."

"The nurse?" Laura asks.

"Had been abusing a friend. Graye . . . takes friendship very seriously," Margaret says, hearing the horror of the words and their implications.

"And Zoe Kendrick? David's TA?" The tension in Laura's voice is growing.

Margaret frowns. She opens her mouth to speak, then looks away.

"She confessed to me she tampered with the girl's car. There was an accident. Miss Kendrick was badly injured."

"For no other reason than . . ." Laura trails off.

"It appears she was simply in the way," Margaret says, unable to look Laura in the eye. "Murder had become a viable option for Graye."

Margaret's words are succinct, restrained. They give no sign of the struggle she faces not to turn and beg forgiveness for allowing this to happen. She abandoned her daughter to walk this twisted path alone, and this is Margaret's burden to bear. Neither Laura nor any of Graye's victims owe Margaret forgiveness.

She suspects not even God will forgive her sins.

51

The jury deliberates for three hours and seventeen minutes before coming back with a verdict in the most sensational trial the country has witnessed in decades.

Graye Templeton, the woman once known as Grace Thacker, America's sad little sweetheart, is found guilty of all charges.

52

LAURA

The drive is long, made longer by Laura second-guessing herself with every mile that passes.

She wishes, not for the first time, that she'd brought Milo, but it's a very long way from the Texas Gulf Coast to Beckworth, Missouri.

The puppy will be happier with Dr. Lawson while she's gone. Laura, too, would rather be home. She can't put her finger on the moment the word *home* became Port Mary, which was always her grandmother's island in her mind, but at some point, New York became a place to visit. Port Mary is a place to make a life. Her place.

Antoine yelling obscenities from the taco stand as Milo barks madly at the birds on the beach is a high point of her days.

The last few months have brought a great deal of change for Laura. "An awakening," her mother calls it.

She doesn't know about that. What she does know is being alone for the first time without parents or roommates or a partner has forced her down the path to discovering someone new. Herself.

The good, the bad, and everything in between.

Some of what she's discovered scares her.

It's difficult to measure the "Graye Effect," as she thinks of it, complete with capitalization. It's touched every part of her. She'll never again be the woman she was.

In some ways, that's not a bad thing. In others, she's still adjusting.

Port Mary has helped. Her family and friends. And Milo, of course, rescued from a shelter and in need of love almost as much as she was.

But there's one aspect of her new life she's kept hidden from everyone, fearing judgment and concern.

Her growing obsession with Graye Templeton.

Once Laura connected Graye with the manuscript of the fictional Fiona Boyd, she found herself drawn back to the narrative.

She'd seen the crime scene photos during the trial. The incongruity of a ream of typewritten papers scattered about the room, some with dark splotches of blood soaking through, many having come to rest on top of David's body, was a bizarre and menacing aspect of an already tragic case.

Graye was correct; the original pages were in police evidence storage in case they were ever needed for an appeal, as Laura discovered when she approached the Rockaway Police Department about the book.

She hadn't intended to. It was a spur-of-the-moment decision to turn her car into the station and walk through those glass doors once more.

She'd been heading to the airport in Houston to catch a plane and spend the week with her parents. Her father was finally retiring, and Lisette was throwing a party.

"If you're not up for it, Laura, we understand. But of course, we'd love to have you. It might be good for you to step off that island once in a while. Remind yourself the world is a big, wide, wonderful place."

Her mother was right, of course.

She needed to get away from the walls staring back at her. Daytime was best, with the sun and surf and the beach always waiting. But at night, the house could become an echo chamber, reverberating words of the past until the volume was unbearable.

David's words. Graye's.

And lately, when she was least expecting it, Fiona Boyd's.

She'd been honest with Graye when she told her the voice in the manuscript was compelling. It had a way of burrowing under your skin and settling in.

The problem came when she wanted it out and it refused to go.

Laura had packed for New York, hoping a change in perspective could help her shake free of her ghosts. But when the turn approached for the police station, Laura changed lanes too quickly, cutting off another car and earning herself a honk in the process.

She didn't think about her reasons, simply let her instincts lead her.

"I'm sorry, Laura," Detective Branson had said. "We don't have those pages in our possession anymore. They were transferred with the rest of the evidence when the case was turned over to the federal authorities."

She'd been expecting that, but her shoulders dropped anyway.

"Okay. Thank you for your time."

She turned to walk out the door. She had a plane to catch, and no business digging up things best left buried in shallow graves.

"Laura?" the detective called out.

Laura's hand stalled on the door and she looked back over her shoulder.

"If you're that interested, I may be able to help," the woman said.

Laura perked up.

"Our sergeant scanned the pages after the lab was done. Or he was supposed to, at least. I don't think anyone ever had any use for the file, but I can see if we still have a copy, if you'd like."

A nervous flutter awakened in Laura's chest, something that felt disturbingly like excitement.

"Yes," she said, keeping her voice sober. "That would be much appreciated, Detective."

"Would you like to wait?"

Laura glanced at the time on her phone. She should be twenty minutes farther down the road if she expected to be at the airport in time to board her flight.

She bit her lip.

"Yes, I'll wait. If you don't mind."

When the plane to New York lined up on the runway, Laura wasn't on board.

She was riding the ferry back to Port Mary, absorbed in the file she'd opened on her phone. It had taken the detective nearly an hour to track down the scanned pages, while Laura waited nervously, wondering what the hell she was doing.

"Mama, I'm not going to make it," she said during the phone call to update her family on her plans. "Next time, though. We'll spend some time just the three of us, okay?"

Lisette was disappointed, and Laura didn't miss the worry in her understanding reply. But that worry would bloom into full-scale concern if Lisette had an inkling of the reason she'd canceled the trip.

Once back home, Laura fired up her laptop and printer. Sergeant Graham had indeed scanned the documents, but had made no effort to put them into any sort of order.

She printed each one and laid them out on the floor in her living room with a glass of wine close at hand. Her stomach seized at the sight of the dark spots marring several of the pages.

It's nothing but light and shadow, she told herself. *A representation. Not real blood.*

The mantra didn't help much, but the second glass of wine did.

Laura spent the evening poring over Graye's words, letting the voice she remembered so clearly take her by the hand and lead her on a journey she now saw with different eyes.

The story centered on a young girl in an orphanage who escapes her drab reality by crafting darkly intriguing fairy tales she burns in an old coffee can, spreading the ashes beneath a gnarled old black cherry tree that grows on the orphanage grounds.

Even if no one listens to her, a child who's never mattered to a soul, the tree is ancient. Her stories will soak into the soil, become part of the tree, and live forever.

But the tree begins to bear strange fruit, with a rich and addicting flavor. The child feeds the tree more and more stories to sustain the irresistible teardrop-shaped black cherries, but the line between reality and fiction begins to blur when the residents of the orphanage eat the fruit and begin to show signs of *becoming* the characters from her stories.

Rereading the main narrative, armed with the added knowledge of Graye's past, Laura could clearly see where Graye drew her inspiration.

The fairy tale sections, especially, stories within the story, resonated with the bleak history both Graye and Margaret tried so hard to escape.

The cinder girl and her golden sister who is separated from her prince and imprisoned to spin gold for their overbearing and narcissistic mother. The sister's revenge. It's not a difficult leap to tie the characters in the story to their real-life counterparts.

And yet, Laura mused, after she'd patched the work back together and read it through from beginning to end, her initial reaction still rang true.

Somewhere along the way, the child narrator of the story becomes more than a fantasist with trouble separating her life from her fictional world. She becomes a liar.

And that was the crux of the dissatisfaction that plagued Laura after her first read-through. By the end of the book, the reader is left with a sense that the little girl is utterly untrustworthy, both in the things she tells herself and the things she tells the reader.

It's something that, as a literary device, often works. But to end the story without acknowledging it or giving the reader at least a glimpse of the truth behind the web of lies is unforgivable.

And that is why Laura is behind the wheel of her car, with her home growing farther away by the minute. She can't put Graye's story aside. Lord knows she's tried. But the voice of the child, of the woman, has burrowed into her mind.

Yet she's not willing to speak to Graye directly. She's not sure she ever will be.

But Graye isn't the only person who knows the truth of her past. The truth Graye can't bear to reveal even to herself, through a fictional fairy tale, within a fictional story.

The truth Laura is inexplicably drawn to seek out. It waits in Missouri like Pandora's box, where a murderer holds the key.

53

LAURA

"I told you on the phone, I've got nothing to say to you." Alexis Thacker's words don't match the gleam that lights up her eyes when Laura introduces herself.

"I was passing through. Thought since I was nearby, I'd see if I could persuade you," Laura says.

Alexis snorts. "You expect me to believe that?"

Laura shrugs and gives her a sheepish smile. "Can't blame a girl for trying."

"Oh, they'll blame a girl for all sorts of things around here. You have no idea. Why do you think I'm stuck working in a grease pit out on the highway?"

Laura glances around. The truck stop is clean, decorated in a throwback vintage style. The clientele, while disproportionately male, seem content to mind their business, drink their coffee, and eat their blue-plate specials.

"Nobody else will hire me. An ex-con is bad enough, but with my history, they can't push me out the door fast enough. Baby sis following in my footsteps made it worse, dragging all the old stories back to the front page," she says bitterly.

"Alex, order up," shouts a man in a white apron from the pass-through window that opens into the kitchen. He's been eyeing the pair of them for the last few minutes.

"Yeah, yeah," she calls back over her shoulder.

"You get that," Laura says. "I'll wait."

"You're wasting your time."

Laura shrugs again. "My time to waste."

Alexis hands over a plastic-covered menu. "Pick something. I'll be back in a minute."

Laura watches her go, studying her mannerisms. She's in her early thirties, only seven years older than Graye, but she could pass for much more.

Several photographs from Alexis's youth are regularly used as staples in any news story about the murder of her mother. As a child, her hair was lighter, along with her expression. She was a vivacious girl, according to the documentaries and true-crime novels. As a teen, she had a glamour that made her seem more than her years.

The constant center of attention in any room, pampered as the favored child of Crystal Thacker, a woman with big ambitions, Alexis performed in pageants from the time she was a baby. None of the news coverage ever mentioned a father, and the cost of the competitions must have put a strain on the single mother's budget.

But Crystal Thacker was determined. Her daughter was going to be a star.

The woman Laura watches now, serving steak and eggs to long-distance truckers, bears hardly any resemblance to the sixteen-year-old girl who committed such a heinous act.

At least, not on the surface. There's no sign of the heavy makeup or careful hairstyles that Alexis favored when she was younger. Her face is scrubbed and lined, dark circles evident beneath her eyes. Her dark-blonde hair is pulled back into a severe ponytail.

"I'll take a root beer and a club sandwich," Laura says when Alexis saunters back to her table.

She raises an eyebrow. "Not gonna do you any good. I'm not talking to you."

"Okay," Laura says. "But I'd still like the sandwich."

"Long way to drive for lunch, lady," Alexis says with a smirk.

Laura shrugs again. It's getting to be her thing. "I've heard good things."

Alexis chuckles. "I'll pass the compliment along to the chef."

Laura eats her sandwich in silence and watches Alexis work. She tries not to stare. She doesn't want her to feel like an exhibit in a zoo.

Alexis may have said she wasn't interested, but Laura catches the way she glances over to her table periodically. Whether she'll admit it or not, she's pleased by the attention.

Laura wipes her mouth on a napkin when she's done and pulls out her wallet to pay the check.

"Giving up?" Alexis asks. "I thought you looked like a woman with more perseverance than that."

And there it is, what she's been waiting for.

"If you don't want to talk to me, there's nothing I can do about that," she says lightly. "And it's a long drive back to Texas."

She lays down enough cash for the tab, and adds an extra hundred as a tip.

"For your time," she says. "I hope life treats you better, Miss Thacker."

Laura gathers her purse and stands to put on her coat. "It was nice to meet you."

She's taking a risk as she walks away from the woman.

Her hand is reaching to push open the door when she hears, "Hey, wait."

Gotcha.

She wipes the smile from her face before she turns and glances over her shoulder.

"Are you driving back right now?" Alexis asks, standing with her weight on one leg, trying to look as if she doesn't care, while Laura does the same.

"I don't know. Maybe," Laura says. "Doesn't seem to be much in the way of entertainment around here."

"You got that right," Alexis says. She runs her fingers down the edge of the hundred-dollar bill. "Listen, there's a motel about a mile up the road. If you need to rest up or whatever before you head back." She eyes Laura's expensive coat. "Probably not up to your usual standards, but there's a bar next door."

Laura pauses, as if she's thinking it over. "Do they have a pool table?" she asks.

Alexis raises both eyebrows this time. "Aren't you full of surprises."

Laura adjusts the strap of her purse on her shoulder. "Do me a favor, okay? I won't hustle you, and you do the same for me. I think we're both old enough to know it's a mistake to judge a book by its cover."

Alexis places one hand on her hip. "If you say so, lady."

"I'll check out your motel, and I'll be at the bar next door. If you happen to drop by after your shift is through, the beer is on me. Your call."

Alexis squints her eyes and looks Laura up and down, but Laura knows her decision has already been made. They're just playing games now.

"I'm on till four, but I might be busy," Alexis says.

"Up to you," Laura says, then turns and walks out of the diner, the bell on the door jingling over her head.

She can play games all day long.

The cost of loosening Alexis Thacker's tongue totals nine dollars, seventy-five cents. The price of three bottles of beer, plus tips.

Laura doesn't ask how the woman's parole officer would feel about her hanging out in a bar. It isn't her business, and clearly Alex, as she prefers to be called, is no stranger here.

"What's your mother like, Laura?" Alex asks, leaning her weight against the pool cue. "No, wait, let me guess."

She raises a finger to her lips and stares up at the ceiling.

"She gets her hair done twice a month. Subtle highlights, classic cut. Your father rolls his eyes at the credit card bills, but she smiles sweetly and all is forgiven. How am I doing?"

"Pretty accurate," Laura admits. She doesn't admit the vague discomfort of listening to Alex talk about her mother.

Alex points the pool cue in Laura's direction. "They take a vacation twice a year, always someplace she chooses, although she lets him think otherwise. Your private school education was carefully monitored. Maybe she was involved with the board of directors? She throws a mean dinner party, but always has time for fresh-baked cookies."

Laura nods. There's a great deal Alex has left out, but she can't deny the truth of it all.

"Is that something I'm supposed to be ashamed of?" She leans over and lines up the cue ball to bank the seven. She takes the shot, and the ball drops into the pocket.

"Ashamed?" Alex says. "Why should you be? You won the mommy lottery, my friend."

A shiver runs down Laura's spine at the word *friend*. Those six letters, in that precise combination, have become permanently associated with Graye in her mind, and not in a good way. But by design, she's only had one drink to Alex's three, so she's able to keep her features casual.

"My mother was a bitch," Alex says. She stares at the balls left on the table, but that's not what she's seeing. She's looking into some dark place Laura's grateful she's never been.

Laura remains silent, unwilling to break the spell.

Alex picks up her beer and takes another swig, then leans over and lines up a shot. It's not hers to take, technically, but Laura doesn't point that out. Alex misses anyway, the cue ball spinning wildly off to one side.

"The lawyers, the judges, the goddamn press, they got it all wrong, you know. I saw that documentary. A load of crap from beginning to end."

A cheer goes up from the few patrons bellied up to the bar at this early hour. A ball game plays on the television behind the wall of liquor bottles, and Alex glances in that direction.

"Haven't you ever wanted to tell your side of the story?" Laura asks carefully, not wanting to lose her now that they've arrived at the slow-beating heart of why she's come. "Set the record straight?"

Alex lets out a dry snort.

"Nobody wants to hear my side of the story," she says. "What planet are you living on? I'm the spoiled little golden child who turned on her doting mother and murdered her in her bed. The bad seed."

Laura wonders if that's a confession. Alex pled not guilty at her trial, just as Graye had. But Alex was only sixteen, and facing charges as an adult by the State of Missouri. Her defense attorney tried to pin the blame on Nick, but the evidence, coupled with Grace's testimony, didn't support that.

"The only reason anyone wants to hear what I have to say is so they can point out what a liar I am. To spit on me. People love a public stoning, but I've done my time. I'm not volunteering for more."

"I don't believe you're a liar," Laura says. Strangely, it's true. Alex is a bitter, angry woman, jaded by prison. By life.

But Laura has an ear for voice, and Alex's is disturbingly and uncomfortably honest, for all her distasteful qualities.

"Ha," Alex says. "Then you'd be the first. Nobody wanted to hear about the hours she forced me to spend honing the perfect baton twirl. Or the way she controlled every minute, every second of my life. Scheduled, timed, trained like an elephant in a circus.

"There was nothing in that schedule about being a kid. Playing softball or making friends or having a sleepover. It was voice lessons and head shots and auditions and dye jobs. Do you know what flippers are?"

Laura shakes her head.

"They're fake teeth," she says. "Partials that fill in the gaps a kid has from losing their own. They're bullshit, and they're painful, but *nobody is going to hire a kid for a commercial if they have a big snaggletoothed smile.*"

She says the last part in a snobbish singsong voice.

"And the funny thing was, this whole time, there's Grace, hanging around in the shadows. God, I hated her."

Laura bites the inside of her cheek.

"It's like Crystal didn't even notice she was there most of the time. Grace was free to do anything she wanted, as long as she stayed out of sight, but she was too stupid to know it. She was always hanging around, getting underfoot, acting like a kicked dog that just wants to get kicked some more."

Alex finishes off her beer in one big drink and holds the empty bottle up to Laura, indicating she could use another.

Laura nods and heads to the bar, taking a moment to gather her thoughts. The childhood Alex describes is so different than her own experience. And Graye, nothing more than a lonely footnote in someone else's story.

With two fresh bottles in her hand, she walks slowly back to Alex.

"You know the funny thing about my baby sister?" Alex asks when Laura hands over the bottle. "All she had to do was keep her mouth shut. That's it, and we could have gotten away with it. It's the one thing she was good at, keeping her mouth shut. Mother made sure of that. But what does she do? For the first time in her life, she opens up and spills everything to a bunch of complete strangers."

Alex shakes her head, held prisoner by an old anger that's been stoked to life.

"I hated her even more after that. Stupid, stupid little bitch. But she got hers, in the end." Alex's lips stretch into a slow, satisfied smile. "Two consecutive life sentences. Does it get any better than that?"

She reaches out to tap her beer bottle against Laura's, then tips it up to her lips. Laura sips her own, taking the time to compose her features.

"So you don't have any doubts Graye did it?" Laura asks, and Alex laughs.

"Doubts? Hell no, I've got no doubts. Is that why you're here? Some misguided idea little Gracie is somehow innocent? Are you searching for something in her past that's going to let her off the hook?"

She stares at Laura incredulously, and Laura shrugs in return. It's not why she's come, but she doesn't need to tell this woman that.

Alex bends at the waist and lets out a deep, loud bray of laughter. By the time it tapers off, there are tears in the corners of her eyes.

"Look at you. Some rich woman on a mission of mercy. For the benefit of the woman who murdered your husband, no less. That's funny, lady. But then I guess she probably did you a favor, didn't she? That guy wasn't exactly winning any husband-of-the-year awards."

She takes another gulp of her beer, watching Laura closely over the top of the bottle, gauging her reaction.

That reference to David wasn't a slip of the tongue.

"How do you know that?" Laura asks slowly.

Alex smiles, a tiger teasing its prey.

"You want to know a secret?" Alex asks. She doesn't wait for Laura's answer. "I was there. I saw her do it."

"What?" Laura says in a low whisper.

"If you repeat that to anyone, I'll deny it to the day I die, and I have parole records to back me up. But I'll tell you just so you can sleep better at night, knowing the person responsible is paying for the crime."

Laura's head is spinning, and Alex is drinking in her reactions like a woman dying of thirst.

"I was on that pretty little island of yours, watching Grace. I followed her from New York, all the way to you."

"But why?" Laura asks, though she knows the answer to that.

"Because she's the reason they put me away! She and Nick, but Nick did his time. Grace owed me, and I wasn't about to let her get out of that debt. I was going to make sure little Gracie, who walked away smelling like a rose, paid every last cent."

Alex grins again. "But it turned out, I didn't have to do a thing. She hung herself on her own rope, and I was there to see it."

"But . . . but how?"

She doesn't need to ask twice. Alex is nearly bursting to share her own brilliance.

"Some of it was luck. A parole officer with a wife, three kids, and a wandering dick is malleable. That was the easy part. Tracking her down was a little more effort, but not much."

"I thought her foster records were sealed?" Laura says.

"Oh, they were. Gotta protect America's little heroine. But Mother had a sister she hardly ever talked about, and that was as good a place to start as any. Once I found the sainted sisters of St. Sebastian's and their Home for Girls, all it took was a look through old newspaper articles listing their good deeds and, lo and behold, there was a shot of little Grace, standing in the back of a crowd of girls. It was grainy and out of focus, but it was her."

Alex rolls her eyes. "Sealed records. What a joke. I'd only been out for a few weeks when I found her living under her fancy new name in New York, but I couldn't stay for long. Stalking costs money, and my parole officer was getting nervous, so I came back here and 'persuaded' him to use his resources to keep tabs on Grace. Do you have any idea how much information they have access to?"

Alex shook her head and took another drink from her beer.

"When Graye bought a bus ticket to Texas, I was right behind her. Right after I talked the parole officer into shelling out for a rental car. I made it there before she did. Saw her get off the bus, rent a car of her own, and head straight to your cute little house on the beach."

Laura sits back on her barstool, shaken to her foundation.

"It didn't take much to get hired as a waitress for your snooty event, and Jesus, it was fun to watch her. I needed to know everything about her life. I needed to know what she loved."

Laura squints at her, trying to understand. "But *why?*"

Alex stared back as if she couldn't imagine anyone could be so dense.

"So I could take it from her," she said, as if stating the obvious. "I spent 5,568 miserable days in prison, all because of my sister. She owed me the same in return. Whatever she loved, she was going to lose. If she had a career, I would sabotage it. A boyfriend, or even better, a husband? Men don't need much prompting to cheat. Mostly, they just need the opportunity."

Alex shakes her head. "But Grace? She was a big, fat zero. No husband. No kids. No house. No car. Not even a cat that could suddenly go missing. All she had was that shitty job as your assistant. How do you ruin someone's life when they never bothered to get one?"

The woman sitting in front of her turns Laura's stomach. Even after everything she knows Graye has done, she can't stop the pity that stirs within her realizing *this* is what Graye grew up with.

Alex laughs. "You know she looked right at me at one point, and didn't even recognize me? I told you, she always was too stupid for her own good."

"Did you actually *see* her kill David?" Laura asks in a sharp voice, tired of Alex's self-congratulatory indulgence and ready to get to the point.

"Oh yeah. She was on the beach the night before, getting shit-faced with some of the loser college kids bumming it for the summer. I was there, watching her. When she stumbled back to her house, she left her phone on the sand. Just left it lying there for me to pick up. What would you have done?"

But Alex doesn't expect her to answer that.

"I knew it might come in handy, so I picked it up with a paper towel. I've played this game before, and I had no intention of leaving my fingerprints anywhere."

The cold-blooded calculation in such an act tells Laura everything she needs to know about the woman sitting in front of her.

"I'd been crashing at a place up the beach with some of the people from the party, but I couldn't sleep. I was too excited, too curious about what kind of crazytown drama Grace had gotten herself involved in. I'd seen that husband of yours trying to punch the guy you were sleeping with, seen the way Grace followed you around like a dog."

She glances up at Laura. "I didn't know what was going on, but it was too entertaining to interrupt. I was up early, before everyone else. It was still dark, and I walked down to your place. Turns out, that was the best decision I ever made. I'm not sure what I expected to see, but it wasn't Grace walking into your house with a big-ass knife in her hand."

"But you . . . you actually saw her kill him?"

Alex nods. "I got up close, watched from the window. She was sneaking around for a while, but then what's-his-name shows up from somewhere."

"David," Laura whispers.

"Yeah, David. So they start screaming at each other. She's acting insane, like she thinks he's done something. And her screaming—I mean, it was getting on my nerves too, and the guy was obviously nursing a hangover. He grabbed her by the arms, yelling at her to shut the hell up."

Alex shrugs. "And she fucking stabbed him."

The apathy and total disregard for life that permeate that statement give Laura chills.

Alex laughs. "And then, it comes out at the trial that guy was actually her *dad*! I mean, can you believe that shit? Like a bad soap opera or something. And there's Grace, acting like she didn't even know."

She shrugs. "I don't know, maybe she didn't. But that never made sense to me. I can guarantee if Crystal knew Grace's dad was some big-shot writer, she'd have hit him up for cash, that's for sure."

Laura shifts in her seat. The truth about Graye's parents was only partially revealed during those weeks the trial had dragged on, and had done nothing but confuse things further.

The prosecution claimed Graye had tracked David down, obsessed over the famous absentee father who'd never acknowledged her. They painted it as a potential motive. The press went wild, of course, but no one realized they had only part of the story.

It was simply assumed Crystal Thacker had been David's lover. They grew up in the same small town, had been near enough the same age. An easy assumption to make. All it would take, even now, is one enterprising journalist with a sense something is off to dig deeper, to discover Margaret and her story. But so far, that hasn't happened.

And Laura has no intention of spilling Margaret's secrets to Alex.

"What did you do after that?" She needs to know. She needs this conversation to be done, so she can get as far from this excuse for a human as possible.

"Well, I backed up in a big hurry, first of all. Grace comes running out of the house, covered in blood. If she'd bothered to look, she'd have seen me, but she didn't. She was completely freaked out, heading back to the little house next door."

She shakes her head. "I couldn't believe it," she says with a smile. "All that effort to make Grace pay, and in the end, I didn't have to do a thing."

"The phone call," Laura whispers. "The 911 call, when Graye confessed."

Alex winks at her. "Well, almost nothing. I sat there for a few minutes, leaning against the side of the house, soaking it all in. But the sun was starting to come up, and the last place I wanted to be caught was outside a murder scene. I remembered the phone in my pocket, and knew I'd made the right decision not to touch it. I dialed with my T-shirt wrapped around it, pretended to be Graye, then tossed the phone into the house. I didn't even have to open the door. Grace left it swinging behind her."

She shakes her head again. "Stupid."

Laura wonders how many miles she can put between her and this woman before nightfall.

"I got out of there fast after that. I didn't want to be seen, and I was jumpy, kept thinking I was hearing Grace coming back. I left on the first ferry back to Rockaway."

Alex lifts her beer and salutes Laura with it.

"That was the best damn day of my life," she says. "And you can rest easy. Believe me, they got the right girl."

That isn't the reason Laura has driven all this way, but she finds she's lost the stomach for any more games.

"Alex, what happened the night your mother died?" she asks outright.

This is the question that keeps her up nights. This is the question she can't get past, the truth she sifts through Fiona Boyd's manuscript hoping to puzzle out.

Alex gives her a slow smile, a smile Laura will see in her nightmares for many nights to come.

"Exactly what they say happened. I killed her. I'm not ashamed of that. I'd do it again, given half the chance."

Laura nods and rises to go. She's done here.

She turns and walks away without a word.

"Hey," Alex calls out. Laura pauses but doesn't turn back. She'd prefer not to see Alexis Thacker again. Ever.

"Ask Nick, if you don't believe me," she calls.

Laura resumes walking toward the door.

If this is what sisterhood is like, Laura is glad she's an only child.

Because the thing is, she does believe her.

Laura may not have had the same amount of alcohol as her companion, but the one beer she did finish over the previous few hours sits sour in her stomach.

Her first instinct is to get as far away as possible, but she can't face the drive back to Texas in her current state.

She also has no intention of renting a room at the motel next door to the bar. She doesn't want to wonder if she's taking bedbugs back home with her, but also, she's loath to give Alex an easy way of finding her.

Not that she will. Laura has a feeling Alex has wrung all the enjoyment she can get out of sharing her truth. Laura serves no further purpose for her now.

She makes it half an hour, just to the outskirts of Kansas City, when she sees an exit proclaiming a decent hotel chain around the corner. She turns the car in that direction.

The desk clerk is friendly, the room is clean, and Laura drops back onto the freshly made bed with a sigh. She stares up at the ceiling.

She wishes she could call her mother. Lisette's voice would go a long way toward cleansing some of the ugly she can feel clinging to her after her time with Alex.

But she's never been able to lie to her mother, even by omission, and Lisette would be horrified to learn what she's been doing. And until Laura can exorcise the triumvirate of Graye Templeton, Grace Thacker, and Fiona Boyd from her thoughts, Lisette would be right to worry.

She pulls the well-thumbed pages of the manuscript she printed months ago from her bag. She removes the rubber bands and sets aside the top three-quarters of the pages.

It takes an hour to pore over the final pages of the draft, words she's read time and again. And still, she can't help feeling there's something there she's just on the verge of seeing.

She hoped Alexis could bring whatever that might be into focus, but instead she's left with answers to questions she didn't want to know, nor even knew to ask.

She sighs and rubs her eyes.

She picks up her phone to dial Dr. Lawson and check in on Milo.

But as she scrolls through the contacts on her phone, her thumb stops on the *B*s and she stares.

Without any real plan, she taps the name listed there. Detective Branson.

It's late. The detective probably won't be at her desk. Laura is debating whether to leave a message when a familiar voice speaks in her ear.

"Branson," it says.

Laura is surprised and speaks before she can think to hang up the phone.

"Detective. Hi. This is Laura West."

"Mrs. West," the woman says, with only the slightest hesitation. "What can I do for you?"

"Detective, I know you don't owe me anything, but I'm wondering if you could do me a favor."

There's no response on the other end of the line, so Laura plunges on. "Can you help me find an address?"

54

The cinder girl has collected the items her golden sister requested. They were difficult to gather, and it had taken time, but she had the spider's help and at last, she was successful.

The down of a black goose, nectar from a moonflower harvested at midnight half past, a section of life cord from a girl baby.

She delivers them all, yet still her sister has more demands.

"My spell has reached my prince and he is on his way," she says. "You'll meet him at the castle gate. Bring a fool's disguise and see him past the guards. Take this potion to keep around your neck. When the time is right, three drops in Mother's drink is all that is required."

The spider scuttles up her leg and arm, then a small vial is tied around her neck. Fear flutters in the cinder girl's heart. "Oh, Sister, I cannot."

"You will find a way." Her voice brooks no argument. "Then we shall both be free."

And so the cinder girl watches and waits. For three days and nights, the prince does not come, but at last, she sees a dark shape on the horizon.

"You've come to heed my sister's call," she says.

"No," he replies, and a new fear awakens within her.

"But you must. She's been locked away and you're her only hope for escape."

She pleads, she begs, but the prince is not swayed.

"Your sister cannot be trusted, child. Did you not listen when I said her heart was mine? It was banished along with me, and see how it has withered and died?"

He opens his satchel and shows her the rotted, worm-infested remains of what was once a beating heart.

"Take my horse and ride from this place while you still can, girl," he says.

"But I have nothing to give in return," she laments.

"That vial of death around your neck is all the payment I ask," he says.

She unties the ribbon and places the little stoppered bottle in his hand, then he lifts her onto the back of his black horse.

"Go now, little cinder sister. Be gone from here, as far as you can go from this place before the sun sets."

"But what about you?" she asks, suddenly filled with worry for him.

"Don't concern yourself with me. I have monsters to slay."

The cinder girl is halfway up the mountain pass when night falls upon her shoulders. She stops and turns back for the first time. The castle burns bright in the distance. The barest hint of smoke tickles her nose, and the big black horse's ear twitches once, then twice, as a faint sound finds them out.

She begins to hum a tune, one she overheard her sister sing when she spun gold. It drowns out the night screams, and the cinder girl turns the horse away.

LAURA

The Wicker Park neighborhood of Chicago is a far cry from a dive bar off Interstate 35.

Laura manages to find a vacant parking spot on the street and walks two blocks to the address Detective Branson hesitantly provided.

The area is sophisticated and thriving, an urban blend of new embracing old. Art galleries nestle next to cafés, converted apartment buildings, and boutiques, all within sight of the elevated trains.

Laura stops and peers up at the historic three-story red-brick building that's her destination.

An intercom and keypad are positioned next to the double front doors. Laura takes a deep breath and buzzes an apartment on the third floor.

At first, no one answers. She's taking a risk by not calling ahead, but she wasn't entirely sure she wanted to go through with this.

Now that she's here, though, the idea of driving home with Graye's words playing incessantly in her mind the entire way fills her with dread.

For better or worse, she began this journey in search of answers, and to give up without completing this loop feels like cheating herself.

She buzzes again.

The intercom crackles in reply. "Yes?" a man's voice asks.

"Nick DiMarco?"

"Who's asking, please?"

"My name is Laura West. I was hoping you could spare a few minutes to speak with me."

Laura waits. She imagines the man she's seen only in old photographs, video footage, and mug shots. A sixteen-year-old boy with long hair and a frown, charged with conspiracy to murder.

She has no reason to believe he'll talk to her, and if the silence from the intercom is any indication, neither does he. She searches for something to say that might change his mind and comes up with nothing.

"I'll buzz you in," he says at last.

She's so surprised she barely manages to get the door open before the lock reengages.

Laura takes the stairs, giving her time to compose herself. The meeting with Alexis has left her wary, guarded.

But other than a shared history, the man who answers the apartment door Laura knocks lightly upon bears no resemblance to the hateful soul she recently left behind.

The man who opens the door and welcomes her into his home is unassuming and surprisingly normal by all outward appearances.

"Thank you for seeing me," Laura says as he ushers her in.

"Can I offer you something to drink?" he asks, his face a bit guarded but polite. "Coffee, water? I have a rather shocking supply of diet soda to feed my addiction, if you'd like one."

Laura can't hold back a small smile. "Okay, sure, if you don't mind."

He nods and walks toward the kitchen. She takes the opportunity to look around at the apartment of the man who was once the boyfriend of Alexis Thacker.

There is a drafting table set up on one side of the large living space, and a computer with several monitors on a desk nearby. The walls are decorated with an odd combination of abstract art and oversized framed comic-book pages.

She turns in a full circle, taking it all in. The juxtaposition works, and the result is one of casual comfort and whimsy.

"Nice place," she says when he returns and hands her a glass filled with ice and soda.

"Thank you." He pauses and looks at her. "I'm waiting to see if you're going to ask how an ex-con and convicted killer can afford an apartment in Wicker Park."

She blushes. "I don't suppose that's any of my business."

He gives her a small smile. "Then you have admirable restraint, Mrs. West."

He gestures for her to take a seat on the sofa and pulls out coasters for their drinks.

"I'm a graphic designer," he tells her. "A very successful one. It allows me to pay the rent while working from home."

"It couldn't have been easy," she says. "Building a life like this, considering the circumstances."

He shrugs. "You can accomplish a lot when you have nothing to lose. There were plenty of lean years full of ramen noodles and canned beans. I've shielded my past, for the most part, behind a company name and logo. And clients are willing to overlook all manner of sins if you work harder, cheaper, and faster than anyone else."

He glanced around. "I'm not the cheapest anymore, but I'm still the best."

Her gaze is drawn to the drafting table, where a large sheet of paper is taped to a board. It's a sketch of a comic page in a similar style to the ones hanging on the walls.

"Is this your work?" Laura asks, pointing to the frames.

"A hobby," he says with a nod. "I publish a comic through an independent press. Under a pen name, of course."

"It's very good."

He nods. "Thank you. I enjoy it. But I don't imagine you've come all this way to make small talk about art."

Laura runs a finger around the rim of her glass. "I have some questions," she says at last. "Questions I haven't been able to find very good answers to."

He studies her, waiting.

"I've spoken with Detective Branson, both before the trial and after. We've become, if not exactly friends, then friendly, I suppose. We were both surprised when you weren't called to testify at the trial."

He takes a deep breath. "I can't say I'm sorry about that. The last thing I wanted was my face in the papers again. I assume I wasn't considered an asset to either side. A risk neither was willing to take."

"How do you mean?" she asks.

"The prosecution isn't going to volunteer that there was a convicted murderer seen hanging around Port Mary in the days leading up to your husband's death, Mrs. West. That would have given the opposing side, as well as the jury, a gift-wrapped alternative theory."

"But what about the defense?" she asks.

"I was interviewed by Graye's attorney. Once she heard what I had to say, I think she understood I wouldn't be helpful."

Laura frowns. "Why is that?"

Nick sighs and leans back against the sofa cushions. "Because Graye was acting strangely during the few interactions we had."

"How is a woman expected to act when confronted by the man who helped kill her mother?" Laura asks mildly.

Nick lifts one shoulder. "A fair question. But the thing is, Graye never had any reason to be afraid of me. Not in the way you mean. I wished her no ill will. I still don't."

"Then why were you there, Mr. DiMarco? That never made any sense to me."

"Because I was concerned," he says, leaning forward and resting his elbows on his knees. "I pled guilty to accessory to murder, Mrs. West, and took a deal. That meant I was eligible for parole long before Alex. I've been out of jail for almost ten years now. Twice as many as I spent locked up. Enough time to come to terms as best I could with what Alex and I did and try to get my life back on track."

He peered at her with a melancholy air that reminded her of a photograph the press had snapped of him as he was led out of the courtroom after his sentencing hearing.

"Then out of a clear sky, the past crashed in on me again. I received a letter from Alex. I'm still not sure what she hoped to accomplish by contacting me. We hadn't spoken in over fifteen years. My best guess is she wanted an audience. Alex always needed attention. Once upon a time, I was happy to provide it."

He rises and walks across the room to where a pack of cigarettes lies on the drafting table.

"Do you mind?" he asks.

She shrugs. It's his house.

He drags a chair to one of the windows and opens it wide, letting in the vibrant sounds of the city, then turns a fan that had been sitting next to the table toward the chair and window.

"Terrible habit," he says as he taps a cigarette out of the pack. "A piece of prison I can't seem to shake."

He lights up and blows the smoke carefully toward the air outside.

"I knew she'd been released, but I hoped, for her sake, she'd put it all behind her. To let go and focus on the future. But she hadn't. Not by a long shot."

He takes a deep drag from the cigarette. "Alex was looking for Grace. She told me she had an idea where to start. An aunt, she said. Mrs. Thacker's younger sister."

Laura hides her surprise at the respectful way Nick refers to Crystal Thacker. By all accounts, she was a horrible person, and Nick *did* plead guilty to the charges against him. He's an odd bundle of contradictions, this man.

"Alex always hated Grace," he says. "I never understood it. She was a nice little kid. But that hatred had only grown over the years. And it didn't sit easy."

He reaches over and picks up a jar half-filled with greenish-tinted water and a few paintbrushes. He sets the brushes on a rag, then taps ash from the end of his cigarette into the water.

"Grace was the biggest victim that night. And the idea of Alex hunting her down to exact some kind of misguided revenge . . ."

He glances over. "Like I said, I was concerned. I hired a private investigator to find Grace. I knew there was no chance she'd ever want to see me again, but I wanted to find her before Alex did. To warn her."

"And did you?" Laura asks.

But frown lines deepen between his eyes. "I found her, but I screwed it up. I was trying to take it slow, deciding how to best approach her, but she saw me. Obviously, her immediate reaction was fear."

"I would imagine it was terrifying to see you again after all those years."

He nods. "It was, I'm sure. But it was more than that. Grace, or Graye, as she'd become by then, was keeping secrets of her own."

Of course, she was. Laura knew now.

"I saw her puncture a tire one morning from the beach. I was considering how to approach her, then I looked up and there she was. I hung around, confused, waiting to see how it would play out. A few minutes later, she's changing the tire she'd flattened. I won't lie, it threw me."

He looks at Laura with regret in his eyes. "I realized I had no idea who that little girl had become, but there was one thing I did know. If she'd ended up as screwed up as the rest of her family, I was at least partially responsible for that."

"What did you do?" Laura asks.

"I didn't know what to do. I had to take some time and think. The look on her face when she pushed that little knife into that tire." He shakes his head. "I had to face the fact that Graye could be dangerous."

Laura closes her eyes. So much might be different right now if Nick had acted on those feelings. She knows dwelling on could-have-been and should-have-been doesn't change what is, but some days that's a hard lesson to remember.

"I didn't fully understand what was going on, but it was like watching a little kid playing with matches. She was going to get hurt—or worse, hurt someone else. I tried to warn her off, but she was terrified I planned to expose her. I even considered doing just that, for a while. I should have, I know that now. But I couldn't do that to her."

Laura tilts her head and gauges his words. They sound sincere.

"But, Nick, why did you feel so . . . so *protective* of her?" she can't help but ask. "I mean, Alex isn't the only one who ended up behind bars."

He chuckles without humor. "Grace didn't put me in jail. My bad decisions did that. Beginning with getting mixed up with Alex. But I was young and dazzled, and I thought she loved me. It's the lamest excuse in the world, isn't it?"

He drops the butt of the cigarette into the paint water with a hiss.

"We weren't supposed to kill her, you know. We were going to tie her up, scare her a little, then take the money she kept in the coffee can in the kitchen and buy bus tickets with it. Get out of there for good. At least, that's what I thought. Alex had other plans, though. For a while after it all happened, I believed she'd changed her mind on the spur of the moment, but I don't think that's true anymore. I think Alex always intended for her mother to die."

Having met Alex, Laura isn't surprised.

"If I had energy to spare on hatred, it would be directed at Alex and at myself. Never at Grace. She was a sad, awkward little girl who'd had a rough time. That woman was a monster, you know. And it took me too long to realize Alex was no better."

He stared out at the L train rumbling past. "I found her once. Grace. She was locked in a closet with duct tape wrapped around her wrists and mouth. Tears and snot had dried on her face. Who knows how long she'd been in there in the dark. Alex said her mother had done it before she'd left Alex to babysit. 'But why didn't you let her out?' I asked. Do you know what she said?"

He glances at Laura, incomprehension in his face. "She shrugged and said *she forgot*."

Nick stands and pulls the window closed with more force than strictly necessary. The relative quiet that engulfs them seems to help settle his agitation.

The anger she'd briefly glimpsed in him banks, replaced by a profound exhaustion.

"Forgive me if I sound rude, Mrs. West, but why exactly are you here? I don't have any great insight to share. The only advice I can offer is to try and move on. Be thankful for every night's sleep that doesn't end in a cold sweat. But somehow I doubt you came all this way for platitudes."

Laura doesn't know how to explain her obsession with Graye's past, with the manuscript written by a sad and disturbed mind, so she doesn't even try. She's imposed on Nick DiMarco enough, and he's clearly ready for her to leave.

"There was a little girl at the home where Graye lived after Crystal's death. She and Graye were close, but the girl died in an accident just before she was due to leave the home."

Nick looks up at her with tired eyes.

"She had a roommate in college, Natalie Ellis. Natalie died of an overdose. The two were close as well. And of course, there was Inez Jeffries. And David."

Nick waits.

"I've been searching for the first domino, I suppose. The tipping point that turned Graye into the person she eventually became. It's stupid, I guess. I spoke to Alex before I came here. She admitted she killed her mother, and you say the same. I just thought if I could get a clearer picture of what happened that night, if I could just *understand*, maybe I could begin to get Graye out of my head."

Nick's face has gone pale. He looks like nothing so much as a haunted man. He opens his mouth to speak, then shuts it again.

Laura's pulse picks up speed. "What is it?" she asks.

He stands, paces like a caged animal. Finally, he stops and turns to face her.

"I hate to think about that night," he says, his voice low and pleading. "I've worked so hard to lock it away."

"Nick, please tell me," Laura says. It's not fair, she knows it's not, but she asks all the same.

Nick runs his hands down his face, then holds them out in front of him, watching the way they tremble.

"She was sleeping," he says when he speaks again. "Wearing one of those little masks I thought people only wore in movies. My heart was beating so hard I'm surprised it didn't wake her up."

Laura swallows back the lump that's formed in her throat.

"Alex was flying, though. I'd never seen her eyes so bright, not even when she said she loved me. We tied her up in her own bedsheets. Alex put the tape over her mouth so the neighbors wouldn't hear her scream."

Wide-eyed, Laura listens to the echoes of a past long dead and buried, resurrected in Nick's words. One night, the repercussions of which are still reverberating.

Too late, she almost wishes she could stop him. Just walk out the door and never return.

But this is what Laura has come for.

55

GRACE

There are noises coming from Mother's room, so Grace clicks off the little flashlight she stole from the kitchen drawer to read under her covers at night. She doesn't want to get in trouble again.

But the voice doesn't sound like Mother's. On soft feet, she steps out of bed and pads to her bedroom door.

"Come on, let's get the cash and go," she hears Nick say. She knows it's him because she listens at her sister's door when he comes to see her.

But he hasn't been here in weeks. Mother was angry after last time, when she found Nick and Alex hugging in her room with the door shut. She told Alex she couldn't see him anymore, which made Grace as sad as it made her sister angry.

She likes Nick. He's nice to her.

Nicer than her sister.

"Wait," Alex says. "I need to get something."

Her voice is excited, happy, and Grace is glad. Since Mother made her break up with Nick, she's been silent or shouting, with nothing in the middle.

She hears footsteps running down the hallway and wonders if Alex and Nick are playing a game. She hopes they don't wake up Mother. She took one of her white pills before bed, but they're being very loud.

"Alex, come on already. Let's go," Nick shouts. He doesn't sound as excited as her sister, but maybe he's sleepy. It is very late.

Grace slides from her bed and peeks around the corner of the door. Her sister will never let her join their game, but she'd like to see Nick again. He always smiles and asks her what's up. He laughed the first time she looked up at the ceiling to see what he meant.

Grace had never made anyone laugh before, and it made a river of warmth run through her body.

Alex is coming back down the hallway, and she's carrying something in her hands, but it's dark and Grace can't tell what it is. She ducks her head inside the door when Alex sees her and runs back to the bed.

"Alex, hurry up!" Nick shouts.

"My sister's awake," she shouts back.

"So what? Let's get the money and go. She won't say anything."

"Gra-cie," Alex says in a voice she only uses when she's about to do something mean. "I saw you, Gracie. You can't hide from me."

Grace pulls herself tighter into a ball. Sometimes Alex can be even meaner than Mother.

The side of her bed dips down, and the covers are yanked out of her grasp.

"You don't have to be afraid of me, Grace," Alex says. She sounds sweet, like she means it, but Grace knows better than to believe her. "I'm going to fix everything. You'll see."

"Is Nick here?" Grace asks, her desire to see him outweighing her fear of her sister.

Alex laughs. "I think somebody has a little crush. Yeah, Nick is here. And we've got a plan. Do you want to know what it is?"

Grace nods. She'll play along if it means she'll have a chance to see Nick.

"Well, come on, lazy bones. Time's a-wasting."

Alex stands up and ushers Grace out of the bed and into the hallway.

"Jesus, Alex, what are you doing out there, baking a cake? Did you get the money or not?"

Grace stops and turns back to her sister, who's walking too close behind her. "Why is Nick in Mother's room?" she asks, her eyes gone wide. "Is she playing the game too?"

Alex doubles over and for the second time in her life, Grace realizes she's made someone laugh.

Alex laughs so hard it makes Grace laugh too.

"Come on, already!" Nick shouts, and he doesn't sound like anything is funny.

Alex wipes her eyes and shuffles Grace forward.

"Yeah, Gracie. Mother's playing the game too. She's the monkey in the middle."

They round the corner together and step into the bedroom, but Grace is confused. She begins to get a bad feeling low down in her stomach.

Mother doesn't look like she's enjoying this game. Neither does Nick. He's holding the bedsheets from Mother's bed where they've been knotted around her, and there's tape on her mouth, but Grace can still hear her muffled shrieking behind it.

Nick is practically sitting on top of her, trying to keep the sheets from coming undone, but Mother is struggling anyway. Her sleeping mask is sliding down her face.

"I don't think she likes this game," Grace whispers, and her sister laughs again.

"What the hell, Alex?" Nick yells. "Why'd you bring her in here?"

"Little sneak was peeking out her door," Alex says with a shrug.

Grace can feel tears building up, but she doesn't want to cry in front of Nick. He's not happy to see her. Not even a little.

"Look, Grace," Alex says. "We've got an early Christmas present, all wrapped up in a bow."

Alex has done something bad. Something really, really bad.

She wants to run back to her room and hide under the covers again and pretend she didn't see anything, but her sister has a hard grip on her shoulder and Grace is frozen in place.

Alex leans down behind her and whispers in her ear.

"Want to hear something funny, Gracie? When I was your age, I thought Mother loved me and hated you. And then when I got a little older, I thought she hated me and loved you. And then I realized she hates us both and the only person she's ever loved is herself."

Grace's eyes go wide. What if Mother hears what she's saying? She doesn't think she does, because she's making so much noise herself, but Grace knows one thing. They're all going to be in so much trouble.

"Alex," Nick says loudly. "We've got to go."

"Just hold your damn horses," Alex shouts back.

Grace doesn't think that's a very nice way to talk to Nick.

"Here's the thing, Grace," Alex says, her voice a whisper again. "I'm going to leave, and I'm not coming back here ever again. When I do, there's not going to be anyone left here for Mother to hate except for you. I know we've never really gotten along, but for once in your life, Gracie, I'm going to do you a favor. I'm going to give you the chance to help yourself. Would you like that?"

Grace whips her head around to look Alex in the eyes. "Is Nick leaving with you?" she asks.

Alex nods slowly, her own eyes big like she's making fun of her. She has a little smile on her face that Grace has learned means bad things.

"Can I come too, Alex?" Grace asks, giving voice to her deepest, most secret wish. "Please, Alex. I'll be really quiet and good."

Alex tilts her head and looks upward, like she's thinking over her answer.

"Please, Alex. I'll do anything," Grace begs.

"Alex, we have to go!"

But her sister ignores him and stares into Grace's eyes.

"Anything?" she asks, and Grace nods so fast and strong that her hair falls over her face.

"Alex!" Nick yells.

But Alex smiles and places something cold and heavy in Grace's hands.

56

LAURA

Nick rubs his hands hard across his eyes.

"It happened so fast. I didn't even know she had a gun, but then she put it in her little sister's hands and I heard her words as clear as a bell. *All you have to do is point and squeeze the trigger.*"

And in Laura's mind, the dominoes begin to fall.

"Grace didn't even hesitate," Nick says, the horror as fresh as if it had happened yesterday. "And I just sat there and watched it happen. I should have grabbed the gun. In my dreams, I grab for it, push it up toward the ceiling, and everyone walks away. But that's not what happened. I sat there like the idiot kid I was, and it was over before I even realized what I was seeing."

He stares at her, trying to make her understand this thing she'd so thoughtlessly sought to find.

"And Alex was laughing the entire time."

Laura has a hand pressed to her mouth. She'd known. Somewhere inside, she'd known the truth was bigger and more terrifying than even she could imagine. But hearing it said aloud leaves nothing but the taste of regret in her mouth.

"Grace dropped the gun and turned back to her sister. 'I'm ready now,' she said. And she smiled. With blood and who knows what else running down her face, that poor, sad, messed-up kid smiled, and Alex just laughed.

"'I'm not taking you anywhere, Gracie,' she told her. 'But don't ever say I never gave you anything, sis. I just gave you the biggest gift of your life.'"

Laura's face is wet with tears.

She came here. She asked for this. She wanted the truth, and now she's got it.

"Alex was ready to go then, but I couldn't go anywhere with her. She was the same monster her mother had been. Worse, because she'd turned Grace into a monster too. I tried to wipe Grace's fingerprints off the gun. My hands were shaking, but I managed it by sheer chance. Later, they picked up a partial of mine and Alex's as well, but no one ever knew Grace had held the gun."

He stares out at the sky outside the window of his third-floor apartment, and Laura doesn't envy him the images playing across his mind.

"I was the one who held her face between my hands and tried to wipe away the blood. I whispered in her ear, 'Tell them it was Alex, Gracie. Say it was Alex, and I'll back you up, but you can never, ever tell them what really happened.'

"I didn't even know if she heard me. The light had gone out of her when Alex said she couldn't go with us. She just sat there, right on the floor of her mother's bedroom, and didn't say a word."

Nick opens the window again and breathes in the city air. He taps out another cigarette and lights it up.

"I heard the sirens then. The gunshot had woken a neighbor, who'd called the police. Alex was throwing things into her mother's car when they arrived. She still thought we were going to get away with it."

"Why didn't Alex tell anyone?" Laura asks. "She blames Grace for her conviction, but she never said Grace was the one who pulled the trigger. Why not?"

Nick looks back out the window.

"Alex isn't stupid. She knew no one would believe her. Not with me telling a different story, and then Grace, once she began to speak. God, I was so worried she'd lay it all out there and Alex would walk. It took weeks for her to open up. Therapists, hypnosis, you name it. But when she finally spoke, she did just what I'd told her to do. She pointed the finger at her sister."

He dropped the second cigarette, only halfway smoked, into the jar of water and turned to face Laura directly.

"But more than that, Alex is *proud* of what she's done. So to answer your question, Mrs. West, yes, Alex killed her mother that night. She just used Grace as her weapon of choice."

His expression is weary, as if he'd like nothing more than for Laura to go now. And she knows she should. She should leave him to whatever peace he's able to find, but she's not sure her legs will carry her weight.

"There are many, many things I wish I'd done differently, Mrs. West," Nick says. "I regret that I didn't tell someone Grace was dangerous. That cost your husband his life. My only excuse for not exposing Grace is that I still remembered the face of that little girl, with blood on her cheeks and hope dying in her eyes."

She looks up and meets his gaze.

"I was always afraid Alex and her mother had ruined that girl's life. It turns out, I was right."

57

LAURA

Laura is wandering aimlessly through the market in Rockaway, but she's having trouble focusing on her list. She realizes she's been pushing an empty cart for ten minutes without once glancing at the aisles. She sighs.

Being home, armed with the answers she'd sought, is supposed to allow her to put her demons to bed, but they're more restless than ever.

The beach has lost its appeal. Her friends speak and she finds herself drifting off, her mind wandering to the stories she's gathered that weigh heavy on her heart and mind.

"Like a car with one low tire, you drift."

Only Milo remains a constant source of joy.

Laura has always been a doer. She gets antsy if she doesn't have at least three big projects to juggle at a time. But her work isn't as engaging as it once was.

She's read the entirety of her unsolicited slush pile in the weeks since her return from Chicago, desperately searching for a voice with enough resonance to drown out Fiona Boyd's, but it's no use.

Her eyes are drawn to a mound of fresh dark cherries piled high in the produce section. She stops dead in the aisle and stares.

The glossy little fruits seem to wink in the light, and Laura's mouth begins to water.

When was the last time she bit into a fresh, tart cherry? She can't remember, but suddenly there's nothing she wants more. She needs to feel the skin burst between her teeth and the red juice coat her tongue.

She picks one up, feels the lightness of it in her hand. She slowly brings it to her lips, tastes the smooth outer skin with the tip of her tongue.

"Mommy, that lady is eating the fruit! You said we couldn't eat the fruit until we paid for it. Is she going to get in trouble?"

"Maybe her mommy never told her not to eat the fruit before you pay for it," the woman across the aisle says, making no effort to keep her voice down. "But I'm your mommy so you have to listen to me."

A small blush rises in Laura's cheeks, but she refuses to be shamed by a stranger in the market.

Laura takes the cherry, unbitten, in her hand and drops it into a produce bag, then fills the rest of the bag full to bursting with more of the dark-red fruit, so dark they're almost black.

She turns her cart toward the checkout and pays for her purchase.

"Is this all for you today?" the checker asks.

"Yes," Laura says, uncaring of the list she's left abandoned in her purse. "That's all."

That night, with her lips stained a deep red, Laura takes a pen and paper and writes a letter to a woman who is not her friend.

A woman who, under the most bizarre of circumstances, has somehow instead become her other half. The moon to her tide.

Her sister.

58

LAURA

After

"Who would you like me to make this out to?"

Cecelia Ainsley glances up, pen poised over her latest novel.

"Why, if it isn't Laura West," she says with a grin. "Look what the east wind has blown in."

The intervening years have been kind to the author. She's as coiffed and regal as she ever was.

"Congratulations, Ms. Ainsley," Laura says with a smile of her own. "The novel is a work of art."

Cecelia waves her hand. "Honey, at this point in my career it could be shite on a shingle and the publishers would still be kissing my rear."

"And with good reason," Laura agrees with a laugh. "I won't take up your time." She throws a backward glance at the line of fans waiting behind her for an autograph.

Cecelia bends her head to write in the book Laura has slid across the table. "Are you back in New York for good now?" she asks.

"Just a visit," Laura says with a shake of her head.

"Why don't you join me for dinner tonight, then? I'd love to catch up before I fly home to the wilds of Texas."

She slides Laura's copy of her book back to her.

Laura's first instinct is to say no, couched in some polite excuse about a previous engagement, but she glances down and reads the hand-scrawled inscription Cecelia has left there.

For the woman who survived the forge, then learned to embrace her scars.

Her overlarge signature loops beneath the words.

Laura is surprised to find a lump lodged in her throat.

"I'd like that," she hears herself say.

"Wonderful. I'm at the Waldorf. Meet me in the lobby at eight."

"Fancy," Laura says, lifting an eyebrow.

"I told you, kissing my rear."

Laura laughs and says her goodbyes, then heads to the checkout desk with the hardback books she's chosen hugged to her chest.

"That will be forty-seven fifty," the clerk says.

Laura slides her credit card into the machine while the clerk begins to bag her books.

"I just finished this one," the girl says, holding up the one on the bottom.

"Oh yeah?" Laura asks. "What did you think?"

"It was fantastic," she says. "I couldn't put it down."

Laura smiles as the clerk slides her new copy of *The Orphan's Ashes*, by Fiona Boyd, into the bag.

◆ ◆ ◆

Cecelia waits until the wine is poured before she leans back in her chair and says, "Tell me a story, kid."

Laura thanks the waiter, then looks back to her companion.

"What makes you think I have a story to tell, Ms. Ainsley?"

"Oh please, call me Cecelia. No one does."

Laura smiles. The imperious woman is easier to like than she remembers.

"Cecelia, then." Laura unfolds her napkin and places it in her lap.

"Don't try to change the subject, dear. I'm a writer. I make a living peering under rocks. You have the satisfied bearing of someone with a delicious secret."

The woman really is extraordinary, Laura muses. She doesn't answer, but picks up her wine to take a sip instead. She imagines Cecelia Ainsley was probably burned at the stake in a former life.

"Besides, I'm old. I'll be dead soon enough, so there's no risk in entertaining me for an evening."

Laura laughs into her wine, then wipes her mouth on her napkin.

"As tempting as the offer is, my secrets aren't entirely mine to share," she says.

The silver-haired doyenne shrugs. "Even better." She leans forward to place her elbows on the table and pushes up her wrist full of silver bracelets. "I have an idea. Start with *'It was a dark and stormy night,'* or some such nonsense, then leave out the boring bits. We'll call it dinner theater."

Laura considers her. She's surprised by the urge to do just that. She's never before been tempted to tell a soul the truth about Fiona Boyd.

Her family and friends would never understand, and she doesn't have the words to explain it to them. But they all agree on one thing: Laura seems to have finally moved past her bout of depression. They were worried, for a while.

Fiona Boyd's publisher, too, is in the dark. Laura acts as a proxy for the author, an eccentric recluse who insists on remaining removed from the spotlight and ferociously guards her privacy.

Laura forwards all communication to Graye through official prison channels, just as the two of them had handled the months of edits and critiques for *The Orphan's Ashes*.

Once it was ready, Laura hand-delivered the manuscript to an old friend of her father's. It was a sensation in the office, of course, just as she'd believed it would be.

The knowledge of Fiona Boyd's true identity could have sold the book on morbid curiosity alone, but neither she nor Graye wanted that. *The Orphan's Ashes* would stand or fall on its own merit.

Laura had little doubt which it would be. She has an eye for spotting talent.

Advance reviews have been positive, and there was an impressive amount of buzz about the book, even before it officially launched a few days ago.

Grace's voice will finally be heard.

And for Laura, a debt is settled.

It's a difficult thing, perhaps the most difficult of things, to have looked eye to eye at the monster that lives inside of each of us. To embrace it, even for a time, willingly. Knowingly.

The morning of David's death, Laura too had woken before the sun was fully up. Or, more accurately, she'd never found the comfort of sleep after the blood had stopped draining from her bruised and battered body.

She'd risen quietly from the bed, not wishing to disturb Rachel or Dr. Lawson, both of whom had finally dropped into sleep. She walked out of Dr. Lawson's house, her wounded soul crying in pain, and she'd stared into the gray morning. In those moments, Laura had known a hatred that left her a stranger to herself.

She walked toward her grandmother's house. Her house. Before David, it was a place that held no more painful memories for her than a skinned knee.

She watched her own feet as they took her forward, toward the man who'd done this to her. She heard nothing except the rush of blood and anger coursing through her veins.

She never saw Graye or Alex. Never heard a commotion that might have given her a clue that something had gone horribly, beautifully wrong in her world.

Laura opened the front door to her home expecting to find her husband passed out drunk, just as she'd expected to find him the night before.

To this day, Laura can't say what she would have done if that had been the case. Her mind shies away from exploring that dark path.

Instead, she found David as he lay dying.

He looked up at her, pain and fear in his eyes, and he asked her for help.

Begged for it.

Logically, Laura understands it was too late for him. Even if she'd dialed 911 or put pressure on his wounds, David had only moments to live. There was nothing she could have done to change that.

But in those moments, his final moments, he looked to her for help and she stood by and watched him die.

For that, she owed Graye Templeton a debt.

One she hoped was now repaid.

Laura smiles and sips her wine. "I'm sorry to disappoint you, Cecelia," she says. "I live a quiet and uneventful life these days. And I wouldn't have it any other way."

59

GRAYE

Graye sits on a bunk anchored to the floor in a six-by-eight-foot room with bars in place of a door.

She carefully opens the package Laura has forwarded. It's been opened already by the guards, of course, but that doesn't bother her.

There is some paperwork from the publishing company that she sets aside to come back to later. Then a letter from Laura. The note is short. She congratulates Graye on her success and hard work. Nothing too personal, which is how their communications have been from the first letter, handwritten in Laura's sloping cursive script.

But Graye understands. Their relationship has always been a complicated one. The complexities only grew deeper after Graye stabbed Laura's husband.

She still dreams about Dr. West sometimes. She knows now he was her father. The lawyers made a big deal about it in court. Strangely, it hasn't altered her perception of him much.

Sister Margaret, Graye's only visitor, confirmed it right after she admitted she was really Graye's mother.

She sometimes stares at Margaret's face, looking for similarities she's never seen before, but for the most part, her parents' identities have had little effect on her.

The dreams come less often now, and that's fine. She's never sure how much of them is based on actual events and how much is a product of her imagination. But she no longer doubts she was the one who killed Dr. West.

The overwhelming feelings of panic at the idea that he'd done something to harm Laura are too real. Graye would have been gentle. Quick. She owed her friend as much. But the scene she found in the West home screamed of drunken brutality and unchecked anger. Typical of David West.

He was never supposed to do that. It wasn't part of the plan.

Memories like these have swept away any lingering doubts that she might have once had. And of course, the sensation of the knife pushing through flesh. There's that as well.

It's different than, say, holding someone beneath the water of a bath or pushing a needle into a vein. Different even than a sudden shove from behind, or the squeeze of a trigger. A knife is more difficult than one might expect. It requires a level of persistence. A level of *conviction* that Dr. West didn't believe she possessed.

But he's dead now, so that hardly matters.

What matters, what was made crystal clear the moment Graye spotted Laura in the Rockaway Police Station, is that Graye's plan was flawed. Oh, the original one was fine, when Laura could be counted on to champion the work of Fiona Boyd, but Graye was forced to make adjustments when Laura didn't connect with the book the way Graye hoped she would.

But her adjustments were shortsighted. The problem wasn't Laura. *It never had been.* The problem was Dr. West all along. Laura didn't abandon her; she'd simply been distracted by her husband's childish needs. By his demands on her time and energy.

Graye can't believe what a huge mistake she almost made.

With David West out of the way, Laura is free. Free from distractions. Free from a loveless marriage. Free to concentrate on doing what she does best.

Recognizing talent.

Seeing Laura alive and well that morning brought everything into absolute focus. The fatal flaw in her reasoning. How closely they'd skirted disaster. Most importantly, how a stunningly perfect solution had fallen into their laps, despite Graye's miscalculations.

The detectives didn't understand her jubilation. How could they? They didn't share Graye's vision.

Graye sets Laura's letter aside. She catches her breath at the sight of what lies beneath. Reverently, Graye picks up the hardbound copy of *The Orphan's Ashes*. Tears cloud her vision as she holds her words, made real and heavy in her hands.

She was right. After everything, all the disappointments and setbacks, all the close calls and near disasters, it was a perfect solution.

The undeniable proof of that was in her hands.

Hugging the book tightly to her chest, Graye's eyes fall onto the pages that remain.

Reviews for *The Orphan's Ashes*, gathered from publications and online sites. Emails directly from readers, with their names and return addresses redacted.

Laura has printed everything—every word, every reaction, every piece of reader feedback she can gather—and she's put it all into a manila envelope that contains nothing less than Graye's entire world.

She reads it all, poring over the words, drinking them in. Then she reads it again.

With tears still streaming down her face, Graye pulls out her supply of notebook paper and her pencil. It's down to nearly a nub. She'll need to get a new one from the prison commissary soon.

Graye smiles widely, and her heart sings as she replies to the readers who've reached out to say her voice has touched their lives.

Laura will send her replies out into the world, as they've agreed.

And as she signs the name Fiona Boyd with a flourish at the bottom of the first letter, Graye spares a passing thought for the little girl she used to be, but only for a moment.

Gracie Thacker died a long time ago. Graye Templeton is gone now too, just a role she has to play sometimes, for the sake of the guards.

But none of that matters. Fiona Boyd is real.

And her voice will live forever.

ACKNOWLEDGMENTS

A book doesn't happen on caffeine alone, but this one couldn't have happened without it, so credit where it's due.

In addition, thank you to the Lake Union team for your faith and support—Danielle, Chris, and the lovely Gabe.

Thank you to Faith Black Ross, for your insight and willingness to hold my hand through the editing process.

Thank you to Katie Shea Boutillier, agent extraordinaire.

To Miriam Juskowicz, for opening this door and graciously inviting me in, thank you always.

Thank you to my family and friends, for the inexhaustible supply of patience and stories.

And a massive thanks to the readers for sharing your time, your love of books, and your generous hearts.

ABOUT THE AUTHOR

Eliza Maxwell is the author of *The Widow's Watcher*, *The Unremembered Girl*, *The Grave Tender*, and *The Kinfolk*. She writes fiction from her home in Texas, which she shares with her ever-patient husband, two impatient kids, a ridiculous English setter, and a bird named Sarah. An artist and writer, a dedicated introvert, and a British-cop-drama addict, she enjoys nothing more than sitting on the front porch with a good cup of coffee.

ABOUT THE AUTHOR

Eliza Maxwell is the author of *The Widow's Watcher*, *The Unremembered Girl*, *The Grave Tender*, and *The Kinfolk*. She writes fiction from her home in Texas, which she shares with her ever-patient husband, two impatient kids, a ridiculous English setter, and a bird named Sarah. An artist and writer, a dedicated introvert, and a British-cop-drama addict, she enjoys nothing more than sitting on the front porch with a good cup of coffee.